J. S. Law started in the Royal Navy as an apprentice engineer and worked his way up through the ranks. He has worked on helicopters, ships and, towards the end of his naval career, submarines. In that time he has experienced first-hand the phenomenal pressures placed upon women and men in working in the military. He is a passionate advocate for education and now works providing nuclear training and education to the defence and civil sectors.

The Coldest Blood is the third thriller in the Lieutenant Dani Lewis series.

Follow J. S. Law on Twitter @JSLawBooks

Praise for the 'Lieutenant Dani Lewis' series:

'J.S. Law's taut crime novel oozes authenticity. I read this in a day and can't wait for the next in what will undoubtedly be an explosive series'   Clare Mackintosh

'Tense, claustrophobic, and totally absorbing, this book should be on every thriller reader's radar – or should that be sonar? Absolutely superb'   Matt Hilton

'Addictively readable'   Patricia Cornwell

'Pacey, claustrophobic and utterly thrilling'   Eva Dolan

'Outstanding . . . Dark and intense'   *Crime Review*

'A taut, tense thriller with a fantastic female lead . . . J. S. Law is one to watch'   SJI Holliday

Also by J. S. Law

The Dark Beneath (previously published as *Tenacity*)
The Fear Within
The Coldest Blood

The Coldest Blood

J. S. Law

HEADLINE

First published in paperback in 2018 by
HEADLINE PUBLISHING GROUP

1

Cataloguing in Publication Data is available from the British Library

ISBN 978 1 4722 2800 0

Typeset in Meridien by Palimpsest Book Production Ltd, Falkirk, Stirlingshire

Printed and bound in Great Britain by Clays Ltd, Elcograf S.p.A.

Headline's policy is to use papers that are natural, renewable and recyclable
products and made from wood grown in well-managed forests and other
controlled sources. The logging and manufacturing processes are expected to
conform to the environmental regulations of the country of origin.

HEADLINE PUBLISHING GROUP
An Hachette UK Company
Carmelite House
50 Victoria Embankment
London EC4Y 0DZ

www.headline.co.uk
www.hachette.co.uk

To my family and friends who supported me on this journey – thank you.

Prologue

'I knew you'd come. I got your message. I couldn't do it. I knew you'd come for me, though.'

Davis could feel the man standing behind him. He hadn't heard him enter the house, but then he hadn't heard anyone enter the house for a long time, not any real people. Occasionally he thought he heard them come home, Mary and the kids. He'd swear he heard the door open and felt the cold air being warmed through with noise and life.

On the odd occasion, when it was particularly vivid, he'd actually get up to go and look. He'd take his bottle with him, attached to his hand like his daughter's phone had been glued to hers, and he'd look across the kitchen, over the dishes and filthy worktops, past the wall cupboards, their doors missing, their shelves empty, and he'd wait and watch, just to be certain that his mind had done it to him, just to be certain they weren't actually coming home – they'd never been there yet.

He'd take a long swig of whatever he'd managed to afford that week; it didn't matter what it was, they all tasted the same by the time he started hearing his family come home.

Then he'd go one of two very distinct directions.

Sometimes he'd cry. He'd feel his once powerful body lose all of its strength in an instant and he'd slump forward, falling against the doorframe as his legs gave way beneath him, his knees pushing against his pallid skin like coat hangers against thin cotton as he lost the strength to stand. He never dropped his bottle, though – he always had the strength he needed to hold on to that.

He'd slump down on to the floor and he'd cry there for a while, sobbing between long swigs of hard liquor, until he eventually passed out; it was often the best sleep he got.

The other direction was the bad one.

It was the way that had made them leave him in the first place. The way that made the wall cupboards doorless, put holes in the plastered walls and broke crockery and the windows. The way that made him bleed.

That way never ended in good sleep. That way led to the memories, to the nightmares.

Sometimes, when the neighbours had had enough, and their children were frightened and unable to sleep, the police would come around and find him slumped on the stairs, still shouting, still screaming, still fighting in his nightmares; he'd fight them all the way to the station.

Now, the cause of those memories, the catalyst of those nightmares, was standing behind him.

'I'm no good to you,' he said, not able to turn around in case doing so made the nightmare even more real.

Davis felt himself start to cry but wasn't even sure why. It wasn't fear; he'd wanted to die for a long time, was ashamed that at one time he'd been able to take the life of another so competently, but now, was too much of a coward to take his own. He'd been the reaper for some and now his was standing behind him.

He looked down at his bare, skinny legs and at his small pot belly above them. He was lying back in his favourite armchair, his only armchair, the one that only reclined now since he'd broken something inside it. He wondered how he managed to be fat, to have a pot belly, when he couldn't remember the last time he'd eaten solid food.

His underwear was stained, and he was wearing two pairs of socks, because his feet were so cold all the time. On his top half, open and unbuttoned, was his combat jacket; the warmest thing he owned, that he hadn't yet managed to sell, lose or have stolen.

'My mum would be ashamed, you know,' he said, chuckling and noticing how weak and quiet his voice was in the cold air of his lounge. 'She always said to keep my underwear clean. "You never know what'll happen and you don't want people thinking ill of you if you have an accident", that's what she'd say.'

He looked again at the yellow stains on his pants; some were old and faded-looking, like dirty tide marks.

'Look at me,' he said, gesturing to his body. 'What the fuck can I do for you? The others are doing better, I think. Fuck knows, I haven't heard from them in years, but what can I do?'

The figure behind him never moved, never made a sound.

Davis began to wonder whether he'd made the whole thing up, whether this was just another beginning, whether the drink was offering him a third direction. Maybe he'd no longer hear the children come home; instead, it would be spectres from his past, sneaking silently into his house to haunt him and kill him.

This felt different.

He wasn't that far gone, could see almost three quarters of his bottle of cheap own-brand cider on the folding table next to him and he was fairly sure it was only his third.

Also, the room felt warmer. It felt as though there was another body in it.

Davis had been a fighter once, a long time ago. There was a time when he wouldn't have been afraid, wouldn't have been alone.

In these early stages, when the alcohol hadn't yet sent him to this dark place, he'd wonder whose fault it all was.

Had it been his, for signing up, young and stupid, joining the Royal Marines and going to fight for his country? As if the country gave a shit about fighting for him. He'd seen and done things that nobody should have to do, that nobody should ever *need* to, and they'd affected him; he'd brought them home with him. To his wife and family.

Maybe it was Mary's fault.

She could've stayed with him, helped him, worked with him to get better and be the man she fell in love with again; maybe he hadn't all but died in Afghanistan, maybe time could have shown that. She could have saved him and brought him back to life.

He wanted that, recognised it now as the tears rolled down his face, touching the corner of his mouth.

Maybe it was the fault of the government, the Ministry of Defence, the Navy Board, the Royal Marines, Taz Lewis and the others who'd all abandoned him so quickly and easily after they got back from that trip to hell.

He felt his fists begin to clench, felt his breathing quicken. It wasn't his fault, he wasn't sure which bastard's fault it was, but it wasn't his and he wasn't going down like this.

'WHAT DO YOU WANT FROM ME?'

4

He bellowed the words as he grabbed for his bottle and turned, throwing it towards the dark figure who was standing against the wall behind him.

Davis was up in an instant, no longer caring that he was wearing only socks, pants, and a combat jacket that stank of his own urine. He charged the figure, for a second almost pleased that the man was actually there, that he hadn't wasted the cider on a false dream.

'I'LL KILL YOU.'

He ran forward, confident and loud, the old muscles remembering and driving him forward as he closed with his enemy.

Suddenly he had nowhere left to go.

He was stopped in his tracks.

His body seemed to fold back on itself, as though he'd been hit so hard, the blow had penetrated what small amount of skin and flesh separated his belly button from his spine.

The figure was on him, stronger, so much stronger.

Blows landed on his emaciated frame and he was sure he heard his ribs crack as he laboured for breath. Then a hand tightened around his throat, the fingers reaching behind his Adam's apple and closing together slowly.

'What do you want from me?' he croaked, choking and retching as he tried to inhale.

He felt the hand loosen its grip slightly and he was able to breathe.

His ribs definitely felt broken.

'I'm no good to anyone. I can't help you. I can't even help myself. I can't do anything,' he said, the words pouring out between gasps and sobs. 'I got your message, but I can't help. I couldn't get there.'

The figure was silent, only inches from his face, and Davis could smell toothpaste on the man's breath as it passed through some kind of thin covering, like a stocking, stretched over the contours of the man's face.

'You can help me,' said his attacker, speaking for the first time. 'I need you to take a message to somebody.'

Davis began to nod, tried to, but his head was held firmly against the floor like a dog being submitted in a fight.

'I'll do that,' he said. 'I can do that.'

He paused, blinking, trying hard to breathe, but never quite getting enough air. The pain was coming into sharper focus as his adrenaline began to subside.

Davis knew he'd need to go to a hospital about his ribs, but he'd just need a few sips of something stronger than cider first, so he'd have strength for the journey.

'I'd need some money, though,' he said quickly. 'To get me there. So I can deliver your message.'

The figure paused, released his throat and stood up, leaning forward and offering a hand, then lifting Davis to his feet in a single, excruciating movement.

Davis limped straight back to his chair, his left arm bent against his side as he stooped over. There was another bottle of cider on the floor and he tried to reach for it but was too sore and instead he lowered himself into the chair and shut his eyes as he tried to distance himself from the nauseating pain.

The figure moved round now, standing between him and the window, silhouetted by the dull grey light that seeped in through the filthy brown net curtains.

'I think you broke my ribs,' Davis said, between laboured breaths. 'When do you need me to deliver the message? I'll need to go and get this seen to, so if you give me a few quid, I can get going.'

'It's gotta be now,' said the figure.

Davis watched as the figure's hand disappeared into his pocket to retrieve something.

6

The man threw it across and Davis looked down at his lap as it landed.

It was a thin piece of wire, with a wooden toggle at either end.

Davis looked up.

'You know what I gotta have,' said the figure. 'You remember. Just the one.'

Davis was already shaking his head.

'No. Please. I never said anything to anyone. I lived with it. I kept it inside. It ruined everything. It's like cancer. It just fucking stayed there growing and eating and taking away everything from inside me. But I kept it in there anyway.'

'Left hand.'

'No. I kept my mouth shut . . .' said Davis, his voice rising.

The words trailed off as he saw the figure move towards him, slowly, almost reluctant, a long sigh slipping through the mask as he crossed the room.

'I kept your fucking secret,' Davis said again.

The man changed pace, moving fast and sudden.

Davis tried to react, wincing as his ribs screamed, but before he could do anything to defend himself, the man was on him, close to him, straddling him like Mary had done in the early days when she'd loved him and wanted him.

He felt the figure close to him, felt his weight bearing down on him and his warm breath brushing past his ear as the man forced his hand up and underneath the bridge of Davis's nose, bringing tears to his eyes and forcing his head back until his neck locked and stars appeared in front of his eyes.

'You're gonna do it, buddy. You're gonna do it now, too. Because if you don't, then I'm going to beat you bad.

So bad that you'll stay in this chair. I won't need to tie you. I'll beat the shit out of you until you want to stay here. Then I'm gonna bring in Mary, Sarah and Joe and I'm gonna make you watch, while I make them take their fingers off, see? I'll tell them that they're doing it because you won't, and they can add that to the long list of things you wouldn't do for them, you useless piece of shit. When I'm done, and I've got theirs, I'll make them each eat them. Then I'll beat and torture your family while you lay here and watch. It'll be like a horror movie.'

Davis was sobbing now, listening as every word seemed to break down another small piece of his resolve.

'Eventually, you'll do what I asked. Though, as seems to be your thing, the damage will all be done, and it'll be way too late. But you'll do it and you'll blame someone else for your dead family and your shitty life. Then, if I was you anyways, I'd kill myself. No way I could live with the shame. But you're not me, so you'll probably just go back to drinking your cheap liquor and being angry at all that's gone wrong for you.'

'I kept your secret. I saw what you did and told no one,' Davis whimpered.

'Then you'll know for damn sure that you don't want me within a hundred miles of those folks you scream about in your sleep. The ones you say you love.'

'I do love them,' Davis said, his voice now a whisper.

The man climbed off him and made to turn away, then seemed to reconsider. He reached back into his pocket and pulled something else out.

'Good. Then put it in this paper bag when you're done,' he said, and leaned against the wall, watching and waiting. 'And be quick. We got some place to be.'

8

PART 1

Chapter 1

She could hear them through the walls.

The sounds were muffled so the words weren't always perfectly clear, but she could still hear them. The only exception was when, for reasons she couldn't tell, they suddenly lowered their voices and then she heard nothing, as though they'd lapsed into silence.

'This cannot go on, Roger. This shall not go on.'

She couldn't always hear Roger's replies.

He'd been her boss in the Crimes Involving Loss of Life team for several years, and her friend for many more years before that. His voice was lower, carried less through the walls, but he'd speak to defend her, Dani was confident of that much; he always had.

'No, Roger. She's an average investigator at best and is often drawn to below average status because she cannot seem to follow our rules and procedures. She thinks she's better than everyone else and acts accordingly and you, for far too long, have tolerated and encouraged these thoughts and deeds.'

The tone of Captain Harrow-Brown's voice meant that his words carried more clearly than Roger's low grumble.

He was Roger's boss, a full captain, three ranks higher than Dani and one above Roger, and he was a career man, a politician in military garb, and he wanted no one in his chain of command who might do anything to draw negative attention and slow his rise.

Dani knew the man hated her and she hadn't had to use any of her investigative skills to discern that; he barely concealed it most of the time.

'Maybe it was the sabbatical, Roger? Hastily arranged and poorly considered. Perhaps taking a year out so soon after screwing up her big success wasn't the best idea. Maybe what she really needed at that time was guidance, leadership, advice and direction from you, to bring her back into the right way of doing things rather than giving her a year's holiday to start building conspiracies in her mind.'

She was sure she heard swearing in Roger's reply.

Roger only had a year left in the Royal Navy Special Investigation Branch, had no chance of promotion, and had been a grizzled and fearless campaigner his whole career. He didn't hold back when he was alone with Harrow-Brown, or 'Captain Hardly-Worthit' as he often called his superior behind his back. Roger also knew why Dani had taken a year's sabbatical.

He'd watched as she'd unmasked Christopher Hamilton, a man she'd known and worked with in the Royal Navy Police, and brought him to justice for multiple murders.

It was widely accepted that Hamilton had been killing for more than thirty years and Dani was certain that his true tally of murders could run well above a hundred, but there were no bodies and little evidence that could be used to convict him.

She'd written a paper about him in the wake of his capture, postulating that he couldn't have killed for as long as he did – and permanently concealed that number of bodies – without help.

The tabloids were already buzzing with stories about a military-trained serial killer who'd twice been seconded to support police efforts to capture himself, and when they ran the story that the investigator who'd captured Hamilton believed there was another killer out there, Dani's career was left in tatters.

Her thoughts and theories on Christopher Hamilton were laid open for all to see, and her naval superiors repeatedly chastised her for writing it and mocked her for suggesting such a thing was possible.

Serial killers working together were rare and, as Dani suggested, working together purely to conceal the victims was unheard of outside family groups – Hamilton had no real family.

It was after this, when her superiors had chewed her up for even writing such a paper and then accused her of leaking it, that Hamilton had reached out from prison to take some revenge.

They'd been waiting for her as she left a remote pub near Portsmouth.

The attack had been fast and brutal.

She'd fought them and escaped, but she could still feel the marks they'd left on her back and she knew they'd never fade.

She'd known it was Hamilton who'd sent them, was certain of it.

It wasn't just the fact that it'd happened on the anniversary of his conviction, it was the way the attack was planned.

The men were going to beat her and humiliate her, to make sure she was left with scars inside and out – a lasting reminder.

Hamilton had all but admitted that he was behind the attack during an interview in recent months, but she'd known anyway.

No one was ever caught or punished for the assault, because, aside from Felicity and Roger, she'd never told a soul, yet Hamilton had known and had enjoyed letting her know that he did.

It was Roger she'd turned to after the attack, Roger who'd cleaned her up, dressed the wounds and arranged for her to take a break, which became a sabbatical, to give her the time she needed to recover.

When she came back, it was Roger who then sent her to investigate a murder-suicide onboard the submarine, HMS *Tenacity*, though it seemed that wherever she went, Hamilton followed in some form or other.

'She's incapable of taking any investigation on and not making it about her, and you damn well know it. That debacle on *Tenacity* – claiming she was assaulted by the crew—'

'If she says she was assaulted then she was!'

Roger's words were loud and angry now, and Dani could hear the threat in his voice; Roger Blackett was not a man to take lightly.

'And yet she didn't report it. Didn't retain any evidence.'

There was a low mumbled response.

'Images of an injury that could have been caused bumping into a valve or other piece of equipment on that damn submarine. It's evidence she was hurt, not evidence someone hurt her, Roger. And even when she could have clawed some kind of victory from this, she chose defeat again – not content to have captured some sailors carting a few bags of narcotic for some extra money, she had to make it a conspiracy, something that went all the way to the top. According to her, she'd discovered the kernel of a criminal empire that was using the resources of Her Majesty's Government to do its evil. She's unhinged, Roger. And now there's this . . .'

Dani waited, wanting to listen and equally desperate not to. She stood by her conviction that the men who'd smuggled drugs on board the submarine *Tenacity* could not have acted alone. They were sailors, not drug dealers – they were mules who liked some extra money and thought they'd get away with it, but they had no way of moving serious quantities of drugs, no network, no protection. It was so obvious to Dani that the situation went deeper, that anger began to filter through the numbness she felt as she lay beneath the crisp sheets of her hospital bed. She knew what was coming next, too, could almost taste it on the air.

'And her fixation with Christopher Hamilton,' Harrow-Brown continued. 'That's gone beyond a joke. She's been watching too much television, Roger. She's hanging on to that connection because she thinks it gives her power, because she thinks it makes her indispensable. It doesn't. This latest shambles has gone all the way to the top. I'm briefing the Chief of the Defence Staff tomorrow morning and I'm struggling to know what I'll say, because her actions are indefensible.'

'As if you'd try to defend anything but your own back-side.'

Dani almost snorted as she heard Roger's response.

There was silence for a while and she imagined the two men staring each other out, Harrow-Brown slowly realising that he couldn't intimidate Roger and that her friend wouldn't back down from his beliefs.

'How the hell did she end up there, Roger? Tell me that,' said Harrow-Brown, his voice quieter. 'What the hell is going on with her? You talked me into approving her assistance with the new Hamilton investigation, and I know she's been in to see him several times, but I had no idea that the body parts of some of his victims had been sent directly to her.'

Dani heard a low rumble as Roger answered. She couldn't hear his words but guessed that he was explaining that that information hadn't been shared with anyone at that stage.

'Yes, I know that,' snapped Harrow-Brown. 'But if the media starts digging into all this, especially with her affinity for headline-hungry actions . . .'

Dani didn't know if he'd left the words hanging or simply lowered his voice for whatever he said next, but she took the opportunity to shut her eyes and turn over in her bed.

This was a laborious process, the pain throbbing in her injured shoulder. She squeezed her eyes shut and willed herself not to listen to any more, but how could she not? She was seeing something bigger. From the very beginning, it had felt as though someone was manipulating her. As though she'd been set in motion, not for justice, but to meet someone else's aim. And yet she knew, in the logical part of her mind, that she couldn't see the big picture, let alone describe it coherently to someone else. She didn't know why it was happening, or when it had started, except that somewhere near the middle, likely at the very centre of all that was happening, was Christopher Hamilton.

He was always there. He always seemed to know where she was and what she did.

'How the hell do you start to investigate a girl who goes missing from a warship and end up beaten half to death in a shop with bodies all over the place and the head of a naval rating in the fridge? We've kept it under wraps for now, Roger, but this is going to go public very soon.

She found the young girl, Roger, she'll take that as a win and it is. She caught Sarah Cox, which is another victory, but all of this will certainly mean the press drawing parallels with the Hamilton case and we both know that that will swiftly lead to the re-publication of Miss Lewis' paper and her outlandish claims that he had help. Questions will be asked and someone will ask the million dollar questions – why was she there alone? And what the hell is going on that she's not telling us?'

Harrow-Brown spoke with the brave certainty of a keyboard warrior, protected from the target of his words as he wilfully missed the point. Not only did he feel he could be rude and overbearing because of the protection allowed him by his rank, but he focused only on the parts of the narrative that aided his point of view.

Dani's last investigation had been to find a missing girl, and she had been found, thank goodness, along with her kidnapper, Sarah Cox, but someone else had been there too, unseen, and they had managed to get ahead of Dani.

The search for Natasha Moore should have ended when Dani found the makeshift cell in Sarah Cox's home, but someone got there first and had taken both Natasha and Sarah Cox, then lured Dani to the abandoned shop in the New Forest, a place she'd been to only once before and had never wished to visit again.

That had to have been a set-up.

Harrow-Brown's voice cut through her thoughts.

'This whole thing, the mess on *Tenacity*, the creation of conspiracies everywhere she goes . . .'

Dani wanted to climb out of bed, hurtle along the linoleum on the military hospital corridor, find Harrow-Brown in the next room and scream, 'What about Ryan Taylor's head turning up in that shop, in a refrigerator? You tried to stop me looking for him and someone decapitated him.'

She imagined herself grabbing his pallid face, squeezing his features and ignoring the shock in his beady eyes as she forced him back against the magnolia wall. She carried on shouting in her head: 'Think about it, you bloody moron! Why would someone decapitate a drug mule and leave his head for me to find? It makes no sense! People selling drugs don't want attention like that – they don't want to give me more evidence to build a case against them. Somebody did it because they wanted to send a message.'

She halted her mental tirade, because the only way she could continue would be to tell him the truth, and she couldn't do that. She couldn't yet admit that when she'd come to after being battered by an unseen figure at that shop, there'd been some men there with her, three of them. Two were known gangsters, crime boss Jimmy Nash and his assistant Marcus, members of an organisation that had the will, knowledge and muscle to shift the types of drugs Dani had found on *Tenacity* – the sort of people who'd be hurt by her actions on board the submarine.

It was their mule who'd been decapitated and their organisation that would eventually come under scrutiny – they gained little from the scene.

And then there was the third person in the room, the person for whom Dani was the message – her father.

Harrow-Brown was speaking again, but Dani couldn't bear to listen. She'd been used to send a message to her father and to Jimmy Nash.

That thought made her furious, that someone could manipulate her and interfere with her investigation to get her to a certain place at a certain time.

Two other things really boiled inside her.

She needed to find out what the message was that was being sent to her father and Jimmy Nash, but more than that, she needed to know who was helping Hamilton to send it.

The article she'd written years before came back to her, as it often did.

She thought about the evidence against Hamilton, or lack of it, the sheer complexity of what he did and how he did it so brazenly.

There was someone helping him, watching Dani, interfering and manipulating her, and she was going to find out who that was – then she'd get to see how Hamilton coped when he was the one who became truly isolated.

She turned on to her back and tried to shuffle up into a sitting position. Her head was pounding, and she saw the two painkillers on the locker next to a small plastic cup half-filled with water.

'Sideline her, Roger. I mean it. Nothing new for her. Make sure she rests up and stays out of the bloody way. She can continue to help the NCA, because I'm not able to turn that tap off so quickly, but I want you watching her. I'll hold you personally responsible for any trouble she gets herself into.'

Dani took the painkillers and sat for a moment, letting her head adjust to being upright again.

Harrow-Brown was saying more, but she was already thinking of other things.

Her father had said he'd come back to explain why he was there when she'd woken up at the shop, and she needed to have that conversation, but first and foremost she needed to get out of here.

Chapter 2

'Have you heard from Dad?'

Dani was shaking her head as she made to reply, though she knew Charlie couldn't see her down the phone.

'Not much,' she said, trying to be more offhand than she really felt.

'Have you actually seen him, to see if he's OK?' her sister pressed.

Dani pursed her lips. She hadn't seen her father for a few days.

He'd called to check in on her and had promised to come and see her soon, but he hadn't actually turned up yet. Dani was pretty sure he was with Jimmy Nash.

The last time she had seen him, she'd been lying injured on the floor of the shop in the New Forest and he'd shown up at the scene along with Nash, a known gangster. It was obvious there was something going on between them, but it was annoying the hell out of her that it was more pressing than coming to see her to explain himself.

'I'm on my way to an interview, Charlie. Can I call you back later?'

There was a pause on the other end of the line.

'Charlie, you know he headed off to some Royal Marines reunion. I know he was with some of his old friends just a few days ago and he called me last night. He's probably spent the past few days drinking and talking like he's still in his twenties, and now he'll be sleeping off the hangover with his head and body reminding him he's literally decades past that.'

'He normally calls in more often than this,' said Charlie. 'And he normally stays at yours. Even Mim's starting to worry about him and you know she doesn't worry about anything.'

'Well, when she starts calling me, I'll start worrying too,' said Dani, pleased with how she sounded. Pleased that she'd managed to inject a little humour into her lies, as though nothing was wrong at all. 'Charlie, I really have to go. I'm due in the interview room now, I've still a way to go and I'm in no fit state to run.'

Her phone rang again as soon as she'd hung up, and she rolled her eyes as she saw the caller's name.

'Hello, Roger,' she said, not trying to hide her annoyance at the call. 'I'm just on my way to speak to Sarah Cox. She's been asking for me. I'll do that and then I'll go home. I won't even pass go or collect two hundred pounds, I'll go straight there.'

The pause at the other end of the line made Dani think she might have crossed a line.

Roger was her friend and a friend of her family and had been for many years, but he was also her boss, two ranks above her in the naval hierarchy and very much deserving of more respect than she'd just given him.

'Sorry,' she said before he could speak. 'I'm tired and I didn't mean to be short. I am just about to go in and speak to Cox, though. Can I call you back later?'

Roger let her go, and Dani dropped the phone into her

21

pocket. She could see Felicity waiting for her at the end of the long corridor leading into the building where Sarah Cox was being held.

The criminal psychologist was upright, tall and slim, with the look of a strict nanny about her. She smiled as Dani approached.

They'd met during Dani's investigation on HMS *Tenacity* and had since become firm friends.

'I want you to know, Dani, from the very beginning, that I am, once again, against this meeting. It can definitely wait until you're fully recovered. However, she wants to speak to you, as seems to be the way with the serial killers and lunatics whose paths you cross . . .'

Dani tried to smile, but she just wasn't feeling it. 'My body's a bit beat up,' she admitted. 'But as she's the one that did most of it, I doubt it'll show any real weakness, and my voice still works.'

'Well, we'll be recording this one,' Felicity said, falling into step beside her. 'She's been interviewed, and she'll be charged in the coming days. Despite her early display of silence, she seems to have already broken down. She's telling quite the story at the moment, but we're confident we have her on abduction and premeditated murder, so she's not getting out anytime soon. Who knows, maybe she'll throw something else into the mix when she speaks to you.'

Dani shrugged. 'We can but hope.'

'You know, Dani,' Felicity said seriously, 'I want to talk to you about everything that's happened. It's important to me that you know you have someone you can speak to and it's really important to *you* to let it out.'

Dani continued to face forwards, avoiding Felicity's piercing gaze.

'If you really don't want to talk to me, for whatever

reason, you know I'm totally OK with that,' Felicity went on, 'but tell me and I can get you in with some of the best people in the country. The key thing here is that you speak to someone.'

'I will,' said Dani. 'I promise. Do you have anything for me, before I go in here? Anything I need to be aware of that I don't already know?'

Felicity was shaking her head. 'No. She's still sticking with her fairy tales. Says she conspired with Mark Coker, Natasha's boyfriend, to abduct Natasha and that Petty Officer Gary Black was in on it too. She says Coker was the driving force and claims he made them do it. She's claiming, though there's no evidence at all to support her, that he'd recorded her during several sex acts and was going to use that to blackmail her – same blackmail story with Black, except with different kompromat.'

'We're still sure she's lying?'

'If Mark Coker was blackmailing her, then he was the worst blackmailer in the world. He recorded the tapes on her hidden cameras, at her house, and let her keep them safe. Hardly a strategy for turning the screw on someone.'

'She murdered him to try and make it look like it was him, but never managed to finish rigging the evidence?' Dani suggested.

'Well, she says she killed him in self-defence and panicked. Claims she had no intention of disposing of the body at sea, but had hidden it down at her yacht, purely because it was the only safe space she could think of. She says that Mark Coker threatened her life, that he made her convert her spare room into a cell. She says it was his idea to try and get Gary Black to rape Natasha. So, according to her version, Sarah's the victim in all this. None of it's her fault and she shouldn't be punished for anything.'

Dani drew in a deep breath and let it out slowly, preparing herself to see this woman. 'She's a lying bitch.'

Felicity nodded. 'We know.'

'What about Stephanie James?' Dani asked. 'The young girl who was supposed to have been lost overboard from *Defiance* a year ago or more?'

'Nothing more about that yet, but rest assured, she won't be forgotten.' Felicity paused. 'I don't have to tell you that this isn't uncommon. We've got what we need for now and we won't stop working to get the rest, but these kinds of defences crumble quickly. Well done you for getting her. I think she'd have killed a lot more people in time. There were no signs of her stopping, only getting deeper and deeper into it.'

'Thank you,' said Dani. They stopped just outside the interview room door. 'Has she spoken at all about her relationship with William Knight?'

Felicity shook her head.

The man had been a serial rapist who'd gone missing some years before and had never had to answer for his crimes. He was presumed to be dead or on the run, though he was actually a prisoner of Jimmy Nash.

Dani had been allowed to speak to him, though she was unable to tell anyone else about it, and though this man had done unspeakable things, she was horrified at the way in which Jimmy was slowly taking revenge for what Knight had done to his daughter.

During the years he'd spent attacking women, he'd been friends with Sarah Cox and had worked for her father and Dani was certain there was something more to their relationship.

'No, we're not dealing with that yet. First, we'll get her convicted and locked up properly, then we'll deal with stuff like that. Knight's been gone for a very long time, so

24

we don't think there's much to be gained by pushing her now. We're only focusing on live, known crimes, the rest will follow.'

Dani passed her phone and keys over to Felicity. 'Her solicitor in there?'

Felicity shook her head again. 'No. She wants to speak with you alone. She's going against her very expensive legal advice, and she knows full well that we'll be filming and listening.'

Dani raised an eyebrow and nodded slowly, a little surprised.

Before she'd crossed Dani's path and been caught abducting and torturing a young sailor, Sarah Cox had been a legal adviser on board HMS *Defiance* and she was lined up for a cushy job at her uncle's law firm after she left the Royal Navy.

That kind of background knowledge would usually make somebody more acutely aware of the benefits of having their solicitor in the room with them during any interview with the police.

The door to the interview room opened and Dani nodded to the guard and entered.

'Hello, Sarah.' She walked to the vacant chair across from Sarah Cox.

She tried not to look at Sarah, tried not to notice how pale she was, or take in the black bags under her eyes and the yellow and purple bruising around her face. Dani didn't want to look, because she'd seen too many women beaten like this over the years, and though Sarah Cox fully deserved all she'd got, Dani didn't want to feel an ounce of pity for her.

'What do you want to tell me that you couldn't tell someone else?' she asked, choosing to be confrontational.

Sarah was looking down, her eyes aimed at her hands.

She looked like a small child sitting on the bottom step, reflecting on the misdemeanour that had resulted in her being sent there, contemplating how unfair the world was that she was to be punished.

'I didn't want to be part of this. I shouldn't be in here,' she said, her voice small and weak.

'No, it really sucks when you kill people and don't get away with it,' Dani said scornfully, her anger building. 'One of the most unfair things about our society is that you can't just abduct people, torture them and rape them for kicks. Or, you know, kill a few folks here and there and just pay Mummy and Daddy's lawyers to make sure everyone leaves you alone. It really does just suck being you.'

Sarah looked up quickly and the self-pitying face was gone, replaced with blazing hatred.

It wasn't the first time Dani had seen Sarah change from one persona to another in an instant, but it still affected her and she had to make an effort not to react to it.

She met Sarah's eyes and held her stare, waiting.

'I'm not guilty,' said Sarah, her voice stronger and more matter-of-fact. 'I was a victim in this and that will be borne out in court.'

'I'm not a judge,' said Dani.

'But you are, aren't you? A judgemental bitch?'

Dani shrugged, trying to appear relaxed. Her injuries, particularly to her ribs, made this difficult, and she knew she was sitting awkwardly. She leaned forward, aiming for confidence.

'What do you want, Sarah?' she asked. 'Because maybe you're right, maybe I am a bit judgemental, but right now I think you killed at least two people and had every intention to torture and kill a third. I think that's what will be borne out in court. Natasha is fine, by the way. Recovering well.'

Sarah stared at Dani for a long time. Then her face dropped, and she whispered something.

With Sarah's head tilted down, Dani was able to see the swelling and scars around her ear that she'd noticed before, when they were in the shop, and she wondered again how they'd got there.

'What did you say?' she asked, refusing to lean in any closer in case Sarah moved within striking distance.

'I'm frightened,' whispered Sarah, this time just loud enough for Dani to make out what she'd said.

'Did you say, "I'm frightened"?' asked Dani, as much for the recording equipment in the room as to clarify it for herself.

Sarah nodded, and Dani saw tears fall on to her grey cotton trousers, turning black as they landed and soaked in.

'As I said, I'm no judge, but maybe you should be frightened, because I think you're going to be in jail for a very long time.'

'No,' Sarah murmured. 'I'm not frightened of going to jail.'

She was speaking very quietly, but Dani still refused to move closer.

'There was somebody else there and you know it,' Sarah said, her voice suddenly cold. 'Someone had been watching me for a long time.'

Dani leaned closer, her attention piqued, the risk now worth it.

'I hadn't been sure before,' Sarah continued. 'It was just a feeling. I thought it was you or that other one that follows you around. At first, I'd thought I was being watched at home, but only at home, never in the dockyard. But then I knew it couldn't be you and I began to think it was just paranoia, because Natasha was at the house . . . because Mark Coker made me keep her there.

27

'I thought I'd been imagining it, but someone knew she was there and they came and freed her.'

She looked up at Dani. 'I was glad she was free,' Sarah said, and Dani couldn't help but roll her eyes. 'I was,' Sarah insisted, 'because, if she was free, then there was a chance that I could also be free of him.'

'Cut the bullshit, Sarah. Honestly, save that crap for someone who gives a shit. Just tell me what you want to tell me.'

Sarah's face distorted with fury for an instant, and Dani was tempted to lean back. She caught sight of Sarah's hands balling into fists, but she held her ground. The cameras and audio equipment would catch their every word, and she desperately wanted to find out who this other person was.

'I never did that to her finger,' said Sarah, seemingly determined not to say Natasha Moore's name. Her voice had dropped again to a low, broken whisper. 'I don't know who did it either. Mark never made me do it and I don't think he did. I don't know who took her from the house. I don't know who took her and I don't know why they cut off her finger, but it wasn't me. I don't know how we ended up at that shop either. I'd never been there before in my life – why would I go there? And look at my ear – I don't remember that happening at all. I just woke up with it like that. I couldn't hear anything. They say I'll never have full hearing in that ear again. The doctors say someone hit me there and it's caused permanent damage, and I have no recollection of any of this – none at all.'

Sarah paused.

'I'm scared, because whoever did that to Natasha, and whoever cut someone's fucking head off and left it there in the shop, they knew everything about me. Where I was and what I was doing.'

Sarah was really crying now, and this emotion looked to Dani to be only the second genuine one she'd seen today, behind the rising fury she'd witnessed before.

Dani watched her closely. It was near on impossible to tell when someone like Sarah Cox was telling the truth, because she didn't simply lie. People like her convinced themselves that what they said was the truth, they believed it, and as such, in her mind, she was always telling the truth.

Yet what Sarah was telling Dani fitted in with what Dani believed herself. Someone had been sending severed fingers from victims of the serial killer, Christopher Hamilton, to Dani's home.

The fingers had been preserved somewhere, many for a period of years. None had actually made it into Dani's home – they'd been intercepted by the National Crime Agency – but it had been the sender's intent that Dani would open the package and discover the severed finger of one of Hamilton's victims.

She'd been the one to catch Hamilton, tracking him to his home and finding the bodies of some of his victims in his garage – the only victims that had ever been found – and he'd recently begun to speak to her, had helped her in the case to catch Sarah Cox, or so Dani had believed.

Hamilton had been the one to tip her off that Cox would be at the abandoned shop – where Dani had found not just Cox, but also the young girl Sarah had abducted, and the severed head of Ryan Taylor, a sailor Dani had been searching for ever since she'd discovered drug trafficking on board HMS *Tenacity*.

There was just no way in Dani's mind that Sarah Cox could have known about all of this. It simply wasn't possible that she could have had access to the bodies of Hamilton's victims to collect and send their fingers – she was far too young to have ever really known Hamilton, let alone to have known him long enough to form a bond of trust – and it was highly unlikely that she could have happened across Ryan Taylor.

A third party had intervened, Dani was certain of it. Sarah had been manipulated, but not by Mark Coker as she was alleging, but by someone who'd been manipulating Dani at Hamilton's behest for many months.

'So, who was it?' said Dani, her voice low, matching Sarah Cox's whisper.

'The fucking devil?' said Sarah. 'How would I know?'

'Did you see them?'

Sarah was shaking her head, more tears falling. 'I never saw anything. I ran from you at the marina. I was frightened after managing to fight Mark Coker—'

'Just get to the point, Sarah,' Dani interrupted.

The fury resurfaced in Sarah's eyes, but quickly subsided.

'I didn't know where to go. I drove towards home, then stopped in one of the parking areas in the New Forest. I must have fallen asleep for a while, I don't really know, but I do remember getting out of the car to stretch my legs. I heard a noise behind me, I think, and that was it. The next thing I knew, I woke up in that shop. Natasha was there, that head was there, and then you were there . . .'

Dani thought about what she was hearing. She believed it.

'But how did they know?' asked Sarah. 'How did they know Natasha was at my house? How did they know where I was? What did they want?'

Dani was silent as she thought about this, certain that Sarah was nothing more than a pawn in this game. She'd been used as a power play, to show Dani how far Hamilton could reach, and to send some kind of message to her father and Jimmy Nash, a message that Dani was still trying to fully figure out.

Sarah was still speaking, and Dani was aware that she'd zoned out, lost in her thoughts, and missed some words.

'Don't you remember him?' Sarah was saying. 'You were on top of me, at the shop, and he dragged you off, choked you until you passed out. You must remember?'

Dani stared back at Sarah.

'Look, you can lie all you want about what happened,' said Sarah. 'But I saw him then. He had some kind of stocking on his head. He was real. He was tall and wiry. He choked you unconscious in about a second. I thought he'd snapped your neck the way he threw you down and you crumpled on the floor. Then he came for me . . .'

She started to cry again.

'What will he do now?' she said, looking to Dani. 'Will he go after my family? What does he want?'

Dani watched, but still didn't speak.

'We need to find out who he is and what he wants,' Sarah said, trying to reach for Dani's hand. 'You need to stop him.'

Dani sat back and felt her mouth drop open. The woman across from her was worried about her own well-being and that of her family. It never ceased to amaze Dani how people could live up to such enormously high double standards.

Sarah Cox could justify in her own mind abducting a young girl for the purposes of watching her be raped and later killed, but the concept of herself, or those she loved, being harmed, was unthinkable to her.

Dani realised now why Sarah Cox had asked her to come in, why she'd opted to be truthful about some aspects of what she'd said.

It was nothing to do with a confession, nothing to do

with making anything she'd done right. It was self-preservation, pure and simple.

This woman who'd nearly killed Dani, knew that Dani was the only person who'd believe that this other party existed, and now she wanted Dani to protect her from him. Maybe Dani would – because she was going to find this person, whatever it took.

Chapter 3

Felicity was waiting as Dani left the interview room.

She'd obviously come out of the observation suite next door to meet Dani in the corridor, and Dani only had to take one look at her face to know that Felicity felt she had some explaining to do.

'Roger's here,' said Felicity. 'He arrived just after you started, so he watched it all.'

Dani nodded and walked slowly towards her. 'Did you get it all?' she asked.

'We absolutely did,' said Felicity. 'But she seemed to be trying her hardest to make sure we didn't. Speaking as quietly as possible and trying to aim her mouth away from the mic.' She gave Dani a searching look. 'Does what she said make some kind of sense to you? Because it doesn't to me and the team. She's now saying there was someone else involved and that she doesn't know who it is. Am I right? She's also saying that this new party took Natasha Moore from her house and delivered her to the shop in the New Forest and they did the same to her.'

Felicity paused, but Dani didn't respond.

'She's saying she doesn't know how she or Natasha

Moore got there,' Felicity continued, 'and she's saying that she didn't kill and behead Ryan Taylor – though that bit isn't new – but she's saying you saw this person and can corroborate her version of events?'

Dani nodded and then shrugged. 'That seems to be about the long and short of it,' she said.

She made to pass Felicity, heading for the observation room, but Felicity stepped into her path.

'She's also saying you were attacked by this person, that she saw it happen and that you know it's true . . .' Felicity looked pointedly at the worst of the bruising around Dani's neck.

Dani sighed. 'Though, as previously discussed, she also says that Mark Coker coerced her, that she killed him in self-defence, and that she knows nothing about the dead body we found at the armouries. The body she had access to and that was killed using her murder kit. So I'm gonna stick her down as not being the most reliable witness we've ever had in the hot seat.'

'No,' Felicity said, her voice challenging now. 'But was there someone else there, Dani? Because you believed her, didn't you? You're lying about something.'

Dani wanted to be outraged. The words hurt, especially coming from Felicity, a woman she'd come to love and respect, and who was among the very small group of people whose opinions she really valued.

But how could she be outraged, when Felicity was absolutely right?

Dani was lying, and she knew it. In fact, since she'd first boarded HMS *Tenacity* to investigate a suspicious suicide, she'd seemed to end up moving deeper and deeper into lies and deceit. She wondered at what point she'd be in so deep that she'd no longer be able to swim back out.

There were some secrets that she'd begun to share. She'd

told Felicity about the attack on her that had taken place exactly one year to the date that Hamilton was convicted, and that she was certain Hamilton had ordered it.

Until the point she'd confided in Felicity, only one other person had known what had been done to her before she managed to fight her way free.

It felt good to be free of that secret, to call it 'my attack', because now she owned it, not the cowards who'd tried to hurt her. She no longer felt that it was her fault; she felt empowered because she'd been able to escape them and then continue after them, relentless. It was her attack, and it would eventually be their undoing.

Getting to that point had allowed her to go and see Christopher Hamilton in prison. But there, once again, she'd been driven to keep secrets.

He'd spoken to her about things she couldn't share, insisting that no audio records be kept, that it was only for the two of them. He'd begun by saying he'd help her with her investigation to show worth and credibility, but really, he was simply manipulating her, and ultimately trying to isolate her.

She couldn't tell Felicity all the things Hamilton had said, and now, here, even when Felicity was calling her a liar, Dani was carrying more secrets, more things she couldn't tell.

She had been grabbed and choked unconscious as she fought with Sarah Cox, and it hadn't been Sarah who'd done it.

Someone else had been there and as Dani got the upper hand with Sarah, she'd felt them close in behind her and slip their arm around her throat, then pick her up clean off the floor. Then there'd been nothing.

She would have reported it in a heartbeat, except, when she'd come to, her own father had been there.

He was hundreds of miles from his home in Scotland, where he should have been, and he was standing talking with two other men who also shouldn't have been there. The men were telling him about the severed fingers that had been sent to Dani, and they seemed to know they belonged to Hamilton's victims. They had all speculated what message Hamilton might be trying to send her.

Dani would take them all down, her father included if she had to, but she needed to speak to him first. She'd hear him out, she owed him that much.

'Look, I have no recollection of anyone else being there at the shop,' she told Felicity. 'No one attacked me. She did this.' She gestured to her injuries. 'I think she's convinced that she's a victim in all this. I bet she's played it over in her mind so many times that she's actually reinvented the memory for herself, adding new characters that further remove her from her crimes. So, do I believe her? Yes. I believe that she believes what she's saying is the truth. Is it the truth, though?'

Dani looked up at Felicity. 'No, it isn't. You know it and I know it and you have no right to call me a liar.'

'I'm sorry,' said Felicity.

Dani ignored her and opened the door into the observation room.

'Dani,' Roger greeted her. He stepped forward as though to embrace her, before seeming to remember who and where he was, and simply reached out to touch her on the shoulder instead. 'How're you feeling? You shouldn't have discharged yourself from the hospital. I was going to come and see you. I was actually there already. I didn't even know you'd gone.'

'I'm OK, thanks, Roger,' she said. 'I needed to get out of there and I knew Cox was keen to speak to me.'

'Hey,' said Felicity. 'You told me you were out of hospital and available. I had no idea . . .'

Dani smiled at her and raised an eyebrow.

'I was out by the time I called you.'

'Well, you shouldn't really be here, Dani. You're supposed to be taking some time out to heal,' said Roger, looking stern.

'It was only talking,' Dani said.

He studied her closely and she was aware of him cataloguing the bruises and cuts that were visible on her face, hands and neck.

'It looks worse than it is. Superficial really. I'm fine. I won't do more than I can manage, and I want to stay busy.'

Roger looked at her a moment longer, then nodded, seeming to accept her decision but visibly unhappy about it.

'That was a bit of an odd interview in there,' he said. 'It seemed like she was introducing new lines, saying someone else was involved, that they attacked you?'

'She's introducing the bogeyman,' said Dani.

They discussed the interview for a while, then Felicity called the lead investigator, who said she'd have some questions once she'd listened to the tapes and read the transcripts.

'Home and rest for you, young lady,' said Roger, immediately looking apologetic as Dani shot him a glance for using a term he knew she hated. 'Sorry. Habit. But you are young, and you are a lady . . . most of the time.'

Dani shook her head, smiling, and looked away.

'I haven't seen your dad for a few days,' said Roger, obviously trying to change the subject and redeem himself. 'I thought he'd be hovering around you, staying at your house, driving you mad?'

37

'I haven't seen him either,' Dani said. 'I've had a lot to do. Better for me to keep busy when I'm like this. I'm going to call him today.'

'Well, send him my regards when you do. We should go for a beer. Tell him we've not had one in a while. It'd do us both good to have a catch up and talk about you.'

Dani knew the last bit was supposed to be a joke, but she ignored it, busying herself with checking some final notes and signing a statement form.

'You know, Hamilton's made repeated requests to see you again, Dani,' said Felicity. 'I think he'd literally call several times a day if he were allowed to use the phone.'

'I thought Twitter was his thing?' Dani said. 'But I guess that's only for reading. I don't want to speak to him. Maybe in a little while, a few weeks or months, and only if we have direct questions we want to ask him, with direct answers that will assist the investigation. I'm fed up with his bullshit, and feeling like I do now, I'm just not ready for it.'

Felicity looked concerned.

'Don't worry,' said Dani, reading her friend's face. 'I'll go in with him again if the investigation needs it, I promise. I just need a few days.'

'There's no rush at all,' said Roger, cutting in. 'I think you'd do well not to speak to him again. No good can ever come from that man.'

Dani nodded.

'I'm more concerned about you than him,' Felicity said. 'We made huge leaps in having regular conversations with him, Dani, but your health and well-being is my primary concern. You're the first and only person he's agreed to speak to in the years he's been imprisoned. I have no doubt that he'll see you again when you're ready, and I do think some good can come from it, it just can't be at your expense.'

Dani felt the tension in the room. 'I know,' she said. 'We all want to find his victims' bodies and see them laid to rest, to give their families a chance to find some peace and to show him he's not smarter than us, or above the law. I guess we just need to find a way to do that together.'

There was nothing in the world she wanted more than to find those women and bring their remains home so they could be laid to rest with some dignity, but she didn't feel that Hamilton was going to lead them there at the moment.

'My taxi's waiting,' she said, heading for the door. 'I have to go. Maybe you should send Hamilton my regards? Also tell him I'll be in to see him as soon as I'm good and ready – those exact words.'

Chapter 4

Dani woke and blinked, feeling a small surge of panic as she realised she was unsure of where she was. She wasn't in her nightmare, no one was pursuing her nor was she being restrained against her will in the impenetrable dark, but she still started as she tried to place her surroundings.

After a few moments, her vision cleared, and she recognised the white swirls of the pattern on her living room ceiling.

She'd fallen asleep on the couch, fully clothed, and this was unheard of for her.

Light streamed in through the privacy nets that lined her patio doors and it should have been a beautiful day, but her dry mouth, dull headache and stinging eyes told her everything she needed to know about how she felt.

She moved around and wriggled her back to see how stiff it was. One of the perks of being what some people would call petite was that she could sleep almost anywhere in reasonable comfort, at least.

The last person who'd slept on the couch had been her dad, and that had been an entirely different matter.

He was far too broad, and his shoulder and one hairy arm always hung off the edge, his knuckles dragging on the floor – a lifelong source of joy to Dani and Charlie who regularly referred to him as a 'knuckle dragger' or 'King Louis'. He was too long as well, and his feet were raised up, resting on the arm at the sofa's end.

They were big, hairy man-feet, like they belonged to a hobbit who'd missed successive pedicure appointments, and it wasn't something Dani relished seeing when she came down to wake him in the mornings.

He'd told her for many years that Royal Marines slept with one eye open, always ready to rise, fight and win, but she'd managed to vacuum the entire room once while he was sleeping on her couch and he hadn't stirred, so that childhood belief had been thoroughly destroyed.

She thought about him now. She needed to find him and speak to him, face-to-face, about why he'd been at the shop and what he knew about Jimmy Nash and Christopher Hamilton.

She picked up her bag and fished for her phone.

He was on speed dial and it went straight to answer.

'We need to talk, Dad, in person. It's urgent, but you know that. It's you and me today, or it'll be a very different conversation after that.'

She hung the phone up and rested it on her stomach, checking that it was switched on and set to ring out loud, then tried not to think about the implied threat she'd made to the man who'd raised her.

The room around her was light, the curtains always open, and only the nets obscured anyone's view from the outside.

The day looked cold and crisp, a good day for a run if she'd been feeling better, but she wasn't, and she considered whether to just let herself nod off again.

She'd no recollection of coming home after leaving the prison yesterday, not really. She must've come in, taken

41

a few moments on the couch to rest up before facing the stairs, and here she was now. She felt as though she could probably go back to sleep – her eyes wanted to – but already her mind was spinning up like a machine, gathering momentum.

She rolled on to her side and lowered her feet to the floor, then used her arm to push herself up into a sitting position. She was stiff and sore and regretted not buying a house with a downstairs toilet. She shuffled slowly to the kitchen, put the kettle on and then headed for the stairs, resigning herself to the fact it'd be a slow journey to the summit.

In her room, a few minutes later, she sat on the bed and then lay down.

She heard the click of the kettle downstairs, but she didn't want a cup of tea badly enough to face the steps again, not just yet.

Thoughts about various conversations were still running over and over in her mind. Not just the one that she needed to have with her father, but the one with Sarah Cox too, and the one she'd overheard at the abandoned shop in the New Forest.

She hadn't known Ryan's head was at the shop, since Sarah Cox had attacked her before she'd been able to look around properly. It was when she'd come around after the fight and heard her father's voice that she'd heard someone say it.

There was a sound downstairs.

Dani listened and then relaxed back to her thoughts as she heard mail being shoved into the letter box.

It was more than just the fact her dad was there, it was the way, like Cox, he seemed to accept that people were hurt and dead around him, and he was fine with that, as long as it didn't affect *his* family or *his* loved ones.

He'd spent her life telling her to stand up and do the

right thing, and she had, but it seemed that for him, the message had had caveats.

All of this bounced around in her head like a silver ball bearing in a pinball machine.

The fact he was there at all left only one real question. What had he done that made him beholden to these people at all?

It was odd to lie on her bed and think about how much she loved her dad, but that's what she was doing now, drifting between nostalgia and anger as she realised she couldn't let it lie. Father or not, she'd go after the truth – there were no caveats in *her* will to do the right thing.

It took considerable effort to lower herself to the floor and to reach under her bed and pull out the lock box that she kept there.

Opening it felt awkward.

Her fingers weren't operating as they should be, and it took her several attempts to get the combination correct.

When she finally got it unlocked, she instinctively shut her eyes as she opened the lid and reached inside. She removed the picture she kept on top and placed it face down on the floor.

Then, when she knew she wouldn't have to look at it, she opened her eyes again and began to flick through the documents that were locked beneath.

About halfway down, she found a file that was an exact copy of Christopher Hamilton's service records.

It showed everywhere he'd been during his years of service in the Royal Navy.

Against many of the entries, particularly the times when Hamilton was working abroad deployed on ships or stationed in foreign bases, Dani had made notes, jotting down incidents, missing persons and mutilated bodies that had been discovered near to wherever Hamilton had been.

She treated all of them as though they might be his victims, and many local police detectives had done the same, but no foreign charges had ever been brought against him due to lack of evidence.

Dani had looked into it extensively. She'd spent her own money during the sabbatical year she'd taken after her attack, travelling to many locations around the world and searching through local records and newspapers, speaking to local police where she was able to find someone willing to do so.

There were bodies abroad, she reasoned, so there must be an opportunity for a conviction, and with that, some kind of justice and peace for those families.

Within the United Kingdom, however, with the exception of the women's bodies she'd found herself on his property on the day she'd confronted and captured him, there were never any bodies at all, just disappearances – it was as though he had a sure-fire way of getting rid of them at home, but it didn't follow him across the sea, not all the time anyway.

This was one of the key factors in why Dani never believed he could have worked alone, and why she wasn't even sure that Hamilton knew where all, or any, of them were.

She looked at the notes now, thinking that if even ten percent of what she suspected was true, then, when added to all the potential cases in the United Kingdom in which he was the prime suspect, Hamilton would have to be one of the most prolific serial killers in recorded history.

She ran her finger down the list, thinking back to the conversation she'd heard between Jimmy 'The Teeth' Nash, Jimmy's assistant, Marcus, and her father.

From the way they'd been talking, it was as though they knew it was him that had called them there. It also seemed that they suspected his sending of the fingers of his victims to Dani was a way of sending a message to them, as well as to her, and that meant that at some point in the past their paths had crossed.

Dani reached for her mobile phone and dialled from memory.

'Josie,' she said, recognising the Leading Hand's accent.

Josie had joined the navy having been recruited from St Vincent and the Grenadines and she now worked for Dani in the Special Investigation Branch offices at Portsmouth Naval Base.

'Hello there, ma'am. I certainly wasn't expecting to hear from you. We were told you'd be off sick for a couple of weeks. In fact . . .'

Josie's voice trailed off and Dani tensed, pretty sure she knew what was coming next.

'In fact, ma'am, Commander Blackett called in just a few hours ago, and he was very, very clear indeed, that you'd certainly be off sick for a couple of weeks.'

Josie's voice was much lower now, likely so as not to be heard by anyone else in the office. 'He said to me alone, ma'am, and I quote, that he'd be "having words, negative tea and biscuits", with anybody who spoke to you about work for at least the next fortnight.'

Dani shook her head in silence. She'd half known he'd do something like this.

Roger did these things with the best intentions, to try and force her to rest, but what he could never quite understand was that it was more stressful for Dani to do nothing than it was to be focused on something important.

'Well, Josie, I did have a favour to ask, but I wouldn't put you in the position of getting in trouble with Commander Blackett.'

There was silence on the line.

'Of course, I wouldn't tell Commander Blackett we'd

45

spoken,' continued Dani, 'and I seriously doubt you would. Sometimes things do need to happen without senior officers knowing. The type of thing I'm after is very much in the weeds, so there shouldn't be any reason for Commander Blackett to be bothered with it . . .'

Dani felt bad as she heard herself speak, but she knew Josie was strong-willed, whip-smart and brave. Dani also knew she wouldn't be able to rest until she had what she needed and there was no way she could go into the RN Police HQ in person to get it.

'So, what you're saying is, ma'am, that Master at Arms Granger is after some information?'

Dani smiled at the mention of her partner, not least because he was still supposed to be on sick leave too.

His arm was recovering from a nasty break inflicted in a fight with Sarah Cox, but he wouldn't have Roger Blackett watching him anywhere near as closely as she did; he could get away with requesting this information and Josie was on the ball to think of it.

'Yes, Josie, that's exactly what I'm saying,' said Dani, half smiling to herself and feeling her shoulders relax. 'Master at Arms Granger is looking for some information on three former Royal Marines. All he wants at the moment are their service records. So, if you could email them to him, he wants records for Royal Marines by the names of Jimmy Nash, Marcus Lowe and . . .' She trailed off.

Josie repeated back the names. 'And the third name, ma'am? Did you say there were three?'

Dani thought about the third name, her father's name, but try as she might she couldn't say it. She leaned her head back against her mattress and thought. She had three data points.

Hamilton's whereabouts and service records were known to her and she'd soon have Marcus and Jimmy's.

Given the very different roles that these men held within the British Forces, she was certain this would be enough to get a location and timescale where their paths had crossed.

If she needed more information, she could go after her father's records then.

'No, just those two, please, Josie,' she said. 'When you email them to Master at Arms Granger, could you please copy me in as well? I just like to keep up with what he's doing.'

'That's just fine, ma'am. I'll be getting on to that straight away.'

Dani wondered what John would think when he received these files from out of nowhere.

They'd worked together many times and she trusted him, not only to be a grizzled and hard-nosed Master at Arms who knew the rules and when to bend them, but she trusted him to know her too.

When he got those files, he'd know she was up to something and he'd call her before he spoke to anyone else about it.

Dani looked down at the files in front of her. She thought about what Hamilton had done and the type of things Jimmy Nash did. Dani had seen enough films and read enough books about police officers who had one case they just couldn't let go of and she knew hers was Hamilton – it was an obsession. But, while she'd always believed that Hamilton had killed many more people than almost anyone else suspected, that he'd used his job in the Royal Navy and the anonymity it brought to travel from country to country committing murder and then disappearing back to sea, she'd never considered that he might take any part in something to do with drugs, or whatever else it was that Jimmy wanted to smuggle into the country.

It just didn't fit with anything she knew about Hamilton.

It didn't seem to fit with what he liked or what drove and motivated him.

She doubted he'd turn the money down, but she also knew that, to him, money was just a means to an end.

He paid an expensive solicitor now, because he'd saved huge sums of money during his career, seemingly only spending what he needed to pursue his killing and present a normal enough lifestyle to cover his activities. Christopher Hamilton disgusted her on every level, but she believed he had a moral code of his own. He would consider the act of importing narcotics to be beneath him.

She looked at the curtains that framed the privacy nets around her bedroom window.

They were open as always, day and night, and she wondered why she'd even had them hung.

Then she remembered her dad hanging them for her.

He'd talked about how she needed to be able to pull them shut when she changed, not listening to her explanation that her privacy blinds blocked all possible view, while still letting in the light.

She always changed in the bathroom anyway, but he wasn't one for listening when he thought something should be done a certain way. She shook her head slowly.

It annoyed her how much he was creeping into her thoughts.

It annoyed her even more how badly she wanted to know what his part was in all of this.

The other people she'd heard speaking with him that night in the abandoned shop, were Jimmy and Marcus.

She knew for a cold, hard fact that Jimmy would tell her nothing. She suspected that Marcus, despite how friendly and genuine he seemed, would also tell her nothing of use.

She checked her phone, although she knew she'd missed no calls.

With her dad not speaking to her for whatever reason, Dani realised she was in the awful position where the only person that might speak to her, that might be honest with her if it suited his need, was a serial killer who'd tried to have her killed.

She laid her head back as she considered the irony. To get some time alone with Hamilton, she would need to be back at work, assisting as the naval liaison for the National Crime Agency's investigation into the link between seven missing women, whose severed fingers had been posted to Dani's house.

They wanted her to speak to him too, but Dani wasn't sure if she could face him yet.

She went back to her first position: she needed to speak to her dad and then go in with Hamilton from a position of strength and knowledge; she was fed up being on the back foot the whole time, always defending and counter-punching – she needed to take the lead and get ahead of him.

She began to put the files back into her lock box, looking at the back of the photograph she always kept on top and placing it in last. She looked away at the final moment as she flipped it face up, a disturbing reminder to her every time she opened the box, of the harm that people can do to others given the right motivation and the right situation.

The lid clicked shut, and she scrambled the combination.

There was a picture beside her bed of her father along with her, Charlie and Mim. It was taken on a sports day, shortly after they'd won the first prize in one of the parent and child events.

Dani looked at it, remembering that day. She loved sports, loved sports day, and she recalled walking into school, her hand swallowed up in her father's giant fist. She'd looked up to him and reminded him, for the hundredth time since they'd left the house.

'Daddy, when they do the games at the end, the ones where the daddies come in and join in, make sure you're on my team, OK? I want to be with you. Don't forget.'

He'd looked down and smiled at her.

'I'm your dad, Dani-bear. I'm on your team for life.'

The letter box snapped downstairs, breaking the memory.

Whatever had been shoved in there earlier had now fallen on to the doormat and Dani rose slowly.

She could see from the top of the stairs that there was only one envelope today and she recognised it, even from that distance.

Going down the steps was hard, but as she approached the bottom, she knew she was right.

The envelope was very thick and embossed.

The handwriting was in flowing black ink.

She knew what it was.

Hamilton had been sending her letters, via his solicitor, for months.

She picked it up, felt it – there was an envelope inside the envelope, she was sure of that.

'Not today,' she said to herself. 'He's not getting into my head again today.'

She knew she needed to speak to him, but she wasn't ready yet and she was too tired to read the bullshit he wrote.

When he had time to pontificate in the obnoxious way he did on paper, he was more unbearable than ever. He'd take time to try and get under her skin, making sure every word had a double meaning and could sow seeds of doubt in her mind.

No.

He'd get his chance to talk to her, but it would be a free exchange, face-to-face and on her terms.

Walking through to the kitchen, Dani dropped Hamilton's letter, unopened, into the bin.

Chapter 5

The information Dani had requested from Josie hadn't arrived and Dani was restless.

She regularly checked her phone, though she knew it hadn't rung, and she switched between daytime TV channels, and between TV and radio, and radio and books, until she finally realised she was starting the same novel for the fourth time in as many minutes and tossed it across the room.

It hit the patio doors and fell to the carpet.

Her phone was next to her, plugged in and charging to ensure it'd definitely be available and serviceable when the time came, and she touched the screen again, just to be sure.

The knock at the door was a welcome surprise and she jumped up quickly, having to pause and catch her breath before she went to answer it.

The knock sounded again.

She walked along the hallway and looked through the peephole.

The man outside was wearing a red delivery-firm jacket and matching baseball cap. He was holding a small package and some kind of handheld device for signatures.

Dani paused, knowing she wasn't expecting anything, and then shouted through the door.

'Who is it, please? I'm not expecting any deliveries.'

The man stepped back, as though he'd been completely unaware she was watching him. He paused, seemed to gather himself and then leaned closer to the door.

'It's a delivery for a Martha Daniels,' he said. 'Your neighbour? She's not in. I've tried twice and if I don't leave it today, it's going back to sender.'

Martha regularly took Dani's post in for her and Dani sighed. 'Leave it there and I'll collect it in a second,' she said.

He was already shaking his head. 'It needs a signature, miss. No worries, though, I've got one hundred and seventeen more to deliver today, so if you won't take it, I have to get going.'

He turned to leave, stumbling a little on the uneven ground.

Dani watched him. 'Hold on,' she shouted. 'I'll take it.'

She stepped away from the door and began to unlock it. Before she pulled the last bolt, she checked again, and saw he was waiting a few feet away. She stepped back, operated the handle and pulled the door open slowly.

He must have run at her, hitting the door at full tilt and slamming it wide open.

It missed her – she'd long since learned not to stand directly behind a door for this very reason – but the noise and ferocity still made her stagger back as the delivery man fell into her house.

He tripped and stumbled, regained his balance and then turned to face her.

She could see now that he was emaciated beneath the baseball cap, his face bruised and pale, so that the marks showed through as dark pastels against a stark white canvas, and his large nose seemed to stretch the skin away from the rest of his face.

Despite her adrenaline, she also smelled him instantly, the pungent reek of alcohol.

Then he was on her, grabbing her by the shoulders and throwing her along the hallway towards the sitting room. He'd dropped his parcel and kicked the door shut behind him, immediately stalking towards her.

'I've got a message for you,' he said, his voice loud and giddy, uncontrolled and frightened. He sounded as though he were trying to remember a script and was panicking as to whether he'd deliver the lines as perfectly as required. 'We can get you anywhere. Here at home. Anywhere.'

He was close to her now and he stumbled as he swung an arm at her.

Dani managed to duck away, stepping back out of the hallway and into her sitting room. She kept a baton next to the front door, but that was useless now, and she looked around for a possible weapon as he approached.

He reached towards her, his hand outstretched.

Dani gasped as she saw dirty bandages wrapped around his left hand – his ring finger obvious by its absence.

'You tell your dad – anywhere. OK?'

The man lunged at her again, as though to slap her, but he was unsteady on his feet and Dani stepped away from his flailing arm.

She watched as it took a second for him to steady himself and then she glanced down at the novel she'd thrown on the floor a few minutes before. She winced as she stooped quickly and picked the book up, throwing it at his head in a single movement.

He flailed to swipe the book aside, and in that instant, Dani stepped forward and kicked out as hard as she could.

She felt her foot land deftly between his legs with a deep thud.

The man went rigid as though he'd been electrocuted. Then he seemed to grab for her again, sheer rage in his eyes, before he folded over on to the floor and let out a long, low groan.

Dani watched him for only a second.

He was lying between her and the front door.

Her patio doors were locked and difficult to open; she had to pass him to get out.

She stepped forward quickly, kicking out hard again and catching him in the ribs, before stamping down on his torso with her full weight and using the momentum to power herself over his body and towards the door. Her hand reached instinctively for the baton as she passed it and she felt better having it in her hand as she opened the door and stepped outside.

'Is everything OK, Dani?'

Dani turned to see her elderly neighbour, Martha, peering out of her house next door.

'I heard an awful noise,' the woman said, her hand held against her chest.

Dani turned to look back into her house, checking that he wasn't following her, then she turned to Martha.

'Someone broke in. Go inside and call the police,' she said. 'Do it now please, Martha.'

The old woman didn't hesitate, and Dani could hear her calling to her husband, Derek, as she moved back inside the small terraced house.

There seemed to be no movement inside Dani's house, no sound at all, and Dani waited, unsure of whether to run, wait, or go back in and try to force some answers.

The man was drunk, but still dangerous, and Dani knew she was better off out here in broad daylight.

A movement caught the corner of her eye and she spun, initially alarmed, until she saw Martha again.

Her neighbour was wearing a dressing gown and slippers as she stepped out of her house with a long, heavy carving knife in one hand.

'Martha, what are you doing?' said Dani, exasperated.

'Derek's calling the police,' she said, matter-of-fact. 'I'll come out here and wait with you.'

The old woman took up a position right next to Dani and began to stare into the open doorway and Dani's hallway beyond it.

Dani knew she had a small frame, but Martha was smaller still, and slightly bent with age. Dani looked down and saw the thin skin of Martha's hand tauten as it gripped the knife handle.

'Martha, go inside,' she hissed.

'I'll go inside if *you* come inside,' the old woman said, her eyes never leaving the doorway to Dani's house.

'I'm not coming inside,' said Dani.

'Then *I'm* not going inside,' said Martha.

Dani looked at her neighbour, frustration ready to burst out of her.

Another movement caught her eye and she looked up to see Derek now exiting the house next door.

He was wearing a thick tartan dressing gown, almost-matching pyjama bottoms and slippers that fastened with Velcro. He was carrying a cricket bat.

'Police are on the way,' he said, as he fell in beside his wife.

Dani felt the urge to laugh as she looked at her two sentinels, standing fearless beside her in their dressing gowns, neither of them knowing what danger they were facing, but standing with her anyway.

There was a sudden bang and an almighty crash of shattering glass from within Dani's house.

All three of them took a step back.

'Was that a gunshot?' Derek asked. 'You two get inside our house.'

Dani wasn't sure. She'd heard gunfire many times before, but not like that.

Derek began to try and hustle Martha indoors, calling to Dani to follow, but both women ignored him and stood their ground, listening.

Dani heard more glass break and, as the sound of police sirens rose in the background, she knew that the man had smashed her patio doors and was making his escape.

'Don't go in there,' said Martha, seeming to sense something change in Dani's posture. 'Please don't go in.'

'He's gone,' said Dani, stepping towards the door.

'You don't know that.'

'I do,' said Dani. 'Stay here. You're not coming in.'

'If he's gone, then there's no harm in me tagging along,' said Martha, her eyes defiant.

'I'm coming too,' said Derek, obviously realising that no one was following him to the safety of his house.

They walked slowly into Dani's house in single file, Dani closely followed by Martha, Derek at the back murmuring his displeasure.

In the lounge, Dani's patio doors were shattered, and her sitting room floor was empty.

'Wait there,' she said to Martha, and moved as quickly as she was able to grab her phone.

As soon as she had it, she gestured for them to retreat back outside to the sounds of police sirens and growing voices outside the house.

A young policewoman was speaking into her radio as she approached the front of the house.

Dani made for her and quickly briefed her on who she

was, why her house was flagged for a rapid response, and what had happened.

'I'll need to get an ambulance to check you over, OK?' said the police officer. 'You'll likely need to go to hospital for a check too.'

Dani nodded. 'I've not long come from there,' she joked. 'I just need to make a phone call first.' She gestured to her mobile phone. 'I need to let my dad know I'm OK.'

The police officer nodded and moved away, then stopped suddenly and looked back.

'You have very good neighbours, Miss Lewis. That can feel a bit rare these days.'

Dani nodded. 'I know.'

She heard the number ring and waited until it went to answer phone as it had done before.

'A friend of yours came to see me, Dad. He wasn't looking great and he attacked me in my home. He asked me to let you know that it might not be the last time he visits and that he can get me anywhere. Speak soon.'

She hung up the phone and checked the time – she was certain now that it wouldn't be long before he rang.

A number of police were heading into her house now, and Dani remembered the letter from Hamilton in her bin.

She walked quickly to the police officer she'd previously spoken to.

'I just need to grab something from the house. It's nowhere near the scene, it's in the kitchen?'

The officer looked around and nodded.

Dani moved quickly into her house and to the bin.

The letter was still there, and she grabbed it and slipped it into her back pocket, just as her mobile phone began to ring.

Chapter 6

Hamilton's Opening Letter

To my dearest Dani,

I hope you open this letter. I know you choose not to read most of my correspondence and so I'll make a copy and keep it for you just in case. I also understand from our conversations that your mail has been intercepted, which sounds very exciting and clandestine, but I think I have sealed this in such a way that you'd know if it had been opened. Unless you've told them, which I doubt you have, it should make it through OK, and that's a good thing.

This letter isn't like the others I've previously sent.

I will ask for your discretion regarding our correspondence and I'm afraid I'll need to proceed slowly, taking some time to trust you with my thoughts and feelings. It's not easy to let someone inside and I need to feel truly comfortable with you before I'm able to fully expose myself.

I would like to say that it's incredibly hard to sit here now, all these years later, and allow my mind to meander back to the good old days. It's also coloured by my rose-tinted glasses and, of course, the natural memory loss of age and time, which can subtly alter the past, often to extremes of positivity or the opposite.

I think I need to try and take myself back, though, for both our sakes. Starting anywhere other than the very beginning will just mean you won't understand where I'm coming from, and that won't do.

I expect that you'll be morally driven to want to share this correspondence at some point in the future. Though I hope we have developed enough trust between us to prevent you from doing so, I accept that you'll want to. But I trust you to know when the time is right, and you should further note that the vast majority of readers simply won't understand it; their intellect won't be sufficiently capable of processing what they read.

The best of my vocation are never discovered. Their existence is never even suspected. I was one of those elite for many years and I will live with the crushing disappointment of my discovery for the rest of my life.

And so, to begin . . .

It feels a cliché, but I do think my childhood is the place to start. If I don't, then further questions will only be asked and all the halfwits who have fumbled around my diagnosis will say I'm repressing.

I went through puberty late in a house where puberty was a very bad thing.

I don't wish to judge my parents too harshly, especially given the way views are changing these days. I think we can all agree that, for instance, some people are born pre-disposed to being gay – some men will always fancy men and some women will only fancy women – I don't believe that all of them are this way – born with it – but I do now, grudgingly, agree that aside from those people who believe that same-sex relationships are cool or the latest fashion craze to make them seem hip and accepted, this predisposition is legitimate and, in recognising this, I have long since come to terms with what could aptly be described as my early years of homophobia.

Society has taken this in its stride and I have never known a time when people were able to be freer in their choices. Society has become more inclusive and welcoming to the fact that some people are born a certain way; they can't help it. I still think we're a way off recognition that, in this same way, some people are born predisposed to desire children.

Society tells us this is wrong, and I agree. But wasn't homosexuality considered wrong not all that long ago? All I would say is that my father did love me in his own way and my mother allowed him to do so; water under the bridge at this point.

It was still, however, at the point of puberty that my relationship with my father became increasingly problematic. He became distant and aggressive towards me, regardless of what I did or offered to do.

By my teenage years I was already highly intelligent, my peers boring me, school dull and uninteresting. I knew that what was happening to me at home wasn't the norm but it was my norm, and I don't feel the shame society believes I should.

My only excitement came when I'd force a young teacher to cry on to her blouse, so I could then spend the lesson trying to imagine running my tongue over the small dark, wet patches her tears left.

While this was happening at school, my home life was disintegrating.

My father no longer wished to hear or see me around the house and any infringement of his demands was met with what could only be termed 'volcanic violence'.

My mother seemed to finally sense his change and she also never wanted to come near me, not to hold me or to even talk to me. She stopped entering my bedroom at all and would lock the bathroom when she was in there. She'd wedge the edge of her towel under the door, so I couldn't have let myself in, even in an emergency.

I had no friends at all at school, or anywhere else, and I was very isolated, though I'm not sure I felt this way. The children around me at school bored me and so I had no wish to be in their company anyway.

I assure you, Dani, that I seek no sympathy from these truths, but as one of the few people who sincerely seeks to understand me, I think it's worth telling you that it was then, at this point, that I think I began to change for what you might perceive as the worse. You've probably gathered by now that revenge is one of the concepts I've wrestled with and clung to throughout my entire life. Revenge was there at the moment I changed and has been with me ever since.

I remember the exact point of my change. I was suffering from acne and my voice was breaking. We had no money at home and my parents had no will to spend time making what we did have look kempt. My clothes were cheap, badly worn and mostly unwashed. My shoes were scuffed and dirty. In school, even back then, these were hardly the ingredients for popularity.

On this particular day, I answered a question in class, as children are often made to do. What started off as an ordinary sound, my voice as I had always known it, descended quickly to a low rumble and then just as suddenly leapt to a high-pitched squeak.

The class laughed and pointed and one girl, in particular, caught my eye – Jenny MacAulay – known as Ketchup MacAulay by all the boys, because she was rich, thick and delicious.

She was a rare beauty, already in full bloom, and her breasts pushed out against her school blouse and caught the eye of pupils and male teachers alike.

She smiled at me and said, 'Cry weirdo.'

Vengeance comes from shaking the very foundations that someone's confidence and being is built upon and leaving them alive, destabilised, living as a different person.

I was angry with Jenny, angry in a way I'd never been before, and so I made up my mind to wait and seek my revenge properly. I did wait too; patience really is a virtue.

Chapter 7

On some level, she was unsure whether she'd be able to even look at her father, let alone speak to him when he arrived to collect her from the hospital.

The police had spoken to Dani at length about the attack on her house and Dani had passed it off as a drunk attempting to burgle her – a daytime home invasion.

She'd made no mention of the message for her father. She'd deal with that herself.

The police woman had said there had been a spate of knock-and-grabs in the wider area, though none were recent or near Dani, but that they'd follow up and be in touch.

Seeing her father after lying to keep him out of the investigation curdled uncomfortably inside her and she was angry at the sight of him.

From the moment she'd heard him speaking with Jimmy Nash, something had changed in the way she felt about him.

It wasn't just that he was in a place she'd never expected him to be, discussing the case she was working on that he should have known nothing about, and doing so with a violent criminal. It was his reluctance to share with her, and it all combined to shake her core beliefs about who her father was.

Jimmy Nash had spoken about her father when she'd met him in a filthy house he ran somewhere on the south coast. A place where people who'd wronged him were held, abused and tortured, and those words echoed in her mind now.

'*Your view of me and my organisation probably isn't great after what you've seen, what we let you see, but I want you to know, that however ruthless and remorseless and lacking compassion you judge me to be, however much the violence sickens you, however frightened the threats make you feel, I want you to know: I've got nothing at all on your old dad.*'

Dani had taken those words as nothing more than an attempt to shake her, but now she viewed them in a different light.

After she'd caught Hamilton, when it was all over the papers, she'd gone home to get away from all the attention.

He'd been waiting for her at the front door – his arms spread wide, waiting to wrap her up – and he'd told her how proud he was that she'd been the one to bring Hamilton down and end his murders. He'd even congratulated her on the paper she'd written that was leaked to the press, where she'd stated her belief that Hamilton hadn't worked alone.

They'd discussed it at length then and again later when it had nearly ended her career, but through all of that, he'd never once mentioned that he knew anything about the man, besides what he'd read in the newspapers.

He was here again now, waiting as Dani was discharged, and she flinched away as he tried to hug her; she couldn't help herself.

His face showed it bothered him, but also that he'd been expecting it.

They walked out together, and he directed her towards his car.

He stepped across her path to open the car door for her. It was clumsy, awkward and he made her stumble as he did it.

She rolled her eyes at the gesture, climbed in and reached out to shut the door herself, but he was there and so she leaned back in the seat and let him do it. She watched him walk around to the driver's side.

Her dad was a huge man, physically and in his personality, but he looked different to her now, and she couldn't figure out why.

It was odd that through her life, she could remember how her perception of her father had changed.

As a child, she remembered him only as her very big, very loud dad.

He was the one who, when he was at home and not away on operations, always brought the fun, chaos, noise and laughter. He was a larger-than-life, strong-as-an-ox, muscle-bound climbing frame with boundless energy and patience for her and her sister, Charlie.

They'd play-fight in the garden, throw balls, Frisbees, water bombs, anything at all they could find to throw at, or to, each other.

He'd throw her and Charlie around too.

Charlie was the more timid of the two, often asking to stop, but Dani would push as far as she could, daring him to throw her higher and higher, knowing there was never any real danger; he'd catch her every time.

He was the one who'd set the garden up as an assault course, and he'd be the one with the watch, timing each of them, deciding how much of a head start she'd get over her older sister and cheering for them both the whole way around.

Back then he was simply the biggest person she knew.

He'd seemed to physically shrink just a little bit when he left the Royal Marines, as though he'd lost something that was visible in the way he walked and held himself.

Dani also remembered when she'd seen different sides of him, like when she'd left home to join the navy, returning a few months later to realise he wasn't just her dad, he was also a human being in his own right.

He had a sense of humour. He had friends. He had a temper, and there were things that cheered him up and things that brought him down, and these things weren't always solely related to Dani and Charlie.

This recognition made him look more serious; not less fun – her father was always good fun – but he just began to look more real.

He was no longer the cartoon giant he'd been until that point.

After he left the Marines, she also began to realise that he was getting older.

His muscle mass was decreasing, his skin becoming loose around his elbows and jawline, and he couldn't sit down or pick something off the floor without grunting as he bent his knees.

Dani remembered these changes, or rather she remembered the moment she recognised them, but they'd all happened slowly, and so throughout, he'd still looked like her dad. She remembered how he'd been on the day he'd turned up to watch her passing out parade with Charlie and her stepmother, Mim.

It was at HMS Raleigh, where all new recruits to the navy, except the officers, go for basic training, and Dani was sure she'd seen his chest grow three or four inches that day, swelling as she'd marched past with the rest of her division.

Now, as she watched him walk around the front of the car, he just seemed to look darker and smaller, more like a stranger, as though she'd never truly known him at all.

He settled into the driver's seat, the car rocking under his weight, and fished his keys from his front pocket, fumbling them once before he started the engine. 'I know you must be dying to get home and have a rest,' he said. 'I spoke to Roger and he's had someone round to board up your patio doors. He says they're solid as a rock, but I can check when we get there.'

The engine of her father's 4x4 rumbled into life, shaking Dani in her seat, then the rows of cars in the car park began to pass her, gathering speed as they disappeared from her periphery.

'I don't want to rest . . .'

She almost said his name, almost said 'Dad', but it didn't feel right, and it caught in her throat before it could escape.

'I'm tired, but I can't rest until you talk to me. I need to know what you've got to do with any of this. What you know, how long you've known it . . .' She trailed off without saying the obvious next line: 'why you didn't tell me'.

She could see his face from the corner of her eye.

'It wasn't a gun that broke your window,' he said, as though he hadn't heard her speak. 'It sounded like one, but it was a hammer.'

He was concentrating on the road, over-concentrating, his jaw tight and his teeth grinding – a bad habit, and one that she'd inherited from him.

Dani turned in her seat and watched him, making sure he knew she was doing so.

They were on the motorway now, and the movement

of the trees whizzing past made Dani feel light-headed. She'd been given some pretty hefty medication over the past few days and, though she wasn't a fan of taking anything, not even paracetamol, she'd been grateful for it until now. It felt like it was starting to catch up with her.

The lack of sleep, the physical exertion and the stress all added to the dawning realisation that her father wasn't going to just open up and talk to her as she'd expected he would.

She could see from his face, the line of his jaw, the bulging muscle on the side of his head as he clenched his teeth together, that he didn't want to tell her, and she could imagine he'd practised what he'd say, how he'd explain that he couldn't tell her, or wouldn't.

Something snapped inside her.

This man, her father, owed her an explanation and she'd have one.

'Dad!' she said, her voice louder than she'd meant. 'I want to know. Now.'

The sounds of the motorway seemed to flood in to fill the silence.

She stared at him.

'You have to tell me,' she said, feeling her breathing quicken.

He was shaking his head.

'Don't shake your head at me,' she said, almost spitting the words at him. 'Don't you dare. Don't you dare shake your head at me on the same day that someone forced their way into my house to send a message to you. And don't give me any bullshit about you and Jimmy just being friends from the Marines, because that might be where you met, but that's not why you were there at the shop, and we both know it.'

She turned in her seat, facing the front again, not sure

what she was going to do next, but knowing that whatever it was would be driven by sheer fury. She glanced across and caught her father's eye.

It was moist, not tears – she'd never seen her dad actually cry – but it was the precursor to tears and it stopped her in her tracks.

'I'm going to sort this out,' he said. 'I promise. I'm working on it now.'

'Jesus, Dad,' she said, feeling her anger disappear, as if it had been snatched away.

She couldn't remember ever seeing weakness in him of any kind, and he'd consider crying a weakness.

He looked smaller now, as though he'd deflated beneath her words.

'I don't need you to sort it out,' she said, her voice low. 'Just tell me what's happened. Who are these people who are trying to get to you, and why? What do they want you to do?'

'I can't,' he said, still shaking his head. 'I know you want to know. I know you *think* you want to know, but you don't, and I can't tell you. Not yet, maybe not ever.'

Dani could feel fury building up inside her – but even through the haze of painkillers she knew meeting her dad head on was futile.

That's who he was: he was the man who met people head on. He was nicknamed 'Taz' after the cartoon character of the Tasmanian devil, the character who'd go through anything, stop at nothing, was indestructible and would never, ever back down.

'You can tell me,' she said, fighting hard to keep her voice even. 'You can tell me now and you can trust me.'

His eyes looked misty, but in that instant, she knew he wouldn't.

'You know, I figured a lot of it out,' she said, watching

him for any reaction. 'Smuggling drugs and other contra-band back in from conflict areas isn't exactly original, but I'd guess using a nuclear submarine to do it might be. Someone needed to have the contacts at one end to have things shipped back to the UK, and I'm sure that's Jimmy. He's probably not the top of the pyramid, but he's up there somewhere. The guys on *Tenacity* were just mules. They probably didn't even know what they were transporting, and they didn't care either. They were doing it purely for the money, and they probably didn't realise, until the bodies started dropping, just how serious the other players were. But when the drugs arrived back into the country, I couldn't understand how a few submariners could distribute that kind of weight. But now I see, that's where Jimmy fits in again. He's the man that arranged for it to be sent and he's the man with the gang who distributes it when it gets here – a gang of specialist military veterans who sell their morals for a few quid. And if it's just drugs, then that's really the whole picture, isn't it? But from what I heard when you were talking to him, it's not just drugs?'

Her father just drove on, his eyes fixed on the road.

'I've got the overview, don't you think?' Dani continued. 'And, as I sit here now, I don't know what else they're bringing into the country, but I'll find out. And I don't know what part you want to play in this, but I do know this much.' She paused, drawing in a deep breath before she spoke again: 'If you tell me everything you know, if you trust me professionally and, more importantly, as your daughter, then you know—'

'Know what?' her father said, his voice quiet but firm. 'What do I know?'

'You know I'll listen to you,' she said. 'You know I'll listen to what you say . . .'

'And then what?' he asked, still focused on the road.

Dani was forced to think for a while longer.

'And then what?' he repeated, turning in his seat and glancing at her. 'What will you do with what you'll know?'

'I'll do what you always taught me to do,' she said, again feeling her temper rising. 'I'll do the right thing.'

He turned away from her, looking out of the driver's side window.

'You know, for someone so smart, you can be really, bloody stupid,' he said. 'Think about who you're dealing with and what they've done so far. Think about it. Sometimes, the right thing isn't the right thing. Sometimes, the right thing to do is just to protect the ones you love. You're not responsible for every wrong in the world, and sometimes you have to accept that and look after the people that matter to you most.'

Dani seemed to hear the words in slow time, as though she were able to examine each one as it came at her.

What was he asking her to do? Was her father asking her to ignore what she'd heard, to do nothing?

She couldn't believe her own thoughts and she took her time before speaking again, choosing her words, putting them in one order and then mixing them up and putting them back together a different way. She didn't know if what she was going to say would come out right, but it needed to be said.

They were turning off the motorway now, heading on to the smaller road that led to the estate where she lived.

'I can't walk away from this,' she said. 'I can't walk away from it, Dad. And if you're involved, then you know I'll find out. The things Jimmy does, the things I've seen him do to other human beings, mean I can't turn a blind eye.'

She stopped and looked at him, watching as he drove, his eyes fixed on the road. She had to have one more go.

The betrayal she'd felt when she'd heard his voice along-side Jimmy's had been crippling, but now, faced with the fact he still wouldn't tell her, she felt paralysed with anger and confusion.

'I want you to tell me what you know. Whatever it is, tell me what you've done. Tell me all of it, even if it's only what you saw. I want you to know I'll listen.'

She stopped for a moment and drew in a deep breath.

'But if you don't want to tell me, then I want you to know I'll investigate you too. And if you've any part in the disgusting acts they've committed, then I'll see to it you get the same treatment as those you're siding with.'

They pulled into the parking space outside Dani's house, and she reached for the door, wincing as she pushed it open, trying to get out of the car before her dad could come around to help; she didn't want to have to look him in the eye.

He was out of the car and round to her side already.

'I was going to stay here with you,' he said, offering her his hand as she swung her legs round.

'I lied for you again today,' Dani said. 'I never told the police you were there at the shop and today I didn't tell them what the guy said at my house. I said he was just a random invader looking to steal stuff, but that's the last time.'

'I should stay with you,' he said. 'It'll be safer.'

Dani walked past him towards her front door.

'You're not welcome,' she said, unable to look at him as she said it. 'I can look out for myself.'

He paused. 'I'll get a hotel closer to here then, in case you need me?'

'I won't,' she said, passing him and not wanting to turn back, not wanting her father to see her face, to see her eyes as she welled up at the thought of the conversation they'd just had.

'Dani,' he said.

She stopped. She was facing her front door, her key in the lock, and she didn't turn around, just paused, standing still and waiting to hear what he had to say.

'When you think about this conversation later, and I know you will, because you're like me – you play things over and over in your mind. But, when you do, do one thing for me? Think about the things you say you've seen Jimmy do and the things you know he could do. Then think about me, about the man I am, the father I am to you, the person you've known your entire life. Ask yourself if I'm like him. You told me to trust you. Well, when you think about all of this later, maybe you need to think about trusting me. You asked me what could motivate me to be involved with a man like Jimmy, well, mull that over too. I've got people I love more than anything else in this world. You're one of them. I don't even know what lengths I'd be prepared to go to to protect you or your sister. So, think about that, and whether it might mean it's time for you to walk away from this.'

Dani waited, without moving, her key still in the lock.

'For years I've known Hamilton had someone helping him,' she said, her eyes on the door. 'I would never have guessed in a million years that you would be helping him too.'

She remained there, unmoving, until she heard her father start his car and drive away.

She thought about what he'd said, the words starting to play back in her mind already, and she realised her dad had changed again in a way she'd never even considered possible: he was afraid.

Chapter 8

'I thought you were supposed to be off work, recuperating and all that good stuff,' said John, shaking his head at her as she opened her front door.

Dani looked at the cast on his arm. 'Well, hello, pot, kettle here, what colour are you?' She realised that she'd been happy to see him through the peephole. 'So, to what do I owe the pleasure? Did Roger send you?'

'Why, my arm is just fine, thank you very much for asking,' John said, brandishing his cast at her. 'And Roger never sent me. Why do you think that?'

He paused, and Dani shrugged.

'No, I'm here because I received an odd email. Turns out I requested some information to be sent to me and I must be getting old because I've no memory of doing it. And even now I see the service docs I've been sent, I just can't seem to recall why I'd be wanting them. So, I decided to read it and see if it would jog my fading memory, and then, when I saw you were copied in on Josie's email, I put two and two together and decided to come here and find out what you were up to.'

Dani smiled and reached out to pat John on the shoulder.

He recoiled a little in surprise and Dani realised she'd done something out of character.

'Sorry,' she said, still smiling. 'I must be feeling unusually tactile. I just have to finish this call – come in and give me a sec.'

She stepped back to let John in, then spoke into her mobile.

'Felicity, it was John.' She laughed. 'Yeah, no panic. But I'll go now. I'll see you tomorrow, OK?'

John was waiting uncertainly just inside the open door. 'If you don't feel like talking tonight, I can come back tomorrow?' he said once she'd ended the call.

Dani looked at his arm and then at the car parking spaces around her house.

His car wasn't there.

'No, it's good. How did you get here?' she asked. 'I didn't think you could drive at the moment.'

'I came on the bus,' John said, grinning as if he'd accomplished something spectacular. 'I have so little to do with my days at the moment, and I got so bored that I managed to decipher the local bus timetables. It took me ninety minutes to get here, but it gave me something to do and I'm hoping to knock thirty minutes off that on the way back. I have it all planned out.'

'Sounds like my gran and grandad,' said Dani. 'They spent their retirement travelling around on the buses all day, every day. It was what they did. My dad told me once that they took a four-hour round trip on the bus to pick up some paracetamol from the Parkhead Forge, which probably cost more than the shop at the end of their road, but I guess it's not always about the destination. Shall I stick the kettle on?'

'I'll do it,' said John. 'You look worse than me. Go and take the weight off.'

Dani nodded and walked through to her lounge, slumping down on the couch and leaning her head back. She felt as though she could close her eyes right now and sleep all the way through till tomorrow.

'So, why have you asked for their service docs?' shouted John from the kitchen. 'I mean, I know who they are, and I can guess what the connection is, but why now?'

Dani remembered things he'd said to her recently about trusting people and taking the help that was there. She also thought about Roger and comments that he'd made to her in the not-too-distant past along the same lines, about her needing to get back into the team, to allow herself to rely on those around her.

John had always proven himself to be a good friend to Dani. He was trustworthy and loyal, and he'd proved time and time again that he always had her back.

'Holy shit,' he said, as he entered the lounge and saw the boards that were fitted in place of Dani's patio doors. 'What happened?'

'You really don't know?' Dani said. 'I'm surprised Roger hasn't burned your ears about it yet. I'll explain it in a sec, but first, I think there's a connection between Jimmy Nash, Marcus Lowe and Hamilton.' She accepted the cup of tea from him and then added, 'And maybe another marine, I'm not sure yet.'

John sat down in the only single chair in the sitting room and dropped a small backpack on to the floor next to him. He couldn't stop looking at the boarded-up doors.

'OK,' he said, taking a sip of his tea and placing it on the ground next to him. 'Well, I popped into the office and got everything I could. Josie was fantastic as always and she's gone well above and beyond what was asked of her. I got their service records, so we can see everywhere they operated, but she's also fished out other things too,

76

commendations, staff reports and a couple of disciplinary reports – all for Jimmy, I should add. Marcus is as white and clean as the driven snow.'

'Thanks,' said Dani.

'I printed them all out for you, so you can look through in slow time, but I also had a quick peek through while I was on the bus, and the time and place that Marcus Lowe and Jimmy Nash worked together the most was definitely during Afghanistan. And when I say worked together, I mean in exactly the same place at exactly the same time in exactly the same unit. Both of them have quite extensive special forces backgrounds and I know it'll frustrate you, but quite a lot of their material's been redacted because of that.'

'Thanks, John,' Dani said. 'That's sort of what I expected.'

'How's your old dad by the way?' he asked. 'I thought he was staying with you for a few days? That's what Roger told me, anyway.'

Dani looked away, focusing for a few moments on picking up her cup of tea and taking a long sip.

'He decided he'd be more comfortable in a hotel,' she said. 'I was too poorly to let him have my bed, and he's way too big for the couch.'

John raised his eyebrows in surprise. 'Taz Lewis missing out on quality time with his daughter? I'm amazed. Last time he came to stay with you, I seem to recall you couldn't get rid of the man. Is something going on with you two?'

'Something like that,' Dani said. 'I'll tell you that later too.'

He didn't push it. 'So, what do you think's connecting Jimmy and Marcus with Hamilton?' he asked. 'I guess the connection between the first two is obvious, but what would Hamilton have to do with any of that? Doesn't feel like his bag at all.'

'I really don't know,' said Dani. She leaned forward and reached for the backpack. 'But let's have a look at these and hopefully we can find out.'

John nudged the bag closer to her. 'This seems like a pretty tame way for you to get the information. If you want to know what links Jimmy, Marcus and Hamilton, I'm surprised that you're not just kicking down Jimmy's door, pinning him to his desk and beating a confession out of him.'

'He wouldn't tell me anything, whatever I did,' said Dani. 'But there's something else too. You know I've always maintained that Hamilton had help?'

'In his murders. I know you think that.'

'Well, I'm certain he's still contacting people outside of the prison too. I know that thought's not new, but I really want to look at how he's doing it and who he's doing it to.'

'Don't the police and prison service look into that?' John asked. 'Don't they vet the guards and investigate?'

'Yes and no,' Dani said. 'The guards are vetted, of course, but drugs and contraband still make it in with relative ease and the police find it very difficult to kick off an investigation unless there's solid proof that it's happening.'

'The solicitor?' he asked.

'Maybe, to an extent, but I think this is more regular than that. I think he's managing to have regular contact with someone, and there's an element of detail to it. I want to find out who it is and cut off his line of communication.'

'Have you spoken to the Crime Agency about it? I'm sure they'd help you if they believe it's happening.'

Dani was shaking her head. 'I will go to them, but they'd follow due process – they'd speak to the guards, and if it is one of the guards, then Hamilton would find out and go silent. I can't risk that. Plus, if they're motivated enough by fear or money, or whatever he's using, they wouldn't speak to the police anyway. They'd just be charged. I want to look into it, but I may have another way.'

John looked sceptical. 'I'm not saying I agree, because for the moment I still need to be convinced, but go on and tell me what you're thinking. Just bear in mind that if we colour outside the lines on this one, then we've no leverage. Whoever it is, is likely to be, as you said, either very well paid – and we've no money – or very, very frightened.'

'I'm banking on the latter,' said Dani.

'OK,' said John, drawing the word out as though he were still a long way from being convinced.

'Well, I think I might be able to get someone to help me who can frighten them even more,' said Dani.

Chapter 9

'I still can't believe someone burst into your house like that,' said Felicity, giving Dani a hug and a kiss on each cheek as they met. 'Are you sure you're OK? I'm furious. I have been since you told me.'

'I'm OK,' said Dani. 'Just some drunk taking a chance. No harm done except my patio doors getting smashed.'

Felicity hugged her again. 'You've been through the mill. Did you get a good look? Did you recognise him at all? Are you certain it was random?'

Dani smiled. 'I've answered those questions already. Hampshire police were very efficient, but the answers are no, no and yes, I'm pretty certain it was just random chance.'

Felicity didn't look entirely convinced. 'Roger's late,' she said, letting Dani into the observation room. 'We've no doubt he's coming, though, and that you're in his bad books. He's becoming more and more against your participation in these meetings as time goes on.'

She handed Dani a page of briefing notes from the investigators at the National Crime Agency and Dani scanned them. There were some questions for her to ask

Hamilton and a few other thoughts about the case, but in reality, Dani knew it was nothing more than hope and speculation.

'I know. He's been calling me incessantly,' she said.

'So, do we wait then?' Felicity asked.

'No. If Hamilton's ready, then I'm ready.' Dani attempted a confident smile.

'He's ready,' Felicity confirmed.

'Same as before?' asked Dani. 'Video, but no audio?'

Felicity nodded. 'We tried to get audio again, but we couldn't, not yet anyway. If he gives you firm information about a live investigation, as in, he confirms he has information and he'll offer it, then we'll go to the judge again, but at the moment, you're just two old friends chatting.'

'Have you guys thought any more about how he's getting some of the information he has?' Dani asked.

She knew she needed to tread carefully around this topic, because Hamilton had told her things that he shouldn't have known, but she hadn't always shared this information with the police.

It'd been him who'd talked to her about William Knight and who'd sent her off down the path that had almost seen her killed.

Dani had shared that with the investigation team and was glad that Felicity seemed to think this was the thrust of her question, but he'd shared other things too.

He'd known about her investigations and her whereabouts and Dani wanted to know how.

'We're always looking at things like that,' Felicity said, 'but, in honesty, I think the police simply don't have the resources to really go after it. The information about Knight was legacy. The man went missing years ago, so although it proved to be a lead of sorts, there's no saying someone told Hamilton that since he was locked up. I've raised concerns with Craig several times and he'd love to get on it, but unless we can provide some proof that it's really happening and impacting what we're doing now, then he simply doesn't have the people to spare.'

'I thought as much,' said Dani. 'But they did preliminary stuff, didn't they? Drew up a list of the guards who come into regular contact and that kind of thing?'

'Yes, they did,' Felicity said. 'Ask Craig if you want to see it, but I wouldn't hold out for much assistance from him. I saw some statistic a while back about the sheer volume of materials that get smuggled into prisons – people using drones to drop stuff in, throwing it over walls, using prison contractors – and that's aside from bribing or intimidating staff. It's a huge problem.'

'I might just ask for a look. Just to scratch an itch if nothing else.'

'I'm sure Craig would prefer your efforts being directed elsewhere, but I can't see why he'd actively stop you.'

Dani nodded, pursing her lips as though agreeing with the scale of the problem and how awful it was, but secretly, she relaxed a bit.

Felicity was watching her closely now, a certain look on her face that said she was thinking about saying something else.

'What?' asked Dani.

'Well,' Felicity began hesitantly, 'I'm just wondering why you're thinking about this now? To open an investigation, we'd need him to have said something and you've only ever said he's hinted at things, or made throwaway remarks. Have you remembered something specific he said that's making you think about this stuff? Because if you have, it could be what we need to get audio in there and to get some serious resources looking into whether he has a route for getting information in and out.'

'No,' Dani said. 'Believe me, I tell you everything he says, and the second he says something that we can use, I'll be right on to it. Is he in good spirits?' She turned to look up at the television screen on the wall.

'He looks as arrogant as ever to me,' said Felicity.

Dani walked to the observation room door.

'Dani,' said Felicity.

Dani turned back.

'Get us something we can take to a judge. Something firm about one of those girls he murdered. If we get audio in there, we can really dissect what he says – analyse his voice, try to get patterns on when he's lying and telling the truth.'

Dani nodded and opened the door. She recognised the guard who was waiting for her.

'Mr Hamilton's ready for you,' he said cheerfully and gestured for her to follow him towards the interview room.

Dani walked behind him, looking down at his shoes. She'd followed him along this corridor before and seen how he leaned heavily on the outside of his right foot, wearing the sole of his shoe on that side.

The shoes he was wearing now were newer than last time, but the rubber heel was headed for the same fate.

When he stopped outside the interview room, Dani made a point of noting the name on his badge.

Chapter 10

As soon as the door to the interview room was shut behind her, Dani knew something wasn't right.

'Dani,' said Hamilton, half standing to greet her as he always did, but being held in a stoop by the cuffs that bound his wrists and connected him to the table.

It always looked like he was bowing to her as she entered.

He was smiling at her and making a show of looking at her hands, as though to see if she was carrying anything. At every meeting since their first, he'd asked her to bring a chess set with her so they could play while they spoke. Dani hadn't yet agreed to that and after recent events was unlikely to.

'No chess set, Chris,' she said, walking to the seat. 'It's arrived, but I had an unwanted visitor at my house making threats, so I burnt it in my garden just in case you had something to do with it.'

She had prepared this line on the way here and was worried it might sound pre-planned and a little childish, but she didn't really care. She wanted to tell him that she'd heeded his request and had bought the chess set, but that he didn't run the show.

She knew she looked terrible, the bruises and marks from her fight with Sarah Cox still fully visible against her pale skin, and it bothered her that Hamilton was able to see the marks that she suspected he had helped to cause.

He sat back in his chair, visibly disappointed.

'You don't look well,' he said, leaning as far forward as he could and making a show of examining her face. 'Looks like a bad trip, a bad shopping trip . . .'

He smiled at her, waiting for a response, as though he'd cracked a clever joke, but Dani ignored him and settled herself into the seat.

He was going through the motions, she could see that, but something was wrong. He was acting, playing the part of Hamilton, but for all his bluster, there was something missing from his eyes.

She'd seen his eyes when they were warm and human, and she'd seen them when they went cold and black, lifeless and reptilian, but there was something different now and she couldn't place it.

'It always amazes me how you know so much about what I get up to, Chris,' she said.

He shrugged.

'How did you get someone to come to my house?'

He smiled. 'How, she asks,' he said. 'Not why . . .'

Dani studied him closely and noticed some very light swelling around his right eye. Not an outright bruise from, say, a punch, but more of a rough mark from some kind of struggle.

He was watching her back and eventually smiled at her.

'How on earth would I do that, Dani?' he said. 'I'm incarcerated. I'm barely allowed to contact anyone. All my contact is strictly controlled and monitored. So, pray tell, how do you think I'd accomplish such a feat?'

'OK, then why did you do it?' Dani rephrased the question.

'As previously mentioned, I have no idea how you'd expect me to achieve such a thing, nor why you'd suspect it was me.'

Dani stared at him and he stared straight back.

'What's the link between you and Jimmy Nash?' she asked, deliberately throwing the question out there, blunt, almost a challenge.

He looked at her and tilted his head slightly to one side. 'You really think there is one?' he asked, seeming genuine.

Dani shook her head. She noticed how his eyes seemed to flit to the camera in the corner of the room, as though they were the only nervous part of his body, which otherwise looked relaxed and arrogant.

'I really do,' she said, watching him carefully. 'Was it him that sent someone to my house for you? If so, the man he sent was half-cut. You need to tell him to raise his game and consider improving the quality of his staff.'

Hamilton seemed to think about this, but again Dani saw him glancing back up at the camera on the wall.

'Tell him how?' he asked, the words coming out in a long sigh as though he were bored with this line already.

'It's just you and I,' said Dani, noticing how he looked to the screen again. 'Video feed for my safety and no audio – not yet, but they're working on it.'

He looked at her and smiled. 'It's never been just you and I, Dani,' he said. 'What did your attacker look like? I may be able to help.'

'He looked like shit. Was missing a finger.'

Hamilton laughed at that.

'Time's running out, Chris,' Dani said. 'They'll get audio in here or they'll get bored, but this won't go on for much longer. Just tell me what's going on.'

'I will not,' he said, and Dani was unsure whether he was genuinely angry or just acting. 'This isn't one of those shitty movies where they seem to have just run out of money and stopped the film halfway through. This is the last part of a good book. Things are coming to a head, but there's still some story to tell – a final twist or two to come. I just don't know how much.'

Dani watched him intently. The pain in various parts of her body seemed to be dampened by adrenaline and her focus was sharper than it had been in days. The way he was talking now was different to the way he'd done in their meetings previously.

'Tell me what I've got to do with any of this,' she pressed, leaning towards him and lowering her voice. 'Tell me what my dad's got to do with any of this.'

For just an instant, Dani could see the old flicker of nastiness back in his eyes, but it was short-lived.

'Yes,' he said. 'I wondered when you'd mention him.'

'I'm mentioning him now.'

'And what did Daddy say?'

'He hasn't said anything.'

'Even when you told him about your attacker and his missing finger?'

'Even then.'

Hamilton seemed to think about that, a broad smile spreading across his face as he leaned back in his chair, stretching his neck and looking up at the ceiling.

His eyes were dark when he looked back, dead and inhuman again, as they often were.

Dani wondered whether she'd actually seen any difference in him at all, or whether she'd imagined the whole thing.

'Tell me something useful, Chris,' said Dani, her voice short. 'Stop talking in circles and tell me what you want from me.'

He paused again, stretching his neck and looking from

side to side, as though warming up before some sporting activity.

'Who's out there now?' he said, nodding to the camera.

'Some folk from the NCA,' said Dani.

'No Roger today?'

'He's coming, but wasn't there when I came in.'

Dani noticed some marks on his neck as he moved, just hidden by the collar of his shirt.

She tried to focus on them, to get a closer look, without him realising that she'd seen them. As a naval investigator, Dani had often seen marks associated with different types of violence, and though she only caught a glimpse of the bruising above Hamilton's collarbones, she recognised the signs of a physical struggle, the markings left behind when someone had been strangled.

He leaned forward and drummed his fingers on the desk, a slow thump-thump-thump-thump.

'I can't keep coming back here, Chris. You know that. You have to give me something I can use.'

Dani gestured to the camera.

'The National Crime Agency's getting tired of me coming to these meetings and we're all starting to think you don't actually have anything to tell. I've said for a long time that you had help, Chris. You're too dumb to have done this alone and too weak to have kept the secrets. I don't think you know where those girls' bodies are at all. If I'm right about that, then the only real benefit I could get by coming here would be a confession, which we both know you're not man enough to give me.'

Hamilton chuckled, but his eyes turned dark and cold. 'You know full well that's not true, Dani. I could give you something that would make you certain of how much of a man I am.'

He was staring at her, but she'd seen this before, was

beginning to realise that she'd seen most of his repertoire and was prepared for it.

'See, it's comments like that that undermine your whole act, Chris. Little comebacks that make me realise you're just like a little boy trying to be taken seriously.'

She met his eyes, watching him as he breathed slowly, a sneer crossing his face and disappearing as quickly as it had appeared.

'You're right, of course,' he said, seeming to relax, though his breathing was still heavier, and Dani could see he was angry. 'It was unnecessary and juvenile, and I apologise. But, regarding your pleas for information, the second I give you anything that's part of an ongoing investigation against me, they'll bug the meeting, and we won't be able to talk freely.'

'So, what do we do? How do we move forward from here? I didn't want to come in the first place, and I think you know I'll stop coming without a second of hesitation.'

'Bullshit,' Hamilton said, his face half-smile, half-sneer. 'You want to find all those women. You're obsessed by it, and believe me, if there's one thing I can spot in a person, it's obsession. But you know what's the most interesting thing here, Dani, is that I want you to find them too and I want to be the one to show you where they are.'

Dani felt her heart start to beat faster as she heard the words, not just what he was saying, but how he was saying it. She didn't dare speak, not willing to give anything away, but inside she knew he was right. She was obsessed, and she needed to find the bodies of those women. She knew she couldn't stop until she had.

'Tell me then,' she said, after a long silence.

'No,' said Hamilton. 'Not yet. I can't.'

Dani felt the urge to reach across the table and force

her thumbs into his eye sockets. To drive them into his skull, to ignore his screams, and to stop only when he finally told her what she wanted to know, when he finally gave up the information that allowed her to give those women and their families some peace.

'And what should I tell them,' Dani flicked her eyes as though gesturing to the people they both knew were watching on the camera, 'to make them think there's anything at all to make it worth my investing time and energy coming here?'

'Tell them whatever you like,' Hamilton said. 'You're a big girl, you've had a few nights out on the town. Think of something.'

He paused.

'List the names of the women who owned the appendages you've been sent, please,' he said, shaking his head like a disappointed teacher.

'No,' said Dani. 'You list them.'

'Just leave, then,' he said. 'If this is how it's going to be, then go.'

Dani watched him, considering him for a moment. 'You haven't been any help,' she said, and pushed her chair back.

'Humour me, Dani. Please,' he said, his voice softened. 'Just tell me the names and I'll see if I can offer something.'

Dani sighed, leaving the chair away from the table.

'Sarah Louise Sharples,' she began, a picture of Sarah flashing in front of her eyes; she remembered them all, and their families. 'Veronica Falvey, Nikki Hislop, Agnes Raggett, Kaisha Holloway, Theresa Olivero Richardson and Irene Dunne.'

She stared at him as she finished, hating the small half-smile on his face as he heard their names.

He moved in his seat. 'Like hearing the names of old

friends,' he said. 'Tell me, Kaisha, was she the one from Yorkshire?'

'No,' said Dani. 'Not even close.'

He nodded slowly, his smile broadening.

They sat for a long moment in silence, before he spoke again.

'Let me think about them,' he said. 'But I promise I'll show you them. That's why I wanted to see you today. I wanted to tell you that and to say you need to be ready when I call you. To come in when I need to see you. I'm serious. I'm going to give you what you want, Dani.'

She waited, but he'd stopped speaking and was watching her now

'And that's it?' said Dani. 'Wait for you to keep your word?' She shook her head and stood up, heading towards the door. 'I don't know what it's like for you in here, Chris, but I have a life to lead, and you must be on drugs if you think you're going to dictate what I do with it.'

'I'm serious, Dani,' he said from behind her. 'I'm telling you and you alone that I will take you to the bodies. If you tell them out there, then we'll never speak in private again and all bets are off. I mean soon, too. It won't be long.'

Dani shook her head and stood there, watching him and waiting.

'You don't believe me,' he said.

'Of course I don't, Chris. You're a liar. You've nothing to gain by taking me to those girls and I see that. You're in here for life and there's not a shred of decency inside you that would give the girls or their families peace.'

He was watching her, still looking her up and down.

'I know it's always difficult for us to understand what motivates people to do the things they do,' he said. 'And

what motivates people to do things that they wouldn't normally do, but I'm giving you my word.'

Dani shook her head. 'More waffle and bluster, Chris,' she said. 'You're not half as smart as you think you sound.'

She turned to leave, but the silence that followed made her turn back to look at him.

He was staring at her again, his tongue pointing through his lips, deliberately looking her up and down with a sickening look of anticipation on his face.

'I've written you another letter,' he said, still eyeing her. 'I can only assume you didn't read my last one?'

Dani shrugged. 'I never do, Chris. So, best if you just stop wasting paper?'

He laughed at her.

'Well, I think you'll want to read these ones, so when you get it, don't destroy it or share it. Read it. It'll be worth it, I promise.'

Chapter 11

Roger was waiting for her outside the interview room.

'I hate him,' Dani said, as soon as the guard had shut the door and left her in the corridor.

It felt like a stress reliever to say it out loud and she shivered as she saw Hamilton's face again in her mind's eye.

Roger looked brooding and angry, and he said nothing, just waited, opening the door to the debriefing room and following Dani in. He stood and watched while Dani lied to Felicity about what little Hamilton had said.

'I couldn't do any longer today,' said Dani. 'I'm sorry, he was really getting under my skin, but we've maintained contact and that's a good thing. He was also being deliberately antagonistic today, so we've lost nothing. I think he was annoyed at the intervals since our last meeting and was trying to punish me.'

She looked at Felicity and tried her hardest to smile at Roger.

'I think he'll start to open up soon, I really believe it. He's talking to me, being an asshole, but I can sense that it's easier for him and flowing more freely. I really think if we just keep at him then we may get the breakthrough we need. Perhaps consistency is the key. Maybe it needs to be a regular meeting, once a week or so, so he knows when I'm coming. It may play on his mind in advance and could help him to loosen up.'

Roger spoke from just behind Dani's shoulder. 'All that talking we could see you doing, and he never told you one single thing that's actually of any use?'

'The fact that he's talking at all is a positive thing,' said Felicity, cutting in. 'I don't need to remind you that he's refused to speak to anyone, in a professional sense, since he was locked up. So even getting to the point that he's in a room with someone is a big step forward, and we need to allow him the time he needs to tell us what we want to know.'

'He'll never tell you anything,' said Roger, walking across the room to face both Dani and Felicity.

He leaned forward on to the table.

'Hamilton's playing games with you. He loves doing it. He did it when he was on the investigative team trying to catch himself. The misinformation he fed into the team caused significant delays and allowed him to go free for much longer than he might have. You, better than anyone else, know this, Dani.'

Dani was silent, and Roger went on.

'Come on, Dani. This is exactly what he does, and that man has never in his life done anything that wasn't for himself. Whether you can all see it or not, he has an agenda.'

Dani thought for a moment. 'He does play games, Roger,' she acknowledged. 'But he is possibly the only person alive who knows the truth about a large number of murders. Families are out there who don't know where their daughters are, some still believing they're alive. Even a snippet of information is worth hanging on for. I think we should float the idea that one day he might be willing to talk or even show us where the bodies are.'

She could see Roger was unhappy. He hated it when anyone argued with him, but particularly her.

'Show you where the bodies are . . .' Roger repeated, with real scorn.

'We need to keep at this,' Dani said, pushing on. 'If we're not here, and we're not talking to him, then there's no way we'll get anything from him. It's my opinion that there's value in continuing to speak with Chris and in chasing down any information he eventually gives us.'

Roger looked stunned. 'Chris?' he said, staring at Dani.

'That's his name,' she said, realising that she'd usually called him Hamilton when discussing him since capture. Chris was what she'd called him when they'd worked together many years before, when he was still a person to her, not a killer.

Roger stood up slowly, removing his hands from the table and stretching his back. He nodded at each of them in turn, shook his head and walked from the room without another word.

'Wait,' said Dani. 'One thing. I think he's been attacked. Can we check any prison records on that? He has swelling under one eye, very light, but I'm sure it was there, and there are ligature marks on his neck.'

Roger turned back. 'He told you he'd been attacked?' he asked.

Dani shook her head. 'The value of being in there isn't just verbal. I saw the marks and I've seen enough domestic violence cases to know what they look like. But also, he was edgy, kept looking at the camera.'

'We noted that,' said Felicity.

'He wasn't right at all. I think we need to speak to the warden and find out if anything's gone on.'

'He was probably just restrained by the guards,' said Roger, his voice dismissive.

'Maybe so,' said Dani, 'but it won't hurt to find out for sure.'

Roger nodded once and left the room.

Felicity walked over to Dani and sat down in the seat next to her. 'He's pissed,' she said.

'He's always pissed,' Dani agreed. 'He needs to accept he can't control every little thing, but he's also getting a lot of pressure from his boss to keep me quiet.'

'They have the knives out for you?' Felicity asked. 'The navy police?'

'Same guy as before – Roger's boss, Harrow-Brown,' Dani said. 'He's hated me from the first time he met me. I'd say he had a problem with women, but he seems to be an asshole to everyone.'

Felicity smiled. 'You know, Dani, you were in there talking a lot in a very short time,' she said, leaning forward so she could look Dani in the eye. 'Are you sure you've remembered everything? That's definitely all he said?'

Dani looked back at Felicity, taken aback by the question.

'Of course,' she said, allowing the shock to show on her face. 'Of course that's all he said, why would I keep anything back? Or am I a liar again today?'

Felicity held up her hands and Dani knew she'd over-reacted and protested too much.

'I didn't mean for a second you'd hold anything back deliberately,' Felicity said. 'I just wanted to make sure it wouldn't be worth going through the conversation one more time, to be certain we had absolutely everything. You were pretty uptight when you came out, I was thinking maybe now you're calmer . . .'

'Look, I'm sorry. I don't know why I'm so uptight. I'm more than happy to go through it again,' said Dani, settling back in her chair. 'It's easy to remember when there's so little actually said.'

Felicity shook her head. 'No, I'm not pushing it. If you're happy we've got it all, then I'm happy too. I just wanted to check. Also, I think you're right. I think there's a lot of value in continuing to speak to Hamilton and I know the NCA do too. What about this idea about him showing us evidence – did he say that?'

'No. I just think that if we're going to push forward, we need to be ready for anything.'

Dani stood up and began gathering her things.

'See you soon?' Felicity asked.

'Definitely,' said Dani, feeling sorry for snapping but not yet able to say so. 'Let's grab some food soon. I'm getting less tired in the evenings and we could use a proper catch-up.'

As she walked the familiar route that led out of the prison's secure wing, she passed the guard with the awkward gait, and smiled at him.

She thought about what Hamilton had said – Hamilton the killer, not Chris, the naval officer.

It troubled her that she'd begun to call him that.

She did it deliberately when she was in the room with him; it was part of making things seem normal and friendly, a way of changing the tempo, but in the debriefing room, it had been an accident. She wondered what had happened to change her mindset and she knew it needed to change back. But she also thought about what he'd said to her and more than that, she thought about the fact she actually believed him.

The glass doors at the exit to the building allowed her to see from some distance that Roger was waiting outside.

She'd expected him to be there, knowing he'd cool off and want to offer her a lift home, likely to take the opportunity to make sure she knew how deeply unhappy he was.

He'd want to speak about her return to work, her secrecy around the NCA investigation that was reviewing how the severed fingers of women widely considered to be Hamilton's victims had been sent to Dani, and her reluctance to talk and confide in him as she'd often done before.

In Dani's greatest hour of need, it'd been Roger she'd turned to.

He'd mentored her for years. He'd tried to nurture her in the ways of policing and the politics of the armed forces and he'd done so with patience and continual forgiveness for her regular transgressions. He'd covered for her, fought her corner, and on the night she'd been attacked and nearly raped, he'd dressed her wounds and comforted her. If he thought for even a second that she was holding something back that Hamilton had said, he'd be hurt and angry. He knew better than anyone when professional discretion was essential. He'd know Dani was duty-bound not to share information revealed as part of this investigation because it wasn't directly a naval matter. She was the one who'd been cleared onto the team to assist, but she knew it'd still bother him. He'd still want her to have the will to confide in him, to *want* to talk to him; in many ways, he was just as obsessed with Hamilton as Dani was.

He was drawing deeply on a cigarette as she opened the doors and stepped outside.

She watched as he inhaled it down into his lungs, held it there for a few seconds as he always did, and then exhaled up into the air.

'Quitting seems to be going well,' she said as she walked towards him.

He appeared not to have noticed her before and now he stopped and smiled.

'I think we have this exchange every time we meet,' he said, taking another drag. 'I figured you'd rather have a lift back to Portsmouth with me than brave the train.'

'Honestly, Roger, I'd rather take a taxi. I'm too tired to listen to you bending my ear.'

She watched him smile at that and couldn't help but smile herself.

'You know, Roger, they'll go directly to Harrow-Brown shortly to make sure you don't interfere any more if you keep showing up here and trying to control something that's not yours to control. I think you're doing it to protect me and I appreciate that, but you have to let me get on with my job. At the moment I'm the only person that Hamilton speaks to and there's no way we can afford to permanently lose the information he might have to offer.'

'Hamilton again now?' he said. He reached into his pocket and pulled out his cigarettes again, pointing at the packet as though asking for permission to have another.

'Have as many as you like,' said Dani. 'I've got nothing to do today. I'm keeping my head down so I can watch you slowly kill yourself all day long.'

He didn't smile this time. He put the cigarette into his mouth and lit it, immediately inhaling the smoke and holding it inside as he watched her, as though making a point.

'This is about more than protecting you, Dani,' he said, exhaling as he spoke. 'This is about us, in the Royal Navy, keeping a grip on how this investigation's run. It may have escaped your notice, but they're using a naval officer to investigate a former naval officer. The embarrassment to the Royal Navy when it was outed that Hamilton was a serial killer and that we twice appointed him as the liaison officer on the case to find himself, was too much. Things to do with Hamilton go all the way to the very top, the Secretary of State for Defence and the Prime Minister – that's how big a deal it all is. You might think that Harrow-Brown will side with you and ask me to step away, but I can assure you, he knows exactly what I'm doing, and he supports it.'

Roger broke off to take another drag on his cigarette.

'I heard you two talking when I was in the hospital,' said Dani.

Roger looked at her.

She nodded. 'He has a loud, whiney voice and it carries.'

'He wants you gone,' Roger said. 'You're ruining his perfect record and bringing unwanted attention to his management chain. He wants you gone, but he hasn't got the balls to just do it himself. He wants it done quietly, no fuss.'

'He wants you to do it?' she asked.

Roger nodded. 'I don't like Harrow-Brown and I don't agree with him a lot of the time. It might be unprofessional to say so, but I think it's well known. Regardless of that, I don't let my personal feelings cloud the areas where I do agree with him and I think you need to remember where your loyalties lie, Dani. I think you need to keep in mind that you're Royal Navy first and foremost, for the moment at least.'

Dani was taken aback. She'd known Roger a long time and he was a lot of things, but he wasn't a company man./

'I know what you're thinking,' he said, taking another draw on his cigarette. 'It doesn't sound like me speaking, but Dani, I don't have a lot and I'll be leaving the navy soon and have even less. I don't want to be remembered as the Chief Provost Marshall who presided over the second biggest press fiasco in the history of the Royal Navy.'

Dani didn't miss his subtle reference to the first biggest media fiasco in the history of the Royal Navy – the release of Dani's academic paper, where she stated her belief that there was no way that Hamilton could have worked alone and that there was someone else, an accomplice helping him along the way.

'Since when did you give a shit about anything like that?' she asked. 'All these years, all you ever bang on about is doing the right thing and that's what I'm doing. Are you saying now I should only do the right thing when it suits the Dark Blue?' She shook her head. 'You know what, Roger, I'll get a taxi back. I'll see you at work in a week or so if I still have a job by then.'

She walked away from him, fishing for her phone to call a taxi.

'Dani, wait,' Roger called. He dropped his cigarette and crushed it out on the pavement. 'Let me give you a lift home,' he said. 'I won't bend your ear any more. I promise.'

Dani paused. 'You need to pick those up and put them in the bin first,' she said, pointing at his two cigarette stubs on the pavement.

He smiled and complied.

Dani watched him, knowing she was always going to accept the lift, that there'd never really been a chance not to.

'I just want you to keep me in the loop, Dani. That's all I'm asking,' he said. 'I just want to know the type of things he's saying, how he says them, how he seems. The things he says to you that might have an undertone of something else, something out of the ordinary, something people like you and I, who know him and have followed this case for years, might pick up on and interpret differently to the police.'

Dani paused for a moment, thinking about where her

loyalties should lie and who she could trust. Was she actually putting her faith in Christopher Hamilton above Roger?

'He said one thing I didn't pass on yet,' she said, stopping and closing her eyes.

She was unsure whether this was a mistake or not, but she'd learned the hard way that she needed to trust people who'd proved they were there for her.

'Go on,' said Roger.

'I said to Felicity that it was just a hunch, because I want them to think about it, but he did say he'd show me the bodies. He said it would be soon, but he didn't know when.'

Roger's brow furrowed as he considered Dani's words. 'He said that to you?' he asked. 'That he'd show you, as in take you there?'

'Yes.'

'And that's it? Think carefully, think about how he phrased it.'

'That's it,' said Dani. 'That's what he said.'

Roger nodded slowly, then turned and began to head for the car.

'I need to trust you with this, Roger,' she said, falling into stride alongside him. 'I can do that, can't I? I need to keep speaking to him because the minute they put audio recording in there he'll clam up and we'll get nothing from him again.'

He nodded.

'You can always trust me,' he said. 'He's likely testing you, but I doubt he has any interest at all in actually helping you. You have no idea how he works, how he gets under your skin and inside your life. He'll do anything to get leverage, and when he does, he'll exploit it.'

'I think I know that more than anyone,' Dani said. 'And

I do think he's testing me. I think he's trying to see how much he can tell me and how much he can trust me. He asked me not to tell anyone about what he'd said. I just don't know why yet. I also don't know how he gets his information in there and how he gets it out.'

Roger seemed to weigh that up. 'He lives to try to manipulate, Dani,' he said. 'The predominant way he can manipulate you is to first isolate you and set up a scenario where he can begin to apply pressure because you've left yourself vulnerable in any way, for instance, by lying to the investigation. When he does try to leverage that, I'll support you. Sharing with me, in complete confidence, is what prevents Hamilton from gaining complete power over you. If we support each other, it removes his ability to manipulate and blackmail you. That's what I'm interested in. I don't want Hamilton to manipulate his way back into the public psyche or into yours. He's like a bloody terrorist organisation; all he wants is for you to be thinking about him and fearing him because that's where the power lies. We need to make sure we're always talking, because then we're never isolated. Do you agree?'

Dani nodded and waited for Roger to unlock the car.

'Is there anything else I need to know?' he asked.

'No,' she said, climbing in. She looked back at the prison and wondered who, if anyone, might be carrying information out of there for Hamilton tonight.

Chapter 12

'How was Roger?' asked John.

Dani shrugged and shook her head.

'He was fine. You know what he's like – once he's vented he calms down. To be honest, I dozed off a bit on the way back, so there wasn't much opportunity for him to say anything in the car.'

They were in the sitting room at Dani's house again, the lights switched on in the middle of the day to make up for the patio doors still being boarded over and blocking the majority of the light that usually entered the room.

'How's it been your end?' Dani asked.

'Grand. I've been reading over those files and trying to find a common link between Hamilton, Jimmy and Marcus. The problem we've got is that Hamilton was Special Investigations for a while, so sometimes he might have been appointed to a job in one place, but not have stayed in that geographical location. So, it's difficult to understand where he could've been deployed, especially considering his records are now locked down.'

'OK,' Dani said. 'I've got some ideas that might help with that.'

John waited.

'Will you be sharing them, then?' he asked.

Dani thought about her lock box tucked under her bed upstairs and the copy of Hamilton's service docs she had in there. She wanted to share with John, to be fully candid, but there were secrets that came with that box that went deeper than she was able to go.

'Sure,' she said. 'No problem. I just think I might be able to get some details from Hamilton's records if we need them.'

John nodded. 'Cool. Well, I've had some time on my hands and the place that Jimmy and Marcus were together the most is Afghanistan.'

'OK, I think we'd guessed that,' Dani said.

'We did, but there's something I want to show you.'

Dani watched as he ruffled through the papers and then held something out to her.

'That was taken before they deployed to Afghanistan. It's the unit photograph. Josie pulled it from God only knows where.'

Dani looked at the picture and immediately knew why John had raised it.

Jimmy Nash was there, looking much younger, and seated on the front row next to him was Marcus Lowe. Only two people along, she saw the hulking figure of her father.

He was sitting bolt upright, looking directly ahead at the camera. His arms were braced, perfectly straight, and each ran down to a clenched fist which rested smartly on his knee.

'I guess there was always a chance they knew each other,' she said, looking at the picture.

'But, if we need information, then your dad may have some. So he could be worth speaking to. Unofficially, of course.'

Dani looked at the picture again and then homed in on a marine in the row behind her father.

The man was tall and slim, his head narrow beneath his green beret and his nose sticking out and slightly crooked, as though it had been recently broken.

She looked closer and then tilted her head. She couldn't be certain, but the resemblance to the man who'd broken into her house was more than passing. She looked again at her father and Jimmy, then Marcus, then thought about what they looked like now, all these years later.

The names ran along the bottom of the picture in three neat rows. She counted them along and saw his name – Marine Davis. She passed the picture back to John, her thumb just above Davis's head.

'Can we find out about this marine too?'

John looked at the picture. 'Sure. Any reason?'

Dani nodded. 'I feel like I've seen him somewhere.'

John shrugged and made a note of the marine's name. 'I just thought you needed to know your old man might be a source of information,' he said, tucking the picture back into his folder.

'It's all useful. I'll call my dad once we have some questions for him. Did you get any more on Hamilton?'

John shuffled some more papers until he found the page he was looking for.

'So, he was on the Afghanistan War Crimes Investigation Unit for a short while, but that's unlikely to have meant he was actually out there, though he could have picked up on an investigation involving Jimmy and co. that he could use as leverage.'

'Possible,' said Dani. 'But he was also on the joint service police task force for a while, wasn't he? They can be deployed anywhere in the world.'

'I think he was,' John agreed. 'Let me look into that

one a little bit more. I know some guys who were there around that time. If I can't find any records, then we can either go the official route and request them, or I can ask around and see what people remember.' He paused. 'Or ask your old man.'

He shuffled through the files again, looking to confirm his theories. 'So, in that picture, Jimmy was a sergeant and Marcus was his lieutenant, waiting for promotion to captain.'

'Bit of a role change, from being Jimmy's boss to being his personal assistant,' said Dani.

'Yeah, well they do say that young lieutenants are told to shut up and listen to their sergeants for the first few years. Looks like these two just took it to the extreme. You know, maybe your dad will remember something. It could save us a lot of legwork. I wouldn't mind speaking to him if you two have fallen out.'

John had met Dani's dad and they'd liked each other. They were similar men and got along easily, but he also knew what Taz Lewis was like. Now that someone had tried to break into Dani's house, he must be wondering why Taz wasn't currently camped on the lawn.

'We've had a small disagreement,' said Dani. 'But, you're right, I need to speak to him anyway.'

'Yes, sure.'

'OK,' said Dani, thinking hard. 'Can you focus in on that time, try and figure out why Hamilton might have been called out there and if he was. Have a look for anything untoward. I don't even know what we're looking for, but you know what sort of thing I'm getting at. Anything that makes you think it's worth a deeper look. If Chris—' Dani paused. 'If Hamilton was sent out there, then there must be a trail. There must've been a reason. We need to try to figure out what it was. It'd also be handy to see any operations reports, anything at all we can get from Jimmy and Marcus to form a picture of what might have been going on.'

'I'm more than happy to do that,' said John. 'But it's going to take me a few days, and I don't know how many of those reports I'm going to be able to access. You know yourself, obtaining that kind of material is all about need-to-know. I can call in favours up to a point and see what's open to us, but it might be that we need to put some more weight behind this. I reckon, at the least, you'll need Roger to sign it off.'

'OK, do what you can and then let me know what you need. If we require more, I'll go to Roger and ask.'

'And you?' John asked.

'I'll call my dad, but I want to do something first. I need to find out who helps Hamilton, and I have a way to do it, but . . .'

'But?' he asked.

'Well, remember we talked about colouring outside the lines?'

He was nodding, his face sceptical.

'Well, I want to go way, way outside of them and I'm happy to go alone – in fact I'd prefer it – but I don't want to lie to you and neither do I want to make you an accomplice to it.'

John gave a rumbling laugh. 'Dani Lewis has grown a conscience!' he said, delighted.

Dani watched him, a small smile fighting through her annoyance at how funny he found it.

'It's serious, John. The NCA don't have the resource and I can't get help for this from the navy, so what I'm proposing is risky. It could lose you your job and pension.'

John had stopped laughing and was watching her closely.

'Well, I'm not letting you go somewhere like that alone.'

Chapter 13

Hamilton's Second Letter

Dani,

A second instalment. I do hope you enjoyed the first, though if you destroyed it, this one will make less sense, and if you shared it with others, then I doubt there'll be a third. Enjoy!

The phrase, 'revenge is a dish best served cold', is very, very true.

The feeling of planning your revenge is incredible. That sense of working towards the harm you'll do someone. Thinking through all the permutations of what might happen.

I cannot overstate the power of these feelings and I would say that this is something that just cannot be rushed, not in the planning and not in the execution.

I was always a people watcher, and so I already knew what made Jenny tick.

She was popular and had a large group of friends, among which she was always the centre of attention.

I was never so sure whether any of them actually liked her, or whether they were just frightened of not being in her group and experiencing the sanctions that might come with that kind of social isolation.

Attacking her through her fake friends seemed like an awful lot of work, for what could potentially be a short-term effect, with only superficial damage.

She'd recover from it, I felt sure.

She had a boyfriend whom she proclaimed to be in love with, but I'd watched them together many times and was confident the relationship's days were numbered. Jenny did what she needed to do, kept him happy, but ultimately, I was certain she was only with him because he was the male equivalent of her; deemed to be handsome, sporty and popular.

She also had a brother, her twin, and yet they were as different in temperament and personality as they were the same in their looks.

Jenny's brother, Michael, could easily have been one of the popular boys.

He was tall, tanned and built like the star rugby player he wasn't. But for all he was to the eye, he was a very different boy in his mind. He was thoughtful, quiet, and loved science and reading. He was never happier than when he was taking samples from the school's pond and then looking at algae underneath the microscope, or some such thing.

Where Jenny would spend every break time out in the yard, Michael would be in the library, or the science laboratories, reading or doing extra study and generally keeping himself to himself.

However, as different as they seemed, they were very close.

In some ways, Jenny was more like Michael than she dared ever show.

She acted like the queen bee, but many times I observed her taking an interest in what Michael was doing, genuinely fascinated as she listened to him talk.

I know what it means to have to act to survive. I know what it is to have to be someone you're not, simply because being yourself wouldn't offer you the status or freedom you need. I felt that I could empathise with Jenny.

I had realised that while Jenny was, for the sake of appearances, the coolest girl in school, the only person with whom she could truly be herself was her twin.

Jenny's house was huge. It was on the outskirts of town and had a large gate that was operated from the main house by an intercom.

I'd never been invited inside, of course. I'd never been inside anyone else's house save my own and some of my parents' friends on the infrequent occasions we'd be invited to parties, but everyone knew which house hers was.

The grounds around the house were extensive. Grass and trees bordered the main building on three sides and a large stone drive lay at the front with a short private road that led from the gate. There was another entrance at the back, a smaller one that led to a play area where there was a small wooden play-cottage, not unlike the gingerbread house from Hansel and Gretel. There was no remote-controlled gate back here, just a wooden panel that was often open and was easy to scale even when shut and locked.

I was over it and dropping down to my usual spot in a jiffy.

Jenny's room was at the back of the house and she had net curtains at the window. (Dani, it must be a girl thing?)

They ruined my view of her, as I believe they make it difficult to watch you, though I could see she was up there moving around, the pink glow from her papered walls shining out into the night.

I watched her for a moment and fantasised.

All this because of the girl I was now watching.

I moved around, hiding against the base of the wall in the late evening shadows until I was at the side of the house.

She also had a small outdoor hutch and in it, four small, fat, contented guinea pigs.

I'd squeaked in class and now they squeaked at me, their mouths open, sniffing and inquisitive. I took them out one at a time, stroking them gently and talking to them in my softest voice as I placed them into my school bag.

You see, though, I'm not writing this to regale you with stories that might offend you or turn you further against me. I'm here to talk about what I learned and how these experiences led me to become the person I am, and this night was a defining one for me.

When Jenny's father saw the tiny trail of blood that led from beneath his daughter's window to the gingerbread cottage he sent the crying children inside.

I wasn't able to be privy to the moment that he found the first of the guinea pigs, dissected and pinned to paper like a real-life science experiment, but I like to think that he was shocked that his quiet, conscientious son would do such a thing.

One of the guinea pigs, or rather its constituent parts, had been separated into various jars, and they'd been labelled so that anybody could tell what was in them.

As he explored further, he'd have found some Polaroid pictures of his daughter taken from outside. There was blood smeared on them and some had been scratched using the pointed end of a set of compasses, her face completely obliterated.

I can only guess as to how he reacted in the immediate aftermath, but I knew he'd have doubts about his son, as any father would, and I knew there was always the chance that Jenny might not find out everything she needed to know.

And so, there was one final card left to play.

As I expected he would, he reported it to the police, because he could not believe Michael, who would have been denying it vociferously, could do such a thing.

I was the weird kid in class and was considered a creep by many, especially Jenny, who now told anyone who'd listen that she believed I watched her and followed her, and sometimes put things in her school bag.

They came to speak to me first.

I'd stolen a new school bag and was only too happy for them to have a look. I cooperated fully, and when I was able to ascertain that animals had been harmed, I went pale in horror. I, of course, held out for as long as I could before I told them about the additional locker that Michael MacAulay was allowed to keep in the science labs. As afraid as I was, they got it out of me eventually.

When they found traces of the guinea pigs in there, and when they found the guinea pigs' coats, sewn together into a bloody pouch, there wasn't an awful lot anyone could do to hide all that had happened.

There were some more pictures of Jenny, and it seemed Michael had scratched the word 'whore' across one of them and smeared the word 'die' in blood across another. (I never said I wasn't a cliché back then, Dani!)

It was an open and shut case and I watched as Jenny reacted in the only way she could.

Had she been a good and decent person, she'd have told people what she knew deep inside, that it wasn't her brother who'd done this, that he'd never do such a thing to her, nor to anyone. But that wasn't the part Jenny was playing. She needed to be at the centre of this drama, being comforted and protected by her boyfriend as she faced her life without her twin, who'd managed to secure a place at a prestigious boarding school in Scotland. (Not far away from your sister's house as it happens, Dani.)

As I watched her act her way through this façade, I saw that after some time, she began to believe herself. The way she condemned her brother's actions changed before my eyes. She was no longer simply acting, playing the role that kept her in the top spot of the social order, but she started to believe what she said, she started to genuinely hate him.

I said very little during the weeks this all unfolded. I was observing and trying to digest and learn from all I was seeing. I watched as she lost weight, too much weight, beginning to look gaunt and far less attractive.

I watched as her confidence crashed. I watched one

114

day as she sat in class, idly drawing a plastic ruler back and forth over her wrists for a whole lesson, and I became obsessed with the skin between her hand and elbow, taking any opportunity I could to look at it, and eventually spotting the small scars she was making there.

I didn't emerge entirely unscathed from all of this and it's important to recognise that everything bears a cost.

When the police had come to my house, my father had been in his armchair sweating, but saying nothing.

I had no real alibi except 'I was in my room', and I was stunned when my father maintained that assertion in a rare moment of support, probably worried about what I might say if the police had me in an interview room.

The police coming to my house was a lesson I needed to learn, and I promised myself that I wouldn't make any of the same mistakes again.

I decided that Jenny had been too close to me.

I'd enjoyed what I'd done to her, but future targets must appear to be random, removed from connection to me by time or distance. You may wonder how someone that removed could then require revenge and I will explain in due course.

Finally, the rage must be controlled, and this is very important.

When I took those guinea pigs out of the bag, my mind focused on what Jenny MacAulay had done. I allowed my rage to take over and the problem here is hard to explain.

When your anger is so intense that you no longer know what you might do; when your vision clouds and your whole body tenses so tight it might never again release; when you want to hurt someone, something, so badly that you know you won't stop – this is the wrong time to take revenge. The rage is too strong at this moment, the emotion too high, and it clouds out the other, better feelings.

When I looked down at the first of the guinea pigs, crushed in my hand, I honestly felt nothing but regret; I promise you it's true.

The pleasure for me could come only from Jenny, and that was much later on.

When she saw me once after school, and we were alone, just the two of us, I squeaked at her and twitched my nose and said, 'Cry weirdo', and her eyes went wide in terror.

She stared and began to shake, her breathing deepening and then shallowing as the first chords of a 'panic attack' sounded. She knew it was me. Knew what I'd done, and she was alone and terrified. Her hands went to her breasts, and she dropped to her knees, wheezing and squeaking like a little asthmatic guinea pig, her eyes large and black as she watched me.

Then the first of her tears grew out like a clear bubble in her eye and rolled down her cheek.

Dani, I ejaculated before anyone even came to help her, such was my joy that she now knew that I had done this to her.

By God, I'd discovered something about myself, something that I think formed the person I came to be and touched the lives of many, many people over the following years. I had discovered, broadly, what I was and what it was that really motivated me – other people's pain and suffering.

Chapter 14

'For the record and to avoid any possible doubt, I am totally against this,' said John.

'I'm happy for you to leave,' said Dani. 'I said I was happy to come alone and I can drop you off at home and come back myself. It's no problem.'

'I just don't think this is necessary,' John said. 'It exposes you to unnecessary risk – physical and in terms of your job – and for what?'

Dani turned to look at him.

He was leaning against the passenger door and looking out of the window, occasionally glancing in the rear-view mirror.

'I've told you,' she said. 'I've been honest. I can't tell the NCA, because if I do, they'll bug my meetings with Hamilton and then he'll say nothing. And if they start pulling out and questioning guards and people who interact with Hamilton, then he'll get wind of it and shut down that line of communication. He's playing well outside the rules and we can't beat him and find out who he's talking to without getting a bit creative too.'

John shook his head but didn't speak.

'John, if he's got to someone and has them delivering information, then unless they're some kind of weird cult follower of his, they're likely just intimidated by him, or, better still, intimidated by whoever's helping him and giving the information. If we break that line of communication, he'll set up a different one and it'll set us back months or years. If we can get the right person and flip them, then we might be able to intercept the messages, find out who he messages and who messages him. If we can isolate him, then that removes a huge amount of his power and gifts it to us.'

John tapped his fingers against the arm rest. He still didn't look convinced.

'You need to stop biting your nails,' Dani said. She reached out and took his hand, holding it up so she could look. 'It looks awful and it must hurt when you bite them that close.'

John was looking at her, but he made no attempt to take his hand away.

Dani let go and looked out of the window, watching as a dark-coloured Mercedes pulled up behind them.

'He's here,' she said, undoing her seat belt and opening her door.

John reached out and stopped her. 'If you think Harrow-Brown is going to oust you, then you must know this will just make it faster and harder, right?'

Dani patted his hand. 'I'm gone whatever happens,' she said. 'I know it and I'm accepting it. This is about doing something good now.'

She climbed out of the car and watched as Marcus Lowe rummaged on the passenger seat of his car, and then slowly stepped out to meet her.

He was wearing a smart, expensive suit and a long woollen overcoat. He looked like a smart banker, or businessman of some description, classy and refined, well-groomed and approachable. He looked nothing like what she knew he was: a gangster's assistant.

'I was really pleased to hear from you,' he said, approaching her and offering his hand.

Dani ignored it and felt John appear at her side.

'I thought we were here as friends?' asked Marcus. 'Aren't we working together towards a mutual aim?' He paused as Dani said nothing and then made a point of looking at her face. 'You look far better than the last time I saw you,' he said.

Dani shot him a look, hoping John wouldn't see it, but needing to silence Marcus on the topic of their last meeting. She'd confided much in John, but she hadn't yet told him about coming around in the shop and hearing her dad speaking with Marcus and Jimmy only a few yards away from where she lay.

He seemed to pick up on it instantly.

'I'm kidding, of course,' he went on. 'You look like you've been in the wars. Can I know how it happened?'

Dani shook her head. 'Line of duty,' she said.

'Well, it's nice to see you anyway, and you too, John.'

John grunted from beside Dani.

'Well, I've done some work on what we discussed and, as you guessed, we do have some contacts inside the facility you're interested in.'

Dani nodded.

'I did a little digging and we identified a few workers who are in regular or semi-regular contact with your man.'

Dani was grateful that he hadn't named Hamilton.

'We have some people in admin and personnel, always handy to be able to get people's addresses and so forth, and so I have that information too.'

'Thank you,' said Dani, holding out her hand.

Marcus didn't move. 'Hold on,' he said, looking around

casually, as though checking there was no one near them, though Dani had picked this spot down near the eastern end of Southsea specifically because it was so quiet. 'I took a bit more of an interest in this than you might think.'

She felt her heart rate increase.

This was the risk with someone like Marcus. He was smart and would do more than just provide information. He would think it through and could potentially get a step ahead of her.

She waited.

'You're trying to find out if he's getting messages out of the prison and who it is and how. Am I right?'

Dani didn't respond.

'So, we've also been thinking about this and have been looking into it. I asked around some of our snitches inside, to see who are the ones that do that kind of thing – smuggling information and contraband – and I have a list.'

He watched Dani carefully as he spoke. 'Then I got to thinking that our man wouldn't want that. He wouldn't want someone who was already doing things for other people, because that type of person might get caught and then squeal about everything so as not to get fired and prosecuted. Am I right?'

Again, Dani said nothing.

'I am right. Good,' he said. 'So, I went back to our snitches and asked again, but this time I wanted to know who the good ones were. The ones that could never be turned. Who were the straight-down-the-liners that never put a foot wrong. You'll be surprised to hear that that was a much smaller list.' Marcus smiled and shook his head as though disappointed.

Dani could feel herself grinding her teeth.

'I then took that list to our friend in personnel,' Marcus continued, 'and asked if any of them had started taking extra holidays, driving better cars, anything like that. Things that a prison guard maybe shouldn't be able to afford. She was quite adamant this wasn't the case, because the prisons are on the lookout for these kinds of things. But she did mention that she knew one of them. She remembered him because a few years ago he had to take some time off after a de-gloving incident when he was working on his car.'

Marcus let that hang out for a while.

'De-gloving?' asked John.

'It's where someone has the skin ripped off the bone of their finger,' said Dani. 'Just leaving the bone behind. I saw it once when a guy was working on an aircraft wearing a wedding ring. He slipped off a maintenance platform and fell. As he tried to grab on, the ring caught on something and it stripped the flesh off his finger.'

'Nice,' said John.

'Indeed,' said Marcus. 'It can be reattached, and, in this case, it was. The guard was taken to hospital and had to have several weeks of sick leave, followed by a period of reduced duties while it healed. It was on his ring finger – apparently he wears a thick wedding ring now to cover the scar.'

Dani was watching Marcus closely and wishing now that she hadn't brought John along with her.

'That's an odd injury, don't you think?' Marcus asked.

Dani nodded.

'It happened only a few months after Hamilton arrived at the prison too,' said Marcus.

They were all silent for a few moments.

The sea wind blew hard from the east and Dani shivered.

'Thank you for your help,' she said, holding out her hand for the folder.

Marcus was shaking his head.

'You know you need me on this,' he said. 'John there's a big lad, but he's injured and doesn't look to me like someone who's got the stones to go all the way. If this guy can work at the prison for years and never be turned, then when we go and speak to him, he's going to need to know that we're serious.'

John bridled next to Dani but said nothing.

'If someone else is prepared to cut the skin off his finger to get him on their side, then he needs to believe that we're prepared to do a lot more to bring him to our team and keep him quiet.'

'I can deal with this,' said Dani. 'I'll keep you in the loop.'

'It's going to be slightly different to that, Dani,' said Marcus. 'This is important to us too, as you know.'

Dani tensed. He obviously knew full well that she hadn't told John everything and he was prepared to use that fact for whatever good it might do.

'I think you know things that we don't, and I think you can be useful, so my offer's simple, you can come and work with us, but we're running the show.'

Dani stepped forward and felt John follow her. 'That's not how it's going to be, Marcus.' She looked at him, willed him to look away. 'I do remember the last time we saw each other,' she went on. 'It was odd, wasn't it, as though I'd seen you somewhere you shouldn't be . . .'

Marcus laughed at her. 'You've no choice,' he said.

'You know what, I do, and I think I've just made it. I'll go with the National Crime Agency and see what happens when they do things their way.'

Marcus shrugged and turned away, heading back to his car.

'You better be quick,' he said over his shoulder. 'We're going to pick him up really soon.'

Dani stepped after him, reaching out and grabbing his arm to turn him back towards her. 'Marcus, don't,' she began. 'We've no idea at all what the situation is. It might

122

not be him and if it is, you could tip someone off just by going near him. We have to deal with this carefully.'

He nodded and gently patted her hand as it rested on his arm. His calm jarred again with Dani's knowledge of what he did for a living and who he worked for.

'Dani, you know who we employ. The guys watching him are expert military intelligence and counter-intelligence operatives with years of experience. We only employ the best our armed forces had to offer. They'll watch and wait and only act when the time's right.' He paused. 'Unless something happens that forces them to act sooner, of course.'

He looked over Dani's shoulder. 'Go and wait over there by the car, please, John.'

John stayed where he was, and Dani turned to him.

'Please, John,' she echoed.

Reluctantly, John turned and walked towards the car.

When Marcus looked back at Dani, there was a hard resolve behind his eyes. 'Did you think I wouldn't know what you were doing? You know as well as I do that this is huge for us. We were called to that shop in the New Forest with no idea what we'd find, and we found you. We need to know who's doing this too. Someone's pulling our strings and we want to know who it is. You've no idea how important that is. We can't speak to the man direct like you can, but if we can find out who he's using on the outside then that matters to us, so it's our way, or you're out.'

Dani waited, thinking hard.

'I need to be the one to speak to him and I want him unharmed. I'm the one that goes in with Hamilton, so he'll have seen me and know who I am—'

'Which will make him clam up and probably tell Hamilton the first time he gets the chance,' Marcus interrupted.

'But if I turn up with you, it will show him that I'm serious and I'm not immediately going to drag the police down on him. We want him scared, I know you can do that, but we want him to think there's a way out too. We want him to know that if he cooperates he can go on with his life, which is likely all he wants to do.'

Marcus thought this over. 'I'll tell you when,' he said.

'OK.' Dani made to leave, then turned back. 'Marcus, did you send a man called Davis to my house?'

'No. Absolutely not,' he said, looking shocked. 'Your dad told me someone attacked you, but it was nothing to do with us. Why do you say the name, Davis? Did the man tell you his name?'

He was lying, Dani was certain of it.

She watched him, waiting, letting the space draw out between them, but he recovered quickly.

'We're making sure it won't happen again,' he said.

'Listen,' she said, the words coming through gritted teeth. 'You need to know, and you can tell my dad as well, that I don't need some thugs protecting my house. If he wants to help me, then tell him I just need him to be honest with me.'

'Your dad's a good man, you know,' Marcus said. 'He's in a difficult position.'

Dani looked away at the sliver of land between her and the sea. A ferry was passing out of sight. 'Will you see him?' she asked.

Marcus nodded. 'I think so.'

'Tell him I'll call him tonight. Tell him if he's not able to talk, then he doesn't need to call me again. Tell him the message I got was from someone called Davis. Judging by your reaction, you know exactly who that is.'

Marcus looked away.

'Tonight,' Dani said. 'Tell him we talk tonight, or we don't speak again. Will you tell him?'

'I will,' said Marcus. 'Keep your phone close by. I'll call you.'

Chapter 15

Her father had called her almost a dozen times and Dani knew that Marcus must have relayed her message about Davis almost as soon as he got back in his car.

She'd ignored the calls.

At first because she was driving in the car with John, but after that, once she was home again and John had left, she wasn't sure why.

She felt nervous about speaking to him and that made her angry. In the end, she knew she had to do it, whether he was prepared to open up or not. She dialled his number and he picked up the phone on the second ring.

'Hello?' he said. 'Dani?'

His voice was urgent, and Dani could tell he'd been on edge.

'Hey,' she said, the speech she'd prepared disappearing from her mind as soon as she heard his voice. 'I want to meet. I think we need to talk.'

'Should I come to yours?' he asked, and Dani was sure she heard him grabbing his keys, the sound of metal against wood noticeable in the background.

'No, I don't want to do it here. Meet me up on Portsdown

Hill, at the car park near that little pub. The one where all the sailors go. Do you know the one I mean?'

'I do. How long?'

'When can you get there?' she asked. 'I can be there in half an hour.'

'Definitely,' he said. 'It'll take me about the same. Will I get us a table if I get there first?'

'No,' said Dani. 'Let's just talk in the car park.'

Her father must have left the second he hung up the phone because he was there waiting in his car for her as she pulled off the road.

She looked at the small pub as she passed it, the rickety windows, the flags of the four home nations hanging in them, and felt her stomach clench as her tyres began to crunch on the stones. She gestured for her dad to follow her as she drove up a small incline to the overflow parking area that was just out of sight behind it. She pulled in, parked up, and looked at the trees all around her, blocking her in, tall and seemingly impenetrable, like a wall on all sides.

It was a pleasant day, chilly but not actually cold, and the trees offered so much shelter from the elements that it was still and almost eerily quiet as the sun disappeared behind them.

She stepped out of her car, looked around and focused on the treeline in the distance that had once saved her life.

Her father pulled up next to her and she watched him lumber out, this man she'd known for her entire life, and she knew that this time, the speech she'd prepared had to go ahead. Family or no family, he needed to know how she felt and she needed to know what he knew.

'Dani,' her dad began.

He walked towards her and reached out, but she stopped him.

'Don't talk, Dad. Just listen,' said Dani, first looking him in the eye, and then realising she needed to look away while she said this. 'We need to talk, and by that, I mean you need to talk,' she said. 'I'm going to tell you what I know already, and I'm going to tell you that I'll find out more, and I want to give you an opportunity to talk to me. Do you understand what I'm saying to you?'

She glanced up and caught his grim expression. He nodded and she looked away again.

'I've spoken to Christopher Hamilton just this morning, and I know there's some link between you, something that's letting him try to drive a wedge between us.'

She was watching him in her periphery, not wanting to make eye contact, but she saw her dad's eyes flit away from her at the mention of Hamilton's name.

Dani felt the urge to close the distance between them and swing a kick at him – his silence made her so angry. She could see in his eyes that he remembered Hamilton – how could anyone not – and it made her feel sick, like a hard punch in the stomach, that he'd kept this from her for so long.

All the times Hamilton had been discussed in their house. The number of times her father said how proud he was that she was the one who'd brought him to justice, all of that, and he'd never once mentioned that he knew him and had met him.

Dani wanted to scream, but she had to stay on script.

The lines she had to deliver were hard and she needed to maintain pace without interruptions.

'I should also tell you I'm looking into everything that occurred in Afghanistan around the time that Jimmy and Marcus were there. I know Hamilton was sent out there,' she said, bluffing and taking a chance to watch her father's reaction. 'I don't know everything yet. But you must realise, Dad, it's only a matter of time now. People are looking into this as we speak. I know you were out there. I've seen the unit photograph with you, Jimmy and Marcus. I think the man who attacked me was in the picture too. A guy called Davis?'

She watched as Taz swallowed hard and then leaned back, resting against his car and running both hands through his short hair. His head had dropped forward, his chin to his chest, and he seemed to be taking deep breaths.

Dani deliberately said no more. She'd decided it would be that way.

If he spoke and confided in her, she'd listen. If he said nothing, then she had only one more card to play before she got back in her car and drove away. At that point she'd call John straight away and tell him she believed her dad was in some way implicated, she'd add his name to the investigation and take it all to the NCA and the SIB; it was her father's choice.

The truth would come out, it always did.

She began a countdown in her head, starting at thirty. That was how long he had.

He was standing motionless, saying nothing.

A flash of temper ignited in Dani as she watched him.

She felt an overwhelming urge to run at him and physically attack him, to scratch him, grab him, do something to get a reaction from him. Her mind began to whir as she wondered what he knew, how long he'd known it for. More importantly, who he was protecting. Her hands clenched by her side as she struggled to control herself, trying to remember where she was with her countdown, the numbers lost in the turmoil of a profound betrayal.

He was still silent.

'Do you know why I brought you here?' she asked.

He seemed to jump as she spoke, as though she'd snapped him out of deep thought.

'Do you know why I brought you to this very spot?' she said, realising that she'd known all along she had to tell him this. 'I brought you here because one year to the day that Christopher Hamilton went to prison, I was in that pub down there celebrating with John and the others. I left early, as I often do, and my car was parked right there.'

She pointed to his car and the spot where he was standing.

'I walked across the car park to where you're standing now and there were three men waiting for me.'

His mouth dropped open and she saw something in his eyes. A mixture of things, maybe fear, fury and terror.

'They'd been sent by Christopher Hamilton, Dad. They'd come to get even with me for putting him away. I don't know how he made them do it. I don't know how he got the message to them. But they dragged me out of my car, just here,' she pointed to the ground next to his car. 'Then they beat me. They forced me over the bonnet and tore my jeans off. Then they used a lash. I heard them say that I was to get thirty lashes. One for every year that Hamilton had been given before he could even be considered for release.'

Her father began to speak, but Dani held up her hand to stop him.

'I fought them off, Dad. Just. I managed to get myself free and run over there to the woods. I was half naked, bleeding, and they chased me. I had to fight another one again, just over there.'

She pointed to a spot near where she'd entered the woods, the point at which the guy chasing her had caught up and she'd spun around, using the knife she'd taken from them to fend him off.

'That was what Hamilton tried to do to me,' she said. 'And I want you to understand that. Hamilton tried to break me. He tried to have me beaten and raped. I still have the scars on my back, but the deeper ones are in here.'

She tapped the side of her head.

'He did it so I'd never forget him. That's why I brought you here. Because I wanted you to know that. I wanted you to know that if you're siding with Hamilton, that's what you're siding with. If you're in any way trying to protect him, then that's what you're protecting and you're no better than the men who attacked me.'

For a moment, Dani was sure she saw tears in his eyes.

His face was ashen white, and his mouth was moving as though he wanted to speak but didn't know what to say.

'How . . . Why . . .?'

She could see the emotions crossing his face as he tried to figure out what he wanted to know, what he could ask.

'I never told anyone,' she lied, knowing that now wasn't the time to tell her father that it was Roger she'd gone to, unable to face a hospital and unable to face the police.

It was Roger who'd helped her photograph the wounds, who'd helped put her back together again, and who'd sorted it out for her to go on a sabbatical year to get some time away and recover.

'Why didn't you tell me?' her dad asked, but his question had no conviction, and Dani was sure he knew full well why she hadn't confided in him.

It was because what had happened would have torn him apart. Because she knew he'd go on a relentless hunt to try and find the person who'd done this to her, stopping at nothing. The only way he'd be able to deal with it would be to hurt someone, to do something to someone. In that instant, it dawned on Dani that her father, knowing what he knew now, could do the things that Jimmy had done. With the right motivation, he could hurt people in the way that Jimmy did. Possibly more.

'I did it to protect you,' she said. 'To protect you and Charlie and Mim, but mainly you. I'm trying to protect you again now.'

He stepped towards her and held out his arms. 'Please?' he said, reaching out to embrace her.

Dani felt cold. Numb. Realising that she'd spoken out loud about what had happened for only the third time in her life. She stepped towards him, but stopped just short, looking up at him.

'Are you going to tell me?' she asked. 'Are you going to tell me how you know Hamilton?'

He nodded as he stepped forward, dwarfing her, enveloped her body in his arms and held her tight.

'Yes,' he said. 'I'll tell you.'

Chapter 16

The sky was dark now and her screen illuminated to show several missed calls from John, a few more from Roger, and a battery that was only just clinging to life.

They were both sitting in her dad's car, the engine running and the heater turned on.

'The thing is, Dani, there's a lot to tell, and it's late,' he said. 'You look beat.'

'I need to know, Dad,' she said, giving him a hard look.

'Look, I'll tell you the bones of it, OK? But we talk it through properly, in detail, tomorrow?'

Dani nodded, and her dad began to speak.

'I was in Afghanistan on operations. This was back in the early days, before the UK admitted it had an operational presence in the region. Before Camp Bastion and all that stuff. I know you're military, Dani, and I don't want to talk down to you, but places like that, when the main forces have yet to be deployed, are like the wild west. The American Special Forces were there too, mainly CIA Special Activities Division. I think, some counter-terror guys, that kind of thing, and we did talk to them, but not as closely as we should have. We were working out of a small forward operating base in Khost, near the Pakistan border, but we were doing long-range work, often heading down into Kandahar and even Helmand.'

His eyes had dropped down now, and he was looking at the steering wheel as he spoke.

'I was on operations, eight men, deep in Taliban country – hell, it was all Taliban country then. We were compromised, and we got into a firefight. It was nasty, really nasty. It wasn't my first, not by a long shot, but this one seemed to go on forever.'

He looked across at Dani.

'They were closing in on us. We were low on ammunition, and I really thought we might be done. All I could think about was you guys. Holding you both in my arms, wanting to watch you become beautiful, strong, intelligent women. You're both so different, but I couldn't love either of you more.'

Dani glanced away.

'You're the more difficult one,' her dad said, and they both laughed, breaking the tension slightly.

'At times like that, that's when I knew what really mattered to me. And I was right, because sometimes, when I see you both now, I literally feel like my heart might burst open in my chest because I'm so proud of you both.'

Dani looked away again, unsure why tears were forming in her eyes.

He rarely spoke like this when sober and she knew it made him as uncomfortable as it did her.

She said nothing and waited for him to continue.

'We had to make a break for it. Laying down cover for each other and working our way towards a line of rocks. We tried to drag our fallen with us, but we couldn't. One other was hit, a friend of mine, Steve, he went down hard.

I tried to go back for him, but there was no way. In the end, I was beaten back, and they took the ground.'

Her father's face was bleak.

'We ran and made it to some cover, but they kept coming and it was hours later that we managed to break away. But when we did, it was because bodies were dropping. Someone was taking them out and we saw two or three of them fall before they even realised what was happening. We didn't wait. We knew someone else was there, someone from the allied forces was supporting us. It was a sniper and he pinned them down while we ran.'

He sighed. 'There's no quick way to tell this,' he said.

'I'm OK,' Dani reassured him. 'Just keep going.'

'We headed for Pakistan. That was dangerous in itself, but better than the option of trying to track the Afghan border. We were the right side of the Dori River when we came to a small village, barely a village really, a settlement. It looked deserted, a little ghost town, half a dozen or so houses, if you could call them that, and all looked empty. We needed to rest, get some shelter, and it'd been days now since we'd had contact. There were five of us left: me, Jimmy, Marcus, who was only a brand-new young lieutenant at the time, and two marines, Davis and Hogben. We moved in and started to clear the houses, checking for anyone hiding or for booby traps. We cleared one house, then the next and the next. Then we went to the last one. It was the outlier, slightly bigger than the others, and it backed on to the treeline.'

He stopped and shook his head, grimacing at the memories.

'Dad?'

He shut his eyes and breathed, raising a hand for her to wait.

The moments passed as Dani watched her father fight

some internal battle with his memories, before he finally spoke again.

'They were all in there,' he said. 'Some were alive. Some dead. Some we literally couldn't tell. Someone had strung up several of the men, we couldn't really see how many, it was just a mass of bloody body parts, but they were bleeding them into a pit in the centre of the room.'

He seemed to be breathing more heavily, struggling to draw in the air as though he were headed for some kind of panic attack.

Dani reached out and touched him.

'Dad, it's OK, take your time. I don't need to know what you saw. Just how it affects what you've done.'

He looked at her and his eyes surprised her. 'To understand what I've done, you need to know what we saw.'

Dani pulled her hand away, something in his eyes sending a chill through her.

'There were a group of girls against one wall, tied and sitting so they'd have to watch. They were alive but had been there for days and the stink of their faeces was thick. There were flies everywhere and when they saw us, they were terrified.'

'It was a Brit?' asked Dani, stunned. 'They were terrified because it was one of us?'

He was shaking his head and Dani wasn't sure if he was answering her question or reacting to the memories.

'We managed to speak to one of them. Marcus speaks some Dari and Pashto and he was able to communicate. The girl that spoke told him it was one of us – a westerner.'

'Dad, that's a war crime.'

He was nodding.

'We tried to free them. Tried to give some first aid where we could, and we shared what water and food we had and could find. They weren't all from the village – some had been brought there and they were sure that they'd been in a vehicle at some point. They were beyond terrified. They'd been made to watch the others die and, though we couldn't get all of it, it was obvious that it had been long and slow, ritualistic. He'd been eating them.'

Dani could barely breathe.

'Two of the girls, and I mean girls, Dani, barely twelve if they were even that, tried to run. We stopped them, but only because we knew they wouldn't survive a night out there and we couldn't risk bringing the Taliban to our location. They were hysterical, and both had suffered serious blood loss. It was then we saw the wounds; they were both missing the ring finger on their left hand. They weren't able to tell us anything, but the other woman, the one who'd talked to Marcus already, she said it meant that they'd been picked – they were next. That was what he did, he took their finger and kept it and that was how they knew. Sometimes they'd be made to wait for days, but when he returned, he always went to those ones he'd marked out.'

Dani couldn't speak.

The silence in the car between her dad's words was absolute; even outside seemed to be silent now, as though showing some respect for those involved.

'Where were the fingers?' Dani asked eventually.

'We don't know. They weren't there.'

'Did you save any of them? Any of the victims?'

Her dad sighed.

'We needed to move, but we didn't know what to do. There were a dozen or more dead, a tangle of other body parts and bones that had been dumped in a latrine hole in the woods, and we had around a dozen sick and injured, all on the verge of dehydration and starvation. We'd been trying to get comms with what allied forces there were in the region for days, but the gear we had then didn't work well in the terrain and we hadn't been able to. We knew we'd need to head higher to get some support; there was no way we could manage it. We thought about all options. Trying to walk everyone out, setting a trap and waiting for him to return, we thought about it all, but in the end, we decided that two of us would head for high ground and call for help and the other three would stay. Davis, who you said came to your house, and another marine called Mike Hogben were the two fastest. Paul was the comms specialist too, so they went while Marcus, Jimmy and I stayed with the victims.'

Dani noticed that his breathing was quickening again, that he was starting to struggle with his words.

'Mike barely made it a hundred feet before a bullet tore half his head off.'

Her dad looked at her, as though trying to make her understand the fear inside him.

'He'd come back. It was the sniper. The one who'd helped us escape – who else could it be? He was back. Davis turned and ran towards us, moving, ducking, changing direction, everything we'd ever been told to do to avoid fire as we ran for cover, but he took two, one in the left shoulder and one in his lower abdomen. He was about fifteen feet away when he fell. He was lying out in the open, alive, but we couldn't get to him and that bastard wouldn't kill him. We tried everything, but the murderer was watching. We threw a line, and a warning shot landed when Davis tried to reach for it. I made to run, and the shot missed me by about the breadth of a hair. We were pinned down, watching a man die, with not enough ammo, and a dozen weak and injured civilians. We could try and get out the back, head for the woods, but there wasn't the cover, not all of us were able, we couldn't leave Davis, and this guy could just pick us off; he'd chosen his location really well.'

'What did you do?'

'We waited for two days and things were bad. Some of the locals were in a state of panic when we got there; by now they were uncontrollable.' He stopped, and a silence stretched out between them.

'Dad?'

'On the morning of the second day a few of them started screaming and running for the door. Jimmy and I stopped them, and Marcus tried to reason with them, but we were screwed. We weren't even sure if Davis was alive and we knew we couldn't get away from there with all of them and neither could we stay there for much longer. We fought them back and looked outside.'

He turned to look at her, his brow furrowed as though reliving the madness.

'There was a note on a post opposite the door – he must have come in close during the night – it said, "just the ones I marked as mine".'

'You didn't give them up, Dad?' said Dani, not sure why she said it, not sure what the other options were.

He shook his head.

'They were starting to fight us now, those that could stand, and the room was full of flies, drawn to the blood and shit. We were going mad. They made one final push at the door, trying to escape, and Jimmy and I looked at each other and we just opened it.'

Her dad was looking at the dash again now, as though watching a movie there of what was happening in his mind.

'They ran, walked and staggered out, some carried their loved ones, and they spread out in all directions. Then the bullets started. It was a few seconds of chaos and we took the chance. We ran out and grabbed Davis and not a single bullet came near us. We ran for the treeline and made it and then we set out, as fast as we were able, for the high ground. We could hear the gunshots and screams behind us, but we kept going. One of the women tried to follow us, the one who'd spoken with Marcus, but the sniper broke her down. He didn't just kill her. He shot her once in the leg, then the hip, then, when she was on the dirt, the abdomen and finally the head, all while we watched.'

'Why didn't he kill you too?' Dani asked. 'It makes no sense to let you get away.'

'We've never known,' Taz said, his words quiet. 'But we carried Davis, on our backs at first, taking it in turns. When we thought we were safe, we managed to build a stretcher. But we weren't safe.'

Her dad seemed to have shrunk again while he spoke, as though the energy taken to tell the story was being converted from his own mass.

'The next morning, after we'd yomped all night, we crossed a ridge where we were sure we'd get a signal for our comms. We saw something on a rock. It was a note, same as before. It said, "our little secret". A few hundred feet later, we found what was left of Mike's head. We kept going, always looking behind us, and eventually we got a signal on the radio. We managed to call in an extraction and we were taken to the American Forward Operating Base at Salerno.'

'And you reported it?' asked Dani. 'Right? It was a war crime, Dad, you did nothing wrong. You tried to save those people, so you had no reason not to report it.'

Her dad nodded.

'We got back there, but our debriefing team was miles away, so I went straight to the only Brit officer who was on the base – it was a young policeman, Lieutenant Christopher Hamilton.'

'But he'd have had to act,' said Dani. 'He'd have had to do something.'

'It was the wild west out there, Dani, remember. We'd lost men, we were covered in the blood of multiple victims, and our story was incredible. There was no record of any other allied operatives in the area and if they checked the village, there was every chance the other guy would have just burned it all out. They wouldn't have found anything to back up our story. They'd likely just have found burnt-out corpses in run-down, burnt-out buildings, and there was no shortage of that out there.'

He was looking at her hard now, as though desperately hoping for her to accept that it was a situation she couldn't fully understand.

'Nothing was going to be done. It was made pretty clear to us that, given the UK wouldn't admit we'd been there at all, if we kicked up a fuss, then the most likely people to be investigated for any war crimes would be us.'

Dani shut her eyes as she tried to process what she was hearing.

This was a war crime and her father was involved.

Hamilton had some proof of this and had kept it somewhere.

She ran through all she'd heard and tried to make sense of it.

'If you have questions, I'd appreciate it if we could get them sorted now,' her dad said. 'It sickens me to think about it and what we did, so I'd rather not keep coming back to it.'

Dani stared at him. 'It's a war crime, Dad, people were murdered.'

'A lot of people were murdered out there. I'm not saying that makes it right.'

'And this is what Hamilton's using?'

'What else could it be?' her dad replied. 'The girls' fingers. All of us who were there. The fact they found Davis and he came to your house.'

Dani watched him and all the while the same question kept running through her mind – 'Why did he let you go, Dad? Why didn't he just kill you all there when he had the chance?'

Chapter 17

Dani could barely wait to get her phone out of her pocket as she left her dad in the car park. She checked she was on hands-free and dialled John's number.

'I have something,' she said. 'It may not be much, and I'll explain in detail later, but I think we need to be looking for a special forces sniper who was live in Afghanistan right near the beginning of the conflict.'

She heard John exhale at the other end of the phone.

'I know,' said Dani. 'Needle in a haystack, but we can go mainstream with this one. My dad opened up about an alleged war crime he witnessed out there. I'm going to have him make a statement and I think that should be enough to pull in Jimmy and Marcus and any others that were there too. There will be records and we can find the location and then go to the Americans. As soon as he makes the statement it'll blow a lot of this wide open and we'll get the go-ahead to requisition documents and personnel records, I guarantee it.'

Dani could hear that she was gabbling. She took a moment and tried to calm herself.

'I don't follow,' said John. 'What has the war crime to do with Hamilton?'

'He was there when my dad witnessed the crime. My dad was out on operations and he found a sniper who was abducting and torturing some locals.'

She almost mentioned that he was also eating them but decided to hold that back until later.

'He was keeping their fingers as trophies, John. It looks as though it was all hushed up, but if Hamilton took an interest, if he somehow managed to locate the sniper, then he could have assisted him somehow.'

'Or entered into some sick mutual love affair,' said John, almost muttering it under his breath.

Dani hadn't said it, but she'd thought it, considered how someone like Hamilton might form a bond with a man who cannibalised other humans. She shivered, the thought making her stomach flip.

'Either way. The fingers as trophies. The fact that Hamilton was there. It's a breakthrough. It's something at least. And it gives us a link between Jimmy and Hamilton. If Hamilton kept some proof. If he had their initial statements. If he had anything to link them to it, then he could be using that to blackmail them.'

There was silence on the end of the line.

She waited, realising how quiet John had been.

'John? What's up?' she asked.

She heard him sigh.

'I'm just thinking that if what you say is right and this is a breakthrough, and if Hamilton in some way blackmailed this sniper and is doing the same to Jimmy, then what makes you think Jimmy and Marcus will support your dad's story? In fact, they stand to lose everything by being involved at all. I'm just saying they're not going to share your excitement, and that worries me.'

He was right.

She'd been so excited to have seen a pathway that she hadn't stopped yet to consider how others might be opposed to it.

Jimmy and Marcus were criminals and they wouldn't want to be involved at all. In fact, if Hamilton was using this as leverage, then they were prepared to go to quite some lengths to avoid being involved.

'You still there?' asked John.

'Yeah, sorry. I was just thinking about what you said. You're right, I just hadn't got there yet, but it changes nothing. This has to be reported and investigated.'

'How're you feeling?' John asked.

Dani frowned at the sudden change of subject. 'I'm OK, I'm just tired. It's becoming my default setting these days. I'm looking forward to getting home.'

There was silence on the other end for a while until John spoke again.

'If you need any help at home, any help getting around, or doing chores, just let me know,' he said. 'I'd be more than happy to come around for a couple of hours. I don't mind cooking dinner or whatever, to let you rest up. You know, anything that helps you to get better really.'

Dani smiled to herself. 'Thanks, John. I really appreciate it, but I think I just want to go home, crash on the couch for a while and get some sleep. I feel grimy after today. I just want to get back, get showered and go to sleep. Hope that's OK? Thanks for offering, though. I really do appreciate it.'

Once they'd said their goodbyes, her phone rang again immediately.

'What did you forget?' she said, but it wasn't John. She could immediately hear that the person calling her was in a different setting, outside somewhere, cars passing.

She looked at the screen and saw the number was withheld.

'Who's this?' she said.

'It's me.'

She recognised Marcus's voice and said nothing.

'It's now, Dani,' he said.

'Wait,' she said quickly. 'I need some time. I don't think we need to lift the guard. I can't explain it to you right now, but I think I have another line on this.'

'That may be the case for you, but we're going now,' Marcus said. 'Am I to understand that you no longer wish to assist?'

Dani hesitated. 'Just give me forty-eight hours,' she said.

'No. You'll be home in about six minutes,' he said.

Dani immediately looked in her rear-view mirror at the cars around her; there was only one way he could have known that.

'Some of my people will meet you there. It's an invitation, though, Dani. If you choose not to go with them then that's your decision, but there won't be another.'

The line went dead.

Chapter 18

She watched the road behind her for the rest of the way home, looking at the lights of the other cars, trying to spot anyone who changed lanes as she did, or kept pace with her as she began to alter her speed, but she saw nothing.

The people employed by Jimmy Nash and Marcus were experts, she knew that.

They recruited exclusively from the ranks of the British armed forces, and the people that she knew must be following her likely had experience in doing so in multiple operational theatres around the globe.

A Ford saloon eventually caught her eye, but by the time it did, she noticed that it was making no further attempt not to.

The driver settled the car behind her and followed her as she left the motorway and made the short trip along much smaller roads to her home.

As she pulled into her driveway, the car stopped, waiting a respectful distance away.

Dani had to sit for a few moments and take deep breaths to calm herself down. That they'd been following her was infuriating, that Marcus was so brazen about it doubled down on that, but for them simply to fall in behind her and follow to her front door and then wait patiently for her to come and join them beggared belief. Dani was livid.

When she'd approached Marcus and they'd discussed lifting the prison guard who was probably taking information to and from Hamilton, it had seemed like a good idea. She'd thought long and hard about the risks of doing so, but they'd made no headway in months and years with the Hamilton disappearances and she'd needed to take the chance, needed to see if she could take a step forward. Now her dad had told her what happened in Afghanistan, and everything had changed again.

She heard footsteps advancing towards the car and saw a man approaching. He was holding his hands up in front of him and moving slowly. She watched him as he went to the passenger side and knocked on the window. Dani lowered the window and waited.

'Miss Lewis?' The man kept his hands in view as he spoke.

His accent was bland, hard to place, and Dani wondered if he'd grown up in the forces as well as serving as an adult. Dani nodded.

'Marcus said you'd be coming with us today. Is that still the case?'

Dani studied the man, noting that he was harder looking than she'd first realised. In the light of the streetlamp, his nose looked as though it had been broken at some point, a slight bump showing on one side. He also had a few old and faded scars around his face and on his hands. Then there were his eyes, friendly but unwavering; he looked like a man who had nothing to prove.

'Can I please have a few moments?' Dani asked.

The man nodded. 'I'll wait in the car,' he said, and immediately walked away.

Dani watched him go, looking at how he walked, his arms swinging, a firm pace, as though he'd marched all his life.

This man was a soldier, just like her father, and it could so easily have been him that had encountered this madman in Afghanistan, as easily as it was her father, or Marcus . . .

Dani swore under her breath. She'd been so pleased that her dad had finally told her the truth and so stunned by what she'd heard that she hadn't realised the most obvious fact of all – Marcus and Jimmy knew everything her dad had told her too and they'd known it for longer. Despite that, and even with their significant resources, it hadn't yet helped them to track down this person.

She grabbed her bag and opened the door; she had to go and speak to the guard.

The former soldier opened the car door for her and let her into the back of the car.

They drove for about forty-five minutes, heading away from Portsmouth and towards Southampton, then they turned off the main roads and headed into a small town that Dani didn't recognise.

There looked to be only a single street with a few shops, an estate agent and a pub, but even though only the pub and one of the shops had some lights on, there were still cars parked alongside the road on both sides with no spaces to stop.

The driver, who hadn't spoken a word for the entire journey, slowed the car and eventually stopped in the roadway.

It took Dani a second to realise that he'd pulled up next to another vehicle and that Marcus was seated on the driver's side, looking directly at her.

'We're here, miss,' the driver said, but Dani was already opening the door.

She moved quickly around the back of Marcus's car and opened the passenger door, sliding in beside him.

Marcus immediately held up a hand to indicate she shouldn't speak and pointed towards the pub.

'Won't be long,' he said quietly.

'I doubt they could hear us from there,' said Dani, looking at where he was pointing.

The entrance to the pub was around a hundred feet away and she had a good view of it. Between her and the entrance was a row of parked cars and a white van.

She noticed immediately that every second street light was out, but that around the white van, others were out too, and it sat in the centre of a long lane of darkness.

'It's not about them hearing you, it's about your mindset,' said Marcus.

'I think this is a mistake, Marcus,' she said.

'I don't,' said Marcus. 'He comes out of that pub every week on the same day at the same time. I've had guys in and around the pub for over a week and there's no one there that shouldn't be.'

As he spoke, Dani saw the door to the pub open and light spilled out on to a small section of the parked cars, then the door closed. She recognised the man who'd passed through, could see from his gait that he was the guard who'd led her to meet Hamilton on almost every occasion she'd visited him.

'If we're wrong . . .' she said.

'If we're wrong, then we better make sure he really understands what happens if he opens his mouth,' said Marcus.

The white van was parked about halfway between her position and the pub, and now two men had stepped out from inside it. They'd left the door wide open and were carrying what looked like a high fence panel.

The guard approached them and then stopped.

Dani could see that the men were chatting, the two with the fence panel seeming to step away from the van to let the guard pass.

He raised his hand to them, as though thanking them for their courtesy, and then passed between the men and the van.

Had Dani blinked she would have missed the instant in which the two men moved, stepping back towards the van. The fence panel seemed to fold, as though it were hinged in the centre, blocking out the vision from her side and most likely the other.

Within a second, the two men were back in the van, the guard was gone, and the van was pulling away into the night.

'That easy,' said Dani, stunned at how quickly she'd seen the guard disappear.

'Two outside and two inside,' Marcus said. 'Exactly how we used to pick them up in Ireland.'

He started the car and pulled out on to the road, driving behind the van as it headed towards Southampton docks.

Marcus reached into the pocket on the driver's side and pulled out a black hood.

'Same one as the last time we took a trip,' he said, handing it to her. 'Feel free to leave your nose and mouth out again so you don't feel claustrophobic.'

Dani took the hood.

The last time he'd passed her one of these was when he took her to see a known rapist who was being held in torturous conditions, but who had since escaped. Recalling the memories of that place and the brutality that was inflicted on William Knight made her shiver. She pulled the hood over her eyes and leaned her head back against the headrest.

'If you've been watching him for a week, then you were already on to him before I approached you,' she said, adjusting the hood so that a little light came up inside to chase away the worst of the blackness.

Marcus said nothing.

'So why do you need me?' she asked.

She heard Marcus moving next to her but couldn't tell what he was doing.

'Because you're good at this. Because you know more about this whole Hamilton piece than anyone else. Because you've got as much invested in this as we have. Because your time's running out. You'll be out of uniform before long, from what we can tell. They're just waiting to find a quiet and palatable way to get rid of you, so there's a win in this for all of us; we find out who's blackmailing us, and you get to solve the crimes you've been obsessing over for years.'

He paused for a long while and Dani could tell he was looking at her.

'Maybe you get to keep your job in the forces,' he said. 'Or maybe there's a job with us for someone who can find things out and follow her nose.'

Dani laughed as soon as he said the words and almost pulled the hood off to check if he was being serious.

'Lots of people laugh when we first speak to them. But think it over.'

'Yeah sure,' said Dani, shaking her head. 'How did William Knight get free? I heard you say in the shop that he was no longer with you.'

Again, there was a long pause.

'Someone broke into the safe house you were at. They

took Knight and the young lad you were looking for and then killed everyone else that was there.'

'Did they take their fingers?' asked Dani.

'They did,' said Marcus. 'The ring finger was missing from all of them.'

'How many did he kill?'

This silence drew out so long that Dani wasn't sure if Marcus would answer at all.

'Not nearly as many as Jimmy's prepared to kill to find him . . .'

Chapter 19

Dani was aware of the light changing as they arrived and parked.

They were inside, she knew that much, though it was very dark, and she could only assume from the smell that they were in a warehouse somewhere down by the docks.

'Just leave the hood on for a second please, Dani,' said Marcus, though he made no effort to get out of the car and the engine was stopped.

They sat in the car waiting, until he sighed and spoke again.

'Last time we brought you to one of our locations, we let you see one side of our organisation. I hope it was enough to make you certain that you'd never want to speak about what you saw or heard – I'm confident it was.'

'Just make the threat and be done with it,' said Dani. 'I think it was my sister you threatened last time. I assume it'll be her again?'

She reached up and took the hood off, throwing it at Marcus as he watched her from the driver's seat.

He was nodding reluctantly.

'I get it. Keep my mouth shut or you hurt my family. Hardly a creative touch, but I get it. Shall we go now?'

Marcus held up his hand to stop her. 'One more thing. We need to put the frighteners on this guy, but I heard what you said about not making it permanent and offering him a chance to go on with his life in peace. I just wanted you to know that I listened. I also want you to know that the vast majority of people that get hurt in this game, get hurt because they deserve it or because they leave no choice but for it to happen.'

'Doesn't seem relevant if we're not going to hurt the man,' said Dani.

'It might become relevant.'

Marcus opened the door and climbed out of the car and Dani followed suit.

They were in a warehouse furnished with row after row of large metal containers, the sort with doors at one end that you could walk inside. Each was around forty feet long, eight feet wide and looked to be about the same high. There were several different colours, but most were dark blues, greens and dull red, and most that Danny could see were locked tight.

She followed Marcus as he walked along one row, his shoes clip-clopping on the stone floor and echoing around the space. It felt as though they were the only ones there.

Eventually, he stopped, and it took Dani a second to realise there was a door in the side of one of the large metal containers. He opened it and gestured for her to enter.

This container had been modified to be used as an office. At one end there was a desk and filing cabinets, arranged to look down the length of the container. Then near the centre was a small meeting table surrounded by a dozen or more ripped, dirty chairs.

Dani also noticed that along one wall there was a dark panel that could have been a window but looked more like a sheet of black plastic.

'Grab a seat near there,' said Marcus, gesturing towards the other end of the container where Dani noticed a very large flat-screen television mounted on a stand.

Dani walked towards it but didn't sit down until Marcus joined her and took a seat first.

He reached for the remote control and turned the television on.

The scene on the screen made Dani's heart beat faster.

'The guys in the room can hear us,' said Marcus. 'And we can hear everything. If you want to ask a question, then remember that they need to relay it.'

'Who's the other person?' asked Dani.

On the screen two men were sitting in what looked like another container. They were each bound to their chairs by ties around their leg and arm and she clearly recognised one of them as the guard – the other's face was covered with a black hood similar to that which Dani had worn in the car, except on this person, it was pulled all the way down and fastened at the neck.

Suddenly the screen was blocked by the face of a man, very white as the light from the camera bounced off his features making him look ghostly.

'Picture's good,' said Marcus.

'Testing sound,' came a voice from the screen.

'Loud and clear also,' said Marcus.

Dani watched as the man then approached the guard and squatted down in front of him.

'Mr Nowak,' the man said.

The audio was clear, and Dani now realised she could hear the guard crying softly.

'Mr Nowak, may I call you Jakub? I want to start by

telling you that there is a way out of this for you,' said the man, still squatting down so he could look up into the guard's face. 'I'm going to ask you some questions and I need you to be honest with me. Do you understand?'

Dani saw the guard nod but couldn't make out any sound.

'But first, I need you to know I'm serious and that if you don't cooperate with me, things will be bad for you; worse than they could be if you help. Is that clear?'

Dani heard more crying and then some words coming faintly through the tears.

'Please don't hurt me,' the guard said, the words almost inaudible.

'That's up to you,' the man said. He stood up now and took a few paces to one side. 'This gentleman here,' the man said, gesturing to the hooded man in the chair opposite. 'He hasn't cooperated with us in the way we hope you're going to. He had the opportunity to be honest with us and he declined. So, I'm going to let you see what happens, OK?'

Dani turned to Marcus, her mouth wide. 'What the hell are you doing?' she said. 'Who is that?'

'It's someone who deserves to be in a lot of pain,' said Marcus. 'If you can't be here, then you're welcome to wait outside.'

'There are other ways,' Dani said. 'At least let me try and speak to him.'

Marcus shook his head. 'This needs to happen and it's going to. We need to show him there's a way out but ensure he realises that we can do worse than whoever else is pressing him. That's what we're doing.'

'No, it's wrong.'

'It's not wrong,' said Marcus, his voice still calm. 'You have no idea what this guy did and who to. You've no idea what we want from him or why. Just because you don't think someone is guilty, doesn't mean they're not.'

'What we're going to do,' said the voice on the screen, stopping Dani from replying, 'is show you what will happen if you choose not to speak to us truthfully.'

The man picked something up from a table that was hidden from the camera and walked back towards the guard.

'This is a one-millimetre drill bit,' the man said, squatting down again and holding something in the guard's eyeline that Dani couldn't see. 'What we do is tie your hand to a thick piece of wood and spread your fingers out and then we drill this through your fingertip, right in the centre of the nail – just one at first. Then . . .'

The man stood up again and walked to the table, picking up something else and returning.

'Then we use these.'

He held something else under the guard's nose.

'These are self-tapping screws. They're about four inches long. Look,' the man pointed to something Dani couldn't see. 'The threads are really pronounced. Well, once we've drilled a small pilot hole through your finger, we then start to screw these through the tip of your finger and fingernail down into the wood below. It takes about five minutes from start to finish, but that's the catch, once we start, we don't speak again until we're finished. So, there's no changing minds halfway through – once we go, we go. Do you understand, Jakub?'

Dani heard the guard sobbing and turned back to Marcus.

'You need to stop this,' she said, feeling panic start to build in her voice. 'There's another way, Marcus. Let me at least try.'

'This gentleman hasn't cooperated,' the man was saying on the screen.

He nodded his head and Dani looked back to see two figures emerge from the darkness behind the hooded man. One pulled the man's hood forward and though Dani couldn't see the man's face clearly, she saw that it was cut before the hood was replaced.

Immediately the man began to beg and plead. His accent was foreign, though Dani couldn't place it, and he spoke in a mixture of English and a second language.

'Shut him up,' said the man who'd been speaking throughout, and one of the other men who'd appeared grabbed the hooded man by the neck, stopping the stream of words immediately. 'This man is getting the full five minutes.'

He nodded and then stepped behind the guard, grasping his hair and forcing him to watch.

The two others began to work, pulling over a small wooden table and tying the man's wrist to a thick piece of wood.

'Stop this now, Marcus,' said Dani.

She saw one of the men fit the tiny drill bit to a cordless drill and step forward.

'Marcus!' shouted Dani, but he continued to ignore her.

The hooded man was talking again, then shouting, but Dani heard and watched as one of the men positioned the drill bit on the hooded man's right index finger.

She heard the drill start, and then she heard nothing but animalistic screams. She flinched and turned away as it continued without let-up.

Marcus sat silent and watching throughout.

She looked back to the screen for a second and could see that one of the men was now driving a screwdriver through the hooded man's finger. He was turning it slowly, a quarter turn at a time and then waiting for a few seconds before he did it again.

The sounds of the hooded man's scream continued relentlessly and Dani covered her ears and looked away, eventually standing up and walking to the other end of the container as the torture continued.

Finally, she stepped outside the container, putting her hands in her pockets so that no one could see them shaking.

The air around her was cold and she took deep breaths.

The sound was still there, faint, and she couldn't tell whether it came from the TV or whether she could actually hear the man's torture in a container nearby. She waited there, her eyes shut, and her feet scuffing on the concrete floor to drown out the noise of another human's pain.

Chapter 20

'It's done.'

The voice cut through her thoughts and she looked up to see Marcus leaning out of the container door.

He didn't wait, but left the door open for her and she followed him in.

She wanted to say so much, to express her anger and to plead the hooded man's right to justice, regardless of what crime he'd committed, but she knew it would do no good, she knew she didn't have the time and she knew that she had risked this the second she spoke to Marcus on the phone and asked for his help.

As she re-entered the room she looked to the screen and saw the hooded man being dragged out of the shot.

A trail of dark splotches appeared behind him and he was limp and silent, likely having passed out due to the pain.

Marcus was already seated again, watching the screen, and he didn't turn to face her until she was seated again next to him.

'She's here and listening,' he said once she was seated, and the man on the screen nodded and approached the guard who was slumped in his chair.

'Do you see, Jakub?' the man said, again squatting down to look up into the guard's face. 'Do you see what happens when you don't help us? And that was just one finger. If that gentleman doesn't change his mind, we'll do all of them on that hand, or maybe alternate with some of his toes. I saw a guy in . . .' the man paused. 'Well, it doesn't matter where I was, but I saw a guy once survive three fingers without saying a word, but the drill bit had barely scratched the surface of his big toenail when he broke.'

The guard was sobbing uncontrollably now, and the man risked a look to the camera.

'Go ahead now,' said Marcus, and the man nodded again.

'So, Jakub. I want you to start at the beginning and tell us everything, but I want to say just two more things. First, we know a lot of it anyway and if we catch you in a lie, it's one finger for the full five minutes, but the second thing is this. If you help us, we'll help you. We'll give you back a normal life, unharmed. We'll protect you until you're properly safe, no matter how long it takes. We'll protect your family too. So, start at the beginning and leave nothing out.'

Dani could hear the guard crying still, and then he spoke, but she couldn't make out the words.

'Audio on our guest,' said Marcus.

Another man that Dani hadn't known was there stepped out from the shadow beneath the camera and adjusted something near to the guard.

'. . . my finger.'

The words came in much more clearly.

'Ask him to go again,' said Marcus. 'Audio now clear.'

The order was passed, and the guard began to speak.

'He cut off my finger,' he said, the words slow and quiet,

broken by crying. 'I didn't want to do it, but he cut my finger off and he was going to do the same to my family.'

Dani made to speak, but Marcus seemed to pre-empt her, holding up a hand.

'Just let him speak for now, Dani,' he said. 'Let him get talking and then we'll get the questions out.'

'That's great,' said the man, nodding and holding a small plastic cup of water to the guard's lips.

'I said I wouldn't,' the guard continued. 'It's not the first time people have tried to get me to take stuff in or pass information, but I've never done that, not once.'

'Of course not,' said the man, offering up the drink again. 'We know you have over twenty years of outstanding service.'

The guard nodded.

'But this . . .' he paused, his breathing quickening. 'This man. He was different. He came into the garage when I was working out there one night, just appeared. I didn't see him coming, but next thing he had me in an arm lock over the car. He forced a rag into my mouth. He didn't say a word, didn't ask me anything, but he had a small knife, more like a bottle opener, with a really short curved blade, and he ran it around the base of my finger . . .'

The guard broke down, his sobs racking his whole body.

Dani looked at Marcus, horrified.

'Military,' he said. 'Hurt them first, then they know you're there for a reason.'

'He cut all the way around, right to the bone, and then used the knife to . . .'

He broke down again as he recounted the attack.

On the screen the man was still watching, and he reached forward again and offered the cup to the guard's lips.

'He skinned the flesh off my finger,' said the guard.

'Then he put it in a little plastic box which had an ice pack in it and he said he'd let me have it back, but only on loan and that if he had to come back again, he'd want the whole lot – bone and all.'

The interrogator was nodding, but he didn't speak, even as the silence drew out between them.

'Just prompt him,' said Dani, assuming that if the man could hear Marcus he could hear her too.

The interrogator waited for a minute or more before speaking again. 'Did he say anything?'

The guard jolted, as though he'd been lost in his own memories of the situation. 'Yes,' he said. 'He said that he wanted me to bring messages from Mr Hamilton.'

'Just let me go in and talk to him,' said Dani, throwing her hands in the air. 'Honestly, this isn't a military specialist that's still holding out. It's a civilian, in his fifties, who's probably filled his trousers three times over and is broken. He's not holding back! We don't need to lure him into telling anything. We just need to ask him the bloody questions we want to know the answers to.'

Marcus was watching the screen.

'Marcus!' Dani shouted. 'Let me go and talk to him. This hardly needs the military's best interrogator. The man's terrified.' She could see that Marcus's eyes were no longer on the screen. 'Why else did you bring me here?' she asked.

He drew in a deep breath and exhaled slowly. 'I'm bringing her in,' he said, and stood up, nodding to her. 'Let's go, then.'

She followed him through the door and along a line of containers, turning left and left again at the end. Dani counted as she went, reasoning when they stopped that they were about to enter the container that had been directly adjacent to the one they'd been in.

Marcus knocked twice, and the door was opened immediately.

Dani stepped inside and was surprised to see just how much of the container she couldn't see on the TV screen.

This one was separated into sections and as she came in she entered a small area with a table and a few chairs. At one side was a suite of equipment where a man sat working on a laptop.

In the centre of the partition wall another large television was mounted showing the same scene she'd been watching in the previous container. To the right of the television was another door.

'Let's go,' said Marcus. Dani tried to take a good look at the man on the laptop, though she couldn't get a good view of his face.

She followed him through the door and saw the guard seated around ten feet away from her.

He didn't look up as she entered.

Around the outside of the room, standing in the shadows, were another four men. They were leaning against the walls, all dressed in black, their faces hidden by some clever lighting that was focused only on the scene at the centre of the container.

The interrogator must have been one of them and Dani looked around, trying to make out his face.

'All yours,' said Marcus. 'I'll be out here.'

Dani nodded and walked towards the guard. She reached for the chair the hooded man had been on, but spotted wet smears of blood on one side and decided against. She looked around until one of the men around the edge pushed a chair towards her.

The guard looked up as she sat down in front of him, and his eyes widened.

'You're police,' he said, as though he couldn't comprehend what he was seeing.

Dani nodded. 'I'm also the reason you'll get out of here alive,' she said. 'Can we untie him, please?'

She looked around at the figures she could make out in the shadows.

'No,' came a quiet, anonymous reply.

Dani stared in the direction of the words. 'At least his right arm?' she asked.

There was a pause, then the interrogator stepped forward and cut the guard's bonds on the right side.

Dani passed him the plastic cup of water that was on the floor near his chair.

'I think you understand the severity of the situation,' she said, watching him drink. 'But I need you to help me now, because I know you want to do the right thing, OK?'

He was nodding.

'I need you to tell me in detail what he asked you to do and how he asks you to do it.'

'Can you keep my family safe?' the guard asked, his eyes pleading with her.

Dani nodded and felt awful for the lie; she had no idea if she could do any such thing, but she'd try.

'Tell me,' she said.

His eyes dropped to his knees. 'All I do is take messages out of the prison,' he said.

Dani watched him carefully. 'Out?'

He nodded.

'The messages are from Hamilton?' she asked.

'Yes. He tells me what to say and I have to come home. I have a pay-as-you-go mobile phone at my house. I take the dog for a walk and switch it on, then I access Twitter. I have an account on there that I was told to set up.'

'What is the account name?' Dani asked.

'TheLewisVendetta,' he said, still facing his knees.

Dani shook her head, not at all surprised that Hamilton had chosen such a name.

'I just put the messages on there.'

'Then what do you do?' asked Dani.

The guard looked up at her. 'Nothing. I log off and wait until Hamilton gives me the next message. When he does, I delete my last tweet and post the next. I don't do anything else.'

'You don't take messages back to him?' she asked. 'You don't take information into the prison?'

'No. Never. Well, only once to confirm I'd set up the account, but never.'

The interrogator stepped forward and touched Dani's shoulder. 'You're needed outside, miss.'

'I'll be right back,' she said, turning and heading back to the small area where she knew Marcus was waiting.

She stepped through and shut the door behind her. 'I'm not done,' she said.

Marcus called her over and indicated the large screen on the wall. It no longer showed the interrogation room, but instead displayed the Twitter feed from the guard's account.

'We should be able to get them all eventually,' Marcus said, 'but for now we have this. All of the tweets are posted as comments to BBC News stories. So, they get lost among the trash talk and debris of the Twittersphere. They all start with a small comment about the story and then have a quote. The last one is this.'

The tweet was below a story about reaction to crime across most counties in South East England. The Lewis Vendetta account had tweeted:

This is bullshit – 'It needs to be now. They're closing in on me. Plan A best, but fish for plan B.'

'What does that even mean?' said Dani.

'I hoped you'd have some idea.'

She shook her head and read the words again.

'Wait. Did you have someone try and assault Hamilton in prison? I saw him, and he had ligature marks on his neck and swelling on his face.'

Marcus didn't answer.

'What?' asked Dani. 'Does a tough, silent stare mean you did or you didn't? Because I don't speak gangster.'

'If we'd wanted Hamilton dead, he'd be dead.'

Dani paused, thinking.

'But you can't, can you?'

'We can't do anything like that until we find out who's helping him,' Marcus said. 'Look, now we know how he communicates out of the prison. Maybe another guard is taking the information in. This one might know which it is, or suspect at least.'

'I don't think so,' said the man working at the laptop.

He turned in his chair and Dani got her first look at him. He was, like so many of the special operations community, unremarkable-looking and very forgettable.

'I don't either,' she agreed. 'It's more likely that he's using Twitter to receive the messages. As part of his prison privileges he's allowed to access certain sites, though he's not allowed to post, but he can read. I bet that he goes to Twitter and knows what to look for and reads the replies that'll be lost among the usual outrage and bile on there.'

Marcus looked to his man for confirmation.

'I think I found some.'

The man used his mouse pointer to highlight a tweet.

'I wasn't sure how he'd do it,' the man said, 'so I figured there must be some kind of way for him to easily scan through and see the tweets for him. So, I searched the exact text that the guard sent.'

On the screen Dani could see a text from another account, identical to the one sent by the guard, and then below it was a thread that caught her breath.

The night is free and with us.

The tenacious absconder has lost his head.

Your friend and mine went shopping and her friends gathered to see her.

Plan A is ready. Plan B is very close, but Plan C is really all up to you.

'It would just look like nonsense to pretty much anyone who stumbled across it, though why would anyone bother?' Dani said. 'But in terms of meaning, it's pretty brazen.'

She read the thread again. 'The first one means that William Knight is free. The second one that he found Ryan from *Tenacity* and beheaded him. The third refers to the shop, to you and Jimmy being brought there to find me.'

'And your father,' said Marcus with a small nod.

'Yes. And my father. But the fourth is obviously referring to some plans they've previously discussed. Do you know anything about that?'

Marcus shook his head.

'Well, let's at least go back in and see if the guard has any further information. He must have seen this guy.'

Marcus snorted.

'What?'

'He never saw him. This guy's too good for that. I don't even have to ask to know he never got a good look.'

'Well, humour me,' said Dani. 'And keep looking for

the conversation. The more we have, the more armed we can be when these plans are eventually started.'

She walked back into the interrogation room and straight over to the guard.

'We know you're telling us the truth,' she said, hearing herself use the term 'us' and shivering at the thought of that association. 'But I need to know anything else you can tell us. This man who came to your garage – did you get a look at him?'

The guard shook his head. 'Not his face, no. He was there and then gone.'

'Did you get a sense of him? Was he a big man?'

The guard was shaking his head again, but he looked ready to speak. 'He felt bigger than me, well, taller. And I think he was thin, very thin, but so, so strong. He was wearing something over his face, maybe a stocking, I saw it for just a second when he was cutting my finger, but all I remember were his eyes. I don't even know if I could see them or if I just imagined it, but he was looking at me the whole time.'

'So, taller than you, very thin and strong,' said Dani. 'Could you place his voice? His accent? Was he from the north? Or south?'

The guard looked up at her. 'He wasn't British,' he said. 'He was American. I don't know where from, but he was definitely American.'

Dani frowned. 'You're certain?'

The guard nodded, suddenly looking very afraid again, tears forming in his eyes. 'I'm not lying,' he said, the shape of his mouth changing as he started to panic. 'I won't lie. I promise I won't.'

Dani reached out and touched his knee. 'I know you won't,' she said. 'And you've helped a huge amount. You're not going to be hurt, I promise you, but you are going to have to work with these men to try and get every bit of information out that you can remember. They'll try to help you pin down the accent and remember the exact words he used and how he said them, and we need to log on to your Twitter account too, but we'll also need you to try and remember everything Hamilton's ever said to you. These men will protect you and your family – they gave me their word – but most important is that when you're finished, and you go back to work, you cannot give even the slightest hint of what's happened. Not the tiniest hint. OK?'

The guard nodded emphatically, like a child acknowledging wrongdoing.

'If Hamilton thinks that something's wrong, or if his friend does, then we can't guarantee your safety.'

'I thought it was only us that made threats,' said Marcus as Dani left the room. 'You forgot to tell him never to mention that you were here, but we'll deal with that.'

Dani pushed him in the chest. 'He needs a psychologist to work with him, not a fucking interrogator,' she said. 'He's scared shitless for himself and his family and he'll likely blow it the first time he sees Hamilton because he's terrified.'

Marcus made to speak, but Dani cut him off.

'No. This was needless and stupid, and I've been a bloody idiot thinking I could work with you.'

'But you did it,' said Marcus.

He was unfazed that she'd pushed him, not even ruffled by what she was saying or how she was saying it, and, in his reply, she couldn't detect even a hint of anger or smug satisfaction. He looked at her as though he understood what she was saying and the reasons behind it and wanted to help her; she hated him for it.

'You did it because you don't really have a choice, Dani. We don't know who's doing this and until we do, we're all hostage to it and we're going to need to do what we can together. So, you can hate us and all we stand for, but we didn't choose to be here any more than you did.'

'Did you know it was an American?' she asked.

'Not until today,' Marcus said.

'And have they contacted you about a plan? Has anyone asked you to do something?'

He shook his head. 'No one has asked me to do anything,' he said. 'Come on. I'll drop you home.'

Dani's phone began to vibrate, and she fished it out of her pocket.

'You can take that,' Marcus said.

She looked down and saw the call was from Felicity, but she ended it without answering and placed the phone back in her pocket.

Within a second, it began to vibrate again.

Dani hesitated, reaching into her pocket and rejecting the call before turning back and following Marcus to the car.

Again, the phone began to vibrate.

'I think you probably do need to answer that,' Marcus said.

Dani sighed and picked the phone up, pressing the green button.

'Hey Felicity,' she said. 'I'm swamped at the moment; would it be all right if I called you back late—'

'Dani,' Felicity interrupted, sounding stressed. 'We need to talk now. I've just had a communication from the prison. One of the other inmates tried to kill Christopher Hamilton this evening. He's stable now, but in a bad way. He's awake and he's asking to speak to you urgently.'

'What happened?' Dani asked.

'We really don't know,' said Felicity. 'He was attacked, but we don't know how or why. Hamilton fought his attacker off. He actually bit a chunk out of the man's cheek, so his attacker's in a bad way too, but he took a beating and there was real intent to kill. He's in the hospital, under guard, but he's repeatedly asking for you.'

'I'm in Southampton,' said Dani. 'I'm about an hour away, but I'm leaving now.'

She ended the call and turned to Marcus.

'I really need to get to the prison hospital right now. Hamilton was attacked a little while ago. He's in a bad way and asking for me.'

'Part of one of the plans?' said Marcus. 'Getting moved to the main hospital?'

Dani shrugged. 'I doubt it. He'll be under heavy guard, but I need to get there now.'

Marcus paused and looked at her for a few moments.

'You look like death,' he said. 'When did you last sleep?'

'I'll sleep tomorrow,' she said. 'Can we go?'

Marcus nodded and started the engine.

Something hadn't been right with Hamilton when they'd spoken. Dani hadn't been sure what it was, but she'd detected something, and now he'd nearly been killed. Maybe they both had far less time than either had realised.

Chapter 21

Dani wasn't sure how she felt as she rushed to the hospital. The long day on top of her recent injuries had taken it out of her, and her body was crying out for a few hours in her own bed. But there was no way she wasn't going to see Hamilton straight away. She couldn't have denied there was a part of her that was glad Hamilton had taken a proper beating, because she, as well as many, many others, knew he sorely deserved one. But she was also worried about him.

She was aware that there was a side to her, possibly a very selfish side, that knew he was her link to whatever was going on, and that he was the only lead she had, or had been until now. In fact her reasons were not purely selfish: she wanted justice for his victims and wanted him punished for *all* of his crimes. Of course she desperately wanted it to be her that gave him what he deserved, but if it was someone else, then so be it; that he was weighed off and justice served was what was important.

She couldn't yet see what part she played in all this, and that pissed her off the most. She'd been a child when Hamilton and her father's paths had crossed. She hadn't known Jimmy before she'd met him a few weeks ago, and Marcus just seemed to be a bit-part player in the whole thing. So her part in this whole saga seemed out of view for now.

Felicity had called again to let her know that Hamilton had been moved out of the prison infirmary and taken to the main hospital. He wasn't in intensive care, as Felicity had first thought, but he was badly wounded. He was in a private room in one of the wings, heavily guarded, and they were looking to move him back to the secure infirmary at the prison as soon as possible.

The diagnosis, from what Dani could tell, was cracked ribs, broken nose and severe bruising in several other areas.

He was badly cut from some kind of prison shiv, but he was conscious, refusing medication and repeatedly asking for her.

Marcus dropped her off and left immediately.

She watched him go, thinking how, on some level, she actually felt herself liking him, even though he frequently showed her why she shouldn't.

The way he'd run the snatch of the guard had been stupid, impulsive and unnecessary.

They could have had the same information as they had now with far less theatrics and effort and she briefly wished that she'd gone on alone – but then realised that without his help, she likely wouldn't yet have known about the guard and Marcus was already closing in.

Either way, for the first time in a long while, she felt as though she knew more than Hamilton, that she was getting ahead of him, and that felt good. He had dictated the pace for far too long, but Dani felt hope that the tide was turning in her favour.

She hurried along the corridors, slowing when she saw the two armed police officers standing outside the room. She walked towards them, holding out her warrant card.

'Lieutenant Lewis, Royal Navy Police,' she said. 'He's been asking to see me. I'm cleared by the NCA to do so.'

The police officer inspected her identification, taking a moment to compare the photograph against her, then nodded. 'Yeah, we've been expecting you.'

Hamilton was a mess, his face swollen and almost unrecognisable beneath the bruising. It looked as though he'd been attacked by a tiger. He had scratches on his face, and she could see more underneath the gauze on his abdomen.

'You survived, then,' Dani said, and saw a pained smile cross his face.

She looked at his eyes, as she always did, and saw some kind of relief at her arrival.

'So, what happened?' she asked, pulling up a chair and sitting a few yards away from Hamilton's bed.

His hands were cuffed to the frame and she was pretty sure his ankles were too. But she was taking no chances; he was always unpredictable.

'Couldn't agree on who picked up the soap when it dropped in the shower?' she taunted.

He remained silent.

'I gather you gave as good as you got, though?' she said.

He smiled now, though it was undoubtedly painful to do so, and because of the damage to his nose, it looked more like a snarl.

'Of course I gave as good as I got,' he said, his words slow and slurred. 'You know me, Dani. If nothing else, I always settle my scores.'

'You asked to see me?' she said. 'So here I am. What can I do for you?'

'I just missed your lovely face and dulcet tones,' he said.

'And I really liked the idea of you driving here, running through the corridors in panic and concern to make sure I was OK. Were you worried sick about my physical and mental well-being? I hope you didn't break any traffic laws on the way to see me.'

Dani could tell he was trying to be witty, trying to speak quickly as he usually did, but the words came slower than usual, missing the comic timing, like a comedian labouring over his act until it no longer sounded funny at all, just stupid and petty.

'Honestly, I don't have anything to say to you at all, except, you know, thanks for coming – it's nice to know I have someone I can count on in my time of need.'

Dani watched him carefully. He was trying to be his usual arrogant self, as though the beating hadn't humbled him at all, but she could tell that something was wrong, something beyond the physical. There was something wrong with his eyes, the way he didn't look at her, the way they didn't move when he spoke.

She looked behind her and saw Roger standing in the far corner of the room. He must have just slipped into the room, because Dani hadn't seen him when she entered, and she did a double-take as she saw him now. As she glanced across at Roger, she caught a small movement of Hamilton's left hand.

His first three fingers were clenched in a fist, and his pinkie and thumb extended in the sign commonly used for a phone call.

He must have seen she'd noticed, because he immediately moved his hand and pointed his index finger directly at Dani. He wanted to speak to her. But he wasn't going to do it in front of Roger.

'Well,' said Dani, standing up. 'It's lovely to see you and all that, Chris. And it's a huge pleasure to see you so soon after you've had the shit kicked out of you. Please don't hesitate to call me any time this happens because, I have to say, seeing your face like that really does make my heart swell. Oh, and, just in case I'm not able to do it myself, please send my heartfelt thanks to the person that did it. Although saying that, I'll probably send them flowers myself or at the very least some cigarettes.' She paused and thought for a moment. 'Are cigarettes still prison currency since the laws on smoking changed?'

Hamilton's hand relaxed and he lay unmoving and silent.

Dani turned away and smiled at Roger. 'Didn't see you there. You staying or going?' she asked.

Roger seemed to pause for a minute, then raised his eyebrows and pushed himself off the wall he'd been leaning against.

'I'll come with you,' he said, following her out of the room.

'How come you were there?' she asked, as soon as they were out of Hamilton's earshot.

'You're not the only one with friends in prison, Dani,' he said. 'I got the call quite quickly. He's still a high-profile ex-navy serial killer, and we like to know what's going on with him. This could well make the news.'

'But why would you come in to see him?' she asked.

Roger shrugged. 'I guess we were friends at one point in our lives,' he said. 'To be honest, I just wanted to see how much punishment the bastard had actually taken.'

He laughed, and Dani tried to smile.

'I want to go back in on my own,' she said. 'I confided in you before, so trust me now.'

He was ready to say no, she could see it.

'If you don't . . .'

Dani didn't finish her sentence, but the implication was clear: Roger had to trust her if he wanted her to trust him.

He was shaking his head, his jaw set, but he wasn't saying no.

'I'm going in,' Dani said. 'Stay here or go home, it's up to you, but I got a lift here and could do with another home if you're willing.'

She turned and walked back towards Hamilton's room. 'I forgot something,' she said. 'It'll only take me two minutes.'

The policeman nodded and stepped aside to let her in.

As soon as she was in the room, she walked over to Hamilton and leaned close to him. 'There's absolutely no way I can get you a phone, Chris,' she said, hearing the anger in her voice. 'And even if I could, I wouldn't.'

He smiled at her. 'I don't want a bloody phone, Dani,' he said. 'I wanted to talk to you, that's all. Without him. Just you and I. That's where the trust lies.'

Dani shook her head. 'There's no trust, Chris, because you won't be straight with me. It's all just bullshit riddles and clues, mixed in with more crap and bluster.'

'Somebody tried to kill me, Dani, and they did it because of what I'm going to tell you. So now you get to understand why you're central to all of this.'

He paused, taking a few breaths as though talking was taking it out of him. 'I'm going to give you what you want. I've already started sending you the letters, telling you the truth, and I'll take you to the bodies. I'll show you everything I can.'

Dani was stunned. She looked at his face, and although she knew Hamilton was a hard man to read, a chameleon, a liar, somebody who spent a lifetime moving among people, pretending to be something he wasn't, she believed him again. For the second time, she actually believed what he was saying.

'I want to show you the bodies. I want to give you what you want. But . . .'

'But what?' asked Dani.

'But I have to show you them myself. You have to get me out of there. That's where you fit in, Dani. Because you're the only one who can do that.'

She stepped back, thinking about what she'd learned before she came here, and wondering how this tied in with Plan A and B and C. The opportunity was enormous, but so were the risks. If the police knew about his Twitter conversations, they'd never let him out, but if they didn't know about them then they might, and she might be doing exactly what Hamilton wanted.

'I'll speak to them and try,' she said.

'You can do it,' he said, his voice weak. 'But one more thing, Dani. Be careful who you trust. No matter how close to you you think they are.'

Chapter 22

Hamilton's Third Letter

Dearest Dani,
I call this Psalm – 'A New Me'.
I must say, Dani, I'm really quite enjoying the experience of writing all this down. It's cleansing.

Having to change schools a year or so after the Jenny MacAulay incident was a real opportunity for me and I grasped it with both hands.

Until then I'd always been the weird kid. I now knew if I wanted to really see myself achieve what I thought I could, then I couldn't let people know how little I thought of them. I had to learn a lesson from Jenny and learn to be friends, to laugh at things that weren't funny, to give people bad advice because it's what they wanted to hear, to flatter people and fan the embers of their ego.

I understood this now and, in short, I wanted to become popular.

It helped that I'm very physically attractive – people

180

just want to like beautiful people. That may seem unpalatable for some, but it's just a fact and one that's benefitted you over your career, Dani. Had you not been slim and easy on the eye, I doubt you'd have the friends and support you do, nor would you get away with some of the things you do.

I'd always had the potential to be good-looking, a poor diet at home left me tubby and my skin wasn't in very good condition. In addition to that, I wore cheap clothes, that were often dirty, and I hadn't discovered the importance of personal hygiene. I was now fifteen years old.

I took up running and showering.

This significantly improved my physique in a relatively short time and it's a habit I kept throughout most of my life, until the point, thanks to your good self, that I was unable to run freely at all.

So, here I am. A few months into a new school, slim, fresh, clean cut hair and captain of the school cross-country team. But I was also at one of the most vulnerable stages of my actual career, though I'll admit I didn't know it at the time.

I had studied very carefully since I killed those little guinea piggies. I went to the library and read everything I could find on murder, serial killers and serial offenders of all persuasions.

After I'd read the first one, which talked about an American serial killer, I began to take notes.

In it, they talked about how, once he'd been caught, they looked back and could see clusters of dead animals in an area around his childhood home – neighbours' dogs going missing, cats and chickens and the like.

So, I mapped out the areas around me, ensuring that I spread my kills out, keeping a ledger in my head of what I took from where and in what time-scales. I worked hard at cycling, too, ensuring I could travel farther afield more quickly when I needed to. I wouldn't be tracked like the moron in the book.

If it interests you, I can actually still remember every single kill, where, when, who, how and, well . . . to be honest, there wasn't always a 'why' that you'd understand.

After that first book I never checked another one out of the library, as after his capture they were also able to see that he'd researched criminals and, in particular, serial killers.

Instead, I read them in the library, tucking them inside a textbook, while I watched the librarian from the corner of my eye.

There'd be no record of a young boy obsessed with killers, not anywhere near me, anyway.

Dani, I'd found some self-control.

I should tell you about a few defining events during these years that I think are worthy of note.

The first of these, which makes me blush a little if I'm honest, Dani, was my first sexual experience. I know you may chuckle at this, and I want you to know that I've often wondered about you in this regard, Dani.

I've often wondered if you're still a virgin. Or whether you're gay. You keep these types of things close to your chest, Dani, and I want you to know you can talk to me if you ever need a sounding board.

I was fifteen at the time I lost my virginity, late according to some of the boys and liars I called friends, but in reality, I was probably among the first.

This was mainly due to the fact that I was 'going out' with a girl who was two years older than me.

This was very unusual, the majority of young girls favouring older boyfriends, but I was very good-looking, extremely intelligent, had no interest in girls who weren't fully developed, and had by now figured women out entirely. (What a disappointing revelation that was!)

She – her name was Paula Day – believed me to be romantic, funny, complimentary and her true soulmate. According to her monotonous wittering, we had almost everything in common, from our love of Duran Duran to our love of lying together and making out, a process that requires a vast amount of uncomfortable fluid exchange.

In truth, all we had in common were abusive fathers and the fact that we were vastly over-sexualised for our ages.

We would, nearly every day, go to her room, push a bath towel under her door so it couldn't be opened – thanks for that one, Mum – then we'd lie on the bed and we'd do what teenagers do, Dani.

Well, sort of.

I did have sex with her, for science you understand, but we both know I don't entirely conform to societal norms in thought or deed. One such way I differ is that I do not like my penis being touched for any reason. I tolerate cleaning it because I must, but I do not touch it otherwise and nor had anyone else from around the time I turned twelve.

I managed to conduct the sex act without hands and penis meeting (a dreadful, messy and unpleasant experience I'd never wish to repeat), but some weeks after, she finally was unable to control herself and breached this most important rule.

Her fingers snaked down and before I knew it she was grasping me.

I asked her to stop, genuinely I did, but as I felt her lips touch the tip, I felt the blood drain from me and I wilted.

I could have been sick, genuinely vomited, and my jaw felt oddly locked.

A little while ago I told you I'd found self-controls; well, Dani, I lost it again at that moment.

My attack on Paula was sustained and brutal, a true exploration.

You may think I never feel sorry for what I do, and that's not true, I do, but just not for the reason you might feel guilt for doing something.

I eventually ran out of steam and I was glad I did; I know with a certainty now that I was close to killing her. I don't know what it was that stopped me, though I like to think it was intellect and the recognition that I would've certainly been caught, and she was definitely not worth that.

I gathered myself as I realised my mistake and remembered all my hard work. I conjured some tears. I was sorry. I lay with her, holding her, eventually untying her and letting her hold me as she too cried.

I considered staying with Paula and practising with her, living out my fantasies; she was so damaged that I knew she'd let me. She'd wronged me with her actions, and I didn't, in my heart, feel I'd got suitably even for how she'd made me feel, but I knew I had to break off my relationship with her, because I'd kill her if I stayed.

I no longer viewed her as anything more than a toy, or a tool, a means to an end, and she was too close to home, too closely linked to me, and not sufficiently prominent in my fantasies to be worth the risk.

But I also knew at this point, that dogs and cats, squirrels and rats, horses and cows and flying bats wouldn't be enough any more. I needed to kill a human being, and while that may sound like an obvious sentiment, given all that has been said before, for me it was the most exciting thing that had ever happened, because I knew I'd do it.

At that moment, for me and for so many anonymous others, a clock started ticking.

Chapter 23

'This could be a huge breakthrough,' said Dani, looking around the room at the members of the National Crime Agency who had gathered.

This day was stretching interminably on and she was fighting off exhaustion, running on adrenaline alone. It was now late evening and she was at the headquarters in London, in a briefing room with several of the investigators from the Hamilton enquiry, including the lead, Craig Rayburn.

'It's got the potential to be a media circus,' said Craig. 'It might also just be a play by Hamilton to get some coverage and relevancy. We've kept what's been happening under wraps so far for the good of the families. This could push it all into the limelight. We all remember Hindley, don't we? Both times?'

There was a murmur of agreement around the room.

'It was on every television station and on the front of every newspaper in the country, and as far as I'm aware, it never led to anything except a rise in her profile. Is that really what we want?'

'I believe him,' said Dani, looking at each of them in

turn. 'I really do. And trust me, if anyone knows how Hamilton can lie, it's me. Something's changed recently. I won't pretend I know exactly what it is, but when I saw him, before the hospital, he was uncomfortable, his eyes flitting around the room, nervous. It was like he was frightened. I couldn't place it then, but I'm sure of it now. Then he's attacked with intent to kill. Something's happened in there and he wants to do a deal. He's only got one throw of the dice and he'll know that. If he doesn't do as he says, then he's never going to leave that prison again and he knows it.'

Dani was speaking with passion. She was excited to be part of such a significant potential development, but she was only too aware that many people would be reluctant to see Hamilton outside of the prison at all – herself included.

The information she had about the various plans had been gained illegally and she dearly wanted to share it, without putting herself and Hamilton's messenger-guard in prison.

There were more murmurs around the room before Craig spoke up again.

'But what does he really think he's going to get out of this?' he asked, not to Dani specifically, but to all the people in the room. 'There's no way that he's getting any years cut off his sentence – he knows he's never getting out. Showing us bodies would, if anything, lead to more convictions and a longer sentence.'

'Confession?' said an officer Dani didn't recognise. 'Forgiveness or absolution? He wouldn't be the first to do it for that. He's never getting out anyway, so what's he got to lose?'

Dani didn't comment, because she'd been wondering the very same thing. What did Hamilton get out of this?

Yes, he got a day trip out of prison and that might be Plan A, and yes, he might end up with some media coverage, but what did he gain from it that was meaningful and motivating?

Also, what did someone trying to kill him have to do with him finally cooperating and helping the police? Was it a transfer he was looking for? A move to a more comfortable, less dangerous prison? She really didn't know, and she was surprised that, if that was the case, he hadn't just asked for it in exchange for talking at all.

Felicity leaned forward and cleared her throat. 'You know, we've always thought that Hamilton would eventually want to cooperate,' she said. 'They all normally do at some point. Once they realise how powerless they are in prison, they want to try and take some of that back. We've seen him do this with Dani until now. She's debriefed regularly on how he tries to manipulate her in interviews. Pushing for the chess set to be brought in so he could play with her, for example. It could be that this is what he's doing again. But,' she looked at Dani, 'I also believe that Dani is the most qualified person to judge if he might be telling us the truth. And if she thinks that he really means it and we might be able to get closure for these families, then I believe we have to take this seriously. This could be our one shot of breaking open not just this current case but multiple cases over more than thirty years. Even if he took us to one body, the additional information we could glean could be worth . . .' She shook her head.

Craig was thinking. 'What do your bosses at the navy think about all this?' he asked Dani.

'I haven't told them,' she said, knowing she'd need to face Roger at some point and that it wouldn't go well. 'I don't think they'd support it.'

'They'll have to be informed,' Craig said. 'At some point,

so they can be ready to deal with any media fallout if nothing else.'

'When they do find out, I wouldn't be surprised if they pull my involvement from it completely,' she said, 'and I'm pretty sure that would put an end to it.'

She wondered if any of them knew that she was potentially days away from being sidelined for good, that Harrow-Brown was working to see her removed from the navy.

It wouldn't be quick when it came, Dani knew that. It would start with her being taken off active duty, there would be an investigation that could take months and then, if she hadn't already quit of her own accord, a court martial or a quiet discharge for services no longer required. Then she'd have no part in this or any other investigation – she'd never work as an investigator again.

'I'm happy enough for someone else to go in and talk to Hamilton,' she said, 'but he's been clear throughout that he'll only deal directly with me.'

Craig nodded, as though he'd already considered that and come to the same conclusion. 'I think so too, but I still don't like it. Feels like he has too much control.'

'I believe we can control a lot more of this than he might think,' said Dani. 'I don't want to speak out of turn, but this doesn't have to be a big blues and twos affair with media all around us. We could make this much smaller, and in doing so, very, very secure. We know he has a following, lunatics on the web who practically worship him, so we need to be ready to deal with credible threats, but secrecy could help with a lot of that.'

Craig was nodding again. 'Yeah, I agree,' he said. 'I'm thinking we head out in a small convoy, three unmarked cars, armed response front and back, armed officer in the middle car with Hamilton, you, and me.

'We'd have another armed response unit standing off a few miles in case there's trouble. We'd inform the local forces at the very last minute that we're bringing a high-profile prisoner through, not tell them who, but make sure they're on standby as we pass through.'

'I think that's the best way too,' Dani said. 'Low key. Take him out, see what he's going to show us, bring him back.'

'We'd have to be prepared for an overnight, I'm guessing,' Craig said. 'There's no way I'm going to a public hotel; we'd have to use a local nick.'

He looked slowly around the room, catching everyone's eye in turn. 'This'll go up to the secretary of state for approval,' he said. 'I know we've floated the idea before and the response was fairly neutral, but this will force a decision and, I suspect, very quickly. So, I'll say to you all, no one outside of this room and those who sign it off will know about this operation. So, if it leaks, you can rest assured, folks, that I'll be coming after each and every one of you. Understand?'

There were murmurs and nods of agreement.

'And the RN?' asked Dani. 'What will we share with them?'

Craig looked sceptical. 'They'll be informed from the top down,' he said. 'You're to say nothing to anyone reference the operations.'

'That's OK with me,' Dani agreed.

'Be aware, too, that I might drive for this to happen very quickly. The longer we wait, the more people will know and the more chance of the press turning up. Once it gets loose within government, there'll always be someone who wants to try and use it for political gain – you all know the drill. So just be ready. If I get a green light on this, we go.'

There was a buzz of excitement in the room now and Felicity looked at Dani and smiled.

'I'll put together a plan for briefing and start passing it up the chain. Until then, it looks like it's back over to you, Lieutenant Lewis,' Craig said. 'Let's get you back in there with him as soon as we can. Find out what he wants and see where he wants us to take him. I'll speak to the chief and find out how long it'd take us to get armed response units in place. I'm not saying it'll wash. I'm not convinced it will. But there's a chance, and we need to be sure that if we take Hamilton out of that prison, we're definitely going to put the bastard back again.'

Chapter 24

'What can I do for you, Marcus?' Dani said. 'I'm just on my way home and I can't see any headlights behind me at the moment, so I'm hoping you've taken me at my word and stopped your goons from following me?'

She heard him laugh, but it seemed genuine. 'We were trying to keep you safe and, to be honest, if you could see them they wouldn't be the best now, would they?'

'I'm serious, Marcus. If I even think that someone's behind me that shouldn't be, I'll call in every favour I've banked over my years in uniform to have every business you own, or are part of, investigated and raided; whatever I'm able to do.'

He laughed again. 'You're probably going to do that anyway, aren't you? Isn't it just queued up in your list of things to do on the crusade for all things right and proper?'

She paused at that, not least because he was right, and she would be trying to look into them more once this whole situation was over, assuming she had any authority to do so.

'Have you found anything more out regarding that information?' she asked.

'Did you find anything out when you spoke to our friend?' he countered.

They were both silent for a moment.

'Is it worth meeting? I know it's too late now, but maybe tomorrow first thing?' asked Marcus.

'Well, I have nothing to tell,' said Dani, knowing that she'd never tell them about Hamilton's possible trip outside the prison. 'But if you have something, I'd be willing to meet you somewhere public.'

He seemed to consider her response and Dani got the sense he didn't trust her, that he thought she was lying to him.

'No need to meet then,' he said, sounding disappointed. 'Only one thing from my end. There was more than one person messaging our friend. I'm not a hundred percent sure of that yet, but I'd say I'm somewhere in the high nineties. It's a different person and the messages were quite different, mainly about you and the navy . . .'

He let that hang out there and Dani couldn't help but be drawn.

'Can you send me what you have so I can look as soon as I'm able to and call you back? It'll save me digging through Twitter and I'm wiped out . . .'

'Most of it's not up any more,' he said. 'We're retrieving it through cache and various other means, but I'll send you what I can. Speak soon, Dani.'

Dani was turning into her shared driveway and as her lights swung past her own front door, she saw a figure waiting.

'Marcus. Wait,' she said. 'Do you have someone at my house?'

'No. It's your dad and Roger Blackett,' said Marcus quietly, and hung up.

She swung into her parking space, braking so hard that

her bag fell off the passenger seat next to her. Then she pushed open her door, narrowly missing her neighbour's car, and looked around, checking all the windows that overlooked her parking area and her house.

There was no movement, no obvious sign that she was being observed.

'You OK, Dani?' her dad asked, stepping towards her.

She saw that Roger had been waiting in his car and was now getting out. Stepping quickly towards her dad, she wrapped her hands around him and pulled him into a tight embrace.

'Tell your friend, Marcus, or Jimmy, whichever one it is,' she whispered, saying the words directly into his ear, 'to leave me alone. They had me followed and they knew you were here waiting for me. I'm sick of it and I won't take it any longer. You tell him that anything else happens and I'll bring the NCA down on them in every way I can.'

She pulled away from him and smiled as Roger approached. 'It's good to see you, Dad.'

He looked down at the ground, like an embarrassed child.

She turned to Roger. 'And you too,' she said. 'Both of you coming together, that can't be a good thing.'

Her dad nodded and tried to smile, but she could see he was shaken by her words.

They entered the house and Dani put the kettle on. Once she'd dispensed tea, they all went and sat in the lounge.

'So,' Dani said. 'It's late and I'm exhausted. Why are you both here?'

They looked at each other, like two kids about to admit to pulling some naughty prank, until Taz spoke.

'Dani, sweetheart, Roger spoke to me today about what's going on at work . . .'

'You've only a matter of days left, Dani,' Roger butted in. 'I know that Harrow-Brown has been in meetings with the Fleet legal advisors. They're finalising some bits, but I'm certain they're going to bring charges against you for your conduct in the past few months. You've cleared some big cases, but the way you've been doing it is unacceptable to him. Your name's still recognisable from the Hamilton investigation and the release of your paper. Harrow-Brown won't risk you bringing the kind of negative attention you got after that, down on him. At the very minimum it would be conduct unbecoming a naval officer and bringing the Royal Navy Police into disrepute. You'll be removed from active duty, dumped in some crappy office somewhere doing God only knows what, and they'll go through everything. Harrow-Brown won't need much to get what he wants.'

Dani felt the blood drain from her face.

It wasn't that she hadn't known this would be going on – she'd been part of enough investigations to know how it went – but hearing it from Roger and knowing it was so close to happening, when she felt so close to a breakthrough, was sickening.

She felt her eyes well up and saw her dad immediately push himself forward to come to her.

'Don't,' she said, raising her hand to stop him. 'Just don't.'

She took deep breaths and looked at her hands as they rested on her lap.

'So why did you both come?' she asked. 'By rights, Roger, you should be telling me this in the office.'

He looked away and when he turned back, he couldn't meet her eyes.

'I will be,' he said. 'It's not official yet and I asked your dad to come to try and make you listen to some reason.

If you step away from this thing with Hamilton, if you cooperate with the investigation into your actions and keep your head down for a while, then I think you've done enough good over your career to get past this. You'll take a hit on seniority and promotion, but you might, if you help and stay low, keep your place in the RN police.'

Suddenly, Dani realised who was talking to her. She recognised the political option she was being given.

'You mean Harrow-Brown doesn't want a fuss and if I'm prepared to cooperate, be a good girl and keep it all low-key, I might get away with irreparable career damage.' She stared at Roger. 'And he sent you as his messenger boy?'

'I'm nobody's messenger boy,' snapped Roger. 'But I do try to look out for my friends and I also know when someone's being thrown a bone.'

'Dani,' her dad said, his voice soft. 'Maybe it's time to listen. You've worked so hard to get where you are, none of us want to see you throw it away.'

'It's only throwing it all away if you do it for no good reason,' she said, standing up. 'Can you both leave now, please? I'm tired and I want to go to bed.'

She watched as they both made to speak, thought better of it and pushed themselves up and off the couch.

'I'll just use the loo,' her dad said.

Roger stood motionless as they both listened to her dad climb the stairs and shut the bathroom door.

'I don't think you realise how much you'll lose,' Roger said quietly.

'You'll find out very soon anyway, so I'll tell you now, because we said we'd trust each other, but Hamilton has agreed to take me and show me where he disposed of the bodies. It's going up the chain now. Once approved, it'll be quick, to avoid any problems with the media. I wanted you to hear it from me.'

Roger's face looked pale. 'In his state?' he asked.

'I don't know when. I just know it's being passed up the chain and they want it to be soon, before word spreads in political circles and it becomes a media frenzy.'

'I don't like that, Dani. It needs to be stopped. It's a huge mistake.'

'I knew you wouldn't like it,' she said. 'But I do appreciate you looking out for me, even if I don't agree with how you do it.'

'I can't really do it any more,' he said. 'I think tonight was the last chance I'll have.'

'I know,' said Dani.

'Just think about what I said. Please. It's not too late. And don't try to contact work. Just be here and recuperate fully.'

Her dad came back and joined them. The two men obviously wanted to stay but knew they weren't welcome.

Dani took the lead, walking towards her front door.

'Charlie asked if you'd call her,' said her dad. 'She's been trying to get hold of you. I think with Liam being away and the baby and everything, she just wants to chat a bit more.'

'I'll call her,' said Dani. 'Pass my other message on too. OK?'

She looked hard at her dad, making sure he knew what she was talking about.

'I will. I'll make sure it stops.'

Roger was looking quizzical but said nothing.

Dani shut the door and pressed her back against it, relieved that they were gone, but suddenly weak at the feeling of how close she was to being removed from active duty. She drew in a deep breath, then reached for her phone and called John.

'Sorry to be calling you so late, but I need you to do

something for me,' she said. 'I did a staff course with an American major. She was a cop, high flyer, really sharp. Can you find out where she's serving now? We lost touch a year or so ago, but I think I may need to speak to her. It's Heather Dickinson.'

'An American?' said John. 'The plot thickens. Can I know why?'

'I'll tell you everything when I see you next,' Dani promised, 'but this is important.'

Chapter 25

She was clutching her torn clothes to her chest, aware of the freezing air touching her as she ran at full pace towards safety. She didn't know if she heard a voice order the men after her, or if her mind had added that to give impetus to her escape, but she heard the sound of shoes on stone as she was pursued.

A hand gripped her shoulder, pulled her back, turning her away from the safety of the trees.

Dani allowed it, allowed herself to be turned, but only for a moment . . .

The repeated knocking on the door brought Dani out of a deep sleep. Her eyes opened wide and she looked at the pale blue dawn light that crept into her room through the open curtains.

Then she heard it again.

She sat up, instinctively checked her phone and saw the missed calls. She didn't recognise the number.

She swung her feet out of bed and pulled on some old, baggy training shorts under the long T-shirt she'd stolen from her father many years before, then wrapped her dressing gown around her for good measure. She also picked up the heavy metal torch that she kept on the floor near to her at night.

It served as a back-up if her bedroom light ever failed, but more than that, it acted as a reassuringly robust baton that was always nearby in case it was needed.

She heard gentle knocking on the door again, as though whoever it was wanted to be heard only by her. She went downstairs and looked through the peephole.

There were two figures outside the front door.

She could make out the silhouettes in the dull blue dawn.

'Good morning,' she said, opening the door as quickly as she could.

'Good morning. Danielle Lewis?' said the police officer, using her name as a question.

Dani didn't recognise her, but she did recognise the uniform of the Hampshire and Isle of Wight police.

'We've been asked to come and get you. We've been told you'll understand what it is and that you'll be expecting to come with us.'

Dani blinked, stunned.

Craig had said he wanted to move quickly to avoid the possibility of leaks and to do so while Hamilton was physically weakened, but she hadn't been expecting anything like this quick.

She'd imagined they'd take some weeks to plan, and yet the trip to take Hamilton out of prison was happening now.

'Let me grab my things,' she said, gesturing for the officers to step inside.

'It's OK,' the woman said. 'We'll wait in the car.'

Dani looked around her, checking to see if anyone was watching, but the street nearby was quiet.

'All OK?' asked the policewoman.

Dani nodded. 'Fine, thanks. I'll be quick.'

She'd heard nothing yet from Marcus and the weekend had dragged as he failed to return her calls and the investigative world seemed to grind to a halt.

John had been round on both Saturday and Sunday and she'd told him most of what she knew, leaving out the prison guard and the information they'd gleaned from him, but he'd not yet found out where Heather was working and Dani knew the woman kept little or no social media presence, so it would need to be through the computers at work, which Dani couldn't easily access.

She'd collected Hamilton's letters and arranged them in front of her. There were three now and she'd read them again and again, trying to see through the bluster and faux-intellect to whatever might be behind them.

Now she headed into the lounge and grabbed the letters, all back in their envelopes, and thrust them into the laptop compartment of her backpack.

Her hand caught against something sharp and hard, the corner of a box, and she pulled it out.

It was a pen box, with a ribbon on it, and she opened the box to see a beautiful fountain pen and a note.

Remember, I'm on your team for life. Dad xx

Dani felt herself start to well up but shook it away – now wasn't the time.

He must have slipped it into her bag when he'd visited with Roger, knowing she'd find it soon.

She looked at the note again and then placed it on the side and tried to focus. She'd been told there'd be no notice and they hadn't been kidding. She'd also been told not to bring her phone and to tell no one where she was going, not that she'd had any time to do that anyway.

She dressed quickly and stopped at the bottom of the stairs.

Her phone clattered to the floor as she fumbled it and missed the shelf.

She left it where it was; broken screen or not, she'd find out another time.

A shiver ran down from the back of her neck as she left the house, but it wasn't only the cold; Dani was excited.

They drove in near silence, Dani gently dozing, until the policewoman pulled into the prison car park. Dani walked over to where Craig Rayburn was sipping tea from a plastic cup.

'Thanks for not forgetting me,' she said, as he turned and smiled at her, gesturing towards a flask on the bonnet of the car.

'Forget you? Hardly,' he laughed. 'Hamilton wouldn't go without you. In the end, aside from the man himself, you're the one person we absolutely had to take.'

She stepped forward and poured herself some tea and wrapped her hands around the cup. 'So what's the plan then?' she asked. 'This was way quicker than I expected.'

'We're going to roll out soon,' Craig said. 'We've moved fast, so there's not enough time for news to spread, but we've kept it simple, exactly like we said. We've got an eye in the sky on standby too, just in case.' He took a sip of his tea then yawned. 'To be honest, I'm not expecting any problems. Not that we won't be ready if we encounter some. Hardly anybody even knows we're going, and of those, even less knew we'd go this quickly.'

'Is Hamilton in any shape to travel?' Dani asked, remembering how he'd been in the hospital.

The police officer nodded. 'He got the all-clear,' he said. 'He was happy to get on with it too. To be honest, I quite like the idea of taking him out while he's still a bit beat up. It'll make him easier to handle, reduce the likelihood of any problems.'

'It's the bloody press I'm worried about,' said Dani, turning to look at the entrance to the prison car park, as though she might see the news agencies driving towards them, ready to film and broadcast their departure.

'Me too,' he said. 'That's why it's been so quick, flash to bang, no time for leaks. You OK?'

'I'm good, thanks,' she said. 'I just hope it's all worth it. The people he killed, and their families, deserve some peace.'

He reached out to pat her on the shoulder. 'Let's hope so,' he said, before turning away to speak to some of the other officers.

Dani watched him go. She respected the way he'd dealt with this operation, because she was all too aware of how she was struggling to focus. She had the story from her dad circling her mind, the details of which were trying hard to escape from her head. She had three letters from a serial killer festering in her bag, and she'd reached a point where she wasn't sure she could easily remember what lies she'd told to who. She just wanted this to be over. Maybe what Harrow-Brown wanted would be a good thing; maybe she'd look at a fresh start and something different when this was done. She'd always wanted to continue her academic studies and she had some money put by.

She heard the tone change around her and noticed a difference in the way the police officers were standing. Those that were armed had their hands resting on their weapons, and the others were moving around more purposefully or watching in a visible state of readiness.

All of a sudden, Dani saw movement through the thick glass doors of the prison entrance.

'Heads up,' shouted Craig, as Hamilton appeared like a watery reflection in the glass.

He was dressed in plain clothes, jeans and trainers with a plain blue top, not prison garb as she'd seen him wear before. His hands were shackled in front of him, and a chain ran down from his wrists to where his feet were also shackled.

He shuffled along, the chains punctuating each step, and there was a prison officer on either side walking him out. He grinned at her, his face bruised but far less swollen, as the guards formally handed him over to the police.

One of the officers signed some papers, and then he and a colleague escorted him to the car.

His eyes widened, and his grin spread further across his face as he moved closer.

'Dani, it's wonderful to see you,' he shouted, his voice shattering the cold, quiet concentration of the morning. 'I know the hour's ungodly, but aren't we all ungodly too? I think we can make this trip worthwhile.'

Dani realised it was the first time since he'd been incarcerated that she'd spoken to Hamilton where other people were present and able to hear. She felt embarrassed at the light, friendly tone and way he looked at her. She couldn't help but look around at the other faces to see their reaction to the way he'd addressed her.

'Do you like my new clothes?' he continued, using what movement he had in his hands to stroke his top and trousers. 'I'm not going to lie, Dani, I didn't choose them myself. Frankly, whoever shops for the prisoners in here has poor taste at very best, but you know what, it beats some of the stuff I've had to wear before now and, even with my current bumps and bruises, I really think I've got the physique to make this outfit work.'

Dani stepped aside as the two police officers marched Hamilton towards the middle car.

'You're in the back with him,' Craig murmured. 'He's going to pass directions to you, and you'll relay them to us. That's how he's said it's going to happen, although, to be honest, we'll only be in the front of the car, so we'll be able to hear, but he was very specific.'

Hamilton was settled in the car, and Craig moved closer to her and whispered into her ear.

'Don't worry about being so close to him. We know what he's capable of, and he'll be shackled to a strong point in the rear. There's no way in hell he'll be able to get anywhere near you, as long as you don't lean over into his personal space.'

Dani nodded, and walked around the rear of the car to climb in the back next to Hamilton.

He was still grinning at her as she sat down. It was as though they were two old friends about to go on a holiday trip. He looked in much better shape than he had in the hospital, though it may have been that he'd simply been cleaned up. The dried blood was gone and the swelling had already started to subside. His voice box had apparently taken no damage and he was back to his usual faux-jovial, arrogant and obnoxious self.

'So,' said Dani, as she realised they were alone for the first time. She wondered whether they were being recorded. 'Where to first?' she asked, looking across at him.

He just smiled, saying nothing.

Craig climbed into the passenger seat and an armed officer slumped into the driver's seat next to him.

'You going to be difficult, Chris?' said Dani, trying to sound nonchalant.

He smiled at her again, although she saw something change in his eyes, and then he seemed to sigh.

'No, I'm not going to be difficult, Dani-bear. Why would I do that? Why would I get you out of bed at this unearthly hour just to be difficult? No, that wouldn't do. I'm going to tell you exactly where we need to go. So, first of all, I'd like you to head towards the New Forest, please, as we agreed. The New Forest National Park. Do you know where I mean?'

Craig turned around. 'I know it's the New Forest, Mr Hamilton, but the New Forest is a big place,' he said. 'I'm afraid you're going to have to be a little more specific.'

'Yes, yes, of course, Mr . . .' Hamilton let the gap hang, but Craig didn't fill it.

Hamilton rolled his eyes at Dani, as though Craig were just plain rude, and then spoke again. 'Head towards the village of Burley, please. I'll be able to tell you more accurately where to go when we get close.'

The officer produced a map and held it up so Hamilton could see. 'Why don't you give us more detailed instructions on this map?' he said. 'And then we can pick out the best route for fuel economy and the environment.'

Hamilton smiled at that. 'I do what I can to make the world a better place, but I'm afraid I don't know the way on a map. I only know by sight. I only know by the landmarks around me.'

Craig shrugged and had a word with the driver, then spoke to the other cars on the radio.

Within a few moments, they'd pulled away from the prison and were on their way.

Dani heard Hamilton start to hum as soon as the car began to move. She wasn't sure, but he seemed to be humming a tune she recognised, a kid's song.

He started to mumble words under his breath to the same tune.

She leaned closer to him, but without getting too close,

trying to home in and see if she could make out the words, and then she did.

He was bobbing his head from side to side in time with the tune.

'The killer in the car plays find the corpse, find the corpse, find the corpse. The killer in the car plays find the corpse, aaaaaallllll daaaaay long . . .'

He saw her looking and stopped. 'Inappropriate?' he asked, looking troubled.

Dani stared at him, saying nothing.

He mouthed something to her silently, so no one could hear, and Dani watched him form the words until she realised what he was saying. He was asking her if she'd read his letters.

Chapter 26

Hamilton's Fourth Letter

My dearest, dearest Dani,

This 'memoiring' business is addictive, though not as addictive as some other things I've done in my time. But I'm enjoying it a huge amount and want to thank you for inspiring me to finally put pen to paper.

So, where were we? Ah, yes. Now, given that in my last correspondence I told you all about Paula, I think you'll be pleased to know that I left her alone after we split up. But for me, and for my understanding of who I am and what I had to do, that one night changed things dramatically.

Killing was no longer something I'd considered, researched and dreamt about. It was now a cold, hard need that burned inside me like dynamite on a short fuse.

I had to kill a human being, but I knew I also had to not get caught.

Now you may be reading this believing you know why I kill but I'd robustly contest that.

Like most people, my needs and motivations changed as I matured and grew.

I knew what I needed to do, and I started to plan. I hoped to select a suitable victim in a reasonable amount of time. I think a kill is a lot more like sex and dating than people realise, and even then, I knew that similar rules would apply.

So, while I didn't wish to kill someone I was close to, or that was, indeed, in my social circle, I also didn't want them to be a complete stranger or an opportunist kill either.

You see, while I was planning my first kill, I'd been out watching a potential partner and was on my way back home when I saw an old man wandering around in a robe and pyjamas.

He was lost, distressed and confused. He was also standing on a small bridge that crossed a railway track.

I knew the local old folk's home he must have come from and it was a fair way away.

He must have sneaked out of the garden and on to the road and I watched him for a moment and then made up my mind. I cycled towards the home, checked there was no activity, no one coming to look for him yet, and then cycled back to the bridge.

He was still there, looking over the edge and along the tracks, and I got off my bike and went to him.

He smiled when he saw me. Chuckled a little bit and reached out to ruffle my hair.

I let him, then grabbed his arm, snapping it like a dry twig as I forced it up behind his back and lifted him over the edge of the bridge. I watched him fall and splat on the tracks beneath me.

He was still moving.

I decided to wait and see the next train hit him. But I heard voices before it arrived, and this was in the days of a nationalised rail service; I shudder to think how long I'd have to wait today.

Anyway, I had to get on my bike again as I didn't want to be seen anywhere near the incident.

That was my first appearance in the papers, albeit my part was anonymous, but the whole thing just felt hollow. It was a complete waste. I didn't know the guy and he'd done nothing to me. There was no revenge, power or motivation.

I had to tell you that. Full disclosure was what I promised, otherwise we'd never be able to trust each other and you'd know I was holding out anyway.

I moved on from that wasted night quickly but never really forgave the old man, instead focusing on what I needed to do to erase him from my memory.

There was so much to do.

I'd picked her, and she was glorious.

A young brunette of nineteen, she was beautiful. She had none of that irritating confidence of a woman who really knows she's attractive and flaunts it. She was energetic and opinionated. I heard her discussing politics in an ice cream bar once and she seemed to really be able to comprehend the ideas she was talking about. I'm not sure if I was in love with her, but she ruined it when she caught me eavesdropping.

One of her friends saw me and whispered to her. Then she threw me a disgusted look, as though I was a parasite feeding off her energy, someone who'd no right to be anywhere near her.

It was probably the only horrible thing I ever saw

her do to anyone, but it was directed at me. In hindsight, it may just have been a bad day, maybe I just caught her at a bad moment, but despite hours and hours of watching her, I was the only person I ever saw her dismiss in this way.

I'm fifteen now and I have to abduct a nineteen-year-old girl, take her somewhere I can do what I need to do, then dispose of her body, all without being seen and without leaving a trace.

Again, I won't lie. I thrice went to do it only to be thwarted or to simply back out due to the risk.

She sometimes borrowed her mum's car, and this was crucial to my plans.

Transporting her on my bike was simply not an option. So, I watched and waited and became frustrated and angry with her when she went for long periods without needing to drive.

However, our night together arrived eventually.

She pulled out of her driveway and turned right, towards the railway bridge where 'you know who' had died.

This was the plan.

She was alone, and I leapt on my bike, cutting across smaller streets and pathways, which meant that I took a route that was over a mile shorter than hers.

I got to the bridge before her, as I'd planned, and once there, I dropped my bike, sat on the ground and waited, my face contorted and upset as I clutched my knee – trying to look younger than I was.

She was there in seconds and damn near killed me, not seeing me at first and not applying the brakes until her bumper was eighteen inches from my head.

She stepped out of the car and came straight over, no hesitation at all, no fear and no recognition from the time in the ice cream parlour. She was more concerned with how frightened I was after almost being hit. She was wearing a white, tight top beneath a baggy shirt and tight jeans that were just a little too short.

I asked for a lift and she agreed. I hid my bike, promising no one would find it and I'd come back later to collect it when I'd calmed down and my knee was better. Then I jumped in the passenger side.

'Where to?' she piped up, cheerful and carefree.

I reached into my sleeve and pulled out the long kitchen knife I'd stolen from the school during my preparation stage. I held it across towards her, pushing the tip into the side of her left breast, just until she squealed, and a tiny speck of blood appeared.

I'd booked us a room; an old abandoned garage along a long dirt track in the woods.

There was a forestry gate that prevented access and I'd previously borrowed a set of bolt croppers to remove the padlock and replace it with one of my own.

This was a dodgy part of the whole exercise, as I had to open the gate but didn't want to leave her in the car, in case she just drove away, but nor did I want her out of the car and leaving footprints.

I made her stop, took the car keys and watched her like a hawk as I opened the gate. I was ready to chase her down if she ran, but she didn't. She didn't even look like she might run. Instead she actually smiled at me, like we were friends who could talk this little problem through.

I locked the gate behind us and we drove on up to the old garage building and parked on the concrete hard standing outside it.

Her name, as I'm sure you're dying to know, was Catherine Rosbottom.

I'm sure her parents, John and Hilda, would want to know, if they're still alive.

In fact, I'll write a little message for them . . .

Dear John and Hilda,

If Dani's ever able to share this with you, then I want you to know you did a great job with Catherine. She was mild and obedient right to the point of death. Hell, in hindsight, she was even easy to cut up and dispose of; a real credit to you both.

Yours aye,
Chris

So, to continue.

I don't like the word torture. I think it cheapens what I do and so I'll say no more on the details, but, Dani, in that first night, I became a proper killer.

I knew that no one would be seriously looking for Catherine until morning, she was a young girl on her way out with friends, but also, she was an adult, and if and when her parents called the police, the response wouldn't be the same as with a minor. I still had her body, a dirty garage full of flesh and blood spatter, her car and clothes, and, of course, my clothes; I was also well covered in blood – so there was work to be done.

I set about cutting her into manageable pieces. The legs and arms are easy enough, the torso gave me the problems. Then I forced stones and fishing weights inside the flesh and wrapped them in newspaper and tied it with string – this was no lapse as you may think, Dani; I wanted the fish and wildlife to get to her.

I changed out of my clothes and washed myself in a bucket of water. Then, I took our clothes, the large blanket I had laid her down on, and the rope I'd used to secure and gag her and placed them in a large barrel outside on the hard standing.

It had been previously used for burning waste and so I doused it in fuel and left it to soak. It was very dark now and the trees all around would hide the flames, while the black night sky would conceal the smoke.

I helped Catherine into the boot and then jumped into the car and had a few goes at driving. I'd done it before in my mum's car, but I just had to check as I didn't want to bring any attention to myself by stalling and juddering along the road. This was probably the most dangerous part of the undertaking, and successfully getting rid of bodies became a crucial and risky part of my career – as you well know.

I have to say, and by no means is this bravado, but I was too excited and elated to be truly frightened. My hands were calm and still as I passed through and re-locked the gate, and while I may have experienced minimal hesitation as I turned on to the road, my confidence was never higher.

This is a crucial thing, confidence.

A winning sports team knows how to win because it becomes a habit. The trust and knowledge that they can achieve victory are as key as their preparation in realising success.

At fifteen years old, I was already massively ahead of my peers, killing in a way that many others could spend years aspiring to and yet never attain.

I put Catherine's body in a large and well-stocked fishing loch near Wishaw.

It was the off-season for fishing, the loch was teeming, and if some paper floated up covered in blood, people would just assume that some illegal night fishing had gone on and the fishermen had cut up their catch and littered as they left.

The car was much more challenging. Wherever I dropped it, I had to walk back from, and that could take a long time.

My running was good, but I was spent, and I knew it.

My limbs felt sore and stiff and I needed food and something to drink. I couldn't have run far or quickly, and teenagers are seldom seen out running at night for any good reason. I drove it into an estate a few miles from my house, kicking myself in hindsight for not putting the bike in the back.

This estate was rough and poor. Many kids, as I had been, were abused and ignored and they roamed around at all hours.

I was later than I'd planned to be. I'd considered that if I left it there before around 2 a.m., then joy riders would likely take it, use it and burn it out by morning, but I'd indulged myself, and it was almost 5 a.m. now. Even the most hard-core tearaways might possibly be in bed.

I found a house with the lights on and music blaring. People were smoking outside, and two young women were fighting, their hands locked into each other's hair like bulls with locked horns as they tried to swing each other around. Their skirts rose up and revealed what should have been private flesh, and their balance, in ridiculously high heels, was the only thing they could really have been proud of.

They disgusted me, but where I could rely on the

fish to play their part in the food chain, I also figured I could count on these animals to play their part in covering my tracks.

I parked the car, left the engine running, turned the lights on to full beam, sounded the horn and was gone.

My muscles ached as I ran, cutting through pathways and down roads. I heard shouts, but no one seemed to follow me, and I didn't wait to see if they took the car; there weren't many people in that estate who'd call the police and I relied on the drink, drugs and bravado to do the rest.

It was almost light when I arrived home and I was truly done. I washed because I knew I needed to, then I bleached the bath and shower after me. I fell into bed around sunrise on Saturday morning, exhausted.

You will, of course, realise that there were numerous lessons to be learned from what I did.

These would be learned in the weeks and months afterwards as I analysed my performance.

Catherine Rosbottom's disappearance made the national papers within a few days. Her car was found burned out in a field a few miles from where I'd dropped it. Her body was never found and no one was ever charged in relation to this crime. For all intents and purposes, I had committed the perfect murder on my first time out – though, regarding perfection, the old man at the railway bridge was never mentioned beyond an obituary in the local rag and I could claim perfection there too if I was minded to do so.

The weeks and months after were a roller-coaster for me.

One evening, in a near panic, I woke from a nightmare, something that would plague my adult life, and cycled down to the old garage in the woods, using my trophy top as kindling and burning the garage to the ground as I began to consider the possibility of my capture.

It was exhilarating to see my creativity on television and in newspapers – to hear people talk about it, about me. I could see now why it would be so tempting for killers to involve themselves in investigations, to gawk at scenes and offer help to the police. The tension I felt was intoxicating. The need to know more information than was publicly available, while maintaining the disinterested demeanour of a late-teen boy, was all-consuming. I read at the library, watched the news every day and would sit near any adults I could find who were discussing it in the hope of hearing opinions, thoughts, or new snippets of information. I deeply regretted burning the trophy; I missed her scent, and now I desperately wanted something to spark my memories. I didn't have to even have it in my house, I just needed to know it was there, but it wasn't. I had destroyed it.

After Catherine, I would sometimes take something to help me remember, but then later I'd destroy or dispose of it, usually after waking up late at night, as I recognised the stupidity of keeping evidence near to me.

I had other problems, though.

I couldn't take another girl from near to me as the focus of the press and police would be too active in this area. I needed transport and was over a year away from gaining my licence and owning a car or van; this became the utmost priority for me.

I couldn't risk a similar abduction as I was worried what the police would discern from my actions – now I realise just how clueless they actually are. None were my equal then or now. Even your good self, or 'she who got lucky' as I like to call you, did so with a healthy dollop of 'Lewis luck'; fate, something you just can't control – it's the known unknown in the killing equation.

But, Dani, listen carefully as this is important, there were more changes and more learning to be had.

First, I knew without a shadow of doubt that I'd do this again. The pressure was already building inside me like a pan on a slow burning hob. I could feel it, even as Catherine began to fade from the press, the sight of her only grew in my mind. I knew I had to do it again.

I also knew now that my anonymity was limited by my age and lack of mobility.

To take another girl from within fifty miles of my home would be folly. Further afield was logistically impossible and far too risky. I needed to become mobile and I needed an occupation that would allow me that mobility, something that would take me to different places where I would neither be seen nor noticed.

And there was one final lesson I learned from sweet, sweet Catherine. This lesson is the one that you, Dani, must recognise from this letter. It is this.

Your safety is a veil. Your locks and burglar alarms are an illusion. What truthfully protects the vast majority of our public, you and your family included, Dani, is not your security systems and locked windows. It's not the bovine police force patrolling your streets.

No, Dani, it really isn't.

What keeps you all safe is simply that your lives are so inconsequential that no one is interested in harming you. It is your worthlessness in the eyes of the predators that protects you.

I saw this now; saw how easily I could access the sheep's pen. How I could walk among you, as one of you, laugh with you and know you.

Catherine Rosbottom had wronged me and it cost her her life, but she didn't die in vain. She will, one day, form a crucial piece of our country's history.

I was now in the most dangerous stage of my career development, but not for me, Dani. Dangerous for you, those you love and care about, and for everyone else who enters my orbit.

If I could continue to be this disciplined, to plan with this level of patience and intensity, I knew now that I could go on doing this, undetected and unchallenged, forever.

Chapter 27

They had stopped for the third time.

As with the first two, Hamilton was sitting silently in the car, staring out of the window at part of the beautiful New Forest.

The first time it had been a small stone landmark and he'd remained motionless and quiet for almost an hour, refusing to let them leave as he squinted and made a show of trying to remember.

After a long wait, he'd shaken his head and ordered them to drive on.

The second time it had been a team of horses in a clearing for almost as long.

He hadn't asked to get out of the car and the only time he'd spoken was when he'd asked the driver to move the car around, so he'd have a slightly different perspective on the landscape.

After the long wait, he'd shaken his head again and given them more directions.

Now they were, once again, parked and waiting. This time in a long lay-by, deep in the New Forest, and Hamilton was looking out of the window, occasionally sighing and scratching his chin, or moving his head a few inches to the left or right, tilting it, as though that might give him the different point of view he needed.

Dani was sitting quietly in the back, trying not to show her frustration. She wasn't renowned for her patience and she was already ninety percent certain that Hamilton had done nothing more than bring them out so he'd see some sights and play some games.

'Is it time for lunch yet?' Hamilton said, turning first to Dani, and then to Craig in the front of the car. 'Only I'm rather hungry, and I had hoped, seeing how we're all out together having a day trip, and with me being helpful and all that good stuff, well, I thought we might be able to have something better than the usual prison slop?'

Craig turned in his seat and fixed Hamilton with a stern gaze.

'Well, you're not particularly helpful, are you, Mr Hamilton?' he said. 'Between you sitting looking at sights and shaking your head, and us driving around so you can do it, we've been on the go for about five hours now, and all we've done is sit in the car in silence.'

'Get angry when I talk, get angry when I don't,' he said, and turned to Dani. 'Honestly,' he said to her. 'There's just no pleasing some people.'

Dani sighed and turned away from him, watching through the side window as the New Forest ponies walked past the car.

'I understand your frustration,' said Hamilton, 'but do you know how many children in this country go to school each day without having had breakfast or a proper evening meal? I'm a regular reader of the BBC news, among other outlets that I'm allowed to access, and I can assure you that you need to read up and understand the impact it has on their brain function, development and ability to learn and retain information. If you want the best from me, and you want me to be able to think back all the years I need to, then I'm going to need to have some fuel in my body, some calories to power my brain, sustenance to give me the stamina to do what we all need me to do. The source of these miracle calories is going to be lunch. Now I don't want to say fast food, because I don't want to be the one to put that idea in anyone's head. I know Dani specifically likes to eat very healthily, but, and I do mean *but*, if we were to go to a fast food joint . . . I don't know, somewhere that might do "fries with that".'

Hamilton winked as he said this and made the sign of a large M with his fingers in the air.

'I can't help but think that it would really, really help me to remember, if you know what I'm saying.'

Craig sighed and faced the front.

'Mr Hamilton,' he said, now speaking to the windscreen, 'there's not one single chance in hell that I'm going to take you to a fast food joint. And, before you suggest it, there's no way I'm going to send one of my guys off to get you a cheese burger, just because you haven't had one in a few years, OK? If you're hungry, we have stuff with us, and I'll feed you, just let me know.'

'What did you bring?' asked Hamilton, his voice petulant.

Craig turned around in his seat again. 'Packed lunches from the prison. Mystery-meat sandwiches, crisps that have never seen flavour, and the cheapest fizzy pop that money can buy. I think there's a piece of fruit in there too, but I'm pretty sure the other officers took all the good stuff. There was a bruised banana and an orange that looked like someone had trampled on it, so I'm going to hazard a guess that one of those will be yours.'

Hamilton scrunched up his face and shook his head.

'Well, that's not going to jog my memory, is it? You guys have got a lot to learn about bribery and getting the best from your people. Perhaps it's precisely this type of attitude that depleted the number of suitable candidates wishing to join the police force in the past few years? That would explain the poor calibre of the officers that have been retained – the good ones always leave.'

He paused. 'It might also explain how you've risen so near the top, Mr Rayburn, like a turd floating in the Irish Sea?'

Craig sighed. 'We're not bribing you. We're trying to let you show us something in return for something you want. I guess some years off your sentence? So why don't you take us where we need to go and then we can all get back and you can get your flash lawyer in to start hashing out the deal.'

Hamilton turned to Dani and gestured towards the policeman with a nod of his head. 'He's not very nice to me. Is he, Dani?'

Dani shook her head and continued looking out of the window.

'OK then. What time is it?' said Hamilton. 'I don't want to eat my mystery-meat sandwich too early and have to endure too big a gap between then and tiffin.'

He made a show of leaning forward and looking at the clock on the centre console.

It was around twelve o'clock.

'So, we eat around one?' he said. 'I always felt one was a good time for lunch. It's very European. Like you sit down at one, finish eating around two, two thirty, and then you're not hungry again until a meal later in the evening, so you can eat around seven or eight and actually take the time to enjoy it. You know what I mean, Dani? You eat late, don't you? Well, when you eat at all.'

Dani ignored the remark. The excitement that she'd felt had faded and she was now beginning to wish this whole day could be over.

'Uh-oh,' said Hamilton, starting to move in his seat. 'I need the toilet actually.'

Craig leaned his head back against the headrest and let out an exasperated sigh. 'You need to stop all this, Mr Hamilton. You're not getting out of the car, and you're not using a public toilet. I don't care if you shit yourself. We're going to take you to a nick and you can use the can there – it's your own time you're wasting because my patience is running out, OK? And all I'm going to do, in a short while, is call this whole thing off, take you back, and put you back in a cage where you belong. Are we clear?'

Hamilton stared at the man for a long time, before he seemed to soften and turned back to Dani.

Although she wasn't looking at him, she felt his eyes on her, before he turned back towards the police officer.

'OK, boss man,' Hamilton said, as though relenting. 'I think I know where we need to go. Head back to Burley.'

'We've just been to fucking Burley,' said Craig. 'We've been through Burley three times now.'

Hamilton ignored him. 'Head back to Burley, it's around there somewhere. It's not on the main road, though. Come off at Burley, and there's a long, straight road that takes you down into the New Forest. Head down there, and I think there are some farms and cottages. Let me go there and have one more look.'

Craig shrugged and passed the message to the other vehicles via the radio.

Dani sat back as she felt the car pull away.

They drove for about twenty minutes in silence, moving back on to the main road before they diverted on to smaller back roads in the New Forest proper.

The track they were on now was for two-way traffic, though it was only just wide enough for one and had passing spaces every few hundred yards along it.

Dani wasn't sure what it was that made her look behind.

Maybe some subtle change in the way that Hamilton was sitting, but she felt as though something wasn't quite right.

She turned and looked again at the unmarked police car that was hanging thirty or forty yards behind.

It veered slightly and stopped in the road.

Dani could see that Craig had been watching too and he was already reaching for the radio.

The traffic around them was very light, and some vehicles stopped behind the stranded car.

'Don't stop, drive on,' said Craig, though their driver hadn't shown any intention of doing otherwise.

Craig was speaking into the radio, trying to ascertain what had happened to the rear car, while making sure the vehicle in front understood the situation.

Dani wasn't sure whether she saw a wry smile start to turn up the corner of Hamilton's mouth, but as she turned again to look behind her, she saw a four-wheel drive vehicle accelerate suddenly and approach them.

Craig reacted immediately. He shouted a code word three times into the radio.

Dani couldn't make out exactly what he was saying, but it sounded like 'hell, hell, hell'. She didn't need to know what it meant because she'd been in the armed forces long enough to know what an emergency call sounded like; it could only mean they'd been compromised and they needed to evade.

The car began to speed up and then the front passenger side seemed to lift suddenly into the air, a loud explosion sounding beneath them, and Dani was thrown around the back seat.

The front of the car dropped back down suddenly, but it was off kilter, low at the front left side and no longer moving.

She saw that the front vehicle was now stopped too and then she began to look frantically around her.

The voices over the radio were coming thick and fast.

She couldn't make it out at first until she heard 'Stinger' and then 'mine' shouted loud and clear.

The driver tried to drive, revving the engine, but the vehicle wouldn't move.

The 4x4 that had been moving up quickly behind them was now next to them, almost touching their left-side light cluster, and Dani could now see three other vehicles closing in fast, two approaching from the other direction, and one from behind them.

'Armed response, one minute out,' shouted Craig. 'They won't breach us. They won't breach this vehicle.'

Dani watched as a man whose face was completely covered by a black balaclava jumped quickly out of the four-wheel drive.

He was armed with some kind of small automatic rifle, and Dani looked around and realised that behind her, the third car in their convoy was also surrounded by figures with similar weapons.

She watched, panicked, as a figure strolled around to the front of the vehicle, heading towards the passenger side, and motioned for the window to be lowered.

Craig said nothing, continuing to stare straight ahead.

The driver had reached for his pistol and was holding it ready but pointing down into the footwell.

Dani then noticed that two other men, both armed, had lowered their rifles, slung them low over their backs, and were now planting lumps of what looked like red or orange coloured plasticine at various spots around the windows of her car.

'No one needs to get hurt here, officer,' said the masked figure by the passenger door. 'You've got about three minutes until your armed response team arrives, not one. We're tracking them, so I can tell you this now: if you open the door, I'm going to take the prisoner, and no one needs to get hurt. If you don't open the door within thirty seconds, I'm going to use this Semtex to blow the windows of this vehicle out. It'll work, we'll gain access, and all you people inside will be deaf, your eardrums will be blown out, and there'll be damage from the glass and debris. I'll shoot you and your colleague in the head and then take the prisoner anyway. I'm going to ask you now, officer, to tell your colleague to lower his sidearm, unlock the vehicle and step outside.'

Dani's heart was beating in a way she'd never thought possible. She looked down and could see her hands shaking and couldn't help but look across at Hamilton and see the smile on his face.

He'd known all along.

The plan had happened, and she now understood what he stood to gain from this.

She couldn't figure out how they knew. How could they possibly have known it would be today? She realised that everything Hamilton had done this morning had been about wasting time, simply allowing time to pass so that they could be here for this rendezvous.

'Twenty seconds, officer,' said the masked man outside.

The other men had now planted the explosive against the windows and were pushing wires into the back of it and running a detonator cable away from the car, to a spot behind their Range Rover.

'Do not open the door,' said Dani, trying to catch Craig's eye in the rear-view mirror.

'Fifteen seconds, officer,' said the voice.

'Don't do it,' said Dani. 'The response will be here; we just have to hold out.'

Craig turned in his seat and looked at Dani, then he looked at the armed response officer.

The radio squawked into life, and a voice said, 'Armed response, two minutes out.'

Dani looked at Craig.

Their eyes met, and they both knew they didn't have two minutes.

'Don't let him out,' said Dani, locking eyes with Craig, holding his gaze and trying to convince him that she was right.

'Ten seconds, officer. These are high explosives. This is your last chance to open the door and see your family again. The safety glass is good but it ain't that good, and you know it,' said the man in the balaclava.

The man began to walk away from the car and shouted to the others.

'Blow it in four, three . . .'

Craig turned to his driver. 'Relinquish your weapon,' he said. 'Unlock the car.'

'No,' said Dani, reaching forward and trying to grab Craig's arm.

There was a moment's hesitation before the driver did as he was asked.

The sound of the car unlocking must have travelled and the man with the balaclava turned back and waited.

As the doors opened, his men raised their rifles and watched the two police officers climb out with their arms raised.

There was a burst of movement as soon as the policemen

left the car, and the armed officer, though he was no longer actually armed, was immediately struck from behind with the butt of a rifle.

They forced him to the ground and Dani watched as two men pounced on him, binding his arms behind his back, binding his feet and then attaching them together, so he was hogtied, lying on his belly with his hands behind his back and pulled tight towards his heels.

The same happened to Craig, and Dani could see now, as she looked around, horrified, that the same fate had befallen the inhabitants of the front and rear vehicles.

She watched as the man who'd spoken came around to Hamilton's side of the car and opened the door.

He leaned in, apparently having taken the keys from the police driver, and unlocked the chains that attached Hamilton to the restraining point.

Dani noticed that the man didn't undo the ones that bound Hamilton's wrists and ankles.

'Out,' said the man, grabbing Hamilton by the shoulder and pulling him bodily out on to the rough ground.

'She comes with us,' said Hamilton, turning back towards Dani. 'That was agreed. She comes.'

Dani saw another figure approaching the car, a huge man, his face also covered by a balaclava, but with a gait that made her look twice. She heard a mumbled voice, and sat, frozen, her heart in the pit of her stomach, as the huge man spoke with some of the others.

Then, he was arguing, leaning in close and talking to Hamilton, but all Dani could hear was Hamilton saying, 'She comes too. She comes too,' over and over again, like a child drowning out any discussion.

One of the men who'd bound the police officers moved towards the car, opened Dani's door and reached for her arm, but the large figure moved quickly and intercepted him, pushing him away and then reaching in the car and gently touching her.

'Get the fuck off me,' said Dani, turning in the seat and kicking out at the man.

He leaned back in and grabbed her more tightly, then he pulled her from the car.

Dani felt his fingers grip her upper arm hard and she allowed herself to be dragged out, watching as he leaned back in and grabbed her backpack. She kicked out at him again, digging her nails into the flesh of his hand as she tried to make him let go.

'Dani, don't,' he growled.

The physical size of the man, the way he moved, these things had all triggered some recognition, but the man's voice was unmistakable.

Chapter 28

Dani was dragged quickly around the back of the police car, her feet barely touching the ground, before she was thrown into the back of the waiting 4x4.

Around her were the escorting police officers, all of them lying on their fronts, their hands tied behind them and stretched back towards their heels as they lay motionless on the roadside of the New Forest.

Some of them looked as though they were bleeding, but all of them looked alive; not a single shot had been fired.

A hood was thrust down over her head.

She'd watched as Hamilton had had the same treatment before her and so she'd expected it.

Her hands weren't bound, and she immediately tried to remove it.

'Leave it!' shouted the voice, and Dani did, almost.

She slowly rolled it up at the front, stopping it just above her nose, so she could continue breathing.

The vehicle listed to one side as a large figure got into the passenger seat. This was a man who she'd recognised just by his walk, who she'd had a drink with as an adult, who'd changed her nappy as a child.

This was a man she'd known for her entire life. Who she'd thought would do anything for her, do anything to protect her.

He'd left her a gift, a pen, only days ago, with a note that said he loved her. He'd dropped that off on the same day he'd come around to her house to try and convince her to make a logical choice.

This was a man who'd just, as part of a criminal gang made up of former military special forces, hijacked one of the country's most notorious killers and freed him from police custody.

Dani felt sick.

Images of her father and the childhood she'd had with him continually flashed in front of her eyes.

He'd been one of the only constants in her life. They hadn't always got on, but she'd known she could always go to him. Had she ever needed him, he'd have been there; she knew it. Yet here and now, what was happening seemed like a thump to the stomach.

He'd told her things that had occurred in Afghanistan, but he hadn't told her everything – not by a long shot – and now . . . Dani realised just how badly she'd misjudged what her father was capable of.

The only possible explanation was that he'd lied to her, blatantly and well, and he was deep in all of this in a way she couldn't yet see. That called into question everything Dani knew about herself, everything she knew about the way she judged people and the way she trusted people.

She remembered the speech her dad had given her: 'Think about who I am, Dani. Think about what you know about me, and the type of person I am, and ask yourself if I could be involved in this.'

That's what he'd said, and here he was, freeing

Christopher Hamilton, and making sure that she came along as he obeyed Hamilton's orders.

Dani wasn't sure why, but she'd expected the next few minutes to be torturous – screeching tyres, the sound of sirens, maybe bullets pinging off the metalwork of the car. But there was none of that.

They drove away quickly, and she lost count of how many lefts and rights they'd taken. But though the vehicle was moving fast, she didn't feel any urgency: they weren't in a police chase. This had been planned far too well for that.

Craig Rayburn had been certain they could deal with anything and Dani had agreed. She'd known Hamilton had a plan, but they'd had armed response units and a helicopter on standby, armed guards within the convoy.

But what Craig hadn't accounted for – and why would he; why would anyone even conceive of the possibility? – was that the people that came to free Hamilton would be highly trained British Special Forces operatives, with years of experience of operations behind enemy lines.

Dani was angry with herself, but on some level, she wasn't sure why. How could she have seen this coming? How could anybody have seen this coming? She'd worked with Marcus and he'd seemed to know nothing about this. In her worst nightmares, she'd considered that Hamilton might try and run away if he got the opportunity, perhaps his mysterious helper might create a diversion, maybe try to stop the convoy with sniper fire. She'd considered he might try to get them to go to a particular café where he had some other accomplices – the drunk guy who'd broken into her house with a stolen pistol or something like that. But she'd been certain that the police would have that covered; they'd discussed things like that on the briefing day.

But what she hadn't considered, ever, was that a team of men, trained to do extractions and arrests in Northern Ireland, Afghanistan, Iraq, the former Yugoslavia and dozens of other theatres around the world, would pull off and execute a slick and decisive ambush against their convoy.

The whole thing was over in less than ninety seconds.

No one had been seriously hurt.

Hamilton was no longer in police custody.

As she sat in the back of the car, her eyes covered, she thought back to the voice that had spoken to Craig to force him to open the vehicle. She reimagined the figure in her head, and she immediately knew who it was. She'd met him before.

It was Jimmy Nash.

She wasn't sure where, but she knew Marcus would be among them somewhere too. She knew it was them and she knew the police had never had a chance.

Out of the bottom of her hood, the only thing she could see was the blue knee of Hamilton's trousers.

He was in the vehicle with her, sitting next to her in the back seat, and it took her a moment to realise that she could hear a sound coming from him.

She listened, trying to hear him over the noise of her beating heart and panicked breathing.

He was whistling.

It took her a few moments to place the tune. It was music she recognised.

It had a strong beat. It was marching music.

She remembered having marched to it at parades during training and many times since, and then it came to her.

Christopher Hamilton, serial killer, was whistling the theme tune to *The Great Escape*.

PART 2

Chapter 29

Dani didn't know how long she'd been in the room.

The hood had been properly pulled down over her head and someone had tied her hands behind her back as soon as she was removed from the vehicle.

She'd managed to lie down, thought she'd fought back the panic attack, but clearly hadn't since she felt as though she'd been there for a while but had no memory of how long.

She leaned on what she assumed was a sofa and used the friction of the hood against the cushions to pull it up again, so it no longer covered her nose and mouth. She drew in a deep breath, closed her eyes and began to count as she warded off another surge of panic. A few moments later, she persevered and worked the hood off entirely.

The room around her had more decoration than she'd expected.

In her mind, it was going to be bare walls, maybe some water trickling down through hard stone as she was held prisoner in a gangsters' lair.

Her memories of the room where William Knight was kept prisoner by Jimmy Nash surfaced and she imagined she'd open her eyes to that level of squalor and know, for sure, that their captors were the same.

This room, however, was nothing like that. It looked old and neglected, but there had been a grand design to it at some point.

The carpet and curtains were busy with patterns and colours – burgundies and reds.

All of the decor was old, from the fifties or earlier, and the dust and cobwebs around the place made it look eerie and abandoned.

The only furniture in the room was the sofa she was sitting on and an ornate wooden table over by the window.

Other than that, it looked as though somebody had come in and decorated it half-heartedly, but realised their mistake before they brought the rest of their furniture in to settle.

The only thing that gave Dani any indication of the time was the window.

It had been light, around noon, when her convoy had been attacked, but she could see now that it was beginning to dim outside, and she knew it had to be early evening or thereabout – she'd been out for a few hours at least.

Her legs were free, and she managed to stand up and walk around the room, though she was unable to free her hands from behind her back.

She listened at the door for a while, not sure if she could hear anything beyond it, then kicked it several times to see if she could break it open or if someone might come.

As it was, she just made a lot of noise and was ignored by whoever might be out there.

Another few laps of the room, a few moments trying to see if she could free her hands using the edge of the radiator, a check of the window, which was painted shut, but still an option if she could free her hands, and she eventually gave up, choosing to sit on the sofa and wait for a while. She felt sure that one of those who'd assaulted the convoy would come to see her soon.

She played over in her mind what had happened at the moment the police unit had been attacked.

How could any attackers possibly have known where they would be and when they would be there? The *where* could be answered: Hamilton had been communicating with someone outside for a prolonged period of time, she knew that. But the when, that was almost impossible.

She hadn't been followed, not that morning. She'd been checking most of the way and the police would surely be aware of such things too. But even if they'd followed her to the prison, the armed convoy were professionals, they'd have been watching for exactly that. She considered whether someone had been watching the prison but knew that must be almost impossible. Craig had to have carried out that kind of basic check to make sure that there was no one around in the hours before they brought Hamilton out, and continuous surveillance on a high-security prison would be nigh on impossible, though not perhaps for the people who'd carried out this attack. She reviewed the strategy they'd used: the armed guards, cars front and back, and the response unit only a few minutes away.

There were only two, maybe three, people who knew when they were taking him, and Dani wasn't even one of them.

The time required to prepare such an attack would be significant, unless, of course, your people were all trained for just such a thing.

The convoy had aimed for low key, relying on the fact that nobody knew what they were doing, but also with sufficient fire power to fend off most attackers.

But they hadn't faced most attackers.

Thinking about the attack brought back an almost physical panic.

The shock and awe of how quickly it had happened, the professionalism and speed, but most of all the recognition that one of the attackers was her dad, overwhelmed her. As that thought passed again, she felt her stomach churn and bile rose in the back of her throat. She didn't believe it was possible she could have misjudged someone so close to her so badly.

Thirst and hunger started to interrupt her thoughts, fragmenting them.

She was also aware that her nose was itchy, and she leaned down, rubbing her face on the sofa, recoiling slightly at the musty smell.

It was at that precise moment that the door opened.

'I'm getting her out of here now,' said a very familiar voice.

Dani looked up from her semi-prone position on the sofa and saw her dad approach.

'Are you all right, Dani?' he said, reaching out to touch her, patting her back and arms as though checking for injuries and breaks.

She recoiled from his touch, stunned he'd come in as if this would be OK.

What started off as an involuntary tensing of her body turned into a kick as she lashed out with her foot, catching him on the side of the thigh and then again on the shoulder, driving him back away from her.

She needed to speak, but she didn't know what to say. She felt her mouth move, but no words came to mind. As she lay on her side, looking up, her father looked down at her, his face red, his eyes not meeting hers, his hands by his sides.

'Get the fuck off me,' said Dani, noticing how her

language made her dad jolt, as though hearing his daughter swear was the most shocking thing.

In a surreal moment, she wondered if she'd ever sworn in front of him before. She was certain she must have, but maybe not *at* him.

'I've known you for my whole life. I've trusted you. Even when we spoke before, you said, "Oh, remember, Dani, remember the sort of person I am", and now this. You've just freed someone who dedicated his life to killing women.'

The words came out jerkily, as though she'd been running and was now out of breath, and by the time she got to the end of her sentence, she was gasping for air.

She felt a sudden rage build up inside her and tried to kick out again, realised she was nowhere near close enough and pushed off the couch with her shoulder to stand up. She spat at her dad before she'd even realised she was going to.

It landed square in the centre of his face.

He didn't even flinch.

She watched her saliva drip down his cheek.

'You don't understand, Dani,' he said, shaking his head, but still not looking at her. 'You don't understand any of this.'

She was about to speak again, to tell her dad she knew everything she needed to know, because she'd seen it with her own eyes, but she was interrupted. Two shapes appeared in the door behind her father and she turned to focus on them.

'Hello there, sweetheart,' said Jimmy Nash.

Behind him, she could see Marcus hovering in the shadows.

'She's got to stay here, Taz,' said Jimmy, walking a few paces into the room, but not coming too close. 'It might only be worse for her if she comes out. We don't know what's going to happen next.'

Taz turned quickly and looked at Jimmy, as though hearing what he'd said as a threat.

'She comes with me,' said Taz, in a tone that courted no discussion.

'Frankly, I'd rather stay where I am,' said Dani, sitting back down on the couch, staring at her father, and then at Jimmy and Marcus in turn.

Taz stepped towards her again, wary this time, as though worried about another kick coming his way. 'Let me at least untie your hands,' he said, as he reached out towards her.

Dani pulled away from him again and shivered; the thought of him being anywhere near her was repulsive.

'I told you,' she said through gritted teeth. 'Get off me.'

He stopped short and looked her in the eye. Seeming to realise he'd get nowhere, he turned and walked towards the door. 'This door's not to be locked,' he said, as he passed Jimmy and Marcus and walked out into the corridor beyond.

Jimmy nodded and turned to follow.

Dani watched the door, waiting for it to be shut behind him.

Instead, Marcus filled the space and walked in. He tried a half-smile as he approached Dani, before he stopped, waiting in the middle of the room.

'If I come near you, will you kick me or spit on me?' he asked, tilting his head and observing her.

'Not if you untie me I won't,' said Dani. 'If you do that, then I'll kick you, spit on you and punch you in your stupid lying face.'

Marcus laughed at that. Not a loud belly laugh, just a sort of chuckle, and it pissed Dani off some more.

'Well, I'm going to untie you anyway, because you'll be much more comfortable if I do. I'd very much appreciate it if, just while I'm doing that, you'd try not to do me any harm or . . . cover me in saliva,' he said.

Dani didn't move to make it any easier for him to access her hands and so he had to sit on the couch beside her and lean back to undo her bonds.

As he released her, Dani realised that it was a mixture of tie wraps and rope, one for speed and one for strength.

The plastic zip ties had pulled her hands tight together quickly, she dimly remembered that, but strong cord must have been added separately to prevent her from freeing herself and she had no recollection of that at all.

'You do know all of you are going to prison,' she said, not looking at him, but bringing her hands around in front of her as soon as she was free.

The blood slowly started to return to her fingers as she rubbed her hands together and flexed them.

'I don't think so, Dani,' he said. 'Can I get you a drink? Some food?'

Dani was hungry and thirsty, but still considered declining, just because she wanted nothing from these people. But she was going to need all her strength, and for the first time she realised she had no idea what she was facing or for how long it would last.

'Marcus,' she said, not answering his initial question. 'Do you actually know what you've done? Do you know who you've released?'

Marcus shook his head. 'We haven't released anyone,' he said, walking towards the door. 'And, for the record, I haven't lied to you. When we spoke, we had no idea about this at all. Whoever helps Hamilton knows what they're doing. We had just enough time to get the gear together and then barely enough to get to the position. I assume this is Plan A, but we weren't privy to it. Now if you want some food, you can follow me.'

Dani waited for a few seconds and then stood up and followed him as he left the room.

Outside was a cold stone corridor and she could see that the room she'd been in was actually the most modern room in what was a very old cottage or farmhouse.

She had no idea where they could be, but, again, seeing the light outside the window and knowing roughly what time they were attacked, she knew they could be almost anywhere within a six- to eight-hour radius of Hampshire's New Forest, which was a lot of places.

Marcus led her along the corridor and into a rustic kitchen.

'Any more from the Twitter messages?' she asked as they walked.

'Of all the things you must want to ask, you lead with that.'

'I ask questions I might get an honest answer to.'

He nodded, accepting her point.

'There's so much crazy on there, it's hard to filter what might be and what can't be, but I have guys working on it still.'

They entered an old kitchen. There was an enormous oak table in the centre of the space, matching the rest of the kitchen around it. The cupboards and worktops looked old and worn, but they'd been high quality in their day, and looked better with age.

The kitchen stood in stark contrast to the room she'd been in – it looked perfectly aged, like the set from an old movie. Around the table at its centre, sitting and drinking tea, were Jimmy and her dad.

There was no one else there, and Dani realised how

quiet it was, noting that very few of those who'd been involved in attacking the convoy had also come here.

'Cup of tea?' said Jimmy, gesturing towards the pot on the table.

Taz stood up. 'She doesn't drink that tea, she drinks green tea,' he said, walking over to the cupboards and starting to look through to see what else was in them.

'I've got one here,' said Marcus from behind her.

She turned to see him holding her rucksack.

He fished through it, going straight to the side pocket where she kept some tea bags, and pulled one out. He tossed it to Dani's father, and then offered the backpack to her.

'I've been through it, and I'm afraid I read some of your mail,' he said, 'but it's all in there.'

Dani snatched it from him. She watched her father as he boiled an old-style kettle over the fire.

He dropped the tea bag into a mug and poured the water using a thick cloth to protect his hand from the heat of the metal handle.

He turned to her and tried to smile. 'This is peppermint, not green. Have you changed what you drink?'

Dani stared at him, her mouth dropping open. He was talking as if they were just standing in the kitchen at home, just the two of them as they often did, with Mim and Charlie chatting in the front room while they made tea for everyone.

'Come and sit down by me, sweetheart,' said Jimmy, patting the bench seat beside him.

'I'd rather not,' said Dani, staring at him.

'Well, it's the seat or the floor, love. You do what you want,' said Jimmy, turning back and cupping the mug in his hands as he took a sip.

Taz handed her the mug, offering her the handle. Dani thought for a moment that if she waited long enough, he'd burn his fingers and she could hurt him in some small way, but she hated the pettiness of the thought.

Marcus was now at the table with Jimmy, and her father walked over and sat with them. There was one space left on the bench, but Dani didn't take it.

'So, what are we going to do then?' said Jimmy, speaking as though Dani wasn't there.

'Well, we know he's got people on the outside,' said Taz, 'someone who's arranged all this.' He gestured at the building around them.

'I think we should just torture it out of him,' Jimmy said. 'I've got a guy who'd have him telling us who his friends are. We torture it out of him and then we take them all out.'

Taz was shaking his head. 'It's too dangerous. We don't know who they are, how many there are and, most importantly, where they are. We can't risk it. We've all got people we care about and we can't guard them forever.'

'Well, we know they're going to come here, don't we?' said Jimmy, looking at Taz and then Marcus. 'This is where we had to bring him, there must be some kind of rendezvous going on.'

'We can't do that,' said Taz. 'You know we can't. His rules were simple. Me, you and Marcus. That was it.'

'And her,' said Jimmy, nodding across at Dani. 'Anyway, I've had this place swept for bugs and there's none. I've got seven guys out in the grounds, specialists, got them dug in deep as soon as we got the location. We'll know who they are as soon as they come close and we can make the call then.'

'Are you fucking crazy?' Taz said, leaning over the table towards Jimmy. 'You're kidding me, right? You haven't done that. You haven't actually put men on the ground after we were specifically warned not to?'

Jimmy eyed Taz across the table. 'You're not in charge now, mate, and just so you know, neither's he. I am.'

'You're a fucking idiot, Jimmy. You always were.'

Jimmy bridled at that. 'And what are you going to do when he tries to take your little girl? Eh? You think he won't?'

'No one's taking her anywhere,' said Taz.

'Yeah, you're right. Because I've got men with guns who'll stop them. Not cos of you, because you're trying to play it safe and think they'll be straight with you – because of me.'

'Wait,' said Dani. 'Just stop a second. We don't know exactly what he has, but we can make a good guess at it. He has one guy, the sniper from Afghanistan.'

She looked around at them and saw how their faces changed at the mention of the sniper. Her father and Marcus seemed to show shame, looking away from her, even if just for a second, but Jimmy stared, hard and angry.

'Just hear me out,' she said. 'I've been working Hamilton for a long time and he has no friends.'

Marcus caught her attention with a wave of his hand and pointed to a door behind her that led off from the kitchen. He pointed at it twice and then put his finger to his lips.

Dani paused and then walked to join them at the table. She took a seat next to Marcus, forcing him to shuffle along a bit, and leaned in to whisper.

'He has no friends. None. He doesn't form relationships like that. Now, this guy, the sniper who cannibalises people, might be an exception to that. They may have some kind of understanding, but my gut feel is that Hamilton, by his nature, would want to hold the power in a relationship. I'd be prepared to bet that Hamilton has something on the sniper, some proof of what he did in Afghanistan, and they may have developed some friendship outside of that, but that leverage would still be there. Hamilton doesn't do friendship and loyalty in the way we might – he doesn't see the world that way.'

'So what?' asked Jimmy, looking at the others to see if they were getting Dani's point.

'So, he's only got one person with any firm loyalty to him, whether that's coerced or not,' said Marcus.

'Right,' Dani agreed. 'Anyone else will be paid or threatened, like the prison guard. They won't have the kind of bond of the main guy, this sniper, and they'll fall away quickly when it's not worth the risk.'

'So, you agree with me?' asked Jimmy, a quizzical smile on his face.

'If you're saying that your part in this was to bring him here, then, unless you're going to be told to just let him go free, his helper has to come here. Though I don't know why they'd do that. It's been so seamless until now, that feels like a slip-up on their part . . .'

Dani's words trailed off.

'What?' said Jimmy.

'Unless they're coming to make sure there aren't any witnesses to the whole thing. In which case, we're all here for them right now.'

Jimmy was nodding. 'I thought that,' he said, though Dani didn't believe him. 'It's a bloody trap. That's why I have the guys out there.'

He looked at Taz. 'I've taken care of everything,' he said. 'Everything. OK?'

Taz shook his head and stood up. He walked past Dani, trailing his hand on her shoulder, and headed out into the corridor.

She followed him.

'What have you done?' she said, watching him stop in

his tracks and turn to face her. 'What could you have done that puts you at the beck and call of Chris Hamilton and Jimmy?' She was aware of how much disappointment was in her voice, knowing that it also carried through her eyes. 'Come with me and report what happened. Tell your story. You did what you could, Dad. Get this off your back and you'll be able to move on from it.'

Her father looked the smallest she'd ever seen him.

'I can't believe you've had any part in this. You're better than this,' she said.

'You need the whole truth,' he said.

He turned and walked away, opening a door a few yards down on his left, leaving it open behind him for her to follow.

Chapter 30

'Lying seems to run in the family, eh?' said Dani.

She'd followed her father into a small, sparsely decorated bedroom.

There was no mattress on the bed and only one chair.

She nodded to her dad to take the chair while she slid down the wall, sitting on the floor so she could face him.

'Go on then,' she said. 'Let's hear it.'

He sat down, the chair creaking beneath him, and looked at her.

'Everything I told you was true, right up until the point we were trapped in that house. Everything I said about those people, the sniper, the death and torture, it was all true. If anything, it was worse than that – being in that house was like being prisoner in an abattoir.'

'But?' asked Dani, feeling a strange unsettling in her stomach.

'But you said to me that you couldn't understand why he let us go.'

She suddenly felt sick.

'It was all true,' he said again. 'Right up until the point we were trapped in that house.'

Her dad moved on the chair, turning half away from her. 'We'd been in there two days. We were pinned down. There was no way we could escape because he had a bird's nest, so even if we went behind the house, we could only go ten, maybe fifteen yards before we were in his sights again. We were trapped in there and we were rotting and dying. The corpses were decomposing, the flies were relentless, and we were out of water. There was maybe a dozen of us alive, about as many again dead and decomposing. On the second day, when they started charging at the door . . .'

Dani looked away now too, for some reason unable to look at her father when he spoke the next words.

'We tried to stop them, for their own good, tried to keep them inside, but they attacked us. They were crazy, starving, dehydrated . . .'

He began to speak and then choked on the words.

The room was quiet for a few moments.

'We opened fire,' he said finally. 'It was self-defence.'

Dani turned, her mouth open. 'Self-defence against unarmed, starving people?' she said.

He ignored her. 'We . . . I shot two of them who were attacking Jimmy, then they were too close. I tried to warn them off. We were shouting, and Marcus was trying to make them understand, then they came at us again and it was close quarters. The next thing I knew, I had my knife and I was covered in blood. The door was open, and the rest were trying to get out. Marcus and Jimmy were covered too, we all had blood everywhere.'

He was looking down at his hands as he spoke now, as though remembering what they'd looked like with red sticky fluid dripping from them.

'The bullets started flying,' he continued. 'He was taking them out one at a time. We ran for it, got Davis and carried him, but not a single bullet came near us.'

'That's why,' said Dani.

'That woman followed us. What I said was the truth. I think she knew we'd wanted to help, but he took her down and let us leave.'

'Dad—'

He held up his hand to her. 'When we got back, we reported it,' he said. 'I wasn't lying about that. We knew we'd done wrong. It was Hamilton that was the Brit policeman out there at the time. He interviewed us all, except Marcus. He'd caught something at the house, some infection, and he was in a bad, bad way; he nearly died.'

'Dad—' Dani tried again, but he silenced her and she wondered whether, if he stopped now, he might not be able to start again.

'We told him everything, me, Jimmy and Davis. We told him the lot and we knew the drill. He'd take it initially, but we'd be pulled out for proper debriefing. There'd be an investigation and we'd go down for it – we all knew we were going to prison. Marcus was in the field hospital and he was touch and go, we'd already lost four in the field; I think we all just wanted to tell our story and for it to be over. Hamilton gave us some time to clean up while they arranged for a full investigation team to be flown out from God knows where. We were sworn to secrecy, and we waited. After twenty-four hours – nothing. Then forty-eight hours and still nothing. It should've been quicker than that. Then, on the third morning, I woke up and someone had left an envelope on my bed.'

He looked at her now.

'I opened it, and it was you.'

Dani frowned. 'What?'

'Inside the envelope were pictures of you. And Charlie and Mim.' Her dad looked away again. 'Someone had managed to get photographs of my family, recent ones, some from our back garden, one of you on the way to school. They managed to get them out to a forward operating base in Afghanistan. Think about the tech at the time, Dani. It wasn't an easy thing to do.'

'And . . .' said Dani, confused.

'And there was a note that said, "Our little secret", and on all of the pictures, your left ring finger was shaded in black pen as though it wasn't there.'

'Someone was warning you?'

He nodded. 'Not just me, Jimmy and Davis too. Both the same – close family, a note and the fingers shaded out. We'd come across a madman and he'd shown he could get to you at home.'

'So you changed your story?'

He nodded. 'We all did, except Marcus. He was too ill and had been unconscious for days. We all went back in with Hamilton and told him we'd made errors, we'd been dehydrated, fatigued and under duress. We said we couldn't remember where it was or what we'd seen.'

He was shaking his head.

'It wasn't the right thing to do, Dani, but after losing your mum, I couldn't risk losing you and Charlie too.'

Dani felt tears well in her eyes.

'We were all family men. We didn't know who it was. Who it was back home who took the pictures. We didn't know how to answer back to the note, or how to protect our families when we were thousands of miles away. So, we lied. We made a pact and we let it go. We changed our stories and we all got away with murder.'

Dani was wrestling with all she'd heard and what it might mean.

Her dad continued. 'Looking back now, it might seem obvious to say that Hamilton was involved. Realistically he was the only one who could have had those pictures taken, but then, we didn't know what he was. He was just a lieutenant – for years we thought he'd been warned off too – we just didn't speak about it. When all that happened, and you got him, I met with Jimmy and Marcus – Davis was already a mess, an alcoholic and a drug user – but the three of us met and we talked about what he could have done. We didn't know. We were just glad he was locked up. Then, all this time later, we got a message to meet. All of us thought it had come from the other . . .'

'He has evidence,' Dani said.

Taz was nodding. 'Our initial statements, the ones we changed. He could well have kept other evidence too. It's possible he even managed to get evidence from the scene, but the messages we've got say he has proof it happened. Maybe he knows who the sniper was, like you say, maybe that's who's working with him now. None of us know, but we all thought it'd come back to haunt us one day. I think I always knew it would.'

Chapter 31

Hamilton's Fifth Letter

Dani,

A short one I'm afraid. I rather got carried away with the last letter and missed some very important information from the end of it. It's stuff you'd very much want to know, and these letters are for you after all.

After the excitement, exhilaration and ecstasy of Catherine, the lows I experienced were terrible, unbearable.

I was bored and unfocussed.

I'll tell you now, Dani, that throughout my adulthood I was rarely without an ongoing project and I think it was then, as a teen, I realised I needed that. Some of my hunts lasted only a few days or weeks until successful completion, some were months long, and others were years, but I was always working towards someone and even before one was dead, I was already looking for the next.

It's a weakness of mine that I was forced to recognise.

While I enjoy the killing, I live for the hunt, for the planning and preparation, the anticipation. I need so little from a victim to allow me to form a link that can be transformed into staggering motivation.

I once tracked a woman for two years, eventually killing her, simply because I saw her eating porridge on a train. Her overconfidence was astounding. She poured the hot water from a small thermos flask and stirred it, the noise irritating all around her. The sound of her chewing made me cringe with every new mouthful as her cutlery clacked against her bowl. She then used her finger to scrape the remnants from her Tupperware pot, sucking herself clean.

All the time she did this, she never once looked at the people around her. Never once wondered what impact her actions were having. After I'd taken her, I challenged her over what she'd done and she had no idea. So selfish was she, so hideously buried in her own activities, that she couldn't even remember what I was referring to, because she did it Every. Fucking. Day.

Sorry, Dani, I digress again, but the point here is that I knew I wasn't able to kill again so soon, but I needed to be in the hunt. It could be practice but I needed focus.

I'd begun to consider a girl for my next kill.

She was a similar age to Catherine, perfect in appearance, though she knew it and her overconfidence and self-absorption would, I knew, make me want to go all the way. She would wear a bikini top and jeans to the shop, flaunting herself without shame, ignoring the whistles and catcalls as though they just bounced off her perfect skin, and she'd had two lovers, not including me, in the short time I'd begun to notice her.

If I may digress, Dani, there is little more unattractive a trait in a woman than overconfidence and you should always guard against it. A little look away when in eye contact, a small blush if lucky enough to receive a compliment, these are the things that add hugely to a woman's attractiveness and charm.

As I watched her, I began to hate this woman as she taunted me again and again, but I couldn't allow myself to kill her. She was protected from me. I needed to move on, to leave her behind and go somewhere that would let me work and build and grow in my career. I needed travel, anonymity and access. Somewhere I could move around unseen in a new place away from Catherine's shadow.

I was accepted into Her Majesty's Royal Navy four days after my sixteenth birthday.

Chapter 32

'Roger? We need to talk,' said Felicity, as soon as he answered the phone.

'It's really not a good time, Felicity.' She could hear him shuffling the phone from one ear to the other. 'I'm in the middle of a meeting at the moment. Well, I've nipped outside to speak to you, but I really need to get back in.'

'I need to talk to you about Dani.'

'You and everyone else,' he said. 'What's she done? Tell me she's not in trouble with you guys too, because I'm in a meet about her now and it isn't going well.'

Felicity sighed. 'Roger, you're not listening to me. I need to talk to you in person and it needs to be now. This is very important.'

There was silence at the end of the phone, and she knew she'd got his attention.

'It's a really terrible line,' said Roger. 'I'll call you back in two seconds.'

'I'm in Portsmouth. We need to speak face-to-face, not on the phone.'

'OK, let me know where you are. Text me the address and I'll be there as soon as I can.'

Felicity was waiting in an interview room at Fratton Police Station in Portsmouth. She could see that Roger was agitated as soon as he walked in. His face was ashen white, and he was jiggling his car keys in his pocket.

'Tell me,' he said without preamble.

Felicity didn't hesitate. 'This morning an operation was mounted to take Christopher Hamilton out of the secure prison unit. He'd promised to identify some locations where he'd disposed of his victims' bodies. He'd agreed to this.'

Roger was completely still, watching her.

'At around twelve-thirty the armed convoy that Christopher Hamilton was travelling in was attacked. They took Hamilton.' Felicity paused. 'They took Dani too.' She felt tears start to well in her eyes.

'You fucking idiots,' said Roger, his expression turning from concern to what looked like pure fury.

Felicity took a step away from him, shocked by his words and tone. 'It was a huge opportunity,' she said, unable to help herself from defending what had happened.

'All you've done is set him free,' said Roger. 'He'd never lead you to the bodies, there's nothing in it for him.'

Felicity was shaking her head. 'We had to try,' she said.

'How did it happen?' he asked, looking down at her, his eyes hard.

'I've spoken to the police commander,' said Felicity. 'This was like nothing they've ever seen before. They had six armed police officers. They had another armed response unit a few minutes out as a back-up. The whole attack, from the moment it started until Dani and Hamilton were gone, took less than ninety seconds. This was a professional job, Roger. One of the policemen that was there, he's ex-army, he said the only time he's seen anything even approaching that type of precision was by special forces units operating in Northern Ireland. The police never had a chance. They're experts at what they do, but they're not military, they're not trained to deal with a military adversary.'

'So, Hamilton's free,' said Roger.

'Roger, did you hear what I said?' Felicity leaned forward and put her palms on the desk. 'They've got Dani. They took Dani with them.'

Roger blinked, seeming to hear her for the first time. 'What do we know? How much do we know?'

'Absolutely nothing,' Felicity said. 'The cameras that were mounted on the cars saw very little. Licence plates were covered, faces were masked, voices were muffled. We have literally nothing to go on, except we're sure it was military. They were carrying military grade weaponry. The sort of stuff that, frankly, we don't see a great deal of in this country.'

Roger seemed to gather himself. 'Is anyone hurt?' he asked.

Felicity shook her head. 'Bumps, bruises, and a lot of damaged pride. But this was an expert job. No one was meant to get hurt.'

'How did they breach the car?' Roger asked.

'They threatened to blow it with Semtex.'

'You can have anything you need from us,' said Roger. 'Let me know what we can do. All the resources at my command are available to you. We need to find them as soon as possible. I've got to go now. But if you need anything, call me and let me know.'

Chapter 33

'Where is he?' said Dani, walking back into the kitchen and speaking to Marcus.

She'd steeled herself before she left her dad's room, unsure what she was going to say to Hamilton, or when, but she needed to get in there now, while she felt confident it was the right thing to do.

Marcus's eyes flitted to a door that led directly from the kitchen and Dani moved towards it.

'Wait,' said Jimmy. 'You can't go in there.'

Dani didn't even break stride. She heard Jimmy start to speak again and then he seemed to think better of it. Then she heard Marcus whisper, 'What harm can it do now, Jimmy?' She unlocked the door and walked in.

This room was a bedroom too and all that was in it was a single bed and a pine bedside cabinet.

Christopher Hamilton was lying on the bed, his hands behind his back, his head resting on a fat pillow; his ankles were bound, but loosely and he had them crossed. He turned to her and smiled as she came in, as though excited to see her, and she saw immediately that his face was an

absolute mess, worse than it had been from the attack that
had hospitalised him.

'Which one of them did that?' she asked, gesturing
towards him.

'Well, it turns out I've rather upset your friend Jimmy,'
said Hamilton, his voice thick and some teeth visibly loose.

He shrugged as though it wasn't much of a deal.

'He got really quite angry with me and lost his temper.
He's a very physical individual, you see, and, well, I suppose
I can't blame him, but I think he broke my nose or tried
at least. The pain's eased a lot since the bleeding stopped.'

'Do you need me to do anything for you?' asked Dani,
looking around the room for somewhere to sit.

'Flay Jimmy alive, slowly, while you make him watch
me do unspeakable things to those he loves?'

Dani ignored him, walking towards the bedroom wall
that was as far away from Hamilton as the room allowed,
and slumping down against it.

'Tell me, how did you manage to arrange all this?'

Hamilton sat up on the mattress. The movement was
awkward because his hands were bound behind him, but
once up, he leaned back against the wall and smiled at
her, though the expression looked more like a snarl due
to the swelling around his nose and eyes.

'Oh, I can do lots of things when I put my mind to it,
Dani. Lots and lots of things. You'd be surprised, actually.
I'm very useful. I'm what you might call a people person,
really. I just seem to bring out the best in those around
me. Whatever I do and however I do it. You know, Dani,
it's not even something I work at, it's just something I
seem to be naturally good at – a gift if you will. I have a
way of making people owe me favours. It's loyalty really
and, frankly, Dani, we need more of that in the world.'

She waited, staring at him. 'There's no way you can

pull this off, Chris,' she said. 'You won't be able to stay on the run for long. You'll be caught again and your friend too. They'll take you back to prison. There's no way this ends well for you. And that's assuming that Jimmy doesn't torture you or kill you before then. I assume it was him that tried to have you killed inside?'

'I'm also feeling confident he won't do that,' Hamilton said. 'I think it's in his best interests not to and I don't think it was him – too cheap and botched. But you're right, people will come after me and I think I'll just have to take my chances. Other relationships had taken a sour turn and forced my hand. Better to live a day as a lion than a thousand years as a sheep and all that.'

Dani desperately wanted to tell him she knew about the guard and the Twitter conversations, but she couldn't risk it yet, not without knowing who the helper was or what they might do if compromised.

'Where do you think you could actually go?' she asked. 'I mean seriously, where?'

He smiled at that and leaned his head back, looking up at the ceiling. 'I know where I'll go, Dani,' he said. 'And I'm going to fit right in. I'm going to be the most patriotic person in the country. They'll love me there, because I love being there. You know how some people wear their Submariner Dolphins on every item of clothing? Or those people that are into climbing or cycling, whatever, and they parade around in T-shirts with it emblazoned all over them? Well, I'm going to be like that. If it was Canada, say, that I chose to go to, then every shirt I wear will have the little red and white flag on it. I'll speak the lingo, support their national team, drink Caesars, sing "O Canada" and wear the maple like I was born to do it. I'm going to set down roots, Dani – not there, of course, but you get my drift.'

263

'You know they have police in Canada too?' asked Dani.

'Oh, I do, but not like you, Dani. You couldn't love a country like I will, because you love your sense of fair play, and right and wrong, far too much. I don't think I ever saw you in anything remotely naval outside of your uniform in all the years we were around each other. It was like you hated being in the navy, were ashamed of it almost, and yet we all know that's not the case. You thrive on it and need it and it keeps you safe, yet you treat it with disdain.'

Dani thought about that for a moment. 'I have some old naval T-shirts I use for painting,' she said.

'In a solitary and non-artistic way, I bet?' he said with a smile. He waited. 'I mean that you're talking about painting the house, on your own most likely, where no one can see you wearing it. You don't mean at a painting class where you'd learn to create something or grow your-self as a person. Where people might see you wearing it and start a conversation – do you?'

Dani didn't answer.

'Do you remember when you used to run most lunch-times when we worked together?'

'I still do when I can,' said Dani.

'Well, I used to watch you and I always noticed a few things. First, you never wore anything naval, not even those horrible T-shirts with all our names on the back that we seemed to get at every course we did. Apparently, there were some on eBay a few years ago with my name on and they were selling well; it's a strange world. It was like as soon as you clocked off, even just for lunch, you'd shed that shared identity that the navy gave you.'

He was smirking now. 'Second was that you always wore headphones, but never played any music. So you were doing it just to prevent people from trying to engage in any meaningful way with you. Again, distancing your-self from those around you. But, and this is most interesting, the only person who you ever allowed to run with you, was John Granger. You still wore your headphones to prevent conversation, but you tolerated him, and I've always wondered at that. Why him? I was and am a far better runner. I could have taken you further and harder, helped you to raise your game and tested you, but you'd never have allowed me to come along, only him.'

'He knows how to be quiet,' said Dani.

'Yes. He knows how to be quiet. He also knows how to do as you say. To run with you and not try and compete. Did you fuck him? I know he wanted to do you. Did he ever make it between your lovely, firm thighs?'

Dani shook her head. 'Why do you always have to revert to being a dick? I don't like what you say, but sometimes, and I mean very occasionally, it's halfway interesting, but then you just go back to being a dick again. I think you think it's clever and a bit shocking, but really, it's just sad.'

Hamilton continued smirking at her, but he didn't say anything.

'But you know what?' Dani went on. 'Yes, I don't like wearing stuff that I feel makes me look like I can't think outside of the armed forces. Yes, I did, and still do, wear headphones so that people won't talk to me, and also, so creeps won't make shitty comments while I'm running. Or, if they do, I can't hear them. And yes, I do tolerate John running with me, because he's not a dick, and I wouldn't have run with you, not because you're not a good runner – I know you're faster than me – but because you're a massive asshole.'

Hamilton laughed out loud as Dani finished her sentence, so much so that the door to the room opened a crack and

Marcus peered in, looking around and then shutting the door again behind him.

'You know, Chris, it doesn't matter where you go. As soon as I get out of here, I'll be straight on to the team coming after you and we'll be coming with everything we've got.'

He smiled again, and Dani realised that the act was actually hurting him, and yet he continued to do it anyway. Such was the importance he placed on letting her know how he felt.

'You won't be coming after me, Dani,' he said. 'Definitely not. I wonder how you'll be when you're no longer with the police. How you'll cope outside the uniform you seem to despise so much.'

Dani tried hard to hide her surprise that he knew this information already.

'You see, I've done you a favour, or rather I will. It's like we've become friends and I have very, very few of those, but the ones I do, I pick very carefully indeed as you can see. So why on earth would you do that? Why would you come after a friend? In fact, I've done you several favours. I'm showing you who people really are and what they can really be willing to do if given the right incentives.'

'I will,' Dani said. 'You know it.'

'No, you won't,' Hamilton said, his voice chirpy as though arguing with a friend. 'Because I'm going to do what I said, Dani. I'm going to keep my word. So many people these days break their words, they say they'll do things, say they'll honour agreements and make pledges of loyalty, and yet they don't. But I'm different. I promised you I'd take you to the bodies and take you I will.'

'And how do you intend to do that while we're in this little predicament?' asked Dani. 'You know, I've seen where Jimmy puts people like you. I've been there.'

The images of the place where she'd met the rapist, William Knight, returned to her again like a recurring nightmare. She shuddered.

'Ah, don't worry about that,' said Hamilton, his voice still chirpy. 'I have it on good authority that you can escape from places like that if you have the right friends. Friends with the necessary motivations and skill sets, who keep their word and repay their debts.'

'And who are your friends?' she asked. 'Is it the sniper from Afghanistan? Is that who's coming to get you?'

He laughed at that. 'For us, Dani, for us. I'd never leave you here with them. And I have something to show you. I have a few scores to settle, but when I'm safe, I'll do just that. You have my word. And in return, I feel sure that after all that's happened, I'm going to disappear, and you'll leave me alone. I'm certain of it.'

Chapter 34

Dani was still in the room with Hamilton. She'd left only once to go to the loo, then once again when her father had stuck his head in the door to say there were sandwiches and drinks for them. Other than that, she'd stayed in there with him the whole time.

It hadn't escaped her, the irony, that of all the people in the house, she spent the most time with a serial killer that she was certain wanted her dead.

She could tell from her dad's face that he'd also picked up on this. But she wasn't going to let Hamilton out of her sight, not for one second.

He'd go back to jail, of that much she was certain; she'd never rest while he was free.

He'd meticulously planned this, manipulating her and making her indispensable to the investigation and building up her worth so that when he offered to do this, they'd listen to her and take the chance of letting him out. All the time he'd been doing that, he had someone on the outside, pulling the strings that would eventually lead to him being freed; she would have admired him if she hadn't known he was a monster.

She thought about what her dad said, about Hamilton and the murderer from Afghanistan. She'd always believed Hamilton had help but he'd been killing for years before then so it didn't make total sense to her. She'd wanted to talk to Hamilton in the hope he might give a hint as to where he was going, who his helpers were, what his plan was. She wanted to listen to what he had to say, and wanting to listen was a good thing because Hamilton wouldn't stop talking.

'So, you see, Dani, I just don't understand the whole "gender fluid" thing. If you're born with a penis, surely you're a man? And if you're born without one and you have a vagina, you're a woman. That's a definition. I mean the definition of male and female is that you are what you're born as, no? Now I'm not saying people don't want to change. I get that. I understand that if you're born a man, but you feel like you're a woman, you could feel trapped in that body. And do you know what? Good. That's fine, you go and get a sex change. I understand that. I get it. And frankly, it's no one's business but theirs. So, I understand that: man to woman, woman to man, born as a man, become a woman. That I get. But what does gender fluid mean, Dani? How can you be something in between one of those two things? Surely gender is binary – the ultimate binary. You're either the one: the one that fucks, or the zero: the one that gets fucked. But if you're fluid, if you're gender fluid, do you fuck, or do you get fucked, Dani? I don't understand it.'

She rolled her eyes and turned away from him.

He'd been trying to bait her for over an hour, discussing various topics, the same ones that he always seemed to want to discuss: feminism, sexism and gender identity – it seemed no one could tell a woman how to do feminism quite like a man who'd spent thirty years killing them.

'Some people just want to be happy, Chris. Gender's defined by societal norms; sex is related to the reproductive function. These people know what sex they are, but at different times they feel like different genders. They understand how they feel and they should be able to do whatever they want; it doesn't hurt anyone else.'

He was nodding emphatically. 'Yes, yes, I'm not complaining that people want to change. All I'm saying is I don't understand it. You know, I'm happy they can do as they please, I couldn't care less. But for instance, Dani, let me put a conundrum to you, something that has bothered me for some time: how is a killer to know?'

He paused and tried to raise an eyebrow, but the swelling prevented it and made his face look contorted.

'You know I always favoured women. I've killed men. I've tried lots of things, but women were always my favourite. But if I were to find a woman, take her back to wherever I used to do that sort of thing and then find out that she didn't consider herself to be a woman, how would I approach that situation? Do I carry on, because she's a woman to me and because I believe gender is binary? Or do I accept that she's gender fluid and that what I'm doing is actually not what I set out to do, and actually, I'm being forced to do some experimentation that's not of my choosing? Do you see the problem? Would I be the victim in that case?'

Dani looked at him, noting once again another idle confession that he was a killer, but also noting that he'd given nothing extra away.

'How do you make people do this, Chris?' she asked, interrupting him. 'Really? You don't have any friends and you never did. How have you managed to do all of this from inside the prison? Tell me the truth about that at least. If you're going to win and walk free, then what difference would it make?'

He stopped and stared at her, his eyes suddenly serious. 'I may have exaggerated our relationship when I said "friend",' he began, tilting his head from side to side as though weighing up semantics. 'Has your dad come clean?'

Dani nodded. 'I think so. You kept proof of what happened in Afghanistan, the fact they changed their stories and lied to cover up a war crime?'

His smile was so broad that Dani realised he had actually lost a tooth near the back of his mouth when Jimmy had beaten him.

'Of course I did, Dani,' he said. 'When I heard their story, I knew that there was an exemplary person out there – one of a kind – a real practitioner, and I knew he needed to be protected. So, yes, I assisted a little, got a close friend to take some lovely pictures of you and did what needed to be done.'

Dani couldn't help shaking her head, though she knew her disapproval meant nothing to him.

'Don't judge me, Dani,' he said. 'Judge them.' He gestured to the door and her father and the others behind it. 'Judge how easily they allowed their own welfare to outweigh the greater good.'

'They did it for their families,' said Dani.

'They did it for themselves,' he said, his tone incredulous. 'So they wouldn't have to live with the guilt and responsibility for the death of their loved ones. If any one of them had stood up and done the right thing, how many more people would be alive now? I'd be willing to bet that my friend has killed literally hundreds. He's insatiable, brutal, violent and thorough; I seriously doubt he'll ever be caught, and certainly not taken alive. At this time, I doubt anyone is even investigating him, but your father could have saved hundreds of lives, instead he chose to save just three – and you think I'm the monster.'

He'd been brazen this past hour, the outside world seeming to energise him, as though the victory he'd had so far was beyond contestation and he'd remain free forever, but now his confidence seemed to have jumped to a new level.

'What your dad did, these past few days, the act of freeing me, he could have said no, gone to the police and told them everything, couldn't he?'

Hamilton waited and watched her, the faux-joviality now gone and replaced by arrogant anger.

Dani didn't respond.

'You know he could. He'd likely have gone to prison, maybe been killed by Jimmy in order to protect the businesses. He'd certainly have had to live in the knowledge that you, Charlie, her unborn child and his new whore-wife would all die, but he could have done the right thing and I wouldn't have been free. Remember this, Dani, there's shades of evil in this world and not all are easy to see, but the very worst shade of them all, the barely perceptible one, is selfishness, and all of those bastards out there have it in abundance.'

'Do you know what?' said Dani. 'Maybe Jimmy should have just killed you today.'

'We'll both be glad he didn't,' said Hamilton, smiling again.

She stood up and walked from the room without looking back.

The door was shutting behind her just as a scream broke the silence of the night and made her heart stop.

It was blood-curdling, echoing around the farmhouse.

Dani turned back and opened the door to Hamilton's room. He smiled at her and shrugged.

A thump came from across the kitchen and Dani looked around to see her father.

'Dani,' he said, pointing at her. 'With me. Now.'

He walked to her quickly, reached down and grabbed her by the arm, then hauled her out of the kitchen.

She resisted, tried to shake herself free, but he was a big man with a firm grip and no intention of letting go.

'Get off me. Third and last time,' said Dani, grabbing his hand and digging her nails into his flesh.

'You can hate me later when you're alive to do it,' he said, and dragged her along the hallway, pushing her into the room she'd first woken up in.

Dani stumbled into the room, turned around and went to take a swing for her dad, but he blocked it easily.

'Stay in here,' he said. 'Please. It's the safest room in the house. Those windows have bars on the outside and the only way in is through that door. I'll be on the other side of it. I won't let anyone hurt you. You need to know, when this all started again, I got sent more pictures, some of you, some of Charlie, some of the scans she had done of the baby. He demanded that he get to speak with you, and we've done that, so stay in here now and let me keep you safe, OK?'

He turned to leave. 'I'm going to lock it behind me.'

'Dad,' Dani said. 'I won't stay in here, whatever it is, let me face it with you.'

Another scream pierced the night, this one closer than the last.

He shook his head. 'I can't lose you. I told your mum before she died that I'd do anything to protect you, anything at all.'

'If you try to lock me in here, you'll lose me forever,' Dani said.

She stared at him for a long moment and then walked back to the door and held it open for him.

There were sounds outside now, a vehicle driving on

rough ground, and Dani followed her dad back into the kitchen.

Jimmy and Marcus were there.

'We've got him,' said Jimmy, pointing towards Hamilton's room. 'So let's end this here and now.'

Jimmy had a pistol and he readied it in his hand and looked to Marcus who did the same.

There was a knock at the door and Dani felt her dad's hand push her behind him a little bit.

Silence.

Then another knock.

Jimmy looked at Taz and then Marcus before shouting, 'Come in.'

The door opened, and Dani instantly recognised the man who'd forced his way into her house.

He stepped inside. 'Got some deliveries for you,' he said and turned to take something from outside, just near the door.

He turned back and tossed a man's head on to the floor, then another and another.

'Five in all,' he said, wiping his hands on filthy jeans when he was done. 'He says to let you know that you shouldn't have brought them and that he's keeping their fingers. He said you'd understand.'

Dani was open-mouthed as she stared at Davis.

He had so much blood over him that he looked as though he'd been working in a butcher's shop. His clothes were so stained that it was hard to see where the fresh marks started, and the old ones finished.

'He says you need to put your weapons down on the table right now.'

Dani instinctively looked around the cottage. Jimmy had said he'd had it swept, but there must be some kind of camera for this man to know what was going on.

Then she saw the small camera.

It was body-worn and visible on Davis's chest.

'I don't think that's going to happen,' said Jimmy.

'Then you're all going to die,' Davis said, his voice robotic.

'I'll take you with me, Davey-boy,' said Jimmy, pointing his pistol at Davis's head.

Davis shrugged. 'I'm going to die anyway,' he said, the words soft but sure. 'And he only wants the prisoner. Put your weapons down and send him out, then you can all go home to your families.'

Dani had noticed Davis's voice change when he'd said he was going to die, as though it had been said without thinking, and then pause before he spoke the rest of the words. She looked at him again, finally seeing an earpiece tucked beneath his unkempt hair.

'He's in direct contact,' she said, motioning to Davis and reaching up slowly to tap her ear.

Davis nodded. 'He says that you have until he counts to five. He says that the last one to put down their weapon loses their daughter first.'

'You'll never fucking find her,' said Jimmy, stretching his neck and staring at Davis down the barrel of his pistol.

Davis paused. 'She's at her aunt's villa on the Costa del Sol,' he said.

The blood drained from Jimmy's face.

'Last chance,' said Davis.

'Davis is unarmed,' said Taz, his voice cutting into the tension as he spoke to Jimmy. 'This other guy could be anywhere. Put the guns down and send Hamilton out.'

Jimmy slowly lowered his pistol and Marcus did the same.

'I'll get him,' Dani said, but her dad immediately stopped her.

She allowed it, watching as he held up his hands and slowly turned so the camera on Davis's belt could see he was unarmed. Then he walked to Hamilton's room and opened the door. He undid the ties around Hamilton's ankles.

'You. Out,' he said.

Dani watched her father step aside as Hamilton limped past him and walked towards the door. She felt the urge to scream, to claw at him, to pull him back, but no one there would be any use dead.

Hamilton didn't look up as he walked past, he just headed quietly for the door, stopping when he reached Jimmy.

'My cuffs please, Jimmy?' he said, his voice bright.

Jimmy reached into his pocket and pulled out the key, tossing it to Davis.

Hamilton followed the keys, waited while Davis picked them up, and then turned his back to let Davis access his wrists.

It meant he was now facing the room.

He smiled broadly at Dani as Davis fumbled behind him and freed his hands.

'That does feel better,' Hamilton said.

Dani watched as Hamilton stretched, hunching his shoulders forward and hugging himself tight. Then he stretched his neck and back, leaning as far back as he could and forcing his shoulder blades together, his hands behind his back as they had been before.

When he finally brought his hands in front of him it took Dani a moment to realise what was different.

Time seemed to slow.

Hamilton had a pistol and he turned it in a single movement towards Jimmy.

Behind him, another figure was filling the doorway, a rifle raised as he advanced through in a tactical stance, his face covered by a thin nylon mask that distorted his features.

Dani watched, saw the smile spread wide across Hamilton's face as he pulled the trigger and shot Jimmy twice in the gut. Jimmy collapsed to the floor, his own pistol dropping unused beside him.

Hamilton turned his weapon on Marcus.

The second figure had fully entered the room now and trained his rifle in the direction of Dani and her dad.

'Well, this has been fun,' said Hamilton. 'Very tense. Dani, come over to me, please.'

Taz stepped forward and raised his hands. 'You got what you wanted. You're free. You got to speak to her. That's it.'

Hamilton turned towards her dad, his weapon following, and smiled. 'I'm a fucking serial killer, Taz. Until everyone I could ever want to be dead, is dead, then I don't have what I want. Dani, with me, please. Now.'

Dani paused, her heart racing. She saw her father move and then heard another gunshot as Hamilton pulled the trigger again.

Her father seemed to jolt, as though he'd been hit by lightning, but he didn't go down, he went forward, rushing towards Hamilton, until the second and third shots sounded, and he crumpled to the floor.

'Unnecessary,' said Hamilton, his voice only just audible as the gunshots still rang in the air.

Dani was frozen in place.

'They're not dead, Dani,' Hamilton said, smiling at her. 'Gut-shots, they'll bleed for a while first. Anyway, I don't want them dead, not yet. I have a little karma for you all. Especially you, Jimmy.'

Hamilton looked over to where Jimmy was bleeding on the ground, clutching an ever-growing patch of dark wet blood on his stomach.

'William?' Hamilton called.

Another figure appeared in the doorway, tall but painfully thin, his face hidden by a hooded top.

Dani's senses were overloaded.

There were too many things going on and she looked from one face to the next and then crouched down next to her dad.

'Dani!' shouted Hamilton. 'With me, now, or the next one goes in his head.'

She stood and walked slowly away from her dad, looking back as he blinked and clutched his wound.

'You'll remember William Knight, Dani,' said Hamilton. 'William, take down your hood, please.'

Dani watched as he did, and she saw the word that had been burnt into his forehead during the years he'd been held captive by Jimmy Nash – the letters made from cigarette burns spelled out RAPIST.

'William, I believe you may have a score to settle with Jimmy.'

Hamilton nodded to the other armed man who passed Knight a long knife.

'Make it slow, won't you?' said Hamilton.

Knight took the blade, his eyes never leaving Jimmy, and nodded.

'Very slow,' Knight said, and knelt down near to Jimmy, watching him, his eyes running over the man's body and stopping at the expanding stain on his abdomen.

'Right, Davis will stay here to make sure the rest of you don't follow, but it's been an absolute pleasure. Thank you all for your help and I hope that we never meet again, for your sakes more than mine.'

Hamilton gestured to Dani to come closer and began to move out of the room.

'Caleb, let's go,' he said, and the armed man began to walk backwards, following them out through the door.

There was a roar and Dani flinched as her father burst to his feet and charged at the door.

She saw Marcus moving now too.

They headed for Hamilton and for a moment it was a melee.

Dani kicked out at Caleb's knee and swiped at his rifle, trying to push it up so that the arc of fire would be above the heads of those around her. Before she could get closer, she was knocked, hard, and she fell to the floor. She looked up to see it was Marcus who'd done it.

He stopped for a second, making eye contact, and then was gone, moving quickly towards her father.

Dani looked down and realised something was on top of her. As he'd pushed her over, Marcus had thrust her rucksack hard against her.

She grabbed it out of instinct and looked around.

Her father and Marcus were fighting with Caleb, the three of them crowding the door.

Hamilton must have been pushed outside.

'Run,' she heard her father shout, though she wasn't sure if it was directed at her. 'Run!' he shouted again.

The fight moved outside, and Dani quickly lost sight of her father and Marcus as they disappeared into the darkness. She looked across, could see Jimmy struggling with Knight, and she stood quickly, taking a long pace towards them, swinging her rucksack at Knight's hand, knocking the knife to the floor. She took another step and kicked out hard, catching him square in the face.

The crunch of bone and tendon travelled through her leather boots and then she saw him roll to the floor, but she was already turning away, heading for the door.

There was shouting and more gunfire, but before she could get there, a sudden silence fell.

She stopped, unsure of what to do, then Hamilton

appeared in the doorway. He still had his pistol, but his face was bleeding again, and he looked to be in pain.

'Let him go,' he shouted over his shoulder.

It was a moment later when Caleb arrived back at the door, also bloodied and panting.

'He's gone,' Caleb said, and Dani immediately picked up on his accent – American, but she couldn't place it more precisely.

Dani smiled at Hamilton.

'Oh, not your dad, Dani,' said Hamilton, watching her closely and beginning to smile. 'He'd never escape while you were still here. No, I shot him again. He's outside, dead. The other one got away, used your dad as a human shield and legged it into the trees, fucking coward. No matter, though, I think Caleb got a shot into him and we'll be long gone by the time he's able to do anything.'

Dani rushed to the door, a feeling of nausea weakening her, making every step feel as though it might be the last one she had the strength to take. As she reached the threshold, she saw a large dark shape lying on the gravel in the near-darkness, an even darker shadow spreading out slowly around it.

'Dad?' she said, but before she could move any closer, she saw Hamilton twist sharply and reach towards her.

Dani dodged and spun round, stepping away, and as he followed, she kicked out. For the second time that week, she aimed for the groin and hit her mark.

He howled and charged towards her.

She managed to avoid the first few strikes. Then she saw the barrel of the pistol just before it impacted against her temple.

Chapter 35

She heard voices as she came to, her eyes opening slowly as she began to regain consciousness.

One side of her face was numb. It took her a second to realise it and she instinctively tried to reach for it, only then becoming aware that her wrists were bound to the bed she was lying on.

There was a moment when she sought to understand whether this was a dream or reality, and she tried to raise up her knees before she realised that they too were tied.

The panic and returning memories rushed in. She felt herself lurching up and down on the bed, pulling at her hands and kicking with her legs. But she felt no change, no give at all, and as she looked around the room, she tried to steady her breathing and take back control.

She must have passed out again.

It was the only explanation, because this time when she awoke, she knew instantly she was bound to the bed, and she stretched her neck, looking up to confirm it.

Her throat was dry and her face was sore. But this time she lay silently, listening.

281

It was there, she could hear it, the quiet sound of people mumbling.

Someone was talking nearby, maybe a room or flat next door, but not far.

She heard some words and recognised the voice.

Hamilton was outside the room. He was talking with the man he called Caleb.

In a flash, the series of events came to her.

She remembered the fight at the cottage and her father's motionless body on the driveway.

The door opened, and she saw Christopher Hamilton stick his head around the door.

'Well hello there, Sleeping Beauty,' he said, coming into the room and switching on the light. 'I heard you wake up earlier, but I thought it best to leave you where you were until the panic passed. I mean, I know it's not the first time you've woken up tied to a bed . . .' He chuckled and raised his eyebrows, as though waiting for Dani to join in.

She didn't.

'Awkward,' he said, pursing his lips. 'I feel like my favourite girl just left me hanging there. Anyway, I didn't want to be here to have to deal with all the emotional stuff you women feel in a moment of panic like that. I'm sure that kind of thing goes deep into your most primal fears; no place for a man. I hope you understand.'

Dani watched him as he walked into the room, limping, and sat down next to her on the mattress.

He sat so that his lower back touched her thigh.

She recoiled from his touch and moved away as far as her bonds would allow.

'I'm really sorry about your face,' he continued. 'But, you know, I could tell you were going to work yourself up into a bit of a state . . .'

He paused, then reached out to touch her cheek.

Dani steeled herself, refusing to flinch.

'I honestly think your attack on me was completely unnecessary, by the way. I don't like touching myself, I've been honest about that in my letters, but I'd like to have the option, and right now I can barely go pee pee.'

He ran his hand along the line of her jaw.

'In my defence, though, I did pistol-whip you like they do in the films, which was kind of cool.'

Dani was silent, watching how the expressions on his face changed as he spoke. It was as though he rehearsed every word.

'I think we also have to take into account when you stabbed me with my own garden shears and, while I accept that's water under the bridge now, I'm someone who always likes to get even,' he said, holding out his hand as though offering to shake.

He looked up, as if seeing her hands wrapped in rope for the first time.

'Let's just call that a gentleman's agreement, shall we?'

She watched him as he moved slightly back on the bed again, just enough so his back was touching her, but her bonds were now at their limit and she had no choice but to lie there, feeling her thigh warm up against his body.

'So, Dani,' he said, 'I'm also sorry about your father, let me just say that right now. I want you to know that I really wouldn't have killed him. Jimmy was going to die for sure, but William was going to do that, and Jimmy was a horrible and cruel man, so I would have felt justified, and not a little poetic, in orchestrating their showdown. But Davis was just going to babysit the others until we were gone. I suspect he'd have killed himself afterwards to be honest, Davis was never the most stable of men. It really doesn't matter now, because your father broke his neck in all the kerfuffle.'

Hamilton raised an eyebrow. 'Had the potential for a horrible degree of violence, did your father,' he said. 'But despite his failings, I want it to be on record that The Mighty Taz didn't have to die. Got it? So, no need for hard feelings about that one, OK?'

He smiled and rested his palm on her stomach as he looked at her, then he readjusted, dipping his finger beneath her top and sliding his hand underneath, resting it against the flesh of her abdomen.

Dani shivered, fear washing over her as she tried hard not to react.

'Let me just lay this out for you, OK?' he said, settling down as though he were going to be talking for a while. 'First of all, I want you to know that I'm not going to kill you at the moment. I know that's what you must have thought when you woke up, and I can see why you might. I'm not hurt by that assumption, as I accept I do have a track record of doing just such things. But I want you to know that I, at this present juncture, have no plans to take your life. So I want to put your mind at ease about that right from the get-go.'

Dani looked at him but could say nothing.

'Now I'd also like to say that, ideally, I'm going to have to keep you in bonds for a little while and occasionally in small dark spaces. I'm afraid some things need to happen, due process, et cetera, et cetera. It's all very dull, but I'm a man of my word, and I want you to know I'll do my best to walk and water you as often as possible, so long as you try not to poop on the floor. I also promised I'd take you to the bodies. I promised you that and indeed I shall. So, I don't want you to worry about that either.'

He raised a finger towards her, as though he were a

teacher, emphasising the point that he was to be trusted; at the same time, his other hand slid an inch further up her stomach.

'Now, finally, I'd like to take you off the bed. You know, being tied down like that must make you feel very vulnerable. It must make you, in many real ways, feel uncomfortable. I mean, you couldn't even scratch your nose if you wanted to. So, what I'd like to do is free you now, and other times when I'm able to. But I'm going to need some assurances.'

He held up the forefinger of his free hand to emphasise the point. 'One: stay in this room unless you need to use the bathroom, in which case by all means knock and ask. And two.' A second digit joined the first. 'Do not try to escape. I haven't done a fire safety brief, which as your host is remiss of me, but I do feel duty bound to mention that the windows of this particular room are barred, and the door is locked. I'm going to need to know that you're not going to be a pest. If you can agree to those things, then I'm going to cut you free. You can move around the room, be comfortable, and I'll bring you in some sandwiches and cola.'

He smiled at her again. 'Now,' he said, their eyes meeting.

Dani realised that despite his joviality, he was deadly serious, his black eyes staring at her.

'One more thing,' he said, and reached into his back pocket, pulling out a letter. 'My letters. The envelopes were opened, so I assume you've read them?'

Dani nodded, remembering that Marcus had too. 'I've started,' she said, and swallowed hard.

'Well, here's the next exciting instalment. I wrote it for you, and I think it's what you want?'

He waited for an answer, but Dani didn't move.

'Well,' he continued, 'whether you know it or not, it is, and I may write more while we're together.'

He was grinning now, his eyes bright and excited.

'I don't mean to be dramatic, but I'll feed them to you hot off the press. It'll be like *Jackanory* – storytime with your old friend, Chris. So, you catch up with your reading and think of any questions, OK? It'll give you something to do to pass the time, and when it's time to go, I'll let you know.'

Hamilton leaned over and reached into his side pocket. The hand under Dani's top slid up another inch, touching her bra, as he did so.

Dani tensed and shivered.

He pulled out a folding knife with a wooden handle and withdrew his hand from under her top as he used both to open the blade.

Then he looked at her for a long time.

Dani couldn't help but feel that he wanted to run the blade over her skin and she stared at him, refusing to show the fear she was feeling.

He seemed to stop, indecisive, as though unsure whether to free her hands or feet first. After a few moments, he leaned towards her, his breath brushing past her ear, and reached for the bond on her right wrist.

'You can have your rucksack,' he whispered. 'A few of those bars you eat are in there along with some other bits. I noticed a sanitary product, but I don't think that's now, is it?'

He turned his head to look at her.

Dani continued to stare straight ahead to the ceiling.

'I always wondered if, because they practise regularly, women could bleed for longer than men and not die, but they can't. I checked.'

Dani shivered and clenched her jaw. Tears welled in her eyes and she hated them for being there.

He paused for a moment, close to her, and then snipped the bond on her wrist.

'I'm sure you'll understand,' he said, 'but I'll leave you to do the rest. I'll be out here if you want me, just knock. If you do need the bathroom, by all means, knock for that too. I'll take you and I promise I'll try not to peek.'

With that, he folded away the knife, stood up and left the room, pulling the door shut behind him.

Dani waited at first, listening, trying to hear the click of the lock, but there was none. Then, with her free hand, she began to undo the nylon cord that was holding her down, all the time glancing between the door and the letter that was balanced on her chest; the images of both becoming cloudy as tears flowed down her swollen face.

Chapter 36

Hamilton's Sixth Letter

Well, Dani,

As you'll be only too aware when you read this, things have changed considerably, and I can now be even more candid with you than before.

I know that you'd say I'm a stalker because, while smart, you're too blinded by your supposed knowledge to know any better. In truth, this isn't the case at all.

As I matured and grew, it became apparent to me that I have an enormous capacity for love; I'm a lover.

I fall head over heels and do so very quickly, and I can't help that I've always been afflicted by this weakness. I fall hard and fast, and I love completely with all I am. I do. I'll sacrifice almost anything to be closer to them. If I'm slighted or hurt or betrayed, then it's this love, not evil, that makes the pain cut so deeply. In many ways, Dani, I want you to know that I love you.

There's no doubt in my mind that I loved Jenny,

but those feelings were a pale shadow of what I felt for Chrissie Bainbridge.

She was there when I arrived at the station in Plymouth to take up my place in the Royal Navy and we were in the same division for the duration of our eight weeks of basic training, along with twenty-eight other recruits.

Dani, she was the most perfect female specimen I have ever laid eyes on.

I once heard another sailor say that if he were to do the dirty on his wife, then the girl would need to be worth it. Well, if I were to move on from Catherine and fall in love again, I'd found a girl that was more than worth it.

The relationship was not without its problems, though.

As you know, the females were housed in a separate block to the males and so we saw little of each other, and even during the day, we were busy running and marching and doing lectures. I tried to go and see her in the evenings but we were often kept apart.

I'd wait till all the others had fallen into bed exhausted and sneak out, hoping to snatch a moment with her.

Once I made it all the way into her mess deck, but she was too exhausted to speak and instead I watched her sleep for a while, touching her long hair and moving it away from her face when it looked as though it might itch and wake her up. I had to do all of this in absolute silence in case her mess-mates woke and saw us together.

Chrissie preferred to keep her distance during the day and I understood this completely. We spoke but kept it light and comfortable. We discussed what we might do when we finished basic training and what would become of us as we moved into the Royal Navy proper.

I knew I'd be happy to go wherever she did and do whatever she wanted to do. I was too besotted to realise the mistake I was making. I do not wish to ruin this tale for you, but to recap . . . I had, at only fifteen years of age, committed a perfect kill – two, in truth, anonymous and without trace. I was an apprentice needing only one more to be recognised as a fully qualified serial killer to the law's standards – I include the old man in my total, Dani, for the purpose of dramatic effect only, but I don't want to hear of him again.

Even now, as I look back, I can see I was ignoring my own rules. I knew I needed separation between myself and the object of my desire, but I was in love with a woman that was closely linked to me. Someone I spoke with daily.

This escalation was a dangerous one, especially in the closely observed environment of a naval training establishment.

Two weeks before the end of training, I was up late one night and reading through some of Chrissie's mail that had been left in her pigeon hole. I found correspondence from her mum, apologising that she and Chrissie's father would be unable to see her on the weekend of leave recruits are allowed at the end of basic training.

Her mum told her that the key to their home would be where it always was and there'd be food and some cash for her on the side.

Her uncle, a Chief Petty Officer at Portsmouth

Dockyard, had agreed to collect her on Monday morning and take her to HMS Sultan in Gosport, where she'd begin the next phase of her training. Her mother wished Chrissie all the love in the world and said she would see her soon.

I was elated.

A whole weekend.

I'll be honest, in that I hadn't told Chrissie how I felt about her, though we were very close and I knew she felt as I did.

This opportunity was perfect, a chance for us to spend time together in peace, away from all the others, for me to tell her how I felt. I didn't tell her that I'd found this clue.

I just planned our surprise weekend.

Chrissie's uncle had been at the passing out parade to watch her receive two separate awards for sports and academia.

I was pleased to have thrown some exam marks to let her have these confidence-boosting wins and I took my second-place prize with me on the train from Plymouth to Portsmouth, arriving at her house several hours before she was due.

Her uncle was driving her down and she'd said she'd stop for a drink with him before coming to the house.

I found the key after a short search of the front and back gardens and let myself in to her home. I placed the flowers I'd bought in the lounge and looked around.

Her room was as I expected, pink in colour and filled to the brim with teddies and soft toys and a pretty single bed in the corner.

I smiled as I went through her drawers and learned so many things about her.

The night drew on, and she didn't show.

I became concerned about her but still felt relaxed.

When it's right, it's right, and there's no need to feel jealous just because she wants a little time to unwind and celebrate her awards, even if the person that had gifted them to her was alone and waiting.

I was wired as the night stretched further, pacing around the house and watching the windows, praying for any sign of her, and when I finally saw her approach, there was a swagger and a stagger in her step as she weaved her way up the path to the front door. I was certain she would have fallen flat on her backside, had she been alone.

They entered the house in a blur of light, noise and giggles, each one like a knife driving into my stomach. I sat on the double bed in her parents' room and listened to them have another drink downstairs. Their conversation wasn't sexy or playful as they thought it sounded, but cheap and vulgar, far beneath her.

When they ascended the stairs, I had no choice but to hide.

I crawled under the king-size bed in her parents' room, planning to slip out and away once they were asleep in hers.

But they didn't go to her room and to my utter revulsion, they tumbled into her parents' room, the light shining brightly, and collapsed on to the mattress only inches above me.

I then lay, as the light was turned out, and listened to the woman I loved being fucked like a beast, again and again, only a foot away from where I lay, the springs occasionally stretching down to kiss my cheek and wipe away the tears that fell.

She did everything he wanted her to, and she did it willingly, moaning in what could only have been faked pleasure as he took her in position after position until she was pre-empting him, doing what she thought he'd want, pleasing him she was working hard for a tip.

I lay awake all night, even as they slept, until I had no more tears left inside me.

He woke first and left quietly at around seven in the morning.

I watched his feet hit the carpet and wished I had a knife to slice through his bare Achilles. Then I watched as he dressed and padded down the stairs.

She didn't even stir as the front door slammed shut.

I eased myself out from under the bed and stood to watch her. I was bursting for the toilet having waited all night, and as I looked down on her near perfect features, I felt that I wanted to mark her. I felt like I could see him on her and inside her. I could smell him in the room, and I knew he would be in her womb and her belly.

The desire in me was so strong, animalistic, I wanted to take her, to fill her with more powerful, better seed – to fuck the other man out of her. It was a strange want for me because physical intercourse was seldom something I actually fantasised about.

When her eyes fluttered open, and she saw me standing there watching, when her eyelids went wide, and her pupils dilated, we both knew exactly what she'd done.

But this isn't about the gore, Dani, we've agreed that already, and no one wants to read torture porn.

It's also worth bearing in mind that Chrissie's fate was well covered by the media during my trial, though it was all speculation.

This is, however, about me, it was always about me. This was about a young man who went from nothing to the peak of his game in too short a time period, like a young boxer who hits his prime but is then ruined by the glory.

The trail between myself and Chrissie was writ clear, and here I stood now, looking down on her disembowelled torso with all manner of things hanging out of it. And I was lost. I'd fallen from grace. I knew I'd need to try and cover my tracks; fire was my only real option for what good it would do.

I had no alibi for the night before and no one to vouch for me.

I was in trouble. I sat down on the bed and put my head in my hands, feeling lost and regretful.

I don't wish for your pity, though it may worry you to know I considered suicide at that point. I was sitting there alone, and I considered hanging myself and being done with all of it. I would've been one of the greatest unsung heroes of our age. No one would have known what I'd accomplished.

I simply couldn't do it.

I couldn't deprive myself of the opportunity for redemption, of the chance to prove to myself that I could do better.

Chrissie had beguiled me and made me do this, made me act on impulse, and I accepted that now.

The times ahead for me wouldn't be easy, I knew that, as I lit a candle in the bedroom next to her, kissed her on the forehead and then went downstairs to snap her parents' gas line to the cooker.

As I prepared to leave in the afternoon sun, I knew I'd need to make changes to survive and develop. I also knew I'd need to plan to run.

What I didn't know, Dani, was that I was being watched.

Chapter 37

'I hope the accommodation's everything you'd have expected,' said Hamilton as he came into the room.

Dani wasn't sure how long it had been since the last time. She had no way of measuring time, but she was sure she could still feel his warm hand on her skin, as though it had left a greasy mark on her. The sight of him made her shiver.

He'd knocked and waited before he'd entered, and the deference he was giving Dani made her feel uncomfortable and wary.

'Any thoughts on my letters so far?' he asked. 'I try to write them in such a way that you'll find it easy to understand the points I make. Do you feel as though you have a greater insight into what makes me tick?'

Dani watched him carefully. He was still walking a little uncertainly, and she was sure she was responsible for the discomfort he was feeling. He also didn't come near her, instead choosing to sit on the floor at the furthest point in the room away in the exact same way as she'd done with him back at the farm.

She constantly felt braced for violence.

'To be honest, Chris, I think they're a little overwritten. And I know you apparently tried your hardest not to be fanciful but, I have to say, just a tiny bit of preening has slipped through the edit.'

She watched his face, trying to read his reaction, but he just smiled.

'Yes, I knew some would. I think it's just in my nature.'

'Or in your nurture?' said Dani, watching as she made him smile again.

They sat in silence for a few moments, each looking at the other.

'So, you left the last one on a bit of a cliff-hanger,' said Dani. 'You're being watched. Is it safe to assume that your friend outside is the one who was watching you?'

Hamilton laughed out loud. 'And you made it as a detective,' he said, shaking his head as though this was the funniest thing he'd ever heard.

'I think you're lying about Chrissie Bainbridge,' Dani said. 'I don't know why you're trying to claim a murder that wasn't you, but you were nowhere near Portsmouth when that attack happened.'

'So the evidence shows, Dani,' Hamilton said. 'What good would a cover-up be if I was linked to the crime?'

She watched him carefully, remembering how she'd reviewed the Bainbridge files herself after she'd caught him. He was never even a suspect in that murder. He'd been in Plymouth still and there were multiple witnesses. The only reason it had come up at all during the investigation was because one of the papers had tried to form a tenuous link because the two had known each other.

Dani was ninety-nine percent sure he was lying; before she'd read that letter, she would have been one hundred.

'OK,' she said. 'So, who sent you the pictures of me as a child that you used to blackmail my dad?' Mentioning him sent a wave of grief through her that might have floored her at any other time, but she needed to be strong now. 'You could just tell me now. It wasn't Davis, because he was there. It can't really have been Knight, could it?'

Hamilton shifted around on the floor for a few moments and then looked at her. 'No, not Knight,' he said. 'You know it's not as comfortable on the floor as I thought it would be. Would you throw me a pillow to sit on? I promise I won't fluff on it.'

Dani grabbed one of the pillows from next to where she was sitting and threw it across the room, watching as it landed at Hamilton's feet.

He dragged it beneath him, nestled into it like a cat going to bed, and then leaned back against the wall again.

'So why doesn't he just kill you?' asked Dani, nodding out towards the other room where she assumed Caleb was waiting. 'He's obviously not a friend.'

Hamilton shrugged. 'A mixture of reasons, maybe,' he said. 'I saved him from almost certain prosecution and imprisonment, so he owes me for that. It didn't take me long with the resources available to me to find out which units were operating out there at that time. After that, I just had to let him know that he'd messed up and that I'd cleaned it up for him. He knew I'd make sure that the evidence that would have seen him locked up never made it further than my eyes...' He let the words hang out.

'You became his mentor too?' asked Dani. 'You looked after him and taught him your ways? Is that right?'

Hamilton furrowed his brow as though giving it genuine thought before he spoke. 'Stop blurting things out and guessing, Dani. It doesn't suit you and it makes you come across as thicker than you actually are.'

He gave her a hard look before continuing. 'And, no, I wasn't a mentor to him, just a kindred spirit, somebody who could respect someone else's calling and encourage him to do it well without feeling that his success in any way diminished mine.'

'So how did this American help you get rid of bodies in the UK?' asked Dani, unable to hide the disgust in her voice.

It infuriated her how casually Hamilton discussed people being hurt, killed or taken from their families. He seemed to be immune to thoughts about what he left behind – the hurt, the pain, the loss.

He discussed killing, and wrote about it, with the same flippancy that people talked about losing small change.

She'd known Chris Hamilton for several years and he'd always been arrogant and aloof, but the letters he'd sent her and the way he was speaking now, were more than just arrogance.

It was as though he was so sure of himself and his actions that he was openly taunting her, daring her to try and challenge him and all he'd accomplished to get to this point.

Hamilton laughed. 'Oh Dani, blurting again! And you really don't listen. Caleb's a friend of sorts. We kept in touch, and he felt he owed me a favour.'

'Ah, sorry,' she said. 'So, he's not the one who helped with the bodies. He's just here now because you have something over him. Don't you?'

Hamilton shrugged again.

'Don't you worry that he'll just kill you? That maybe he's starting to think you don't have any proof about what happened in Kandahar?'

Hamilton tilted his head slightly.

'Daddy was honest in his last hours then. That's good. But anyone who deliberately comes into Caleb's orbit and who likes their fingers, would do well to have some concrete insurance. We have an agreement and I'll honour it, as he's doing.'

'And what you have on my dad,' she said, 'it's the same? So you were using that one thing over all of them?'

Hamilton frowned and looked at her carefully. 'Well, he's dead, Dani, Jimmy too, so only Marcus would be affected over here. But you're right, it's the same thing and I won't put the Afghanistan information in the public domain just out of badness, because it would impact Caleb too. That info falls into my agreement with him.'

'Who tried to have you killed in prison?' Dani asked.

Hamilton beamed. 'A very old friend.'

'Tell me who it was,' she said.

'I will,' said Hamilton. 'I promise you, in good time, I will.'

'Was it the friend who helped you conceal your victims' bodies? Is it the same person who was watching you?'

Hamilton stood up. 'You are inquisitive,' he said. Dani wasn't sure whether he'd just answered her question or not and she made to ask again, but he raised a hand and spoke before she could.

'Get some rest,' he said, heading for the door. 'We'll be going soon.'

Chapter 38

She was clutching her torn clothes to her chest, aware of the freezing air touching her as she ran at full pace towards safety. She didn't know if she heard him order the men after her, or if her mind had added that to give impetus to her escape, but she heard the sound of shoes on stone as she was pursued.

A hand gripped her shoulder, pulled her back, turning her away from the safety of the trees.

Dani allowed it, allowed herself to be turned, but only for a moment . . .

Then she was running again. She broke the treeline as though it were the ribbon at the end of a race, but someone else was coming, a different pursuer . . . she couldn't stop to look back, didn't want to know what had happened to the man who'd grabbed her . . .

Dani's eyes opened wide the second she felt the warmth of someone's hand touch her arm. She heard a gasp and knew it had come from her.

She was disorientated in the dark and turned on her side to push herself away from the hand, moving until the wall that ran along the back of the bed stopped her retreat.

'Dani, it's me. It's Chris.'

'It's dark,' said Dani, feeling her breath start to quicken as a panic grew in her chest.

'Ah yes,' said Hamilton, his voice thoughtful and concerned. 'I popped in after you fell asleep and turned out the lights for you. I'd forgotten you're not too keen on the dark. Let me fix this.'

The mattress moved as he stood up and she heard him walk across the room to the door.

Within a moment the light was on, and the room was bright.

Dani blinked as she waited for her eyes to adjust.

'The time's come for us to leave this place,' said Hamilton, speaking from the door. 'I got you a croissant for breakfast, but time's at a premium and I'm afraid you'll have to have it cold.'

Dani licked her lips, not at the mention of food, but because her mouth was so dry, and her lips felt cracked.

'Just water, please,' she said.

Hamilton nodded and walked quickly across, dropping a bottle of mineral water on to her bed with a small bow.

'Grab your stuff and put your shoes on,' he said. 'Use the bathroom before we go, because we won't be stopping unless we have to, or unless I need a cheese burger.'

He smiled and made to leave, but then stopped.

'Don't you think I'd make a great parent?' he said, turning back to Dani and smiling. 'Don't you think I've got all this stuff down? Go to the toilet. Pack your stuff. Get your shoes on. Honestly, with more shouting and screaming, and maybe the odd expletive thrown in for good measure, I think I'd make somebody the perfect father.'

He smiled at her again, a broad, beaming grin. 'Maybe

you and I together . . .' he said, raising a questioning eyebrow at her.

'I'd rather die,' said Dani.

'After the nine-month gestation period, you could do just that,' he said and left the room.

Dani took a moment to calm her breathing and licked her lips again. She felt panicked, not only about how she'd been woken up but the fact she'd been able to sleep at all. She had no watch and no phone and no idea what time it was, where she was or where she was going. She checked the bottle, made sure it had an intact seal, and then opened it and drank about a third in one go. Then she pulled her shoes on and tied them tight, ready to run and fight if she got even a sniff of a chance.

Her backpack was on the floor next to her bed, but she had no other stuff with her that wasn't already in there, except the seventh letter, which she dropped into the laptop compartment at the back.

There was a knock at the door, but this time it opened immediately afterwards, and she saw Caleb enter.

He was wearing the same thin, stocking-like face covering and had an individually wrapped croissant in his hand. He stopped a few paces inside the door, tossed it underarm on to the bed and turned immediately to leave.

'Caleb,' Dani whispered, taking another swig from the bottle as she tried to catch him before he shut the door.

He turned to look at her, his face distorted and expressionless beneath the mask.

She paused, unsure of what she'd wanted to say. For a moment, she felt glad that he continued to hide his face from her, because it meant that on some level he still considered that she might be able to identify him, and to do that, there must still be a chance she'd be released alive.

He was still watching, not moving. Maybe he thought she'd beg him to help her, that together they'd be able to take Hamilton down and back to jail. But there was something about this man's eyes, even through the thin mask, that told her she had little chance of assistance from him.

'Do you know where we're going?' she asked, hoping to get him talking and gauge his reaction.

He nodded.

'Can you tell me?'

He shook his head.

'Can you speak?'

He nodded again.

'Then why don't you?' said Dani, asking a question she hoped couldn't be answered with either a nod or a shake of the head.

He shrugged.

'Can you help me?' she asked, her voice quieter than before, her eyes meeting his.

He smiled at her, a broad smile that showed large white teeth, and then shook his head.

'I think I could help you,' Dani whispered.

He stood looking at her, saying nothing.

'The proof he has of what you did in Kandahar, the crimes you committed out there? It's the same as he used to blackmail my dad and the others who rescued him from the convoy, but it's going to come to light very soon. It won't take long for people to figure out who you are. You'll be found.'

She was speaking quickly and quietly, trying to get as much out as possible in a short time.

'But think of this, if he'd had to use the information from Afghanistan to punish my dad, he'd have had to throw you to the wolves at the same time, regardless of whether you'd kept your word or not. There's no way out of this for you, but if you help me, if you stop him and let me go free, then that will count for something. You know it will.'

A small flicker of a frown crossed Caleb's face, but it could have meant anything, and Dani pressed on.

'Caleb, he's only got one hand and he's massively overplayed it. Help me and I promise I'll help you.'

They looked at each other for a few moments.

'What are you two kids talking about?' said Hamilton. He bustled into the room. 'I mean, don't get me wrong, it's great that you're making friends but we really do need to get going. We have a very long journey ahead of us.'

'Where are we going?' asked Dani, now looking at Hamilton.

'We're going to the bodies,' he said, without missing a beat. 'But it's a long drive, and we really need to drive at night. So we're going now.'

Dani felt a sudden surge of fear, as though she'd known this room was safe and that she wouldn't die here, but now there was only uncertainty again.

'Are you going to kill me, Chris?' she asked, fixing him with a stare, challenging him.

But Hamilton smiled at her. 'If I was going to kill you, Dani, I'd have already done it. Caleb here wanted to do all sorts of horrible things to you last night, but he didn't because I asked him not to.'

Caleb nodded and grinned. He reached down to his belt, to the scabbard of a large knife that hung there, and withdrew it just a few inches. With his other hand, he reached across and nicked his thumb on the revealed section of the blade, then put the bloody thumb into his mouth.

Dani watched as he wiped the blood on to the tip of his tongue and showed it to her before he swallowed it.

'To be honest,' said Hamilton, 'Caleb and I had to stop

talking about you. I thought he was going to work himself up into a frenzy and that he'd simply reach a point where I couldn't stop him, but I like your fingers where they are.'

'I thought fingers were your thing, Chris?' Dani asked, playing for time.

'Not me. The idea originated from Caleb. It was all his work, I just stole it for a little while. Fingers are so small and easy to keep, they're very individual and defined by the fingerprint, but as much as I like to know there are trophies, it was never really my bag. Anyway, I digress.'

Hamilton turned and patted Caleb on the shoulder. 'I think you showed marvellous restraint last night, my friend. Don't you agree, Dani?'

Dani felt sick as she saw Caleb's smile and the way his eyes moved over her body.

When the convoy was attacked, she'd been frightened. She'd seen what was happening around her, but there was something in the back of her mind that told her she'd be OK, that it had been planned so that people wouldn't get hurt.

In the farm, when she'd heard that man screaming, and the bullets had started flying, she'd been too pumped on adrenaline to consciously acknowledge the fear.

When she'd woken up in this room, she'd felt fear, but there had been some part of her that seemed to know she wouldn't come to any harm while she was in this place. She had no idea how she knew that, but she did.

Now, as she sat on the bed and watched Caleb licking blood from his thumb, while Hamilton approached her ready to carry her rucksack out to their car, she felt as though she was going to vomit. She felt weak, hungry, light-headed and nauseated all at the same time as she thought about the sheer hatred that Jimmy and her dad had set free – two cold-blooded killers, two men with the coldest blood there was.

The light in the room seemed to dim for a few moments and before she knew what was happening, Hamilton was moving towards her.

He held her up, put his arm around her shoulder and lifted the bottle of water to her lips.

'Take a drink,' he said. 'You're tired and probably dehydrated. I blame myself, really, I should have encouraged you to drink more clear fluids.'

Dani choked a little bit on the first mouthful and then tried to swallow.

'You look faint,' said Hamilton, reaching around and putting his hand on the back of her neck, massaging it gently as he felt how hot she was.

'Need to lie down,' said Dani, trying to breathe in through her nose and out through her mouth, trying to regain some control.

'We really don't have very much time, Dani, and I think you're going to need to keep your fluids up.'

He held the bottle to her lips again, tipping small drops into her mouth.

She pushed it away.

'What did you give me?' she asked, looking up as she slumped against him.

He grinned at her, and then at Caleb, like a child whose prank had been discovered.

'Just something to help you sleep,' he said, 'now drink up.'

Dani wanted to fight, but she was already drifting away.

Chapter 39

She tried to open her eyes, but her lids were so heavy that, at first, she just couldn't do it. She was awake, but her body was fighting it, trying to convince her to settle back into a restful sleep.

There was something inside her, though, something that was screaming that she needed to open her damn eyes and pay attention to where she was.

She made a conscious effort to force her eyelids open, reaching up with her hands from where she was lying in the foetal position.

Her hands were tied together in front of her and she was in near pitch blackness.

She tried to stretch out but couldn't. She was in some kind of very small, cold and confined area.

As her senses started to return, she recognised a steady noise around her, light vibration and then the sound of passing vehicles. She was in the boot of a car.

The panic started to rise.

She couldn't tell whether her eyes were open or closed, couldn't see her hands properly in front of her face, and she quickly realised there was something attaching them to a point on the floor.

The scream arrived before she even realised it was brewing and she had a moment of uncontrolled panic, where she kicked and thrashed, shouted and screamed, and did everything she possibly could to free herself.

It did no good. The bonds were tight and, as the panic subsided, she tried to work at the ties with her teeth. But they were solid, hurting her mouth as she bit them, and she knew it was going to make no difference.

More sounds started to creep into her consciousness.

She could hear a radio, something local, and then shortly after that the sound of two men talking.

Still shaking, closing her eyes as if by doing so she wouldn't have to face the dark, she tried to slow her breathing, quieten her heartbeat and listen.

'I think your girlie's awake.'

She heard Caleb speaking.

'Well, in her defence, Caleb, she's been remarkably well-behaved for hours. We haven't heard a peep from her and it's about time we did what's needed. There is a place not far up here where we can pull off the road.'

'OK,' said Caleb.

Dani tried to keep her mind focused. She opened her eyes again, hoping to let them adjust to the darkness around her, and she started to think. She needed to find anything she could use to free her hands or something she could use as a weapon. She moved her hands as far as she could, but there was only a tiny range of flexibility and she was certain that she was the only thing in the back of the car.

She felt the metal strong-point on the floor and tugged at it, but it held firm.

She rolled around as best she could, trying to feel for any loose articles again. But there were none. She'd seen somewhere on the internet that if you're in the boot of a car, you should kick out the rear light cluster so that other vehicles can see you. They'd placed her in the boot facing forward, so the opening would be behind her, and that's where the lights were. She twisted around as far as she could to look for them, hoping that some light might spill in, but there was nothing. She took aim at where she thought the cluster might be, towards the back of the boot on the outside, and she tried to kick at it with her heel.

Her feet were also bound together and also attached to a point on the floor of the car.

She swung with all her might, but her foot reached the edge of its travel and the bonds dug in tight, causing her to yelp in pain. She wasn't even close.

She could feel the car slowing down, felt the turning forces push her to one side.

They slowed down again, and she heard the tyres move from hard tarmac on to some kind of grit or gravel. Eventually, there was near silence as the vehicle came to rest.

She lay now and waited for the boot to open, without any weapon for defence or attack, and not easily able to turn her head to even see them when they came.

She heard them walking around, listened to some mumbled speech and a groan as one of them, likely Hamilton, stretched and complained about cramp. Then they moved away from the car, the sounds becoming distant until she couldn't make out the words. Dani tried to brace herself, to contain the panic and compose herself for when the boot eventually opened.

It seemed like forever before she heard the footsteps of someone approaching.

A pale light flooded in as the boot was opened. She tried to look behind her.

'Well, hello there, sleeping beauty,' said Hamilton.

She felt his hand on her hip as he reached forward and patted her.

'How's your journey so far?' he asked, jovial. 'I know it's not first-class travel, but needs must and all that.'

His hand lingered on her hip and she shuddered as she felt the warmth of his palm slip down to her bum.

'You know what, Dani, you've got a perfect backside. I've always thought it, admired it from afar. I'm not sure if it's all the running and exercise you do, or maybe just that you eat well. Hell, maybe you're just genetically lucky in the butt department. But, whatever it is, I wanted you to know that.'

Dani tried not to flinch as she felt him move his hand over her bum and around the top of her legs, his fingers slowly drifting towards her inner thigh.

She clamped her legs together as tight as she could and felt his hand meet the resistance.

'You're no fun at all, Lewis,' he said, slowly withdrawing his hand. 'There was me thinking I might be able to give you some happy thoughts for the rest of the journey. You know, you could pass the time a little bit turned on, thinking about what might be between us, but no, the celestial gates are shut.'

Dani had turned away from him, resting her head back down on the floor and facing the back of the rear seats. She tried to send her mind away, to go somewhere else.

He paused and she heard him chuckle. Caleb did the same. It was as though they'd exchanged a glance and the joke was on her.

'You thirsty?' Hamilton asked.

'No,' said Dani, although she was. Her lips were dry,

and her tongue felt swollen and heavy, sticking to the top of her mouth and seeming to push against her teeth.

She knew she'd been given something, some drug to make her sleep, which was making her mouth dry and furry.

'The thing is, Dani,' Hamilton began, and Dani had the sense that he was playing to Caleb in the way he was speaking. 'I'm going to need you to take a drink, for your own good really.'

'Fuck you,' said Dani, not moving, still looking into the darkness of the boot.

'Well, Dani, it's funny you should say that because if you don't take a drink, I might well fuck you.'

Dani felt herself tensing up. She said nothing because there was nothing she could say.

'I'm sorry,' said Hamilton. 'That was crude and unnecessary. I'd chosen not to be like that with you and yet here I am breaching my own agreements. I won't really fuck you, though Caleb and I did discuss gifting you a dream threesome, but I told him you wouldn't appreciate our gesture. I am, however, going to need you to take a drink. And realistically you do have a choice. You can have a drink, swallow it, four or five mouthfuls, and you'll go back to sleep. Or, Caleb has offered to choke you to sleep. It really is your call. I'm all for equality – women deciding what happens to their own bodies – and so I want you to decide what's going to happen to yours.'

She heard them laughing again, but said nothing.

'What's it to be? Drink or choked? I always wondered if you were a bit kinky beneath your prim, aloof exterior. I guess we'll find out soon enough.'

Dani was silent again.

'Caleb's hoping you choose the latter. Just saying.'

Dani closed her eyes.

'Caleb,' said Hamilton. 'You're on, buddy.'

She heard Hamilton step away from the car, heard other footsteps approaching.

'He'll sell you out the second he can,' she said, hoping the words reached Caleb. 'He'll control you forever. It's what he does. He'll never let go.'

She felt a hand tighten around her neck and felt her eyes go wide and her mouth gape as the grip tightened against her throat.

'Water,' she gasped, angry at how urgently the word came out.

'Water what?' said Hamilton, his voice further away than it had been before.

'Water!' The words were barely audible even to her.

'Yes, I understood that, Dani, but I'm not a dog. I've been nice to you; I'm even keeping my word. So, a little show of manners occasionally would go a long way.'

Dani tried to swallow, but there was no moisture in her mouth and Caleb had a tight grip, his fingers digging in behind her windpipe.

'Water, please,' she said, the words quiet.

'Sorry, Caleb,' said Hamilton, and Dani heard his voice moving closer again. 'I'll make it up to you, my friend, I promise.'

Caleb released her and must have got back into the car because she felt it move and heard a door slam before she felt Hamilton touch her again.

He leaned down into the boot, his palm on her hip, and held the bottle of water to her mouth.

'I need you to drink half of this,' he said.

Dani took small sips, pretending to swallow, and letting the water trickle out of her mouth and on to the black carpeted interior.

'No more of that please, Dani,' said Hamilton. 'Drink it all and swallow it or we go back to option two.'

She felt him move, realised that he'd climbed into the boot with her.

He grabbed her hair with one hand and turned her face, so she was looking upwards. He was on top of her, and she felt a pinch as he forced a knee between her body and the rear seats so that he was straddling her.

He held the bottle to her mouth and watched carefully as he poured the water in.

'Good girl,' he said as he watched her swallow one mouthful.

He fumbled around in the boot. 'Somebody put a tracker in your backpack, Dani. Did you know that?'

Dani shook her head.

'I didn't think you did. I suspect it was one of Jimmy's crowd, trying to keep tabs on you. They didn't do the greatest job of hiding it.'

He held up the pen her dad had given her.

'They were supposed to watch you, so they'd know when you were coming to take me out for the day, not use technology that could be easily found. But somebody wanted to keep tabs on where you are.'

He dropped the tracker next to Dani's head. 'It's had no signal, just so you know. We found it straight away.'

He poured more water into her mouth.

Dani spat it out, choking.

'You're pissing me off, Dani,' he said.

She felt his weight increase as his hand gripped her face, squeezing round her mouth and distorting her features.

He squeezed tighter and tighter, as though a wave of rage was surging through him and he was fighting to control it.

After a few moments, the pressure eased, and she heard him exhale slowly.

'Drink, please,' he said, holding her face and pouring more in.

Dani swallowed as little of the next mouthful as she could, storing some in her mouth and then coughing it out.

He paused and Dani tensed, waiting for another attack, but then she felt him start to climb off her. She felt his weight move off her chest and she was free to breathe more easily. He stopped and leaned in close until Dani could feel his breath on her face.

'This might be goodbye, Dani,' he said, though his words were starting to sound thick.

Her head was groggy, but not as much as it had been back at the house.

He was close again, really close, and she felt his hands on either side of her face as he leaned in and kissed her.

She had nowhere to go, no way of fighting. She wanted to bite him, but her brain wasn't sending the signals to her teeth. She felt his tongue in her mouth, moving against hers, his lips tight against her.

As he withdrew, his teeth caught her bottom lip and bit down on it, gently pulling it taut before he finally let her go.

'It's been a pleasure, Dani.'

He climbed off her.

She was numb, the whole episode a nightmare as she felt him touch her again just before he shut the boot.

This time it was different, and, in her haze, she realised he'd slipped something into her back pocket.

Chapter 40

The force of the impact drove Dani head first against the side of the boot.

There was a horrendous bang and the sound of metal against metal.

Dani's arms and legs felt as though they were going to be ripped from her sockets as her bonds reached their limits.

The pressure eased off for a second, but Dani knew instinctively that their car had been hit.

She could feel it was still moving, but sideways, and the noise didn't change at all. She was sure she could hear Hamilton and Caleb shouting from the front and then she heard gunfire, two or three shots.

There was nothing she could do except close her eyes and hope.

She'd almost been out, maybe had been, but she was wide awake now.

Her jaw clenched tight as she braced for more impact and she tried to tighten her muscles, unsure of which direction it might come from.

More shots were fired – they rang out over the sound

of skidding tyres – and she heard shattering glass, then the car came to a halt, rocking and unbalanced.

She felt herself hyperventilating in the darkness of the boot. She had no idea of where the next sound or force might come from and she curled up as small as she could, hoping to avoid any possible chance of being hit by a stray bullet.

She was sure she heard the car doors open, some more gunshots, shouting, and the sound of voices moving further away.

There was a voice at the boot now, saying her name. It was familiar, but she didn't dare to hope.

'Dani, move as far to the front as you can,' the voice shouted. 'Do it now, Dani.'

She did as she was told, shuffling as far as her bonds would let her to get away from the opening, but they didn't wait.

There was an almighty bang, and then another – Dani was sure her eardrums would burst – and then the boot opened, and daylight flooded in.

'John?' she said, her partner appearing in the gap.

'Let's go,' he said.

'Tied,' Dani said, only managing one word.

She saw him drop a large sledgehammer on to the floor, before he leaned in with a knife.

She tried to move to show him where she was lashed to the strong-points and he leaned in over the top of her, working quickly to free her from the car. Then, without hesitation, he tucked the knife into his pocket and leaned forward towards her. One of his hands snaked under her legs and the other behind her neck and he dragged her towards him. The cast on his arm was hard against her skull, but as soon as she was close to the edge, he held her over his shoulder and began to run.

'I can run, just cut me free,' she shouted, but he either didn't hear her or ignored her.

The motion of his running knocked the wind out of her and she heard more gunfire, but realised that it wasn't aimed at her; John hadn't come alone, and someone was firing past them, keeping Hamilton and Caleb's heads down as they made their getaway.

He threw her body into the back seat of a waiting car.

'Where's Hamilton?' Dani shouted.

'We just have to stay here,' John said, sliding in beside her and leaning over to cover her from the direction of the now sporadic gunshots.

He was working with the knife again, trying to free her hands and leaning heavily against her.

She pushed him away as she tried to get out of the car, but he was easily two and a half times her weight, and he barely moved.

'One second,' he said. 'Almost there.'

With a grunt, he pulled the blade across the final knot and Dani's hands were free. He immediately sat away from her, pulling her legs up on to his lap to start cutting at the bonds.

She could see outside clearly for the first time.

They were somewhere quiet, lots of trees, grass and not much else.

The car she assumed Hamilton and Caleb had been using was twenty yards away, the front passenger side crumpled from impact, and a second vehicle was next to it, the rear window smashed.

Beyond, she could see a small ditch, some fencing and a thin treeline that led to a larger field and wood behind it.

She could see a man crouched by the car, a weapon in his hands aimed in the direction of the field, but no other movement.

A loud squawk from within the car made her jump and she looked in the front to see a radio transmitter.

'We have one,' came a voice. 'The other is in the treeline somewhere. Shall we pursue?'

There was a moment's hesitation and then some sound that was laden with feedback that Dani couldn't make out.

'Negative. Law enforcement is on way. Bring what you have and pull out.'

She heard them acknowledge what had been said and watched the treeline closely.

It was only a few seconds until she saw three figures approach, moving at speed, and one had the unmistakable shape of a man slung over his shoulder.

'I need to see,' said Dani.

'Just stay here, we were told,' said John.

'You were told,' said Dani, 'and I need to see.'

She opened the door on her side and got out of the car.

The man who'd been crouched down was now standing and Dani recognised Marcus instantly.

'Who is it?' she asked. 'Is he dead?'

The three men arrived back and approached their car. The one who was carrying the body moved quickly to the boot and one of the others opened it.

The body flopped over on to the carpet, but even before she saw the face, she recognised the long limbs and pale skin.

'It's not Hamilton,' said Dani.

'It's the one who killed five of my men,' said Marcus.

He spat on the man's body and turned away.

'Is he dead?' asked Dani. 'Is Caleb dead?'

'We have to go,' Marcus said, walking back to the car. 'The police are only minutes out. We need to go now.'

He grabbed Dani's arm and tried to move her towards the car, but she was staring at Caleb, noting several wounds.

319

'His mate used him as a bloody shield,' said one of the men, speaking to Marcus. 'Literally dragged him in front of him and legged it while he took the bullet.'

'Was the other one hurt or injured?' asked Dani. 'Was he hit at all?'

The man shrugged and slammed the boot shut.

'Get out of here,' said Marcus. 'Meet you back at the clubhouse.'

The men nodded and Marcus began to push Dani back towards the other car.

John was standing outside, watching them and studying the road beyond.

Dani jerked her arm free of Marcus and jogged back alongside him.

Within seconds of her climbing inside, the car was moving, following the other vehicle out on to the road.

In the front of the car, Marcus was driving, an MP5 submachine gun cradled on his lap.

'Go back,' said Dani. 'Give me the gun and take me back, we need to finish this. He can't go free.'

Marcus and John were both looking at her.

'Now!' she screamed, reaching out and grabbing the headrest of the passenger seat to pull herself forward. 'Take me back now, we can't let him go. You know what he'll do – he'll go after our families. We have to get him now, before he gets too far.'

Marcus was watching her in the rear-view mirror and she saw his eyes flick from her to John and back again.

'We're not going back,' he said.

Dani looked to John.

'We have to go back,' she said, lowering her voice, trying to convince him with her eyes.

'If we go back there, someone will die, and we'll certainly be arrested,' said Marcus.

Dani stared from one to the other.

'They killed my dad,' she said. 'We have to go back.'

Marcus was shaking his head. 'He's not dead.'

Dani felt a flood of relief spread through her body. 'What?'

'He's in a bad way, but I got an ambulance to him after they left.'

She slumped back in her seat and let her head fall forward. She'd spent so long being angry at him that her relief he wasn't gone felt all the stronger.

'Someone needs to go after them,' she said, her eyes shut.

John reached out and rubbed her arm. 'The others will tip off the police,' he said. 'They'll mention Hamilton's name. There's a nationwide manhunt underway for him; they'll have him, and it won't take long.'

The adrenaline was subsiding and whatever Hamilton had given her seemed to be on the edge of taking hold again. She tried to fight it.

'No,' she said, 'they won't get him, you know that. He's got time, he'll disappear, and when he reappears, he'll come straight after all of us.'

She reached up, cupped her hand, and slapped herself hard on the back of the neck, three times. Her eyes were shocked open. 'They gave me something,' she said, in answer to John's look of surprise. 'Don't know what. Makes me sleepy.'

'You can sleep now,' said John. 'I won't leave you until you wake. I promise.'

Dani tried to force her eyes open and looked around at the landscape. 'Where are we?'

'We're south of Kilmarnock,' Marcus said. 'They took a long route, sticking to the A-roads and back roads, but they've been heading north since they started driving.'

Several questions hit Dani at the same time. 'How do you know?' she asked.

'Tracker in your bag,' said Marcus. 'Your dad did it.'

Dani stared at him. 'They found the pen,' she said. 'Hamilton said he disabled it.'

He nodded. 'The pen was easily found, it was turned on and it would've worked, but it was there to be found. We hid two more. One in the lining of the top pouch and one wrapped up in your rain poncho in the little pouch at the bottom.'

She wanted to ask why he hadn't just told the police where she was, but the answer was obvious: Marcus was a wanted man, people were dead, and her dad was injured. He wanted to know what Dani would say before she was able to speak to the police.

'Jimmy?' asked Dani.

Marcus shook his head.

'Hamilton said my dad killed Davis?'

Marcus shrugged. 'He's dead. I didn't see by who.'

'William Knight?' Dani asked.

There was a long pause before Marcus replied. 'He's back where he should be.'

The car was silent for a long time.

Dani was thinking about her dad.

'Why did you leave my dad,' she said. 'Hamilton told me you ran and left him.'

Marcus sneered.

'Hamilton's a pathological liar,' he said. 'I read those letters and they stink of bullshit. Your dad had asked me to go if it all went south. He wanted to make sure that someone got out safe and could look out for you. We agreed a plan and I stuck to it exactly as he asked me to.'

The relief of knowing her dad was alive seemed to give her renewed energy and she felt fully awake again.

'Thank you,' she said, turning in her seat to peer out of the rear window and seeing a signpost in the opposite direction.

The sign said that Glasgow was forty miles away.

Hamilton had said he had an old score to settle and he'd been driving north, into Scotland.

'Where's Roger?' she asked. She turned to John. 'I assume Marcus came and got you? Told you what's happening and asked for help?'

John nodded.

She turned to Marcus, leaning forward in her seat and gripping his shoulder.

'Did you try and get Roger as well?' she asked. 'Why did you bring so few men?'

'We're a little light on manpower at the moment,' he said. 'With Jimmy, I'm down six good men.'

'And Roger?'

'I couldn't find him. Time was running out, I only needed one more capable guy. Knew you wouldn't trust one of mine and knew he'd do what it took to get you back.'

Dani sat back again, her head swimming, but she noticed a look pass between them in the rear-view mirror.

'What?' she said.

'Marcus told me about how Hamilton was communicating,' John said. 'He told me about the Twitter accounts and the guard.'

Dani nodded. 'And?'

'And, well, there was a second person communicating with Hamilton. His people couldn't figure out what was being said, but when I looked, it was obvious.'

John looked away from her, seeming to wrestle with what he was going to say.

'Jesus. Just tell me,' Dani said, her voice rising almost to a shout.

'Someone was sending in snippets about you, Dani. How you were, what cases you were working on. It was quite detailed. So detailed that it could really only have come from a few people . . .'

'Like who?' Dani asked.

'Me,' said John. 'But I would never do that.'

There were only a few people who really knew what she was doing at any one time, what cases she was on and how she was pursuing them. Hamilton had always been a step ahead, always known what he shouldn't have, and she realised now that she'd been blinkered all along. Hamilton, the great manipulator, had more than one person feeding him information.

'It was Roger,' she said, knowing the answer. 'Roger's done nothing but try to warn me about Hamilton's manipulation all the way along. He's tried to keep me away from him. He's constantly asked me what Hamilton says and implies, because he's been feeding him information the whole time, hasn't he?'

John nodded.

'It seems to have started a few months after you went on sabbatical. It increases and decreases in volume over time, but he's been telling Hamilton what you've been doing for months. No one else knows that much about your movements. It has to be him.'

Dani was silent for a few moments, the weight of the betrayal like lead in her stomach.

'He was on his way to Roger's house,' she said. 'And if you can't get hold of Roger on his mobile, then that's where he'll be too. There's no signal up there at all.'

She made eye contact with Marcus in the mirror.

'We have to go,' she said. 'Hamilton might be looking to disappear, or he might not, but he's got some kind of score to settle with Roger and that's where he's headed.'

She held out her hand to John. 'Give me your phone,' she demanded.

He dropped the handset into her palm without hesitation.

'Turn the car around,' she said. 'Head for the Faslane naval base.'

She scrolled through John's saved numbers until she found Roger's name then pressed call and waited.

The call went directly to answerphone and she heard Roger's familiar voice asking her to leave a message.

'Roger, if you get this message, call me back on John's phone. OK? Call me back.'

She hung up and looked at Marcus and John in turn. 'I said turn the car around,' she said.

'No,' John said. 'I'm taking you back to the New Forest, to near the cottage. The story is that both you and your dad were taken. You don't know why or how they got him, but likely as leverage over you. You both escaped, he got shot in the process and you made it into the woods. I'll take you back to within a few miles and we'll wait and watch you until someone finds you, so you're not alone, but that's what we're doing.'

'No,' said Dani. 'All of that is fine, except when my dad escaped and was shot, they took me in a car and drove north. We can figure out between us how I ended up at Roger's, but if you want me to support your story, that's where we're going.'

They drove on in silence for a few minutes.

Marcus kept looking at her in the rear-view, as though checking her resolve. Every time he glanced, she was waiting, looking right back at him.

He shook his head and fiddled with the sat-nav.

'There's one more thing you should know before you speak to Roger,' he said, as he indicated to pull off the

325

motorway. 'He approached us, well, Jimmy, a few weeks ago. He wanted us to help him. He wanted to pay us to have someone take care of Hamilton inside the prison.'

'So, it was you,' she shouted.

'No. It wasn't us. We said no. Too risky and, at the time, we had no reason to do it. But I wanted you to know.'

She began to think about Hamilton, the attack made on his life, the letters he'd written. She remembered the feeling of him slipping something into her pocket before he'd climbed off her. She turned in her seat, reaching to her back pocket and searching for the letter.

Chapter 41

Hamilton's Seventh Letter

Dani, I was in trouble. Big trouble!

I was in trouble, and the police were closing in.

There was no physical evidence that linked me to the house – my hours of study in various libraries had paid dividends in allowing me to cover my tracks meticulously.

The forensics back then weren't anywhere near as good as they are now, and the explosion had destroyed the house and most of the ones either side of it. But I'd been seen leaving, though not clearly identified, and I had no alibi.

Now, Dani, I promised to be candid, and I will. Like many talented but desperate people in my situation, who lack the experience to correctly cover up their mistakes, I began to hunt the police officer that was in charge of the investigation, and this is a grave error. I went to his house, watched his family and used the short time I had before I'd surely be arrested, to plan how much hurt I could inflict upon him before he tried to destroy me. I was out of control, but I knew I had to get my revenge in advance of this one, while I was still able to do so.

It would lack the time and meticulous planning I normally allowed, but needs must.

One evening, I waited in his garden, watching his young children, neither older than seven or eight. Only the glass of the patio door protected them from the night, and from me. I heard someone behind me. I spun. I knew it wasn't the police officer as I'd seen him only moments before when he'd last checked on the kids.

I was carrying a large pruning knife with me – they'd become something of a fascination at the time, widely available, untraceable, brutally shaped and deathly sharp – and I held it tight and prepared to fight.

But what was waiting behind me was no attacker. It was an angel of mercy, and I was, all at once, damned forever, and ultimately saved.

I'm afraid I'm somewhat in a hurry as I write this, Dani. I have a long journey ahead of me, and I need to get going. For reasons I'm sure you're acutely aware of, I can't travel conventionally.

I have to say, it's been a pleasure to go on this journey with you and I hope you feel you understand me more than you did before. I've wanted to kiss you and touch you for such a long time, so thank you for that – a dream come true if you will.

But onwards, for the end is nigh . . .

Now, Dani, imagine a football manager who could spot talent in young players. Imagine he were able to sit and watch thousands of young men and women pass through his field of vision every year. Imagine that all the men and women who passed through this field of vision were of a particular type. The sort of people who'd be particularly predisposed to being good at football, people who had the family background, the personality, the drive and ambition, the tactical awareness and planning, or at the very least the potential for all of it. Then imagine that manager, this spotter of talent, had near unique access to every part of their life and history, so he could truly spot the talent, the balance, the poise, the eye for the game.

How many footballing superstars would be found, if this manager had weeks and weeks to assess each and every one of them, and to check that they had the right level of mental robustness to perform any task that was asked of them?

Now, Dani, imagine if it weren't football you were looking for.

Imagine that the predisposition required was different.

Imagine if instead, the candidates you were looking for came from rough backgrounds, broken homes and incomplete families.

Imagine if you were looking for people who wanted to leave where they were from, to start a new life and gain a new family and new friends.

Imagine if these were individuals who needed to prove themselves, to be part of something greater than themselves, to have their lives mean something.

Imagine if these people were young and impressionable, hungry for attention and like dry sponges ready to absorb guidance, leadership, advice and direction.

Then, suppose you were looking for one other thing, something that knows no social bounds, or backgrounds, something that can spring like green grass anywhere in the world that humans exist. Imagine you were looking for evil.

There was someone looking for me, Dani, and he found me.

That night he took me away from the police officer's garden and he helped me.

The next day I went to the police and explained that I did have an alibi, I'd hidden it as I was ashamed, but I'd been in Plymouth that night and had spent much of the evening with a prostitute.

My new friend arranged it, and the woman, an intelligent, high-end escort, played the role perfectly, though to what end I've never known.

Her detailed statement and the photographs that we took at her apartment, completely removed me from the investigation and I was free again.

But, and this is a hugely important point in what I'm trying to tell you, I had learned that there were others like me, others who were smart and worked at their craft. I learned that there were some who were subtly different, yet drawn to do things that complemented what I wanted to do.

I'd never had a strong authority figure in my life, one whom I could trust and who had proved their loyalty and asked nothing of me in return, except they be allowed to help me. I was wide open to receive these gifts.

My new mentor taught me and tutored me and protected me. I was a 'god among men', he told me, and I would 'continue on to greatness' under his tutelage and with his loyal assistance.

We would always work together, in support of each other's activities.

Even when I was incarcerated he continued to help me, passing information and knowledge. We would always be partners in what we wanted to achieve together, from that point on.

The trust between us was complete and he is the only person I've ever really trusted.

We worked together in harmony for more than three decades. Trusting each other, staying loyal to each other, assisting each other, and feeding each other.

He provided me with knowledge, support, discipline and coping mechanisms to spot when I had begun to unravel, and to deal with that constructively.

He taught me not to crave recognition for what I did, as that was a false pleasure. He reinforced in me the knowledge that there were killers out there that weren't even known to be operating. He taught me to listen to my instincts, while still following my heart. He communicated with me, offered me guidance and he was the one who suggested I move across into the Navy Police to further my career; he was the father that I'd never known I wanted.

We became a team.

He never left me, even as he helped me to meticulously plan what I wanted to do to you.

I didn't want you to die for me, Dani, that would be too easy, too final.

I want you to live for me. I want you to know hurt that will shake you to your core. I want you to recognise that your own selfishness has blinded you to what is really happening. It is through the people you trust and those who are most important to you, that you will be made to pay.

Chapter 42

'What are you doing?' said Dani, as she watched Roger bustling around in his large open-plan kitchen.

His house was up in the hills above the Faslane naval base. It was beautiful and remote, and if you were prepared to walk to the very edge of the property and stand on the wall set against an old outhouse, it had stunning views of the whole Gare Loch.

It was as remote a place as Dani had ever been – only a single road led to it – and she had no idea where its nearest neighbour was.

Roger had owned the place for as long as she'd known him, but it was only as he neared his retirement from the Royal Navy, that he'd really seemed to spend significant time up here.

He'd done a good job on the place too. The interior was modern, clean and functional, and he'd achieved it without changing the original exterior.

She wandered closer to him and tossed Hamilton's letter on to the large central island in the kitchen. 'You need to start locking your front door. I think Hamilton's coming for you.'

She watched him carefully, checking for a reaction. 'Why did you come straight here when you knew Hamilton was free?' she asked. 'You did know, there's no way you weren't informed straight away.'

Roger didn't reply.

'Hamilton's trying to fit you up as a person who's helped him over the years,' she continued. 'He hasn't named you, but that's what he's saying.'

Roger looked away from her, concentrating on wiping a worktop.

'He says you spotted him at Raleigh, when he stalked and killed Chrissie Bainbridge, says you gave him an alibi and helped him after that.'

Dani felt anger begin to rise slowly within her.

He wasn't reacting at all and a dread began to settle inside her.

She'd often thought of Roger as a second father, had trusted him sometimes when she could trust no one else.

The very least he could do now was be outraged, furious, tell her it was all bullshit, that it was what Hamilton did. He could explain to her how Hamilton tried to get inside your mind, to shake you at your foundations, but he didn't. Instead he squirted more antibacterial cleaner on to the marble worktop and began to wipe it clean.

'A lot of what he says does fit,' said Dani.

She pulled out one of the bar stools lining the worktop and perched on it.

'You were at Raleigh when he was there, have been several times since. I remember the re-examination of the Chrissie Bainbridge murder from his trial. He had an alibi and had been dismissed as a possible suspect early on. There were few details beyond that, which is something you would have known how to make happen.'

He flinched at that, then finished wiping the worktop

with a cloth and turned, tearing a few sheets of kitchen towel from the roll and using it to buff and dry the damp surface.

'He says you helped and mentored him. That you liked the bodies and you helped him get rid of them.'

Roger put the kitchen towel in the bin and turned to put the kettle on.

'He says that you were supposed to hurt me for him, to punish me because I caught him. You two had agreed you'd do that.'

Roger was watching the kettle boil and Dani couldn't see his face.

She saw his shoulders rise up and then drop as though he'd let out a long sigh.

'And why didn't I?' he asked, speaking for the first time. 'If I did all those things and supported Hamilton for that many years, why didn't I hurt you?'

Dani said nothing as she watched him open the cupboard doors, pull out two cups, and then search around in another cupboard until he found a small box of green tea.

'If I was supposed to hurt you, then why have I spent almost your entire career doing the very opposite of that?'

'He says that's why you two fell out. He says he doesn't know why you wouldn't do it either, but that's why he's got a score to settle with you.'

Roger poured boiling water into the cups and slid Dani's across the worktop towards her, leaving the tea bag in, which was how he knew she liked it.

She looked at the tea, unsure even though she'd watched him make it. 'Tell me why you came here, Roger. I know they'd have told you Hamilton was free, that he'd taken me, and you've come straight up here.'

Roger added some milk to his cup and then took a sip of his tea.

'Hamilton was bringing me here,' she went on. 'It was as though he was bringing me to see you. He sent several letters explaining to me how he liked to gain his revenge. He likes to shake someone at their very core, and to do that to me, he was bringing me here. He was supremely confident that when we got here, that would happen. So why did you run here, Roger?'

Roger gave a hollow laugh. 'I'll tell you why, Dani. Because after I spoke to the police and they told me, and I realised you'd gone and allowed Hamilton not only to leave the prison, but to get himself into a position to escape, I knew my career and my life was over.'

He took another sip of his tea.

'The highest profile naval prisoner in the country was free and on the run. The person I considered to be my closest ally, my long-time friend, had pushed for it to happen after ignoring everything I told her about how he works, how he manipulates and gets to you. If you must know, I spoke immediately with Captain Harrow-Brown. I informed him of the situation and I resigned my commission.'

Roger seemed to tear up as he said the last words, as though he'd finally found some emotion.

'In light of the circumstances, he accepted my resignation and I'll remain on gardening leave until the administration can be completed. Then I'll be discharged from the service. I came up here to get the place ready, to take some time, prepare to move up here for good.'

He looked around the place, his lips pursed, as though accepting within himself that this was home.

Dani felt conflicted. Everything he said made sense, and yet, so did so much that Hamilton had said and written.

'Did you know Hamilton when he was at HMS Raleigh in basic training?' she asked.

'You've asked me that many times before. Yes, I knew of him. He was an arrogant little shit from what I could tell, but I worked in a different part of the base. So, I knew *of* him, but I didn't know him.'

'Did you encourage Hamilton to join the Royal Navy Police?'

Roger shrugged. 'I neither encouraged nor discouraged him. I did some of his initial interviews when he applied to change branches. He was smart enough, seemed to have matured a bit since he was in basic training, was either less arrogant, or better at hiding it, but as you know, I wasn't the head of branch and I didn't sign his transfer papers.'

Dani's throat was dry. 'My dad's in hospital. He's in intensive care,' she said, watching as Roger seemed to truly react for only the second time since she'd arrived. 'It was him, with Jimmy Nash and a load of Jimmy's boys, who took down the convoy.'

Roger nodded; it was obvious that he'd already thought as much. 'There aren't many organisations in this country with the skill set to pull off something like that,' he said, 'but I no longer hold a warrant card as a member of the Royal Navy Police, so it's not my place to speculate on such things.'

Dani took a sip of tea, her hands cupped around the mug, and felt herself blink as the hot liquid touched her lips. She felt a tear run down her face and in an instant, she felt so weak that she might not be able to hold the cup for even a moment longer.

Roger was watching her. 'It's what he does, Dani,' he said. 'I won't lie to you. I'm hurt you could even think all that of me, but it's what he's an expert at. He manipulates people, putting together facts and linking together situations to make you question everything, even those people you might consider to be your closest friends.'

He looked for a moment as though he might try to come to Dani, to comfort her, but she raised a hand to stop him.

'He hates you, Dani, regardless of how he may seem when you meet him, how jovial he pretends to be and how little he pretends you mean to him. He hates you with all his being. I told you that and you allowed him to be set free.' He watched her, standing motionless as he spoke.

'For what it's worth, he hates me too.'

'Then why didn't he just kill me?' Dani said, not even sure if it was a question to Roger, or whether she was just thinking out loud.

'Because he can do that any time. What he wants to do is isolate you, break you and make sure you feel alone in here.'

He tapped his head.

'And more importantly in here.'

He tapped his chest.

'Because when you're alone, you're weak. Not just you, everyone is. No one can really make it on their own. That's why I'm so frightened to leave the navy, because I don't know how I'm going to do on my own.'

Dani bit down hard on her lip. She was biting in the same place as Hamilton had when he kissed her, and she felt blood begin to flow inside her mouth.

'Maybe he was going to leave you here,' said Roger. 'Maybe his plan was to see how deeply he could drive a wedge between us.'

'We know about the Twitter feed, Roger,' said Dani.

She watched him closely but needn't have.

At the mention of the Twitter feed Roger seemed to almost fall down, as though his legs were going to give out from under him.

'You've been messaging him about me for months. It

was you that was keeping him up to date with where I was and what I was doing. It was you, the person I trusted the most . . .'

Dani seemed to just run out of words, or the energy to speak them.

Roger staggered, put a hand on the counter to steady himself.

'Did you think we wouldn't find out?' Dani asked. 'Did you think you'd get away with it?'

He couldn't speak. His mouth was moving but Dani could hear no words.

'Roger!' she shouted.

He pulled a stool towards himself, slowly, as though it was near impossible to do, and climbed on to it.

'Why?' she asked.

'For you,' he said faintly.

Dani looked at him. 'You gave him power over me.'

'I tried to stop it!' Roger shouted. 'I never stopped trying to get you away from him. But you listen to no one!'

Dani watched the anger flare up and die away again quickly.

'I went to him after he sent those men to attack you in the carpark, after I'd helped put you back together again,' said Roger, his eyes looking down at the worktop. 'I told him I wanted him to leave you alone. I knew it had to have been him. That in some way he'd managed to get it done. I told him he had to forget you.'

'And?' asked Dani.

'And he said he would, but he wanted a favour in return. He wanted me to find some things out for him. He said it would help his defence against another round of charges. It seemed innocent enough. He wanted to know about old crimes. Things that had happened in Afghanistan. He wanted to know if they were being investigated.'

'And you did this?'

'It was easy. A call to an old friend. A quick check. No one knew anything about it. So I told him that. A stupid, pointless bit of information traded for your safety – it was a deal I felt I'd strike anytime.'

Roger sighed.

'But then he had a little bit of me. He had me exposed and he reached out and asked for more. He threatened you again, wanted you to come and see him. Said he wouldn't talk to you if I did as he asked. It was simple and inane stuff too, at first. Find a marine called Davis. Find out little bits here and there. Each step seemed like nothing on its own, but they began to build up and before I knew it, it had changed. He was never going to leave you alone and I was in so deep I didn't know how to stop. I told you again and again, that's what he does. He does nothing for anyone else, he doesn't know what loyalty is and there's always an agenda.'

'But you could have stopped anytime,' said Dani. 'You could have told me at any time and we could have faced it together.'

He sniffed, and Dani wasn't sure if he was crying.

'Then there was Caleb,' said Roger, his voice trailing off.

'You knew?' Dani asked.

He was shaking his head. 'Not really. Not at first, but he was the one who really started to turn the screw. He wanted more information, more favours. I was compromised, and I would have lost everything, my pension, my job, my only real friends. They had me and I danced to their tune. I swear it, Dani, I started off trying to protect you and by the end I was trying not to lose you. I thought I could do it, that I could keep you safe on the outside and keep him quiet in there. But he has no human in him at all. He has the coldest blood of any creature I've ever known.'

'Is that why you tried to have him killed?' Dani stood up, the stool scraping backwards the only sound in the house, and turned towards the door.

'I've lost everything,' said Roger from behind her. 'When this all comes out and people know what I did, I'll have lost absolutely everything and everyone. He got me to be completely alone, don't let him do the same to you.'

Dani walked towards the door. 'You'll have plenty of company where you're going,' she said, unable to turn round and face him. 'Goodbye, Roger.'

Chapter 43

'How are you?' asked Felicity.

She walked over to Dani and leaned in to give her a kiss on the cheek.

'I'm fine,' said Dani.

'You've been to see your dad, haven't you?' Felicity said.

Dani nodded. She'd been to see him twice – though he'd been asleep throughout both visits – and had been assured that he would recover in time.

'I'll go and see him again soon,' she said. 'Any word? Any sightings?'

'Nothing at all. And believe me, everyone's looking.'

Dani relaxed back on her sofa, adjusting a cushion behind her. 'And Roger?'

Felicity drew a deep breath and shook her head slowly. 'Dani,' she said, sitting closer to her friend and resting a hand on her arm.

Dani saw tears well in Felicity's eyes. 'What is it?'

'Roger took his own life in the early hours of this morning. He hanged himself.'

Dani felt sick. For all Roger had done, he'd been a friend and mentor to her for as long as she could remember.

'We know that he was communicating with Hamilton and we're digging into that now. Well done for figuring that out. But in terms of what Hamilton is saying in the letters, about Roger helping him beyond the Twitter information, we found nothing, Dani, no evidence at all. It looks as though Hamilton was lying.'

Felicity sat down next to Dani and reached out to hold her hand. 'They've checked every inch of Roger's land and his house, but there's nothing there. It's horrible, Dani. I wish Roger could have seen that there's no weakness in being manipulated by a man like Hamilton. You have to understand that Hamilton spent years waiting to get even with you. He spent years planning it . . .'

'And he had help,' said Dani.

'We're looking into that, but there's not much to go on regarding who this helper was. Not yet anyway.'

Felicity sat up straighter. 'Dani, I said I'd ask and I need to understand this. The convoy was attacked in military fashion – the police have been clear on that – do you really have no idea at all who it was that took you?'

Dani sighed. 'I really don't, Felicity. Their faces were covered all the time. They were working for Hamilton, I think. I still don't know what they wanted from me. Perhaps they thought having my dad would mean they could control me. I don't know if it was a car accident or what, I don't really remember how I got free, but once I was and I realised where I was, I just headed for Roger's house. It felt like the safest place I could be. I don't know what they'd given me – it's all so hazy.'

Felicity was staring at her and Dani knew, deep inside, that her friend knew she was being lied to.

'If you remember any more, please tell me,' said Felicity neutrally. 'I have to shoot. I'm sorry. I'll come back and visit you again as soon as I can.'

Dani noticed that Felicity didn't offer her a kiss on the cheek, or a pat on the arm, no sign of affection as she left this time. She leaned her head back against the sofa and wondered how much damage all the lies would do to her friendship with Felicity. She thought about Roger and how alone he must have felt, and then about herself and how few friends she had to form a barrier between herself and loneliness.

Felicity knew she was being lied to and was tiring of a relationship that was never based on trust.

Dani's dad was lying unconscious in hospital, with seven bullet holes in him; her list of allies was thinning.

Hamilton couldn't have pulled this off without his friend Caleb. Even though what bound the pair was blackmail, not trust, the relationship had still worked to Hamilton's advantage.

Now Hamilton was out there alone.

She felt as though it was one against one now.

They were even.

So far, she'd been outmanoeuvred and outgunned, but that needed to change.

Roger's implication and now his death was a huge blow to her, but it would also buy her some time.

She reached for her phone and dialled John.

She heard a phone ring nearby and glanced towards her front door before she heard a knock.

'One second,' she said, ending the call and going to answer the door.

'What did you want?' he asked as she let him in.

'Help,' she said. 'But don't I always?'

He laughed. 'How're you feeling? I saw Felicity leaving, but she didn't look very happy.'

Dani ran her tongue around the small sore patch on the inside of her mouth where Hamilton had bit her lip after he'd kissed her. It had become a habit, a nervous tic, and she knew she was making it worse by continually probing at it, but she couldn't help it.

'Roger hung himself last night, John.'

John stopped in his tracks, his mouth open. 'I . . . I had no idea.'

'I only just heard myself,' said Dani. 'But John, this one's on Hamilton too. And I want payback. Did you get hold of my friend Heather? The American?'

John nodded.

'I need to speak to her soon,' Dani said. 'She's straight down the line, but I think that when I lay out for her what a US citizen has been part of, she might be able to help us. We need to identify this Caleb. It's probably not his real name, but she would be able to find out who he is from the information we have.'

'OK,' John said, 'looking for him sounds like a plan, but what next?'

'There'll be time to grieve for Roger soon, but until then, I need to know as much about his movements as possible. I know he was feeding information to Hamilton about me, but he was doing other things for Caleb too. He told me as much. So, I want you to look at his movements and see where he went and who he spoke to. See if there's anything out of the ordinary.'

Chapter 44

'Dani, are you serious?' Heather took a sip of her extra-large coffee.

Dani looked at the crowds milling around Waterloo Station. A number of men walked past their table, all of them noticeably clocking her friend.

Heather Dickinson was beautiful, part Native American Indian, but what they couldn't see while they looked or leered, was that she spoke eleven languages, had degrees in Psychology and Law Enforcement, and had been, around the time she had done some courses with Dani, widely tipped to be moving towards the top of the US military intelligence community.

'Look, Dani,' she said, leaning in closer. 'Look at the way things are between our countries at the moment. I appreciate you being honest with me, but the whole concept of a war crime being committed by United States special operations forces, then being discovered and compounded by members of the British special forces . . .'

Heather shook her head. 'It's not something anyone is going to want to be anywhere near. And what you're asking me for, I just can't give you. We don't hand out lists of our veterans who've been on operations to anyone. The whole idea of handing over the names of our special forces and CIA operatives from the early days in Afghanistan – that's crazy. You're a crazy lady.'

She took another sip of her coffee and then leaned close again. 'Take a minute to think about how the Iraq Historical Allegations Team went, the thousands of cases that were opened after that conflict. Now imagine what would happen if this story came to light, while we still have troops on the ground in Afghanistan. God, it just doesn't bear thinking about.'

'There's proof,' said Dani.

Heather's demeanour changed. 'You said they were allegations. That you wanted help to find someone involved.'

'That's true, but someone was blackmailing those involved, and to do that, they have evidence.'

'You're one hundred percent on this?'

Dani wasn't certain, but she needed to play a strong hand. She hadn't told Heather that Caleb was dead, his body taken by Marcus's men to God only knew where.

'Yes. One of your guys is in the UK now. I've met him and seen him.'

'Then tell me what he looks like,' said Heather.

Dani paused, already regretting her last sentence. 'His face was covered, but I'm sure he's Caucasian, average height, av—'

'Average build,' interrupted Heather. 'Nondescript features, not too big, not too small, just the sort of guy you'd forget you saw as soon as you saw him. I get it. They all look like that. That's why they get picked for those kinds of operations.'

Dani tried to keep her cool. 'If we're not careful, then we will end up in a situation where this comes out and we don't control it. That has to be worse for everyone. I don't know much about this guy, you're right, but I do know he's a sniper of some kind, and he was on the ground before the official deployment of US troops into Afghanistan. The name I've heard from him is Caleb, but I'm almost certain that's fake, or some kind of code name. All I need is some way of identifying him.'

'Then what?' asked Heather.

Dani paused. 'We bring him in. We control the narrative. We share the glory.'

Heather smirked, the only expression that Dani thought made her look less than beautiful.

Dani knew what she was thinking. People like this Caleb didn't get brought in for questioning, because there was too much danger that they might actually talk.

'Hey, gorgeous.'

Dani and Heather both turned to see a young man standing a few feet from their table.

'You two ladies must be exhausted, because you've been running through my mind all morning.'

'Go fuck yourself, dipshit,' said Heather, and turned back to Dani.

The guy hovered for a few moments and opened his mouth to say something else.

'That means go away and bother someone else,' said Dani, before he could speak. 'Go,' she added, shooing him away.

'Fucking whores,' the man mumbled under his breath as he walked away from them and was soon lost in the crowd.

'You want to go after him?' asked Heather. 'We could follow him somewhere, pretend we'll do a three-way with him, then kick his stupid ass all over the room.'

Dani smiled. She loved this about Heather.

The woman was a badass through and through. She

347

took absolutely zero shit and didn't care who liked it or who didn't.

'Look, Heather, we're going to find your boy,' said Dani. 'I came to you first, because I want you to be part of it, so we can protect both militaries when this comes out. If it goes bad, you at least had fair warning . . .'

Heather took a deep breath. 'If you're even halfway right, then this is bigger than us, Dani. You know that?'

Dani nodded.

'Thanks for the coffee,' Heather said, taking a last swig and placing the cup on the table. 'Let's get together for drinks soon, OK? We can go out in London together. It might be fun to do something a bit different?'

'Sure,' said Dani, and she stood up to embrace Heather before her friend disappeared into the crowds.

Chapter 45

Dani arrived at John's house just as the light was fading. He ushered her into his dining room, where Josie was tapping away on a computer.

'Did you speak to the Yank?' he asked as soon as the door was shut.

'I did,' she said.

'No dice?'

Dani paused, thinking.

There had been something in the way Heather had spoken to her that made Dani feel as though her message had got through. Heather was sharp and driven, she'd understand the risks and would pass them up the chain in a way that would be understood. Dani was hopeful that some help might come from their meeting, though she didn't know what.

'No dice on the list,' she said, not wanting to get hopes up prematurely. 'But I don't think it's a total dead end.'

John seemed happy with that.

Dani glanced across at Josie tapping away at the keyboard. 'Hey, Josie. You good?'

'Oh, I'm good,' said Josie, without looking up. 'I'm very good.'

Dani gave John a quizzical look.

'Well,' he began, 'we're running through Roger's diary to see where he's been, but Josie had the idea of checking all of his travel claims. He's on the road a lot, and we have his fuel receipts which tie in with where we think he was according to his diary.'

John faltered, as though he'd reached the end of his understanding.

'I'm just putting them into a map, for goodness' sake,' said Josie. 'It's hardly magic, but I can then get a time stamp of everywhere he was and look at it easily, day by day.'

John looked chastened. 'It's at times like this that you realise you're a dinosaur,' he said. 'Fortunately, our girl wonder here knows exactly what to do.'

'It certainly isn't rocket science,' said Josie, still not looking up.

Dani turned to John. 'Marcus promised me everything he had on Roger's secret Twitter account today too. The police will be digging into it, but he's ahead of them, so we can start trying to work through that.'

'Marcus . . .' John echoed. 'I suppose he's the boss there now, after you saying Jimmy's gone?'

Dani nodded. 'I guess so.'

Marcus always seemed like he could be a decent person and she couldn't reconcile that with what he'd got involved in. If he was now the boss of Jimmy's old criminal gang, she would have an even tougher job.

She looked around John's house. It was fairly obvious that a single man lived here. The sitting room was reasonably tidy, but it somehow looked as if things had been hastily stowed out of sight before she and Josie had arrived.

The sofa looked nice enough, and Dani knew he'd bought it since splitting with his wife, but the cushions loosely arranged on it looked worn, and while there was a tenuous link in the colours, they certainly didn't match. The curtains and carpets were also completely colour-independent of the other soft furnishings.

'Can I grab some tea?' she asked. 'You guys want one?'

'I'm good,' said Josie.

'You haven't finished your last one,' said John.

Dani glanced at the cup next to Josie's right hand: it wasn't exactly clean. She knew instantly why Josie hadn't drunk it.

'You know what,' Dani said. 'I think I'm good too.'

John looked genuinely hurt. 'I've some cartons of orange juice,' he said. 'Or I could go and wash up some glasses and get you some water?'

Dani wasn't sure why – maybe it was the accumulation of stress – but she began to laugh, and Josie soon joined in.

'What?' asked John.

'Nothing,' Dani managed. 'I'm just busy and not sure I need a dose of botulism at the moment.'

'I hear you,' Josie said, pointing to her mug. 'I only wish my husband was that dirty.'

John ran his fingers around the rim of the mug. 'That's all right,' he said. 'I washed that.'

'But you know you have to do it every time,' said Dani.

He looked from her, to Josie, and then began to laugh with them.

'I guess maybe I got wash confused with rinse,' he acknowledged. 'I'll go and wash up properly now, with liquid and everything, then I'll make you some more tea, OK?'

Dani and Josie were still laughing, but Dani nodded.

John walked out of the sitting room towards the kitchen.

'And the spoon,' shouted Josie, before he disappeared from sight.' Don't forget to wash the spoon.'

Dani stood behind Josie and rested a hand on the back of the chair. 'Thanks for this,' she said. 'Who's got the kids?'

Josie was typing away, concentrating on the screen, but was easily able to talk at the same time. 'Their dad has them tonight,' she said. 'It'll do him good to get some bonding time.'

'How long to finish with this?' Dani asked.

'Not long,' said Josie.

Dani watched for a few moments then wandered through to the kitchen where John was boiling the kettle.

He made to speak, then paused.

'Just say it,' Dani said.

'I just don't feel good researching Roger like this. He was my friend . . .'

John's voice wavered, and Dani looked at him for a moment, realising that she'd focused so hard on not letting Roger's loss affect her, that she'd completely forgotten about how it might be affecting the others.

She walked over quickly and put her arms around him, pulling him close. She felt his body shake and she waited, giving him a moment, fighting to control her own emotions.

'Hamilton killed him,' she said. 'Not directly, but he turned the screw. I'm going to find him and make him pay and then we can mourn Roger and celebrate him like he'd want it to be done. OK?'

John nodded and wiped his eyes with a dishcloth, then he turned back to the sink. Dani stood next him as he washed the cups. She picked up the drying up cloth and bumped him along a bit with her hip, so she could reach the wet cups on the draining board.

'Hamilton's tried for months to isolate me, John. He achieved that with Roger, but he'll never do it to me again.'

He turned to look at her, their bodies closer than would normally have been comfortable for Dani, and she looked up at him.

'He's tried to break all of my relationships and he managed to make Roger believe he was alone. But now, with Caleb dead, I think Hamilton may well begin to know what it's like to be isolated.'

'And then what?' John asked, but Dani could see in his eyes that he knew the answer.

'He'll probably come for me, because it's all he can do, and we'll be waiting. He was always going to come for me, John, I can see that now,' Dani said. 'It isn't if, it's when. I think the difference is that he's now coming alone, and even though we've lost Roger, I have a lot more friends around me than he ever realised.'

'Helensburgh, on Gare Loch?' said Josie from the door, startling them both. 'It's not in his diary and not official duty as he never claimed for it, but he spent a lot more time in Helensburgh in the past few months.'

'He has a house near there,' said Dani. 'Up in the hills. He's been going up more regularly to get it ready to move in when he leaves the mob. He would just put Helensburgh in his diary because people would recognise it.'

Her phone began to ring. 'Hello?'

'It's me,' said Marcus. 'I've sent you across what we have from Twitter now. It's all zipped up, or some such thing – my people tell me you'll know how to get to it.'

'Thanks,' said Dani.

'That's OK. We'd appreciate it if you'd let us know if any of it means anything to you. We want Hamilton out of the picture as much as anyone.'

'I understand,' she said.

'There is one thing that came up that I wanted to ask you about. There was one tweet from Roger that said, "Kaisha's dad has agreed to meet her. He'll do as asked to see her again." It's the only time a name is mentioned, so it stood out. We did some digging and Kaisha was the name of one of his victims. Does it mean anything to you?'

'Kaisha Holloway was one of his victims, that's for sure,' said Dani, her mind racing. 'Let me think and I'll call you back if I come up with anything.'

She ended the call and looked at the others.

'Kaisha Holloway was from Helensburgh,' she said. 'She was one of the only victims to come from so close to a naval base.'

'You don't think he's kept some of them alive?' asked John. 'That couldn't be possible, could it?'

'No, but when I spoke to Hamilton, he asked me to name all the victims whose fingers had been sent to me. When I named Kaisha, he said, "Is that the one from York?", which just pissed me off, because I think he remembers all of them.'

Dani was already heading for the door.

'Kaisha's dad is a boat owner up there. He works ferrying sailors to and from naval vessels and running people and supplies around on the water. He was re-interviewed after her finger was identified. If Roger was playing errand boy for Hamilton, then it's worth a look. He could easily have spoken to him.'

'You're going up there now?' John asked. 'It's eight hours or more to drive up there.'

Dani tapped her fingers. 'Josie, can you check flights?'

Josie headed back to her computer.

'You won't get anything tonight,' said John.

'I'll drive up overnight,' said Dani. 'I can get a hotel up there and sleep once I've spoken to her father.'

Her phone rang again.

'It's me again,' said Marcus. 'I think we should drive up and speak to Kaisha's family tonight. I've just checked, and her dad runs a company that moves people and stores around. He also goes between the UK and Ireland. If Hamilton was trying to get a lift from the mainland, that might be a decent first step.'

Dani looked at John.

He was shaking his head.

'They're in Helensburgh,' Marcus continued. 'No flights, but we can be there by morning if we leave now. You in?'

'Pick me up from my house,' said Dani.

Chapter 46

She parked up in a hurry, looking for Marcus's car as she climbed out of hers, but he wasn't there yet.

Footsteps sounded on the pavement behind her and she spun around to see a large man walk up and lean against her door. He didn't try to approach any closer, but watched her and waited, his hands in his pockets, his muscles bulging beneath a tight hoodie.

'Hey,' said Dani, reaching slowly into her bag for her pepper spray.

'Hey,' he replied.

She stared at him, her heart rate starting to increase, a small sheen of sweat breaking out across her brow.

She couldn't really guess his accent from one word, but if she'd had to choose at that point, she'd have said he was American.

'What can I do for you?' she asked.

'I'm looking for someone,' he said. 'My friend Heather, she said my friend lived round here, but can't find his house.'

Dani relaxed the tiniest bit at the mention of her friend's name. 'What's the name?' she asked. 'Maybe I'll be able to help you find him.'

He nodded. 'Maybe you can. His name is Isaiah Michael Caleb Dunne.'

Dani felt as though she were struggling to breathe. 'Thank you,' she said.

He nodded and reached slowly inside his jacket pocket, pulling out a business card and holding it out for her.

She edged towards him, her fingers still tight around her spray, and took the card.

There was no name on it, just a number.

'He's our problem. If you do find him, you call that number before you go anywhere near to him, you hear?'

Dani nodded and stared at the card as he turned, walking slowly away from her house.

Her phone nearly fell to the floor as she fumbled it.

John answered on the second ring and she simply blurted it out.

'Isaiah Michael Caleb Dunne,' she said, spelling the last name.

'It worked?' asked John.

'It did,' she agreed. 'Find out everything you can and get me a photograph and an address.'

'I'm on it.'

'Let me know soonest,' Dani said, her excitement and fear subsiding a little. 'Then be ready to go, OK?'

Her hands were shaking as she put her phone back into her bag.

Chapter 47

The conversation had been light, Dani dozing for a long period and then finally persuading Marcus to let her drive his car so that he could snatch a few hours too.

She'd watched him sleep fitfully in between surreptitiously checking what speed she was doing.

The roads were nearly empty for most of the journey and they stopped outside Glasgow to swap back over for the last leg into Helensburgh.

'Different to driving your little car?' Marcus asked.

'Well, I am a girl, so the bigger steering wheel really caught me out, but thankfully it was mostly straight lines and I managed.'

He shook his head and laughed. 'I didn't mean it that way, but there must be a difference between your hatchback and a top-of-the range Mercedes? I mean, if there isn't, people need to know.'

'People are stupid and would still pay for the badge anyway, but yes, your car's a nice drive. Is it making up for deficiencies elsewhere? Or is that all myth and rumour?'

He laughed again and glanced across at a coffee shop over the road.

'Doesn't open for hours,' said Dani.

He nodded. 'I think we should head straight to Loch Long. I know he keeps his boat there. I don't know a lot about it, but I guess they head out early.'

'Not this early,' said Dani. 'Head into Helensburgh and we can check his home first. It might save us a few hours' driving.'

There were people moving about as the town slowly came to life.

They drove down the front, the Clyde out on their left.

'Do you know the way?' asked Marcus.

'I do. My dad's house is only a few hundred yards that way and my sister's is less than a mile from there. My dad was 45 Commando and we settled here when we were kids. He was on Comacchio Group, guarding the deterrent at one point. This is my old stomping ground.'

Marcus was smiling, and Dani recalled that he already knew most of that, since he'd served alongside her dad when he was a young Royal Marine officer.

'Let's use the sat-nav.' Dani input a postcode and house number into Marcus's navigation system. 'Head there and I'll call him.'

It was only just 5 a.m. and she hesitated before dialling but went ahead anyway.

'Hello?'

The voice that answered was deep and rough, the strong Scottish accent obvious even in a single word.

'Mr Holloway. My name is Lieutenant Dani Lewis and I'm with the Royal Navy Police. I've just arrived in Helensburgh and I'm sorry it's so early, but I would really like the opportunity to speak to you as soon as possible.'

There was a long silence. 'What did you say yer name was?' he asked.

'Dani Lewis. I'm with the Special Investigation Branch of the Royal Navy Police.'

As she said the words, Dani wondered whether those credentials would check out now if he called the Faslane naval base and tried to confirm who she was, or whether she might find herself being called in by the local police for overstepping another mark.

'I'm no' free today,' he said, after another pause.

'It's very important,' said Dani. 'Are you at home now?'

'Aye, but I can't talk.'

Dani turned to look at Marcus, a frown on her face.

'Weird?' she mouthed to Marcus.

'If you can't meet me, I can come to your house,' she said, straining to hear every sound at the other end of the line.

'No, don't do that. I won't talk to you, so don't come.'

There was a noise at the end of the line, then a bump.

Dani heard a sound like the handset dropping to the floor and then a gurgling sound before it was picked up again.

'Mr Holloway,' she said. 'Are you OK?'

She could hear breathing on the end of the line.

'I'm very near your house, Mr Holloway,' Dani said, gesturing to Marcus to drive more quickly. 'I could pop in now, very quickly?'

There was another long pause.

'This one's on you, Dani.'

The voice sent a shiver down her spine.

'This one could have lived. He was going to find out where his daughter's body was and now, instead, because of you, he's gone to join her.'

Marcus was speeding along now, turning into an estate where the roads were lined with cars.

'You're a bloody fool, Lewis,' said Hamilton, his voice

rising. 'I told you not to follow me, but you're a stupid bitch. I would have been gone.'

Marcus slowed suddenly, peering at house numbers. The houses were arranged as terraces, with five houses in each block. He pointed to one with a red door in the next terrace, then he leaned over to whisper in Dani's ear.

'That one,' he said. 'You're on a landline, so he's in there. Keep him talking.'

He leaned away from her for a moment and reached under her seat, pulling out a small black bag.

Dani knew what it was before he even put it on his lap to open it.

The pistols inside looked clean and modern. He handed the smaller one to her, showing her the safety on the side and gesturing to her to just point and shoot.

'You're a fool, Chris,' Dani said, allowing Marcus to place the pistol on her lap, but not wanting to touch it yet. 'You thought you had us all running around, but you're not half as clever as you think you are.'

Marcus opened the car door slowly and Dani changed ear to try and mask the sound.

'You know, we found out who Caleb is,' she said. 'It didn't take us long.'

'Well then, indirectly, I've taken you to the bodies after all,' he said. 'Do have fun picking the bones out of that one.' He laughed. 'Pardon the pun.'

'You're going nowhere, Chris. Just come in now.'

She watched as Marcus ran past the pathway that was next to the car, and took the path one terrace further along, which would lead him around the back of the house that Hamilton was in.

'Did you read my letters, Dani?' he asked.

Dani paused as she heard something in the background, but she wasn't sure what it was.

361

It sounded like chinking glass.

'I did, Chris. I have to say your staff work needs a little effort. You forgot the old accuracy, brevity and clarity in your writing.'

He chuckled.

Dani looked at the terrace, trying to catch a sign of Marcus, but he'd disappeared behind them now and all was quiet and still out the front. She looked at the pathway immediately next to the car.

It would lead her to the back of the houses in the next terrace and she wondered about leaving the car and taking a different route to support Marcus.

Then she looked back to the front door.

It would be fifty-fifty whether Marcus caught him or not. Her moving around would just make a pursuit more difficult; she needed to keep him on the phone, that would give them the best chance.

'What did you take from the letters, Dani?'

'That you're an enormous asshole,' she said. 'You seemed to labour that point, as if there's anyone who doesn't already think it.'

He was silent.

Dani checked the screen of her phone; the call was still live.

'That you always get revenge,' she added. 'That you like to shake people's lives.'

She heard a noise at the end of the line again and wondered whether she'd lost him, whether he'd left it and run.

'Are you there, Chris?' she asked.

'I'm here,' he said. 'I was just thinking about how to tell you a few things. You see, you're such a self-centred whore that it never occurred to you that a large portion of what I was doing wasn't about you at all. It seems like my revenge on Roger is complete, though. I gather he took the coward's way out?'

Dani said nothing.

'Yes, I can almost hear the hurt. You know, Dani, you'd be even more hurt if I described to you just how easy it was to get Roger working for me. I was going to take you to him, to let you two talk it out, but I gather that already happened?'

Dani looked frantically for any sign of Marcus, but still there was nothing.

'But here's the thing, Dani. I don't think you cared enough about Roger for it to really shake you to your selfish core, so that wasn't really about you. No. But you do, believe it or not, have a weak spot for a few people.'

Dani felt as though her stomach was about to drop out through the seat of the car.

'Charlie,' he said. 'The penny has dropped at last, hasn't it? Her and her unborn child.'

'No,' said Dani. 'No, you haven't. Don't you dare. She's safe.'

'Yes,' Hamilton said. 'Yes, I have, and I do dare. She was safe, Dani. But you didn't hide her well enough and now she's safe with me.'

'You're a fucking dead man, Chris,' Dani said, grabbing the gun from her lap and opening the car door.

'I can imagine,' said Hamilton.

Even in her rage, Dani heard a sound that made her stop.

At the other end of the line she heard the clinking of bottles.

She turned in the street, looking behind her, and saw a milk float stopping a few houses away. The bottles clinked as the vehicle jerked to a halt.

'You and your friend also forgot about cordless phones,' said Hamilton.

Dani spun around, just as she saw him step out from the pathway next to her.

He must have left the house before Marcus could have seen him and looped around the back of the terraces. He had the drop on her, the gun in his hand already raised and pointing at her as she stood with the car door still open. He smiled, the phone still to his ear, though she could have heard him easily enough without it.

'You don't get to die until you know she has.'

He fired twice and for a moment Dani was frozen in time.

She willed her body to move, to jump out of the way, but her legs were lead. She heard another gunshot, knew it must have been Marcus, but knowing it made no difference as she felt hot metal burning through her hip. She collapsed back against the car, falling against the passenger seat, the second bullet missing as she crumpled into the footwell. As she looked up, her vision beginning to blur, she saw Hamilton running. He was being chased, but Marcus was way behind.

Hamilton reached a red estate car and was inside in a second. Then he was pulling away.

Dani could see it all unfold before her.

The glass on Hamilton's driver's side window disintegrated, but the car kept going.

'Dani.'

Marcus was back with her now, looking at the wound in her upper leg. He took off his jacket and pressed it against her.

'We need to get an ambulance,' he said. 'You're losing a lot of blood.'

Dani grabbed at him, missing at first and then finding his hair. She turned his face towards her.

'He already has my sister,' she said. 'That's why he came here. He was always going to get her. We have to get him now. No time for an ambulance.'

Marcus made to speak.

'Now!' shouted Dani.

She struggled to get herself up and fully into the passenger seat again.

Marcus seemed to pause for a moment and then picked her up in a single movement, placing her on the seat. He was back inside and driving a moment later, the car screeching down the road.

'Go right,' said Dani. 'I know these estates. Left just takes him in deeper. He has to go right.'

Marcus did as he was told, and the turning forces threw Dani against the car door. She reached for the seat belt and put it on, realising she was still clutching the pistol in her right hand.

Hamilton's red estate was at the end of the next road.

'There,' she shouted.

But Marcus had seen it and was already gunning the engine.

The estate turned, and it was obvious to Dani that they would catch him soon.

His vehicle wouldn't be able to gain distance on them. He was on the main road now, heading north out of the town.

Before long the Gare Loch was on their left as they both accelerated hard.

Ahead of her, Hamilton swerved around a white van and stayed in the other lane, driving towards the oncoming traffic. He held his position, facing down a large delivery truck, until the very last second when he veered back on to his side of the road.

The truck slammed on the brakes and Hamilton shot

past on the inside as the truck's trailer began to slide out across the road and into Dani's path.

Marcus dropped a gear, steered on to the grass verge and aimed for the gap between the trailer and the now stationary white van.

There was a loud bang and a grinding of metal.

Dani shut her eyes, but they were through and Hamilton was still in sight.

She recognised the Faslane Peace Camp as they passed it. It had been there as long as she could remember to protest against the Vanguard class submarines that were berthed in the Faslane naval base and which carried the United Kingdom's nuclear deterrent. She knew there were few places for Hamilton to go. It was a long straight road.

Marcus was up behind Hamilton now and he reached for his pistol and held it out of the window, firing at Hamilton's car.

The rear window of the red estate shattered, but Hamilton drove on.

Dani watched, feeling the weight of the pistol in her hand and watching the back of the estate car as the rear light cluster fell from it.

'Stop shooting,' she shouted, pointing at the car. 'There's someone in the boot.'

As if on cue, she saw something pale, a small hand, stick out of the gap left behind by the rear lights.

Hamilton jerked the car to pass another vehicle and the hand was gone.

Marcus began to slow down.

'What are you doing?' asked Dani.

'If we force him to crash . . .' said Marcus.

Dani watched the red estate pull away from them.

'No,' she said. 'He's going to kill her anyway. He was always going to. We have to stop him.'

Marcus nodded, and the car lurched forward again.

Ahead of them, Hamilton disappeared from view.

'He's turned up Glen Fruin,' said Dani. 'On the right.'

Marcus took the corner at speed, almost leaving the road as he joined the narrow track.

Dani was thrown around as he took the bends and she winced as he misjudged a small bridge, scraping the car along the stone sides and then sliding on the cattle grid that immediately followed it. She knew that any oncoming vehicle would be the end of the chase – there was no room for two and they were going too fast to stop. She knew this road well, had travelled it many times with her father, stepmum and sister.

There were lots of tracks leading off the main route and she looked down each one, trying to see if Hamilton had turned off in an attempt to lose them.

'There he is,' said Marcus.

They entered a straight bit of road and Dani saw the red estate speeding away in front of them.

Hamilton took another corner, disappearing from sight, and Marcus pressed on harder.

They reached the corner, crested a small hill and then they saw him, stopped in the road.

Dani reached across and jerked the wheel, steering them around the red estate where her sister was captive and off the road into the grass and heather.

The car flipped and Dani was thrown around, her body limp as the forces of the crash pushed her to the limits of her seatbelt.

Then there was silence.

She looked down. Her jeans were thick with blood and her vision was fading in and out of focus. She heard him almost immediately.

He was clapping.

'Bravo,' Hamilton shouted, from somewhere near to her. 'Excellently done.'

Dani looked across at Marcus.

He was lying across the bonnet of the car, his hips where the windscreen would have been and the airbag deflating under the weight of his thighs. His trousers were ripped, and his skin stained with blood. He wasn't moving.

'See, Dani. You should always, always wear a seat belt. And this is why.'

Dani couldn't see him and wasn't able to move. Her leg was so painful that she couldn't feel past the wound, wasn't sure if she could still feel or move her toes. She tried to flex her fingers, testing her right hand and feeling the weight of the small pistol still gripped there.

'So, here's what I'm going to do,' said Hamilton, his voice closer now, as though he were just outside the car, but remaining out of sight. 'I'm going to get you out of there. I'm going to shoot holes in the trunk of Mr Holloway's car. I'm going to hope that something dramatic happens, like some of your sister's blood dripping through one of my bullet holes, because that would be really visual, and it could be one of those iconic pictures that wins prizes. Then, Dani, I'm going to open the trunk and strangle you while you look at your sister's corpse. But we'll need to be quick, because I suspect we've ruffled a few feathers during our chase.'

Dani waited in the car, unable to move. She looked again at the sheer amount of blood that had come from her bullet wound.

She said nothing, unsure of how long her consciousness would last.

Then he was there, beside her window. He pretended to knock, although the glass was shattered.

'Knock, knock,' he said, his smile broad. 'Are you awake, Dani? Your eyes are open, but is anybody home?'

Dani kept her eyes dead ahead as she felt him only a few feet away from her.

'Come now, let's get you out of those filthy clothes,' he said, stepping back and reaching for the door handle. 'I'm starting to think about you naked again, Dani, and I'm getting to wondering whether pregnancy with my child would be the better course of action than strangulation.'

He was tilting his head at her as though he was frustrated at her inaction.

'We have things to do, Dani, people to kill, revenge to be taken, that kind of thing. Come on now, don't be a spoilsport.'

Dani turned her head as he swung the passenger door open. She looked at him, made sure she had eye contact, waited until he smiled at her, his eyes gleaming, then she raised the pistol and aimed it at his face.

The shock as he saw it was unmistakable, his mouth dropping open as he tried to step away from her. His hands rose as though they could defend him from bullets.

'You're not as smart as you think you are, Chris,' she said as she pulled the trigger again and again, cycling it even after he'd fallen from sight and only the click-click of metal against metal broke the silence.

Chapter 48

It was cold when the taxi dropped her off and she huddled into her jacket as the driver carried her bag to the door.

Her neighbours were there to meet her in an instant and she knew they'd been watching for her.

Martha hugged her as Derek watched, and they hovered and bustled and offered to help, but she begged them to let her rest alone and they eventually relented.

She stepped inside, using her crutch to get over the small threshold. She was grateful for the silence and locked the door behind her, picking up the mail that was scattered on the floor. She limped through to the new patio doors at the back of the house and drew the curtains shut.

As she stopped to look around, she saw a handwritten envelope among the mail and recognised the writing.

My dearest Dani,

So, this is a bit of an awkward letter to write, because I'm writing it before things happen and I don't know how they pan out. It may be that Roger has wormed his way out of his crimes against you and you've repaired some kind of relationship together. Part of me hopes so, but I feel like the death of your sister and her unborn child, whom I have christened 'Christopher the Second', will quash any joy you feel at a relationship rekindled.

Oh, Dani! I just had a thought – what if Roger killed you to protect his secret? That would be dramatic, and I suppose it would mean that it would be your dad reading this letter. In which case . . .

Hey, Taz, hope you're all well and the grieving is coming along nicely. Sorry I killed both your offspring. Chris xx

I don't know if I'm just letting my imagination run away now, Caleb says I am, but maybe you killed Roger instead? Fought and killed him in a desperate life-or-death struggle, which I think we'd both have to admit would be kind of poetic. Either way, it was a great position for me to be in, because I didn't really care who won the fight, I just wanted to hurt you both and so, as with many things, I really couldn't lose.

I'll be out of the equation now as you've probably gathered. I'll be wearing the emblem of my adopted country far across the sea, being the greatest and most committed citizen they've ever known. I'm ripe for a fresh start and I'm going to take some time out, relax after my prison ordeal, and see if I can find myself and remember who I really am.

I very much enjoyed writing these letters to you and I've considered I might write my memoirs, properly and for the purposes of publication. Perhaps you might be willing to give me a foreword? Something to discuss another day.

I also wanted you to know, that I know.

You said you'd follow me and hunt me down and if you're reading this, then I'm sure that killing your sister won't have done much to dull that desire. Remember, Dani, that pain is good for us. It reminds us that we're human. As the pain of your sister's death slowly takes over your life and you can't visit your family because of the reproachful looks and the knowledge that it was all your fault, I feel sure you'll be more driven than ever to track me down. But don't, because you now know that I know.

So, I wanted you to know that I know your secret, the thing you did, the thing that plagues you and keeps you awake at night, and I have proof of it too.

That night in the car park, when you were attacked on my behalf, you escaped, such is your tenacity, but you were followed, attacked again, and you defended yourself. I want you to know that the day I found out you'd stabbed that young man in the chest, was one of the greatest days of my life. Before then, I only wanted sweet, cheap revenge: I wanted to put you back in your place and to punish you and I've achieved that. But when I saw what you could do when you were properly motivated to act, hell, Dani, I just knew I had to think bigger. You killed a man – in self-defence, but killed him nevertheless. You're a good investigator, so I know you'll have identified who it was, probably have pictures of him at your house, such is the way you like to flagellate yourself over things.

For what it's worth, I don't think you have what it takes to take life again. I think you were so scarred by what you did and that it is buried so deeply in who you are, that even in self-defence, you don't have the stones to do it, and I'm seldom wrong about such things.

So, no chasing me, please, there will be quite enough people doing that anyway, and your murderous secret stays safe with me.

Finally, I don't know if they've let you keep my letters, but I'm sure you could get good money for them on eBay. As you know, there are some fairly sick people out there who'd pay big bucks for them. You'll note I signed each one – no need to thank me for that little bit of extra (and valuable) authenticity.

If you wish to publish them, you have my permission. Show this to my lawyer and he'll act on it.

I'd much prefer you edited them somewhat to preserve at least some of my modesty, but I understand you very likely won't, and I've made my peace with that.

Dani, the pictures that were sent to your father, the ones of you and your sister that motivated him so admirably, do I need to send more to you? I know you have little regard for your own well-being and my promise of keeping your secret may not be enough, so I ask, must I send you pictures of your stepmother and father to ensure my freedom from Danification?

I want you to know that we're done. I'm finished. I have no intention now of ever returning to the United Kingdom, and so, as long as you remain there, we will never have to meet.

I've gained a certain kind of respect for you over the past few months, Dani. You have a killer instinct and I think you now truthfully understand what revenge is all about.

I'm heading off to the new world, Dani, and I will

leave you with your pain – goodbye. As I've said many times before, I hope we never meet again.

Chris xxx

Dani leaned back on her couch and thought about the image at the top of the lock box that she kept under her bed. The first image she made herself deal with every time she opened it. It was of a young man, missing, presumed dead. He was Navy, had gone missing the night that Dani was attacked in the car park on Portsdown Hill. He was the young man that Dani was sure she'd killed.

She started as she heard the knock at the door. She walked slowly towards it, limping with each step, and looked through the peephole.

It was John.

She opened the door and let him in.

His mouth dropped open as he saw her face.

'Holy shitballs,' he said.

'I know, I'm a proper hottie, eh?' Dani joked, reaching up with her free hand and touching her swollen face. 'How's things?'

'Better than you,' he said, following her back into the lounge.

'Any news?'

He was nodding. 'Hell, yeah. Caleb lived in a place in Wales. He had loads of land, like a big quarry. He bought it when he left the forces and lived off his pension. The police are getting into it properly, but apparently the place is like a mass grave. They literally have no idea how many human remains are there. I spoke to one of the guys on the team, on the quiet.'

John tapped his nose. 'They know this is going to explode soon. They can't keep it under wraps, but he says that in the house they found a huge freezer and cold store and it was full of fingers. They were all laid out and marked. Loads were lying in big trays of formaldehyde. This guy had been doing bodies for years and years. My source said that some were dried and stored, and others were in jars. The freezer and fridge were loaded with body parts. It's pretty grim, and from what I can tell it's gonna cause an international incident. One sick, sick man.'

Dani thought about things Hamilton had said to her.

He'd said many, many times that the really successful killers were the ones that no one was even looking for, and here was Caleb, just like Hamilton said.

But they were both dead and that was all that mattered.

'Heather called me,' Dani said. 'She didn't say it in as many words, but they're investigating over there too. Looking into when Caleb moved here after Afghanistan and checking the places he lived when he was in the States.'

'Have you heard anything about you?' John asked.

Dani shook her head. 'Suspended without pay pending a full enquiry.'

'What about your sister?'

'She's OK and the baby too. Beaten up and bumped around, but they make the Lewis clan out of stern stuff. Her husband's being brought home from operations for some leave, so that will help her too.'

John nodded. 'That's good. Can I make some tea?' he asked.

'Sure,' Dani said. 'Can you pull the door to on your way out? I need to make a quick call.'

John did as requested, and Dani picked up her phone and dialled.

'Hello.'

'How are you?' she asked.

'I'm alive,' said Marcus. 'Can't say much more than that at the moment.'

'I need to ask you a question,' Dani said, pursing her lips. 'When you came and got me from Hamilton, you had a shootout. You said that you got one and not the other, then you took the body away . . .'

The silence drew out for longer and for a moment Dani thought he'd ended the call.

'I never got to see him and I want to ask you now, Marcus, was Caleb dead?'

'I'm afraid I don't have a clue what you mean, Dani,' said Marcus as the line went dead.

Acknowledgements

Thanks to Roe, Elizabeth, Sammy, my mum & dad, and Vicky & Alan.

Thanks to my friends Martin & Mary for reading and critiquing, in the nicest possible way, and also to Sheapy, Mike and Mac for their naval knowledge and ongoing support.

To Alice Lutyens at Curtis Brown and to Toby Jones, Katie Sunley, Jenni Leech, Joe Yule and Lucy Bennett at Headline, you all have my greatest appreciation for your work and support to get me into print.

All your help and support is very much appreciated.

And finally...

To all my brothers and sisters in the Armed Forces who are deployed around the globe, away from their loved ones – be safe, look out for each other, and remember - never let the truth get in the way of a good story!